I0647417

# Home
## from the
# Meadows

## Gerald Names

**The E. B. Houchin Company**
Est. 1992

The E.B. Houchin Company
Salt Lake City, Utah

Copyright 2011 by Gerald Names

Trade Paperback ISBN: 978-0-938313-02-1

Library of Congress Control Number: 2011913278

All rights reserved, including the right
to reproduce this book or any portion thereof
in any form whatsoever.

Printed in USA

# Come, Come, Ye Saints

# 1

The early morning sun was just illuminating the hills on the north side of the river as James Marshall, shoulders hunched because of the cold, went to make his daily inspection of the millrace. The rest of the workers were at breakfast.

He saw it, but he didn't see it. Not at first. He turned to go, and it beckoned to him. Like a long-forgotten memory, a thought, an image entered his mind. Marshall bent down and looked at the delta of sand and gravel beneath the trickle of water at the end of the millrace. Gingerly he climbed down into the millrace, and squatted down, sifting the sand and gravel with his fingers. Marshall arose with the glittery stone and turned it in his hand, examining it. He held it up in the early morning sunlight, and his look of wonderment changed to a smile. The gold nugget was nearly as big as his thumb. Marshall pounded it between two rocks. It bent, but it did not break. Marshall removed his hat and placed it on the ground beside the millrace. He placed the nugget into the crown of his hat and went back to digging, sifting the dirt looking for another shiny rock.

Captain John Augustus Sutter, a German Swiss, who had immigrated to Mexican California in 1839, had received a land grant of eleven leagues in the Sacramento Valley from Governor Juan Bautista Alvarado. The grant came with the understanding that Sutter should function as political authority and dispenser of justice. Alvarado wanted to stop the invasion of adventurers from the United States and the hunting and trapping by companies from the Columbia River region. Sutter had other ideas.

He built a fortress, which served as a focal point for the increasing tide of covered wagons bringing settlers from the United States. Profiting from their trade, the captain encouraged their passage, and because his rising power had made him a feared and mistrusted figure among the Mexicans, he heartily endorsed the American conquest of California.

As prelude to the expected arrival of American immigrants Sutter decided to build a sawmill on the American River at Coloma. Except for Marshall, the camp cook and her husband, and some local Indians, all the workers at the mill were former soldiers of the Mormon Battalion.

The trouble began when the waterwheel at the new sawmill had been set too low and would not turn. Digging the millrace deeper was judged by Marshall, the chief carpenter and supervisor of construction, to be an easier solution than raising the wheel. But increasing the depth had proceeded slowly of late because the workers had reached the granite bedrock. At the end of each day they turned the water of the American River into the millrace to flush out the day's diggings.

That morning, January 24, 1848, as they always did before breakfast, three men had shut down the head gate and had thrown in dead leaves and sawdust to make it tight. And, every day, before work could begin, James Marshall made his daily inspection.

Marshall called out to one of the "Digger" Indians working at the mill. "Go fetch me a plate!"

When the Indian returned, Marshall dug out a handful of mud, plopped it onto the plate, then proceeded to wash it in the trickle of water. Within minutes, more shiny pebbles appeared. Marshall climbed out of the millrace, carrying his newfound treasure in his hat.

"Boys," he said loudly, "by god, I believe I've found a gold mine."

Marshall carried his old white hat in his arms and placed it on a workbench in the center of the mill yard as the curious mill hands gathered round.

"What do you think, boys?" said Marshall, holding up one of the shiny nuggets that lay in the crown of his hat. "If this ain't gold, it's a darn good imitation."

"Praise the Lord!" Exclaimed one of the onlookers.

"No such luck," said another.

One of the men retrieved a five-dollar gold piece from his pocket and compared the coin with the shiny bits of metal.

"Looks like the genuine article to me," he said.

"What's all the commotion?" asked Isaac Delaney, as he returned from breakfast.

A deep silence fell over the men. Each man's thoughts turned inward as they stared longingly at the gold, but soon they were looking at each other, some grinning and others trying to look stoic. All Delaney could think of was his beloved wife Molly, who he had left behind in Nauvoo with their son John. Oh, how he longed to share this with her.

The men of the Mormon Battalion were members of the Church of Jesus Christ of Latter-day Saints, and had endured much pain and hardship for the cause of their religion. Joseph Smith, founder and Prophet of the church, had been murdered, with his brother Hyrum, by a mob at the jail in Carthage, Illinois, on June 27, 1844, while awaiting trial on a false charge of treason. By the winter of 1846 the Mormons had been driven out of Nauvoo, Illinois, and forced to flee across the frozen Mississippi. The graves of many of the faithful marked the trail of their emigration, from Nauvoo to Winter Quarters, on the east bank of the Missouri River in Iowa. Dispossessed of its property and almost penniless, the church had been in need of a miracle. It arrived as if on schedule.

The United States was prosecuting a war with Mexico. For the Mormons, the conflict proved to be a godsend. The government required a battalion of volunteers to assert American claims in California.

By inspiration and the voice of the people, Brigham Young had succeeded Joseph Smith as leader of the church. His call for volunteers was quickly answered. The United States army issued the men arms, fed and clothed them, but the church received their pay. Five companies, totaling 541 men, mustered in on July 16, 1846, and marched from Winter Quarters on the east bank of the Missouri River to Fort Leavenworth, Indian Territory.

After completing the longest infantry march in American history, the men of the battalion were discharged on July 16, 1847, in southern California. On that same day an emigrant company of Saints camped less than a week away from the Great Salt Lake Valley. Brigham Young had decided that the Mormons would only find peace if they relocated to a place so desolate that nobody else would want it. The desert valley on the southeast shore of America's "Dead Sea" was just such a place.

Eighty-one men of the battalion re-enlisted for six months, but most of those who were discharged started for the Great Salt Lake Valley. After crossing the Sierra Nevada Mountains, they came upon Sam Brannan, a fellow-Mormon, guiding a party of Mormon soldiers to Monterey to get their discharge from the army. He carried a letter from Brigham Young and the Twelve Apostles as well as letters from family and friends for the returning soldiers.

The Prophet's letter counseled the soldiers of the Mormon Battalion to return to California to earn money to fit themselves out properly, and then come to Salt Lake the next spring. Provisions were scarce at Salt Lake and the church leaders foresaw the coming winter filled with hardship. Thus, the Mormon Battalion veterans accepted employment by Captain Sutter to build his sawmill on the American River.

# 2

Isaac Delaney had not hesitated to return to California with the other battalion veterans. For Delaney the commandments of the Lord came through Brigham Young, his longtime friend.

Delaney stood an even six feet, lean and muscular with large, powerful hands gnarled from a life of carpentry, a quiet man, humble, sincere. Those who knew him well, found him to be pleasant and likeable. An Anglican by birth, Delaney had converted to the Church of Jesus Christ of Latter-day Saints, Mormons to the Gentile world. A true believer and steadfast in the faith, he personified the Mormon scripture, "I will go and do the things which the Lord hath commanded, for I know that the Lord giveth no commandments unto the children of men, save he shall prepare a way for them that they may accomplish the thing which he commandeth them." Leaving his wife and child to serve with the battalion had pained Isaac Delaney as much as any man, but it was the will of the Lord as far as he was concerned.

Delaney, his wife Molly, and their son John had enjoyed a very tranquil existence in a little cottage near Manchester, England. The cottage had only three rooms, but was snug and cozy in the winter. Molly had kept a garden in the rear every summer, and Delaney had owned a carpenter shop that adjoined the house.

As if following a familiar road and coming suddenly upon a crossroads, Delaney's life had taken a new direction, never to return. While plying his trade on an unusually hot day in the summer of 1840, Delaney wiped the sweat from his brow, glancing through the open door as he did. A stranger approaching from a long way off caught his eye, but Delaney paid him no mind until the man finally appeared in the doorway, doffed his hat, and inquired, "Isaac Delaney?"

"Yes?" said Delaney, looking up from his workbench.

"I have come all the way from America," said the stranger, "To deliver you a message."

Delaney continued working on the chair he was making, only slightly interested in the stranger's words. Peddler, he thought. Perhaps a bookseller. A seller of something for certain. He would give the man half an ear.

"You have?" said Delaney. "And from whom might it be?"

"The Lord Jesus Christ has restored His gospel to the earth, Brother Isaac, and He has a work for you to do."

Delaney dropped his mallet and chisel, and looked carefully at the stranger for the first time. The man appeared to be of a common sort, poorly attired but clean-shaven. "How is it you know my name?"

The stranger smiled and said, "I'm sorry. My name is Brigham Young. Last night I dreamed of a carpenter who was called forth to labor in the Lord's vineyard. This morning I inquired of the names of the local carpenters. When I heard your name, I knew you were the man. We are engaged in a great work, building the Kingdom of God here upon the earth. Hear the Lord's message and become a part of our great undertaking."

"You're joking, of course."

"Not at all," said Brigham. "The Lord has need of good men such as you."

Delaney stroked his chin. He had a far off look in his eyes. "Just where is this kingdom you mentioned?"

"America."

Delaney's countenance brightened at the word. "America?" His eyes darted around and the hint of a smile appeared on his face. "I'll be talking this over with my wife."

Brigham Young came everyday for more than a week, preaching the message of the restoration of the gospel to the earth. In the end Isaac and Molly accepted the Mormon religion enthusiastically and were baptized into the Church of Jesus Christ of Latter-day Saints.

In the spring of 1844 they sold the cottage and all its furnishings and with only what they could pack into a large steamer trunk, they set sail for the place Brigham Young called Zion, then at Nauvoo, Illinois, to be gathered with the Saints under the leadership of the Prophet Joseph Smith.

The Delaneys arrived too late to meet the Prophet. An apostate had set up shop as a newspaper publisher and was taking editorial potshots at Smith and his followers. Being the mayor as well as prophet, seer, and revelator, Joseph Smith had declared the newspaper a public nuisance and ordered its printing press destroyed upon a vote of the city council, which proved to be a fatal and tragic error. Rather than flee their enemies, seeking justice, Joseph and Hyrum had gone to meet their fate at Carthage, Illinois. While the Smiths and their companions were being held under guard, a mob stormed the Carthage jail and killed both Joseph and Hyrum.

# 3

By the following Sunday, January 30, 1848, the Mormons at Sutter's mill had extracted an aggregate of some seven ounces of gold, worth slightly more than $100 at sixteen dollars per ounce. Each man gathered gold flakes and nuggets on the sly as if they thought they might be accused of theft. They discussed the subject of gold in the millrace quietly, and then only in groups of two or three.

As was their custom the Mormons gathered privately for a brief worship service that Sunday. Henry Bigler took his turn conducting the service, and he quickly warmed to the subject on every man's mind.

"Brethren, I can't help but see the hand of the Lord in this," said Bigler. "When Brother Brigham asked us to enlist, he promised us, if we were obedient and did our duty, then we would be blessed. Though we marched off to war prepared to fight, we were not called upon to shed blood. When we were asked to stay in California, I'm sure there is not a man among us who wouldn't rather have returned home to his family. But we saw our duty and accepted it like men. We were told that each dollar we could take to Salt Lake would be worth five times as much. Now we have the opportunity to bring back more money than could be earned by an army of men doing common labor."

"What about the mill?" asked Delaney.

"We're all honorable men here," said Bigler. "We took on an obligation to build a sawmill, and I suggest we see it through. Besides, we're paid a fair wage here, and if we were to leave off to look for gold, we might lose more in the long run than we would make."

The men agreed. They had plenty of time after work to search for the yellow metal that seemed to be everywhere. Each man spoke of what he could do for the church with this newfound wealth. But the unspoken truth deep in their innermost thoughts said they were also thinking of what they could do for themselves.

Delaney hoped that Brigham Young could be persuaded to bring the Saints to California. Here they would prosper. The days of persecution would be behind them. The gentiles had no respect for Mormon religious views and practices, but money appealed to everyone.

The days grew into weeks. As winter passed into spring, all work gradually stopped at the mill. Everyone had gone to the hills to dig gold. Each day Delaney retrieved the likeness of his dear Molly from among his belongings. It was a Daguerreotype he had obtained in Nauvoo before departing with the battalion. Molly had jet black hair, an ivory complexion, and rosy red cheeks. She looked how Delaney imagined Snow White to be in the fairy tale. Delaney couldn't wait to gather her and their son and return to California. Surely, this was the promised land. But that would have to wait. Because the mountain passes were closed by snow, he couldn't leave for Salt Lake.

By the middle of May, the lust for gold had completely captured Delaney's soul. Each day he looked to the snow on the mountains, as it slowly retreated to the higher elevations. He worked harder, knowing that when the passes were clear, the men of the battalion would start for the newest gathering place of the Saints in the valley of the Great Salt Lake.

Delaney took his leave of the California gold fields on June 24, 1848. With him went one hundred twenty-three ounces of gold, worth nearly two thousand dollars, and his dreams of a better life. As soon as he could fetch his family, he would be back.

The Mormon Battalion veterans, who had remained in various locations in California, gathered at a rendezvous place in the mountains. With Delaney's arrival, the company had grown to forty-five men, one woman, four hundred head of cattle, and seventeen wagons. They elected Jonathan Holmes to be their leader. Then they organized themselves into groups of four to share the work of setting up camp, cooking the meals, driving the team of oxen, and doing sentry duty. Early on the morning of July 3, they struck their tents and began the arduous journey to the valley of the Great Salt Lake.

The wagon train progressed slowly. The men built the road as they went, bit by painstaking bit. Sometimes they spent days in camp while scouting parties searched for the best route. Once they worked the road for four days to advance only five miles. Hauling wagons up mountains, over snow drifts, and down into valleys, by August 12, they reached the main emigrant road and came to the Truckee River, never realizing the magnitude of the work they had performed in building what would become the main road of the California emigration. For the first time in nearly two months they knew where they were and how much farther they had to go. They made camp and offered up thanks to God who had delivered them safely from the wilderness.

With another two days travel, the company camped nearly forty miles closer to Great Salt Lake City. After the tent was set up, fires started, and food put on to cook, Delaney decided to improve the time by writing a few words in his journal. He situated himself as comfortably as possible against a wagon wheel, and was just organizing his thoughts, when he heard the creaking and rumbling of wagons on the move. He looked in the direction of the sound and broke into a smile.

Leading a cloud of dust was a train of about a dozen wagons, the first sign of civilization Delaney had seen in nearly two months. The entire company turned out to watch the wagon train's approach.

About ten minutes later the emigrant train turned off the road some fifty yards short of the battalion camp and formed into the usual double semicircle corral with the wagon tongues pointing outward. In another twenty minutes teams were staked out, cook fires were started and tents were pitched. As the other camp prepared their evening meal, the Mormons joined them, mingling and sharing news and good-natured conversation.

Delaney put aside the idea of writing in his journal and joined the others at the emigrant camp. As he approached the group, he heard, "...and there's lots of it. Why, every man here has some. Here, take a look at this."

The speaker pulled his purse from his pocket and emptied the contents, about an ounce of gold, into the palm of his hand. Grinning, he slowly stirred the gold dust with his index finger.

Suddenly, one of the emigrants, an old man of about seventy, jumped to his feet, threw his old wool hat on the ground, jumped on it with both feet, and then kicked it in the air.

"Glory, hallelujah!" he shouted. "Thank God! I shall die a rich man yet!"

The joyous scene that followed repeated itself in various fashions with each emigrant train the Mormon company encountered on the trail. The word was out. There was gold in California!

North central Nevada presented a bleak contrast to California. The landscape was a treeless scene of sand, sagebrush and bare rugged hills of basalt. The road was as good as any the Mormon Battalion had ever traveled, but the wagon wheels and oxen hooves ground it into a dust as fine as white flour that found its way into everything. When the wind blew, it was worse than a winter snowstorm. Water was scarce and in many places it was warm and brackish, its wetness being the only thing to recommend it.

The battalion's course took them north and east along the Humboldt River, a stream that ran mostly underground in the summer. The mornings were cool and pleasant, but from noon to four the heat was insufferable, forcing the company to travel only in the morning and then again in the late afternoon and early evening.

On Sunday, August 27, they laid by in camp all day near the headwaters of the Humboldt River. At three in the afternoon the men came together for a prayer meeting. Just as worship service concluded, a train of eleven mounted soldiers with pack mules came up from the northeast. Above the sound of the tramping of hooves could be heard the tinkle of the bell mare as she led the mules along the road. Every one of the Mormons turned out to greet them. On the trail each passing train was a combination newspaper, post office, and trail guide. They wondered what news this one would bring.

Leading the soldiers was a captain, a man whose weather-beaten face gave no more clue to his age than to place it in the range of twenty to thirty-five. He spurred his horse over to the Mormons and stopped. Touching his hat in a casual salute, he said, "Good day. Hensley's the name, Sam Hensley. Mind if we camp here with you?"

Jonathan Holmes stepped forward, his hand extended. "Jonathan Holmes, sir. The company elected me to be leader for the time being. You're welcome here. Pick a spot. There's plenty of water and grass."

Hensley reached down and shook the outstretched hand. "Thank you, sir," said Hensley. He turned to the other soldiers and said, "We'll stop here, men."

The soldiers dismounted and set to work. The mule herders unloaded the pack saddles, and drove the animals to the river. Hensley turned his horse over to a private and brushed the dust off of himself as he walked back to the Mormons.

"Any news?" asked Holmes.

"None to speak of," said Hensley.

"Well, then, how are trail conditions ahead?"

The captain looked puzzled at first. "Oh," he said slowly, "You're headed back to the States."

"No, sir," said Holmes. "We're bound for the Great Salt Lake Valley."

"Then you must be Mormons," said Hensley.

"Yes, sir," said Holmes proudly. "We have all served under Lieutenant Colonel Cooke in the late war and are now on our way to join our families."

"Then you'll be interested to know," said Hensley, "that we were in Great Salt Lake Valley only eighteen days ago."

A murmur of excitement swept through the Mormons. Delaney pushed forward, his innards fairly bursting with longing for his wife and son.

"But how is that possible?" asked Delaney. "Surely, it must be at least another five hundred miles."

The men were confused. The road to California followed the Oregon Trail from Fort Bridger to Fort Hall near the Snake River, then branched off to the southwest, a very round about way. Two years earlier Lansford Hastings had blazed a trail through the west desert from the south end of the Great Salt Lake. Only the ill-fated Donner party that became stranded in the snow that year had taken that path. Since then no one had ventured to go that way again. No water for more than a hundred miles.

"If you go through Fort Hall and Fort Bridger, yes. But we have taken a new route, around the north end of the Salt Lake. Plenty of grass and water. I reckon it to be not more than 380 miles. I should think you would save at least eight to ten days by going that way."

"But you're a pack train," protested one of the men. "What about wagons?"

"You might have to cut down a few stream banks," said Hensley, "but I think you would be able to make a very good wagon road without too much labor."

"Just where is this new road?" asked Holmes.

"Have you heard of the City of Rocks?" asked Hensley.

"Yes."

"Just before that place is Steeple Rocks, two very tall rocks at the crest of a ridge. The road passes between them. About a mile this side of Steeple Rocks, look to the right for our trail. A valley about a mile or two wide extends some fifteen or twenty miles to the east. Before you reach the end of it, you should be able to see the northern end of the Salt Lake, if you have a mind to do some climbing."

"Could you prepare us a waybill?" asked Holmes.

"Be happy to. Got some paper and a pencil?"

"I have some," offered Delaney, holding forth his journal.

And so it happened that the route of the Salt Lake Cutoff was first recorded in the diary of a Mormon pioneer. The Mormon Battalion veterans thanked the captain. Had it not been Sunday, they would have broken camp and continued their journey. They were like thirsty animals, who could smell a water hole somewhere in the distance.

# 4

The company broke camp the morning of September 28, 1848,

with the knowledge they would be reunited with family and friends before the day was over. The road was as Captain Hensley had described it. The past four days they had traversed the length of the Great Salt Lake from the Bear River crossing on the north to a point about twenty miles below the Weber River. Though only early autumn, a feel of winter was in the air. The sky was mostly clear with only scattered clouds. To their right was the Great Salt Lake. A gusting wind whipped the water into little whitecaps of foam. A foul stench filled the air, created by the dead, decaying sludge being stirred up on the lake bottom. The setting was appropriate for the sight that greeted the men of the battalion as they passed the hot springs below the west side of Ensign Peak.

Delaney was near the end of the train of seventeen wagons as one by one they ground to a halt. A wave of joy and shouts of jubilation swept over the men as they rushed to the head of the line for their first full view of the Great Salt Lake Valley. Like the fading echo of a clap of thunder, the veterans of the Mormon Battalion fell silent. The Saints had been here for more than fourteen months. Where was the city? Where were the houses? The stores? The farms?

About two miles to the south was a squat-looking stockade. To the northeast of the fort was a solitary log cabin and nearby a bowery, the community's open air meeting place. Several plots of land were under cultivation, and here and there some twenty houses were in the first stages of construction. After the towns, ranches and lush valleys of California, it was a depressing sight.

The Battalion's arrival in the valley did not go unnoticed. Some of their brethren had gone ahead the day before. By the time they reached the fort a large crowd had turned out to greet them.

On closer examination the fort was much larger than it had appeared at first. The original structure stood on a ten-acre site with two additions on the north and south more than doubling it in size. Two-room houses constructed of timbers and adobe shared common walls and formed the exterior walls of the fort. The rooms all opened onto the public square and had small windows on the outer walls for defense and ventilation. Entrance to the fort was a gate on the east side of the center square. Two other gates connected the north and south enclosures. The fort housed nearly all of the valley's population, slightly less than two thousand people.

A crowd stood around the liberty pole at the center of the fort, waiting for the new arrivals. The battalion veterans were bone tired, but the joy of once again being united with their loved ones washed away their fatigue.

Isaac Delaney looked at the faces in the crowd, searching for his wife and son. He was about to ask their whereabouts when Brigham Young and Heber C. Kimball, counselor to the Prophet, strode through the east gate of the fort. The Prophet plunged into the throng, shaking hands with the men of the battalion. Upon seeing Delaney straining to find his wife's face, he went immediately to his old friend.

"Brother Isaac," he said, "it's good to see you again."

"Thank you," replied Delaney, still craning his neck around. "Have you seen my wife?"

President Young slipped his arm around Delaney's shoulder. "Come," he said, "let's walk awhile and talk. I'll show you the city."

The crowd parted respectfully for them as they headed for the main gate. Delaney felt a tightness in his stomach and a prickly sensation on the back of his neck.

Outside the fort two horses were saddled and waiting, as if Brigham and Isaac were expected. They mounted the horses and started in a northeasterly direction. In a few minutes they arrived at the bowery, a few yards southwest of where City Creek forked. "City" was a rather generous description of the area. Wishful thinking would have been more appropriate.

"This is the temple block," said Brigham. "Here we will build the House of the Lord, so we may worship God in the tops of the mountains."

To the east, on the east fork of City Creek, stood a log house, the first house in the new city outside of the fort. The two men crossed the north fork of City Creek and started the long climb to Ensign Peak. When they reached the top, they dismounted. From that vantage point President Young described the layout of the unbuilt city, which had been laid out in ten-acre blocks. He showed Delaney the various improvements built since their arrival the previous year: bridges over Mill Creek and the Jordan River, as well as a grist mill on City Creek and a sawmill on Mill Creek.

Eventually, the Prophet ran out of things to say about the new Zion. For a long time the two men sat looking out over the valley. The sky began to clear from the west, and the wind subsided.

"You have a fine new daughter," said Brigham in a subdued voice. "She was born a year ago last March."

"What about my Molly?"

"Her name is Elizabeth. She is the image of her mother."

"My wife. Where is she?"

"She's not with us, Isaac. She returned home to Heavenly Father this past May. I'm sorry."

Head down, fists clenched, and jaws clamped as tight as a vise, a cry of anguish escaped Delaney's lips such as the Prophet had never heard before. His senses reeling, Delaney collapsed in a heap on the ground. He buried his face in his hands and mourned the passing of all he had ever hoped and dreamed for. Molly, sweet Molly. How could it be? How could it be?

Holding the reins of both horses in his hands, Brigham Young crouched down next to Delaney and looked out over the valley, saying nothing. A great orator, the Prophet also knew when to be silent. As for Delaney, he was glad his friend did not speak. Words would not comfort him. The initial pain was sharp and unrelenting, but eventually gave way to a numbness that permeated his entire being.

After several minutes Delaney turned to the Prophet and in an almost matter-of-fact tone asked, "How did she die?"

"She died of consumption. During the first winter you were gone she took sick during her confinement. It didn't appear she would live to bear her child, but she did, and her health began to improve, though it was never as good as before her illness. She insisted on coming west in the spring to be with you. We buried her along the trail. It was a restful spot, in a stand of trees near the mouth of Ash Hollow. I understand her last words were of you."

"I had hoped to take her to California next year," said Delaney. "It is a bounteous land, Brother Brigham. The church could grow and prosper there."

"I'm sure it is," said the Prophet. "Perhaps one day I'll visit it. Come, let's go meet your new daughter."

"And my son?"

"He's being well cared for."

Brigham stood up and mounted his horse. Delaney looked up at him, let out a heavy sigh and nodded. The sun was low in the western sky and it was time they should be getting back to the fort.

Few words passed between the two men on the return trip. Delaney had much to think about. His entire body ached to hold his darling Molly. Now he could only embrace her memory. How she would have loved California! Now, how could he go? And what about the children? John was ten years old, a resourceful lad, but Elizabeth was only a baby. Delaney didn't know what to make of this surprise. After John was born, Molly had experienced several miscarriages. Neither she nor Isaac expected to have more children. The girl had been born eight months after his departure with the battalion. If Molly had known she was with child, she hadn't told her husband. Perhaps she hadn't wanted to trouble him during the long infantry march of the battalion. In any case, Delaney had to provide a home for the children. It was too late in the season to return to California. He had heard about the tragedy of the Donner Party just two years past. A grisly business. By the following spring he would need a new wife to be mother to his children. He didn't like to think of that, but he had to be practical. When the battalion had departed two years before, Brigham Young had promised great blessings for their faithful service. In spite of his sorrow, Delaney intended to grab hold of all he could.

Delaney had gone to the mountain a humble, willing follower of the Prophet. By the time he reached the fort he was a changed man, tempered by the fire of tragedy, firm in his resolve to return to California and make a new life.

## 5

During the next few days the story of gold in California was voiced abroad in the community. When the pioneers arrived in the valley in 1847, some had questioned the wisdom of locating in this desolate place, some even to the point of leaving the valley the following spring. Those who had kept their doubts to themselves now also began to think seriously of moving to California. Only the oncoming winter prevented many families from starting immediately for the gold fields.

Before the arrival of the battalion veterans, Brigham Young and the other church leaders had set the people to work building homes and fences. Now, the work began to suffer.

Ever the practical man, Isaac Delaney didn't let the talk of gold distract him from what needed to be done. No one could leave for California for at least six months. He put his back into it, and soon had a good beginning on the house on his allotted piece of ground.

Church services were held in the bowery on the ten-acre plot designated as the temple site. At the first Sunday services attended by Delaney and the other new arrivals, the Prophet announced the first efforts to build a temple would be expended in erecting a large wall around the temple block. As the meeting adjourned, Brigham Young asked the men of the Mormon Battalion to stay to hear a few remarks prepared just for them.

"Brethren, you have done a great service," said Brother Brigham, "and I bless you in the name of the Lord for your fidelity to the kingdom of God. It is not generally understood why we raised the battalion. We had friends and enemies at Washington. When President Polk could do us a favor, he was disposed to do it, but there were those around him who felt vindictive toward us, and kept continually harping against us to him, and who thought themselves wise enough to lay plans to accomplish our destruction. The plan of raising a battalion to march to California by a call from the War Department was devised with a view to the total overthrow of this kingdom and the destruction of every man, woman, and child, and was hatched up by Senator Thomas H. Benton. They thought to prove our disloyalty to the United States by our refusal to accept the call. But you have proved them wrong to their everlasting shame. You went as honorable men, doing honor to your country and your calling. I am well satisfied with all of you. If some of you have done wrong and transgressed and been out of the way, I exhort you to refrain therefrom and turn unto the Lord and build up His Kingdom. As you can see, we have a great labor before us. Let each man do his duty with all diligence and soon we shall have a city that shall rival the greatest in the world.

"We recognize your sacrifices, and I regret we are unable to provide clothing and other necessities, but we will share such as we have."

"Brother Brigham," shouted one of the men, holding up his purse, "we'll buy what we need. There's gold just lying on the ground in California!"

President Young gave the man a piercing look and continued. "Brethren, I would sooner wear skins or do without than go back to the States to buy clothes. Trust in the Lord. He will provide. If we were to go to San Francisco and dig up chunks of gold or find it here in the valley, it would ruin us. Many want to unite Babylon and Zion. It's the love of money that hurts them. If we find gold and silver, we are in bondage directly. To talk of going away from this valley for anything is like vinegar to my eyes. They that love the world have not their affections placed upon the Lord.

"Now those of you who wish to receive farm land as an inheritance in Zion may report yourselves to the clerk's office."

Delaney went away from the meeting disappointed. He had thought his discussion with the Prophet up on the mountain would have persuaded him that California was a better place for the church to grow and prosper.

During the next few days Delaney threw himself into his work. He had neither the time nor opportunity to discuss his feelings with Brother Brigham.

A huge banquet, planned for Thursday, October 5, to celebrate the return of the battalion, was postponed because of rain. On Friday the semiannual conference of the church began, and, after opening exercises, promptly adjourned so the festivities could begin. Tables were placed in the bowery and a sumptuous feast laid out for everyone to enjoy. The band played, the people danced, and most everyone had a good time. Except Isaac Delaney. Everywhere he went, he heard discussions of the gold strike. He thought of his dear Molly and the wonderful life they would not be sharing.

As was usually the case in public gatherings, Brigham Young

attracted a sizable group of people, all wanting to be close to the church leader. Delaney hung around on the fringe of the crowd, hoping to have a word with the Prophet, but not daring to speak up in front of so many. Eventually, Brigham Young noticed his old friend and excused himself. He slipped his arm around Delaney's shoulder and drew him off to one side. "A fine celebration, wouldn't you say, Brother Isaac? The people rejoice in the battalion's return and the service rendered."

"Brother Brigham, I've come to tell you my resolve is firm to move my family to California next season. When you asked some of us to stay there last year and work for wages, I was reluctant, but now I see it was a revelation from the Lord showing the way for the people of His church to grow and prosper. I know how the Lord tried the children of Israel in the wilderness before allowing them to enter the Promised Land. I see the same grand principle at work here. I hope you'll take the opportunity of this conference to announce to the people that the church will continue on to California in the spring. I'm sure you've noticed the mood of the people."

"I certainly have," said the Prophet. "And I have spent a great deal of time in prayer concerning this matter. Of course you're right. I should address this issue during conference. Thank you for opening your heart to me. I admire a man who speaks his mind."

Isaac Delaney went away from the celebration with his spirits lifted.

On Sunday morning, at eleven o'clock, the entire community turned out for conference at the bowery. The strong voices of the orators more than made up for the poor acoustics in the open air setting. The meeting lasted nearly two hours and consisted mostly of sustaining the various church leaders to their positions.

The conference reconvened at three in the afternoon. When at last the Prophet rose to speak all eyes turned to him in anticipation. Though lacking in formal education and lacking the skills of a polished orator, the power in his sermons reached deep inside his listeners. As he stood before the assembled congregation Brigham Young seemed to grow in stature. His eyes swept the crowd until there was total silence. Then he spoke.

"I am thankful that the weather has become so mild that we can again meet in this bowery, which is large enough to accommodate the congregation. It is said that short visits make long friends, and short sermons perhaps make interesting meetings. I am sure this is the case sometimes.

"When I address the throne of grace in prayer, I am happy to be able to thank God that the Latter-day Saints are striving to order their lives before Him. I am pleased because of the progress this people are making. And yet I see how easy it is for a person to slide backward, and get into darkness and blindness of mind. The adversary of our souls is constantly watching to decoy us from the path of truth and duty to God, until we become reckless in our disobedience to His commandments and to the counsel of His servants. There is but one path to the light of the Lord, which is, as it were, a compass to direct the Saint to the haven of safety, and it will not vary, for its directions are sure.

"We have many duties to perform, and a great work is before us. We have Zion to build up, and upon this we are all agreed. We may differ in our choice of method, some of us wishing to follow the dictates of our own inclinations. There is folly in this.

"I exhort my brethren continually to live so that they may have the light of the Holy Spirit in them, to know their duty, and when they know their duty fully it will be to follow truly those whom God has placed over them to lead them as a community, as a people, as a kingdom of God, it will be to obey the counsel given them from time to time. What does the man who understands the spirit of his religion believe with regard to his own affairs, with regard to his life, with regard to his business transactions? He believes that it is his privilege to be dictated by the constituted authorities of the church of God and the spirit of revelation in all things in his mortal life. There is no part of his life that is exempt from the guidance and dictation of the Priesthood of the Son of God.

"We have recently welcomed among us a number of our brethren bringing tales of gold and easy wealth in California. This has created a great excitement among the people. Even now plans are being laid by many families to relocate to California in the spring. This is contrary to the mind and will of the Lord. I would counsel all such to remain here in the valleys of the mountains, make improvements, build comfortable houses, and raise grain against the days of famine and pestilence with which the earth will be visited.

"There are those with a god of gold in their hearts. The Spirit of the Lord is not in them. If they do not speedily repent, they will be destroyed in the flesh as well as in the spirit. If you elders of Israel want to go to the gold mines, go and be damned. I advise the corrupt...and all who want...to go to California and not come back, for I will not fellowship them. Prosperity and riches blunt the feelings of man. If the people were united, I would send men to get the gold who would care no more about it than the dust under their feet, and then we would gather millions into the church. Some men don't want to go after gold, but they are the very men to go."

Slowly, Isaac Delaney rose to his feet, fists clenched, his lower lip trembling. He couldn't believe what he was hearing. Did the

Prophet intend that they should live in squalor while such abundance awaited them less than eight hundred miles away? Blessed are the faithful, for they shall be poor? No! He wanted to shout, a thousand times no!

The Prophet paused in his speech when he saw Delaney stand up. He turned and looked at his old friend steadily. His eyes were kindly and the hint of a smile was upon his lips. The fire in Delaney's heart went out. He suddenly felt very tired. Bowing his head, he sat down.

"Now, I have spoken harshly," the Prophet continued, "even as a father would to a wayward child. The scriptures are abundantly clear on this point. The Lord has said, 'Lay up for yourselves treasures in heaven,' and 'seek ye first the kingdom of God and His righteousness and all these things will be added unto you.' May God bless you all and guide you in the days of trial to come, I pray in His holy name. Amen."

About an hour after the meeting Delaney was about to sit down with his children to the meal he had prepared for them. Through the window of his unfinished house he saw the Prophet approaching through the grass and sagebrush of what was supposed to be a street. A feeling of nostalgia came over Delaney. He felt transported back to that day when he first met Brigham Young. "John, go ahead and eat," he said, "but feed your sister first." Then he went out to meet the Prophet.

"Brother Isaac," Brigham called out, "I would have a word with you."

Delaney stepped forward, his demeanor cool and unfriendly. He could not hide how he felt. The Prophet extended his hand. Delaney hesitated for a long time. He looked at the hand. Then he looked into Brigham's eyes. He saw love, compassion—and strength. Delaney averted his eyes, ashamed. The Prophet's extended hand reached out and touched Delaney on the shoulder. A gentle tug and Delaney found himself walking with the Prophet toward the east fork of City Creek.

"I grieved, too," said Brigham, "when I heard of your wife's passing. She was a precious gem."

"Then why was she taken?" demanded Delaney. "You said we would receive blessings if we went with the battalion."

"Your Molly was not the first to die for the sake of her religion, nor will she be the last. As for blessings, what greater blessing can a man have than to know his wife has been sealed to him for time and all eternity. Molly will be yours forever...if you continue faithful."

"It is more than I can endure," said Delaney, his voice breaking.

"You will endure it," said the Prophet soothingly, "for the sake of your children...and for the sake of your religion. You are a fortunate man, Isaac. Only a man highly favored of the Lord would be so sorely tested by the adversary. Do you remember the day we first met?"

Delaney nodded.

"I told you then the Lord had a labor for you to perform. The Lord is not through with you yet, Brother Isaac. Do not forsake Him. He has not forsaken you. Stay with us, here in the valley, and I promise you in the name of Jesus Christ you will prosper and become the instrument of much good. Your joy will know no bounds."

"How can I know that?"

"That is something only you can answer. When you next approach the Lord in Prayer, remember the scriptures that say, 'whoso believeth in God might with surety hope for a better world' and 'ye receive no witness until after the trial of your faith'. The Lord is with you, Brother Isaac. Are you with Him?"

"Yes."

"Then ask Him if these things are not true. If you feel a burning within your bosom, you will know of a surety that what I have spoken is true. Will you do it?"

"Yes, I will."

"Then I'll leave you now, Brother Isaac. I am confident you will remain with us in the spring. If you ask sincerely, there can be no other answer. God bless you, Brother Isaac."

Brigham Young extended his hand again. Delaney shook it tentatively. The Prophet turned and started back, while Delaney continued on to the bank of City Creek. He wanted to walk awhile and think. He had sacrificed so much for the sake of his religion. He still intended to go to California in the spring, but he couldn't ignore the tugging on his heart that urged him to stay in the Great Salt Lake Valley. He pondered, what would Molly have him do?

# 6

Lack of timber was probably the greatest shortcoming of the Great Salt Lake Valley. The pioneers built their fort primarily of adobe bricks, which they called "dobies." Timber was to be had in the canyons, and, with a concerted community effort, sawmills were built and the necessary material for building real houses was becoming available, though not at a rate sufficient to meet the demand.

Delaney would have preferred to build a real house for his children, but he recognized the necessity of getting the job done before the winter snows came. So he elected to build a small, two-room log cabin, which he finished before the first of November.

Timber was useful for more than just building houses. It was the only fuel available to the pioneers besides sagebrush, which burned too hot and too quickly. Nearly every day Delaney took a wagon up Millcreek Canyon to cut firewood. The distance was greater than to City Creek Canyon, but competition for the firewood was less keen. He was able to gather enough for himself and still have some to sell, his only means of support besides the gold he had brought from the gold fields. His intention was to save the gold and use it to get back to California in the spring.

On a beautiful, sunny morning in late November, Isaac Delaney went up the canyon again to cut firewood. A strong, warm southerly wind was blowing when he left home. By noon the sky was completely overcast and the temperature began to fall. Delaney barely noticed the cold. Woodcutting was warm work.

At two o'clock Delaney turned his wagon around and started back down the canyon. A light snow began to fall. Soon the flakes were being whipped about on a swirling wind. He had gone barely a mile when the wind quit blowing, and the snow turned into a blizzard. In no time the track that was called a road was indiscernible. Delaney had seen snow before, but never like this. He pressed on, realizing he had to find shelter from the storm before too long. He estimated he must have gone at least eight miles up the canyon. He decided to try for the sawmill about four and one-half miles distant. He thought of the many times he had passed that way and how he had ignored the residents at the mill when they had greeted him. He hoped they would be more gracious than he had been.

Time passed. Ten, fifteen, thirty minutes. The snow got deeper. Visibility was down to only forty or fifty feet. Side canyons and twists in the trail slowed Delaney's progress. He wasn't sure he was on the right track or not. An hour passed and still the snow didn't let up. Delaney thought of his children. He had to make it back for their sake.

At last Delaney came to a spot that he didn't remember seeing before. The trail seemed to lead through a narrow gap between a large rock and the bank of the stream. Delaney pondered the situation for a moment. Could he make it through? He had to try. Going back was not an option. He started forward. Two thirds of the way through Delaney felt a lurch. The wagon shuddered and, before he could jump clear, he felt himself flying through the air.

Delaney landed in a snow bank and tumbled into the creek, which at this time of year was only about a foot deep. Before he could move, the wagon and its contents came sliding down after him.

Delaney was cold and wet and pinned beneath a wheel of the wagon. *Oh God, don't let me die out here,* he thought. He looked the situation over. The wagon was still upright, as was the horse. Delaney whistled and hollered at the animal, but succeeded in only getting the horse to look in his direction. He needed a whip and didn't have one. Plenty of rocks lay in the streambed. He picked one up and threw it as hard as he could against the horse's rump. The animal jumped and started to move, momentarily lifting the weight of the wagon from off of him. Before Delaney could move, the horse had stopped and the wagon settled once again onto his leg. He got another rock and tried again, this time accompanying his throw with a stream of shouts and curses that would have made a sailor blush. The horse pulled forward, and strained against the load long enough for Delaney to drag himself to safety.

Delaney examined his leg. It was cut and bruised and hurt like the dickens, but he couldn't tell if it was broken. It didn't matter if it was. He would have to walk on it or die. Delaney pulled himself to a standing position, and slowly, painfully worked his way up the stream bank, unhitched the horse from the wagon, and climbed on its back. The animal stumbled forward in the ever deepening snow.

After what seemed like half an hour, the snow was up above the horse's knees. The wind was blowing the snow into deep drifts, completely obscuring the trail. A few minutes more and the horse was heaving and jerking, trying to move in the deep snow, but unable to get anywhere. Finally, the beast collapsed, exhausted. Delaney lay next to the stricken animal, listening to its labored breathing and feeling the warm columns of steam coming from its flared nostrils. This was the end, or ought to have been, but Delaney was not a man to take dying lying down. He got to his feet and pressed on in the snow and gathering darkness.

More minutes passed. How many, Delaney didn't know. He just kept plowing a path through the knee deep snow. Finally, the snow stopped and breaks appeared in the clouds above. He could see stars here and there. And then, coming around a bend in the trail, he saw the mill a couple hundred yards in the distance. *Thank God! A light in the window!*

Delaney tried to move faster, but his limbs refused to respond. They moved as if they had a life of their own. He tried calling out, but his voice had been reduced to a croak. He kept trying, and by the time he had covered half the distance was managing a fairly respectable volume. The door of the mill house opened, a head stuck out, and then it seemed as if in an instant a man was beside him, helping him to the open door where two women stood watching.

Inside the house the man and his two female companions immediately stripped Delaney of every bit of clothing. No time for modesty. This was a matter of life or death. They laid him next to the fire and covered him with quilts and a feather bed.

"How did you come to be out in this weather?" asked the man. Delaney was trembling so violently he could barely get out the word, "firewood."

"Let him be," said one of the women.

The second woman came with a steaming mug of coffee. Delaney gulped down two cups of the stimulating drink. After awhile, he quit shaking. And then sleep, blessed sleep.

The following morning Delaney awoke to the sound of a woman's voice singing. He opened his eyes and looked around. The younger of the two women he had seen the previous night sat next to a window singing softly to a baby in her lap. The child appeared to be six to eight months old. Through the window he could see the sun shining and water from the melting snow pouring off the roof of the mill house.

Delaney tried to raise himself up, but the sharp pain in his left leg caused a low groan to escape his lips. The woman stopped singing and looked in his direction.

"Good morning, sir," she said. "You gave us quite a fright last night. Are you feeling better this morning?"

"I...I think so. My leg is quite sore, and my feet also. My fingers feel quite stiff and useless."

"I'm not surprised. Brother Porter says you'll be lucky if you don't lose some of your toes."

"Brother Porter? Is he your husband?" asked Delaney.

"Not likely," said the young woman, laughing. "He's my sister's husband. It was she who gave you the coffee to drink."

"I'm sorry. When I saw you singing to the child, I naturally thought it must be yours."

"And she is."

"She's a beautiful girl," said Delaney.

"Do you really think so? I think she quite looks like her father, and I would hardly have called him beautiful. Handsome, maybe."

"Shall I have the pleasure of meeting him?"

The young woman's face darkened and she looked down at the floor. "No," she said. "He died last year. He drowned while ferrying our wagon over the North Platte."

"I'm sorry," said Delaney. "I know just how you feel."

"Do you, then?" she said, sharply.

"Yes. My wife died this past spring."

"Oh, dear," said the young woman, dismayed. "I'm sorry for being so curt. It's just so easy to feel pity for oneself, that I sometimes forget that others have troubles, too."

"I know just how you feel," said Delaney.

They both looked at one another and laughed. "I thought I would never laugh again," said Delaney.

"Nor I. Do you have any children?"

"Yes, I do. Two children. And I should be getting back to them. If you could fetch my clothing, I'll be dressed and on my way."

"Brother Porter said you would probably want to leave. He says you are a man of great determination. He also said I was not to let you leave until he returned. Besides, I shouldn't think you would get very far in your condition."

Delaney realized she was right. This was a terrible turn of events. What good could he be to the children?

"If I am going to be here awhile longer, perhaps I should introduce myself. I'm Isaac Delaney. And what might your name be?"

"Harriet. Harriet Brimhall."

Just then the door opened and Brother Porter entered. "I see you're awake," he said. "You're a lucky man, sir. I found your horse...alive... and I was able to get your wagon here in one piece."

"Good," said Delaney. "I was just telling Sister Brimhall that I should be getting back to my children."

"No, I think you had better stay with us awhile," said Porter. "Can't your wife look after them?"

"I'm a widower, Brother Porter."

"I see. Then you just tell us where they are and I'll see that they're taken care of."

Of course, they were right. As long as the children were properly cared for, it was best that Delaney not further endanger his health.

The days grew into weeks. The children were brought to the mill for Christmas. It was a joyous celebration, far more so than Delaney would have expected. He couldn't help but notice how his son John seemed to bond with Harriet. He saw John laugh and play again for the first time since Delaney had first left him in Nauvoo.

Sure enough, Delaney lost two of his toes, just as Brother Porter had predicted. Harriet acted as his nurse and was jealous of any attention paid to him by her sister. She was only twenty, but in spite of the difference in their ages, Delaney found himself thinking of her as more than a nurse.

As part of his recovery Delaney began to take short walks with Harriet at his side. His thoughts kept returning to California, and Molly with him there. But every time he thought of Molly, the image of Harriet crowded her out. In a way he felt guilty, as if he were doing something wrong. John needed a mother. Isaac needed a wife.

On one of their walks Harriet stumbled in the snow. Delaney managed to catch her arm and stayed her fall. "Oh, dear," she said. "I should be more careful."

Delaney looked at her intently. He had never touched her before. Harriet smiled. Delaney blushed. "Harriet... I..." his voice trailed off. He knew what he wanted to say, but didn't know how to say it.

"Yes?" she said, in an encouraging voice.

Delaney drew within himself, thinking that maybe this wasn't the right time, but finally he found the courage to speak. "Have you ever considered going to California?"

Harriet's face took on a look of bewilderment. "California? Never!"

"But it's a wonderful place."

"*This* is a wonderful place. The Lord has brought us here for a reason. If He wanted us to go to California, we would be there."

The simple logic of her statement made perfect sense to Delaney. Maybe Brigham Young was right. Maybe he *did* have a god of gold in his heart. Delaney felt a swelling of emotion building within himself. A hint of tears appeared in his eyes. "Harriet..." he began again. "When my wife died I thought I could never love again... but..."

Delaney couldn't find the words. He didn't need to. Harriet took his hand in hers and smiled. "You don't have to say it," she said. Delaney pulled her close and they embraced warmly. He felt whole again. His life would begin anew.

By the end of January, Delaney was ready to return home. Harriet and the Porters rode with him to the city. Only the Porters returned to the sawmill. Harriet accepted Isaac's proposal to be his bride, and the Prophet himself married them.

Together, Isaac and Harriet would heal each other's hurts as they built a new life in the valley of the Great Salt Lake. For Isaac Delaney, California was only a fading memory.

# I Have Seen the Elephant

# 7

The lure of California reached far beyond the confines of the Great Salt Lake Valley. It beckoned men of all classes, occupations, and religious persuasions to come west to seek their fortunes. First rumors, then newspaper reports, and finally government confirmation of the gold discovery had awakened a spirit of adventure in the hearts of thousands. A revolution in the ordinary state of affairs was happening. Emigration across the continent, a mere trickle before, had instantly been transformed into a flash flood. So great was the press of gold seekers that one tribe of Indians began to make plans to relocate to the east, for surely there could be no more white men left in the States.

Most of the adventurers had no skills as miners or as prairie travelers, but it mattered not what they had been in their former situations, for now they were Californians, on their way to "see the elephant" and someday return to home and family with "a pocketful of rocks." They came from everywhere, by train, steamboat, in wagons, and even on foot, to the great "jumping off places," St. Joseph and Independence.

The two sleepy river towns had suddenly become bustling cities of many thousands, attracting the lowest forms of human life. Brothels, saloons, and gambling dens lay in wait to shear the unwary sheep. For weeks the population grew as the emigrants waited for the prairie to dry out and the grass to green up sufficiently to feed the teams of mules and oxen. What had cost ten dollars back home, cost twenty dollars at Independence. Business was good and the local merchants prospered.

The rush was on. There was gold in California. The word had been spread everywhere by the spring of 1849, even to a small farming community in Mississippi.

# 8

The rock only weighed about homespun pants. Though only March, this was Mississippi and Deaton didn't think he was working hard enough if he didn't sweat. The only things easy to grow were weeds and rocks. MacKenzie Deaton had been pulling rocks out of this field for nine years, but every year he harvested a fresh crop. He was a big man, five foot ten with a farmer's powerful arms and shoulders. Though only twenty-nine, his brown hair had an occasional touch of gray. When he removed his hat, the white of his upper forehead contrasted with the fiery sunburn of the rest of his face, a testament to his occupation.ten pounds. It made a sound like billiard balls colliding as MacKenzie Deaton heaved it onto the rock pile in the corner of the field. Deaton removed his hat and wiped his brow with the blue bandanna he always carried in the pocket of his

The Deatons were a clannish family. When they moved from North Carolina in 1820, everyone had come; brothers, sisters, aunts, uncles, and cousins. MacKenzie had been the first Deaton born in Mississippi, named for Robert MacKenzie, some distant ancestor on his mother's side of the family. He could read and write, no small accomplishment on what was then the frontier, but that was the extent of his education. He had married Sarah Burns when he was nineteen and she had given him two children, Joel Oliver, eight, and Laura Jean, six months.

Deaton had farmed this same forty acres of bottomland along the Yazoo River near Greenwood since before he was married. Except for last year, he had always brought in a fairly good crop. Now he was getting ready for the new growing season. He replaced his hat and started back toward the plow, when he saw a rider approaching from the opposite end of the field. The horse made no sound nor created any dust as it came. The moistness of the newly turned earth cushioned the pounding hoofbeats. The horse stopped a few feet away from MacKenzie Deaton, and Eli Bennett was sporting a broad grin.

"How're y'all doin'?" said Bennett, as he swung his right leg over the horse's neck and slid off the left side. The horse had no saddle.

"Mighty fine, Eli," said Deaton, "and yourself?"

Bennett extended his hand and Deaton shook it.

"I'm a Californian," said Bennett.

"You're a what?"

"A Californian...or soon will be. I'm goin' to the diggin's."

"Well, I always knew you was goin' to the dickens, but to the diggin's... that's a mite surprisin'. What about your farm? Y'sellin' out?"

"Don't reckon I will," said Bennett. "I aim to come back soon's I get myself some of them rocks. What about you? Y'want to come with me?"

Deaton gestured toward the rock pile. "Got plenty o' rocks," he said.

"I mean the kind with gold in 'em."

"I know what you mean, Eli, but I'm a farmer. Don't know nothin' about minin'."

"You don't need to. I hear it's just layin' around on the ground, just waitin' for someone to come pick it up."

Deaton looked down at the ground and kicked a few clods of dirt. "That sounds pretty good," he said, "but my daddy taught me to always know the difference between need and greed. Everything I need is right here. I know things are different with you now that Clara is gone, but I got a family to look after and I gotta get my seed in the ground. Then someone's gotta look after it. Joel's only eight."

"You got family 'round here, Mac. I'm sure you could get someone to look after things. You'd only be gone a year or so."

"Can't do it, Eli."

"Chance of a lifetime, Mac. When you're an old man sittin' by the fire with your grandkids, you can tell 'em how you went on the great gold rush to California."

"How soon are you leavin'?"

"Day after tomorrow," said Bennett.

"Be sure an' stop by 'fore you leave. Have dinner with us."

"You won't be comin' with me?"

Deaton shook his head.

"Can't change your mind?"

"Not likely."

"Well, then," said Bennett, "guess I'll be goin'."

Bennett grabbed his horse's mane and jumped onto its back, balancing on his stomach. With a twist and a grunt he got his leg over and sat up. "Be seein' you, Mac," he said, then turned his horse's and headed back the way he had come. Deaton watched him for awhile, then went back to his plowing.

# 9

Eli Bennett had made a bigger impression than he realized. Less than a week after his departure for California, MacKenzie Deaton walked through the office door of Samuel Tyler, president of the Greenwood bank.

"Afternoon, Sam," said Deaton. "Got a minute?"

"Of course, MacKenzie," said Tyler, displaying his best banker's manners. "Come in and have a seat."

Deaton took a chair opposite the banker and tried to get comfortable. He was nervous. He hadn't even discussed this with Sarah. "I reckon you've heard of the gold strike in California?"

"Yes, I have," said Tyler in measured tones.

"I'm giving serious thought to making the trip myself," said Deaton.

Tyler's eyes seemed to bore a hole through Deaton, but he said nothing. He was a man with a nose for a good deal.

"If I go," said Deaton, "I'll need eight hundred dollars."

"Am I correct in assuming you want me to put up the eight hundred dollars?" asked Tyler.

"Somethin' like that. I take the physical risk and you take the financial risk. We split fifty-fifty."

"Frankly, MacKenzie, I'm not predisposed to take any kind of risk on the bank's behalf. This is a conservative financial institution. Our depositors expect us to handle their money carefully. Somehow financing a gold mining expedition doesn't fit that definition. Tell you what, though. If you give me a mortgage on your farm with a note due, say November 1, 1850, and you pay me back the eight hundred dollars plus half of all you earn, I think maybe we can make a deal."

"Wait a minute," said Deaton. "You want me to take all the risk while you take half of the profit? It ain't fair. If you want half the profit, you gotta take half the risk."

"No, MacKenzie. If you want to go to California, you take the risk and I get half of the profit. Besides, I'll be using my own money and not the bank's, and the loan will be interest free."

"You call fifty percent interest free?"

"Sometimes when we want something bad enough we have to be willing to sacrifice for it," said the banker.

Of course Tyler was right. He held all the cards. Either way Tyler would come away a winner. He would either share a bonanza in gold or own the Deaton farm. Deaton knew he was taking a gamble, but it was an opportunity that might never come his way again. He was willing to take the risk.

MacKenzie Deaton grimaced as he strained to push his rowboat into the river. Loading it on shore had proved to not be a very good idea. He had caulked all the leaks, but still wasn't sure the boat was up to the trip. It wasn't much to look at. It just had to get him to Vicksburg.

"Y'all be careful now," said Sarah Deaton. "It's gonna be hard enough lookin' after this place while you're gone. Ain't got time to be lookin' for a new man."

"Woman, don't worry yourself about me," he said. "You'll have plenty of help till I get back."

"If you mean that shiftless brother of yours, I'd get more help out of Laura Jean."

MacKenzie looked up from his exertions. Sarah stood a few feet away holding Laura Jean on her left hip. Their son Joel was leaning up against her right side. For a moment MacKenzie felt a twinge of regret. It would likely be two years, maybe more, before he next saw them. Then he remembered why he was going. It wasn't only for himself, but for Sarah and the kids.

"Don't you get started on my family," said MacKenzie. "It's your family, too."

Sarah looked away, her head nodding and a sarcastic grin on her lips. MacKenzie heaved once more and the boat slid into the Yazoo River. He tied it to a stump on the shore, then turned to his wife and children. Sarah's eyes were starting to water. She had promised herself she would be strong, but she just couldn't help it. MacKenzie came to Sarah and embraced her and the baby.

"I ain't much for goodbyes," he said.

"Just be careful," said Sarah, her lower lip trembling. "Come back to us."

"I'll be back. I'm gonna get me some of those rocks, and then we're gonna live the good life."

Deaton looked down at Joel and tousled the boy's hair with his left hand. Then, squatting down, he said, "You're gonna have to be a big help to your ma while I'm gone."

"Yes, Pa."

"You ain't a man, yet, but you're gonna have to act like one. I'm countin' on you now. D'you understand?"

"Yes, Pa."

MacKenzie stood up and kissed his wife. "Be seein' you," he said.

Sarah clung to her man, unwilling to let him go, but also knowing that it was the only way she could keep him. Deaton slipped from her grasp and untied the boat. He stepped aboard and pushed away from the riverbank with a long pole. The current took the boat, and the distance between MacKenzie and Sarah grew faster than either of them wanted. In moments it was fifty, then a hundred yards. At the bend in the river Deaton stood up and waved. Sarah shouted something, but he couldn't understand what it was. Joel was crying. A tree blocked the view, and then they were gone. MacKenzie Deaton felt more alone than he ever had before in his life.

The day was new and the air felt crisp and clean. Deaton maneuvered the boat to where the current was swiftest. Mile after mile of Mississippi countryside slipped by like a panorama show he had once seen at the fair. The banks were heavily timbered with cottonwoods and pines. Occasionally a farm or plantation came into view. Deaton took note of one plantation in particular. A large house, a barn and stable, and several Negro huts. This was about the bottom of the scale as plantations went. A reminder of what was beyond his reach, but not so far that he couldn't dream about it. Slaves worked in the fields. The faint strains of singing carried on the breeze and several of the black children came down to the river to wave. Deaton returned the gesture of friendship and thought of his future. One thing he understood well was that wealth was not money. Wealth was property, be it land or slaves.

Just before dusk Deaton rowed the boat beneath a large cottonwood and tied it off. Half an hour later he was relaxing next to a crackling fire. In the fading sunlight he scribbled a few lines in his diary:

> *Sat. Apr 14th—Sed goodby to Sarah and kids Should make Vicksburg by Monday and Saint Louis in a fortnight made about 50 mi today.*

When darkness fell Deaton rolled up in his bedding, glad that the first day of his great adventure was over.

# 10

The city of Vicksburg sat on a hill. Everything seemed to be vertical, the buildings clinging to the sides of the steep hills. The people spoke of "going up" or "going down" to visit friends. Above the waterfront the bluffs rose some two hundred feet, affording a majestic view of the Mississippi River and the Louisiana shore across the way. Viewed from the river, church spires punctuated the skyline, while mansions of varying degrees of elegance and dignity embellished the slopes and hilltops.

The city of approximately five thousand was a creature of the river, one of the principal stopping places for the sidewheel steamboats plying the route from New Orleans to St. Louis. From its wharves and warehouses the farmers and planters of the area shipped their produce and cotton to the great cities in the North. Its location in the center of the Mississippi steamboat traffic was Vicksburg's greatest virtue, as well as its greatest curse. The rougher elements from Natchez and New Orleans were attracted to Vicksburg like fleas to a dog. As well as riches and prosperity, the river brought driftwood and scum. The waterfront was home to every form of skullduggery and vice, as if it were the natural order of things.

Shortly before noon on Monday, April 16, 1849, MacKenzie Deaton and his rowboat were ejected from the mouth of the Yazoo River. The current was much stronger in the big river and landing the boat would be a tricky affair. As Deaton steered for the Vicksburg landing, he sighted a column of black smoke away to the south. In moments a steamboat rounded a bend in the river, blowing its whistle and churning the muddy brown water into white foam. *It must be a fairly new steamer,* thought Deaton, for most of the old steamers still had bells instead of whistles. If it was the steamer for St. Louis, the timing was perfect. Deaton would have plenty of time to book passage, but not enough time to get into trouble. Vicksburg wasn't the place for a country boy.

When the steamer *Tempest* arrived at the Vicksburg landing, Deaton went aboard to inquire about passage to St. Louis. A crewman directed him to the clerk, a short, dark complexioned man with longish hair and a prominent nose.

"Good day, sir," said Deaton. "Are you going to St. Louis?"

"Yes, sir. It's twelve dollars. Twenty if you want a stateroom. I have a few left."

Twenty dollars was more than Deaton wanted to pay, but sitting out on deck for two weeks wasn't very appealing either. He thought it over a minute. It would be four or five months on the trail to California, and he had no idea what the cost to get outfitted in Independence would be. The clerk's head was tilted to one side and the frown on his face indicated his growing impatience. Deaton decided this was no time to be extravagant. He pulled twelve dollars from his purse and handed it to the clerk. The clerk's expression changed little, if at all, as he counted the money and filled in the blanks on Deaton's ticket.

"We'll be leaving at two o'clock," said the clerk as he handed over the ticket. "Don't be late."

Deaton disembarked and then returned with his few personal belongings and climbed the stairs to the cabin deck. He stacked his gear next to a bench and made a quick tour of the boat.

The *Tempest* was the newest boat on the Vicksburg, Natchez & New Orleans line. She was 287 feet long and 32 feet wide. Fully loaded with two hundred tons of cargo and two hundred sixty passengers, she drew only thirty-three inches of water. Empty, she fairly skimmed over the water's surface at only twenty-one inches. The boat essentially had only three decks. The eight boilers and two engines were located on the forward section of the main deck. Cargo was carried below in the five-foot deep hold and to the rear on the main deck. The next deck up was the cabin deck. In the center was the main cabin, an oblong room surrounded by thirty-six staterooms, so-called because of the former practice of naming each room after a state instead of giving it a number. Each stateroom had two doors, one that opened onto the deck and another that opened into the main cabin. The passengers traveling cabin class took their meals in the main cabin and otherwise used it for a lounge. Deck passengers had to fend for themselves. Perched above the main cabin was Texas, a small group of cabins for the officers and the crew members who did "clean work." Surmounting everything was the pilothouse, nearly forty feet above the water. Two iron chimneys rose above the forward part of the boat and a decorative letter "T" in wrought iron was suspended between them. An aquatic scene of a raging torrent with a mermaid sitting on a rock adorned each of the sidewheel housings. As Deaton enjoyed his tour of the boat, one of the boat's officers approached him.

"Are you a cabin passenger?" he asked.

"No. Deck."

"Then get down below with the other deck passengers. This deck is for cabin passengers only."

A flippant reply flashed through Deaton's mind, but disappeared as quickly as it had come. They could just as easily throw him off, and getting a refund of his fare was unheard of, so he meekly gathered up his meager possessions and removed himself to the main deck. The view wasn't as good, but it had its own advantages. At least he would be out of the weather, unless there was a real blow.

By two o'clock the *Tempest* had taken on a load of cotton bales, fresh water for the boilers, several cords of wood to stoke the fires, and a total of seven new passengers; four for St. Louis and the other three to various destinations. Deaton had no way of counting everybody, but he guessed nearly two hundred passengers must be on board. He made himself comfortable on an overturned cotton bale and watched as preparations were made to get underway.

Two Negro tenders had been stoking the fires for several minutes while the chief engineer went around checking the safety valves and the main steam lines to the two engines. The engines were designed for operation at one hundred sixty pounds of pressure, but without gauges safety was more a matter of instinct than an exact science.

The captain, standing on the hurricane deck, called out in a loud voice, "Are you ready?"

The mate, standing on the forecastle, the fore part of the boat on the lower deck, looked to the engineer, who shouted, "Steam's up!"

"Aye, aye, sir!" shouted the mate to the captain. Then he turned to the several deck hands waiting near the iron mooring rings, their hands on the big lines. "Cast off!" he shouted.

The deck hands lifted the lines and the captain turned to the pilothouse behind him and shouted, "All clear!"

Three deck hands poled against the levee as bells jangled and the panting of the engines grew faster. The great boat trembled as if it were alive, then it was free and backing out into the river channel. The paddles stopped and the *Tempest* was caught by the current and began drifting south. Then the engines reversed, churning up great billows of foam and checking the boat's southward progress. Slowly, the steamer gained speed and in minutes it rounded a bend to the northwest, leaving only the heights of Vicksburg in sight. It was all lost on Deaton, though. The heat from the boilers and the throbbing of the engines had overcome his interest in steamboating and he was fast asleep on his bale of cotton. He awoke some five hours later in darkness. It was completely quiet except for the sounds of the river and muffled conversations. The *Tempest* had tied up for the night. Deaton could only guess where they were.

# 11

The days passed in a slow monotony that almost numbed the senses. Cast off at dawn and tie up at dusk, stopping at some river settlements that nobody ever heard of, while passing others by. The method of their selection was a mystery to all but the captain, but the stops were a welcome opportunity for the deck passengers to purchase food and other necessities. Sometimes the steamboat stopped at clearings next to the river where some enterprising entrepreneur had cut and stacked firewood for sale at two and a half dollars per cord.

On the eighth day out of Vicksburg the *Tempest* landed in Memphis and Deaton had his first real encounter with the evil that the world had to offer. Memphis was a bustling city of some twenty thousand souls, the largest city in Tennessee. Situated on the Mississippi at a place formerly called Chickasaw Bluffs, the great city had been founded in 1819 by three wealthy landowners, one of them the late President Andrew Jackson.

It was past noon when the *Tempest* gently nudged against the Memphis levee. The waterfront was alive with activity and MacKenzie Deaton decided to use the two hours of the layover to see the city. His wanderings eventually led him to the public marketplace where he bought food for the next leg of his journey. He had decided to start back for the steamboat when something caught his eye. A crowd of men was pressing to enter a large wooden structure too big to be a house and not big enough to be a barn. Deaton went to see what it was all about.

The building was all white and above the door was a sign that read, "Marston & Waddell." Once inside, Deaton was disappointed to see a cattle auction in progress. The interior was rough framed like a barn. The auctioneer stood on a two-foot high platform toward the back of the room and was auctioning a critter that stood in front of him. The sale was made and another animal led in through a side door. A barefooted black man crouched near the door, broom in hand, ready to clean up after the cattle. This animal sold quickly, too, and as Deaton turned to leave, he stopped when the next item of sale came through the door: a group of six slaves. A man, a woman, and four children ranging in age from about ten down to a child barely old enough to walk. They were quite probably a family and had a look of fear in their eyes such as Deaton had never seen before. An older gentleman accompanied them, and from the sad look on his face Deaton guessed he was the owner and sorry he had to sell his property. Deaton had lived around slavery all his life, but this was his first time at a sale. Slaves were the invisible people. Like cattle, they were always there, but hardly ever noticed, particularly if you didn't own any.

Deaton looked around him and noticed the makeup of the crowd had changed. The cattle-buying farmers began to leave while those who remained were well dressed and didn't look like they had ever done an honest day's work. They were businessmen, and their business was slave trading.

"Gentlemen," called out the auctioneer, "I draw your attention to the block of nigras offered for sale by Mister William Bolt of Fayette County. Tom is a prime field hand and skilled in carpentry. Patsy is a house servant and cook, but works well in the fields. You may inspect them before the sale begins. It is Mister Bolt's wish that they be sold as a group, rather than break up the family."

The slave traders gathered around and began inspecting the merchandise. They pulled up eyelids and peered at teeth. It could just as easily have been a horse auction.

"Get your shirt off, boy," said one of the slave traders. "Let's have a look at you."

The slave Tom removed his shirt, revealing a lean, muscular torso.

"Turn around."

Tom turned around slowly, his head bowed. The slave trader made a derisive sound and said, "This nigger ain't worth nothin'. There ain't a mark on 'im. First time you lay the lash to 'im, he'll be runnin' for sure."

"On the contrary," said the auctioneer. "That just means he

don't give nobody no trouble. Ain't that right Mister Bolt?"

"Tom's a good boy. Best nigger I've got. Never been any trouble."

"There you are," said the auctioneer. "Now, Mister Bolt wants one thousand dollars for Tom and seven hundred for Patsy. Anyone who'll take them all can have the children for only five hundred dollars."

"Each?" asked a buyer.

"Total."

A murmur of approval went through the buyers. The bidding began with restraint. This was only the first sale. The bidding would become livelier before the day's business had concluded.

"I'll give two thousand dollars for the lot of them," said one of the buyers.

The auctioneer looked around the room for another bid. His eyes fell on Deaton, who suddenly felt very uncomfortable, even sullied, by being present. Deaton began edging toward the door.

"I'll give twelve hundred for the buck," said another buyer. "Got no need for the girl."

Interest in the slave Tom grew rapidly and he was sold for thirteen hundred and twenty-five dollars. His new owner led him from the room as Patsy cried out, "Please don't take my Tom!"

Tom looked around at his family for the last time. He wanted to say something, but couldn't. His new owner cuffed him on the ear and said, "Get movin', boy! We got us a long road to travel."

Deaton pushed his way through the buyers and out onto the street. It had long been his ambition to own property. A lot of land and slaves to work it. Now he wasn't so sure anymore. He pulled his watch from his pocket and saw it was time to be heading back to the steamboat. He hadn't got twenty yards when he heard a commotion behind him. He turned around to see the girl Patsy being dragged from the auction house screaming, "My babies! My babies!" From inside he heard, "Mama! Don't leave us! Mama! Come back, Mama!"

"It ain't right," said Deaton half aloud. He thought of his own family, and his resolve to go to California completely disintegrated. In ten days he could be home. Think of it! That black family would give anything to be together and he had willingly parted from his own. Depressed and guilt-ridden, MacKenzie Deaton trudged back to the levee. The sky had darkened and it was beginning to rain.

Deaton boarded the *Tempest* and went to his usual place near the boilers. He gathered up his things and was checking around to see if he had missed anything when he heard a cackling laughter from behind him. Deaton turned and peered into the shadows by the boilers. There, sitting on a stack of firewood, was the Negro tender who had stoked the fire all the way from Vicksburg. He sat all scrunched up with his legs crossed and his arms resting on one knee. In his right hand was a pipe emitting a faint wisp of smoke. Deaton had barely noticed the man before, but he took a good look at him now. The black man had on an old slouch hat and wore only dirty denim pants held up by gray suspenders, and a rough pair of work shoes. His grizzled growth of whiskers made him look older than his real age and the whites of his eyes looked almost yellow. A mixture of wisdom and sadness was reflected in those eyes, and they were looking directly at Deaton.

"Gwine ter leave de boat?" asked the black man.

"Yes. I've decided to go home."

"And where might dat be?"

"Up the Yazoo...near Greenwood."

The black man cackled again and shook his head. "You ain't de first man gwine ter California dat has gots de cold feet."

"How did you know I was going to California?"

"Ain't much on dis boat dat 'scapes my po' eyes," said the black man. "See over dere dey is two men drinkin' out of dat dere jug an' playin' cards? Dey's two of de worst men on de river. Dey's gamblers. You plays cards wit dem and you be a po' man sho 'nuff."

Deaton looked at the two men. They sat on crates with a steamer trunk between them, playing cards. On the deck was a jug of something and they were taking turns at it. As they played, their eyes never rested, flitting here and there, looking for a likely prospect.

"Never seen them before," said Deaton.

"Dat's okay," said the black man, cackling, "long's dey don't see you."

"Well, I'll be going now," said Deaton. "Gotta find me a boat to Vicksburg."

The black man appeared not to hear Deaton. He took a puff on his pipe and continued speaking. "More 'n one way ter make a livin' in dis ol' world. Some folks work all day, but dem gamblers, dey get rich skinnin' travelers. Some folk's po', but dey's too proud to steal. You a po' man, dat's why you is gwine ter California."

"I *was* going to California."

"Some day when I has 'nuff money, I is gwine ter California."

"Do you think the captain will let you go?"

"It don't make him no nevermind."

"But you belong to him, don't you?"

Deaton saw a light in the black man's eyes as he spoke in a low voice, full of emotion and pride, "I don't belong ter no man. I is free."

"I hear tell that slavers take free black men and sell them. Ain't you afraid that might happen to you?"

"Yassuh, but a man does what he has ter do. My Tildy, she ain't free. When I has 'nuff money, I is gwine ter buy 'er, den we's gwine to California."

"You'd risk that much for your wife?"

"Yassuh. A man does what he gots ter do, but you been know dat."

Yes, that was something Deaton already knew. Somehow he had forgotten it. Going to California was for Sarah and the children. Going home was strictly for himself. Deaton put his things back and lay down on the cotton bale. When the *Tempest* pulled out, he was fast asleep.

# 12

The assessment of the two gamblers was right on target. Myron Lang and Walter Kelsey didn't call anywhere home, unless two rooms above a saloon in New Orleans could be so designated. If two men of lower character existed on the Mississippi, they had not yet been found. While some men had a streak of dishonesty, this pair was the mother lode. Like chameleons, they could blend in with almost any environment. They could be the suave, gentlemen gamblers in the salon or the rough and ready river travelers among the deck passengers. They had set up shop on the boiler deck before the *Tempest* left Memphis. They started out playing poker just between the two of them, using a crate for a gaming table, but before long they were joined by other passengers looking for fun, relaxation, and perhaps a chance to make an easy buck. The games were loose and easy, win a little, lose a little, as different players drifted in and out of the game.

For bait Lang had a bankroll of nearly five thousand dollars, which he was losing in small amounts...all of it to Kelsey. It was all part of the act. They were looking for an appropriate victim. Someone with a lot of cash, and greedy, and stupid. By the second day out of Memphis they had found their fish, a gentleman farmer from eastern Tennessee on his way to California, had set the hook, and were about to reel him in.

MacKenzie Deaton had long since lost interest in the gamblers. He knew how to play poker, but his mind was set on getting to California. Playing poker was not on his schedule. He was on the third page of a letter to his wife when Joshua, the Negro boiler tender, came up and sat down on one end of Deaton's cotton bale.

"Dey has catched demselves a big'un dis time," said Joshua.
"What?"

"Dem gamblers. Dey is gwine to take dat man's money."

Deaton looked over at the poker game. Only three men were playing. Lang on the left, Kelsey on the right, and the farmer in the middle. "How do you know they're going to take his money?" asked Deaton.

"Dat man, he been winnin'. When he gots 'nuff money, dey switches de cards."

Deaton put his letter aside and turned his attention to the game. He had heard of cheats, but he had never seen any in action before. Kelsey shuffled the cards while the farmer looked on.

"How much of my money you got there?" asked Lang.

The farmer took a quick inventory of the money in front of him and replied, "More then a hundred dollars, I reckon."

"Cut?" asked Kelsey, offering the deck to the farmer, who cut the cards a third of the way into the pack.

"Well, I got a whole lot more," said Lang, opening his purse to display his bankroll. While the farmer took a closer look, his eyes fairly gleaming with greed, Kelsey set the deck down next to his hat and quickly moved the hat to cover the old deck while exposing a new one. The farmer never noticed the switch.

"I'm gonna get my money back," said Lang, "and I don't want to spend all day doin' it. What say we raise the stakes?"

The farmer stroked his chin, looked at Kelsey, then at Lang and his bankroll. The last time he saw that much cash was in a bank. Hundreds of dollars lay on the crate they were using for a table and he couldn't think of a good reason why more of it shouldn't belong to him. Smiling confidently, he said, "What's your proposal?"

"Ten dollars to open, and no limit to raises. Table stakes, of course."

"Hey, that's too rich for my blood," said Kelsey.

"What're you complainin' about?" demanded Lang. "You've got plenty of my money, too."

"Yeah, an' I aim to keep it."

"We'll see about that," said Lang. Then to the farmer he said, "What about it, mister?"

The farmer took out his watch and looked at the time. It was a gold watch and looked expensive. He smiled and looked out at the passing countryside. He didn't want to appear to be too eager. Finally, he said, "Well, I reckon that'd be all right."

"Deal the cards!" said Lang, pointing his right index finger at Kelsey. The fish was on the hook.

Kelsey quickly dealt the cards. The game was five-card draw poker. Each man picked up his cards, one at a time, and arranged them in his hand. As the farmer picked up his cards, he couldn't conceal the look of growing excitement on his face. His eyes darted around nervously. His hands trembled slightly. He had a winner. Did it show? He wondered. If he played it right, he would soon be a good deal richer. He had been dealt four nines and a king of hearts. How should he play it? If he stood pat, they would know he had a cinch hand.

"You gonna open?" asked Kelsey.

"Yes, ten dollars," said the farmer.

"Raise ten," said Lang.

"Call," said Kelsey, pushing twenty dollars into the pot.

This was better than the farmer had hoped. They must have really good hands to be betting twenty dollars, he reasoned. He hesitated for a long time before pushing another ten dollars into the pot. He didn't want to appear too eager.

"Cards?" asked Kelsey.

"One," said the farmer. Maybe they would think he had two pair. And of course he did...two pair of nines. Kelsey deftly dealt the farmer a card from the bottom of the deck.

"I'll take three," said Lang.

*Must be a pair of aces or a pair of kings*, thought the farmer.

"Dealer takes two," said Kelsey.

A pair and a kicker or three of a kind? It didn't matter to the farmer. He was going to make money from both of them.

"Twenty dollars," said the farmer cautiously.

Lang carefully squeezed his cards, making their value appear one at a time. He looked at them for a long time. Then he pushed them together and held them in his left hand while he fingered his money with his right. He looked at the farmer intently, then he said, "How much?"

"Twenty dollars."

"See you and raise fifty."

"Call," said Kelsey.

This was too good to be true. They both had hit something good. Lang wanted to play big stakes? That was just fine with the gentleman from Tennessee.

"Raise you back, hundred dollars," said the farmer.

"Your hundred," said Lang, "and five hundred more."

"I'm out," said Kelsey, throwing in his cards.

The farmer counted the money in front of him, then said, "I ain't got five hundred."

"Then you lose," said Lang, reaching for the pot.

"Now hold on a minute! You can't do that!"

"Table stakes, mister. You gonna cover the bet?"

"But...but...I'm good for it. I've got it in my cabin."

"What do I look like? A money lender? How 'bout your watch? What's it worth?"

"You can't have my watch," said the farmer. "It belonged to my daddy."

"Tell you what," said Lang, "We're all gentlemen here, right? I'll let you call the bet with what you got in front of you, but if you lose it'll cost you another thousand. Fair enough?"

A shock wave of relief went through the farmer. It didn't matter that he didn't have a thousand dollars. He was holding a winner.

"Yes, that's fine."

"Show me your cards," said Lang.

"Four nines!" said the farmer triumphantly, as he turned his cards over.

"You jackass," said Lang, showing his cards. "I've got a straight flush, queen high."

The farmer raised halfway up from his seat, his mouth hanging open. This couldn't be! The man drew three cards! No one is that lucky. Lang pulled the money in and began stacking it into a neat pile.

"You owe me another thousand," he said. "Go get it."

The farmer stood up, looking dazed, and slowly walked away. Lang and Kelsey exchanged smirks.

MacKenzie Deaton turned to Joshua and shook his head. It had been so obvious, and yet so easy.

"See what I done tole you?" said Joshua. "Dey has done took dat po' man's money."

"It ain't right," said Deaton. "Somebody ought to do something."

"An' what might dat be? He is a growed man. Ain't no law 'gainst bein' a fool."

"Well, it ain't right."

"Some day someone's gwine ter get eben wit dem gamblers. I hopes I gets ter see it."

Joshua got up and shuffled back to the boiler. The fire was low, so he began throwing chunks of wood in. Deaton looked at the gamblers with loathing. They didn't notice his look of disdain, but if they had, they wouldn't have cared.

"Don't look like he's coming back," said Kelsey.

"Reckon he ain't. We'd best be protecting our investment."

Lang and Kelsey gathered up their cards and disappeared up the stairs to the cabin deck. Deaton watched the gamblers until they were out of sight. Joshua came up behind him, shaking his head.

"Lawdy," he said sadly. "I hopes dat man has got de money, or he be knowin' how ter swim."

"Swim?"

"Yassuh. Dey wants dere money. Ain't no way dat man's gwine ter walk away widout payin'. Nosuh! He gots de big trouble."

Deaton and Joshua watched the stairs for awhile and made small talk. After about thirty minutes Lang and Kelsey reappeared. From their countenances it was easy to deduce they had failed to get their money. They looked around as if trying to find another sucker, but they were too agitated to play poker. They talked and kept looking at the stairs. Eventually, the two gamblers gravitated to the rear of the boat and Deaton lost interest in them.

At sunset the *Tempest* pulled out of the main current and tied up for the night. Lanterns were lit and deck passengers broke out their foodstuffs. Deaton ate and Joshua worked. The black man put in a good store of firewood by his boiler for easy access the next day. The wood supply was getting low. They would have to put in at a wood seller's tomorrow or the day after. If they didn't come upon a wood seller, the captain would tie up in a convenient spot and the passengers would forage for wood.

During the day the steady rumble of the steam engines and now the quiet sound of the river as it swirled past the boat were very soothing. The boat moved gently and the ropes tying it to trees on the riverbank groaned their displeasure. The deck passengers had gathered in groups and the air was filled with the drone of muffled conversations. Slowly, the steamboat went to sleep and the sounds of crickets and other insects took over.

Deaton lay on his cotton bale a long time, unable to sleep. He couldn't get that farmer out of his mind. The man had gone to his cabin, but had never returned. Surely, Lang and Kelsey wouldn't have dared to provoke a confrontation in broad daylight. Why were such men allowed to prey on unsuspecting travelers? Something ought to be done about it.

Deaton drifted into a dreamlike state somewhere between sleep and consciousness. Images of home and family came and went.

Deaton sat up suddenly. He didn't know how long he had been sleeping. From the position of the moon, now in its first quarter, he guessed it must be about ten o'clock. It was very quiet, but something had awakened him. He looked around. The stern of the deck was bathed in the faint moonlight. He saw no discernible shapes. Nothing moved. Then he heard something.

The sound came from the top of the stairs on the cabin deck. Deaton couldn't make out what it was. He then heard what sounded like a grunt. Deaton looked in the direction of the sound and saw a dark something silhouetted in the moonlight falling from the cabin deck, followed by a loud splash. Deaton got up from his bale and started for the railing.

"Ain't no use tryin' ter hep dat po' man," said a voice in the darkness. "He has been kilt fer sure."

"What makes you think so?"

"Dey ain't gwine ter throw no live man into de water. Dey sometimes comes back. Where dat man gwine, dere ain't no comin' back."

"There must be something we can do."

"Cain't do nothin' for dat po' man. It's just like de river. Dere is big fishes an' little fishes, an' de big fishes eat de little 'uns."

"You seem to know a lot about these two men. Why don't you do something about it?"

Joshua cackled in the darkness. "What you 'spects dis po' nigger do 'bout dat? My mammy din raise no fool! Nosuh! Let de white folks take care of dere own probbems. I gots probbems 'nuff jes bein' a nigger."

Deaton couldn't fault Joshua's logic. It was a white man's world and for a black man to get along he had to go along.

"You said there was big fish and little fish. Which one am I?" asked Deaton.

Joshua laughed again. "I 'spects you wants to be de fisherman."

"Could be."

"Well, suh, just you 'member de first thing what you do is you gots ter let de catfish run wit de bait. Dat way he thinks he's smarter den you. Den you sets de hook, an' you has catched yo'self a catfish!"

The two men fell silent and the sounds of night returned. MacKenzie Deaton had learned a valuable lesson. Pity the poor farmer who had learned it the hard way.

Deaton didn't sleep well that night. Before Joshua began to fire the boiler in the morning, Deaton had been awake watching the starry sky turn to gray and then dissolve in hues of orange and crimson. This business with the farmer and the gamblers troubled him greatly. He began to doubt his own good character. Obviously, greed drove these two men to their criminal acts. Deaton wondered if he was much different. Wasn't it greed that was driving him on to California?

In the ensuing days the farmer's disappearance was talked about only nervously in quiet conversations. Something resembling a bloodstain had been found near the railing on the cabin deck. The popular, public speculation was that he had slipped ashore to avoid paying his debt. But privately many thought he had settled his debt by paying the ultimate price. In any case, Lang and Kelsey found themselves temporarily out of business, a fact that seemed not to bother them. The two miscreants parked themselves at the rear of the boat with two jugs of "corn squeezin's" and spent the remaining days to St. Louis in various degrees of intoxication.

# 13

It was past midday when the great city of St. Louis came into view. As MacKenzie Deaton lounged on his cotton bale the cry went up that their destination had been sighted. He stretched and yawned, then shuffled over for a view of the western shore. It was a dazzling sight for a country boy. The St. Louis levee stretched several hundred yards until it disappeared around a bend in the river to the northwest. As far as he could see along the waterfront stood the great white steamboats like a row of monstrous wedding cakes. Gaudy packets with tall stacks, some of which emitted columns of black smoke ascending into the clear blue sky. On the sidewheel housing of each boat was its name in huge letters. It was like a roll call of the river. The *Baltimore,* the *New Orleans,* the *Quincy,* the *Natchez,* and the *Grand Republic.* Deaton counted twenty-eight in all.

After several minutes the pilot nudged the *Tempest* into a vacant spot on the levee. The gangplank was lowered from the bow of the boat and passengers began to disembark. MacKenzie Deaton gathered his few belongings and turned to go. Joshua sat on a chunk of firewood next to the boiler, his ever-present pipe clenched firmly between his teeth.

"Well, suh," he said, "It's been right pleasure'ble knowin' ya. I hopes dat California be up ter yo' ec-spec-ta-tions!"

Joshua smiled and cackled as the latter word rolled off his tongue, as if he had been practicing and saving up the word just for this occasion. The two men shook hands as Deaton said, "I've learned a few things on this trip. I'm obliged. I hope you get your wish. You've made me appreciate my family more than ever before."

"Thank you, suh," said Joshua. "De Lawd bless you now."

Deaton nodded and headed for the gangplank, his excitement building with every step. The big city was a feast to his senses. Bells were ringing and from the river came the mournful sound of a steamer whistle. On the sunny wharf, sweating Negro stevedores pushed bales and boxes and barrels over gangways. Delivery wagons pulled by huge Clydesdales clattered along cobblestone streets. Cobblestone streets! Everywhere! Deaton marveled at the number and variety of people. He had never seen so many people together in one place. Finely dressed gentlemen and ladies were arriving and departing in carriages. There were two kinds of frontiersmen: those who were and those who would be. The latter were easily distinguishable by the newness of their frontier clothing.

The chatter of men, women, and children mixed with the shouts of workmen. Above it all was the whine of deck winches. One boat was taking on new wagons, their covers gleaming white in the sunlight. With both eagerness and trepidation, Deaton plunged into this maelstrom of humanity. He suppressed the desire to sightsee. He would have plenty of time for that on the return trip.

The first order of business was to book passage to Independence, Missouri. Schedules were nonexistent. Arrivals were whenever the boat showed up at the levee. Departures were whenever it suited the captain. Sometimes departures were printed on handbills and posted on rectangular bulletin boards along the waterfront. Some boards were on buildings, but usually they were mounted on two 4 x 4 posts in the open so handbills could be posted on both sides. Sometimes departure information was only available by going aboard the steamboat.

Deaton slung his knapsack over his shoulder and started making the rounds. At his third bulletin board a small knot of travelers had gathered around a man, listening intently. As Deaton approached, he heard the man say, "...and I hear tell there's twenty-seven cases of cholera right here in St. Louis."

"Any of 'em died yet?" asked a second man.

"Any of 'em?" snorted the first man. "All of 'em! I ain't never heard of nobody that lived through it."

"I don't think I want to stick around here then," said the second man.

"Where y'headed?" asked a third man.

"California. Isn't everybody?"

"Won't do no good to run. I hear every boat going up the river has had at least one case of cholera."

"Is that a fact?" said another man, incredulously.

Cholera. Deaton had heard of it. It was out there, like a bear in the woods, lurking in places unknown. Like the bear, it was deadly, but one hoped that by treading lightly and in the right places, it would be possible to traverse the wilderness in safety. Unlike the bear, however, the dread disease had an appetite that could not be appeased, nor was it a respecter of persons. There was no known cure. The malady started as a mild stomach complaint, but rapidly turned to raging diarrhea and severe abdominal pain. Then came the unquenchable thirst, followed by vomiting, and finally death from shock and dehydration, usually within twenty-four hours. Only a fortunate few managed to survive its deadly embrace.

Deaton pushed on. He had much to do and to linger too long in one place was an invitation for trouble. He checked every bulletin board on the waterfront and several of the steamers. No luck. After nearly two hours, he found himself standing in front of

Greenhalgh's Emporium on Market Street. A large, hand lettered banner in the window proclaimed:

*CALIFORNIA OUTFITS!*
*WAGONS! MINING TOOLS!*
*EVERYTHING NEEDED FOR THE MINES!*
*BEST PRICES BEFORE THE FRONTIER!*
*Ernest Greenhalgh, Prop.*

Deaton was about to enter when a boy of about ten approached passing out handbills. "Hey, mister!" said the boy. "Are you a Californian?"

Deaton nodded and the boy handed him a handbill, an advertisement touting the goods and prices to be had at Independence, and offering the persuasive argument that it would be more prudent to buy at Independence and avoid paying heavy shipping costs up the Missouri River. Deaton decided to check out the local merchandise anyway.

The Greenhalgh Emporium seemed to indeed have everything a gold seeker could possibly need: pistols, rifles and shotguns of every sort, picks, shovels, cooking utensils, barrels of bacon, and sacks of flour, sugar and coffee. Out back a crew of seven men was busy building wagons.

Although persuaded to buy his outfit at Independence, nevertheless Deaton couldn't resist buying two items: a gutta percha raincoat and a .32 Cal. Pocket Colt.

"You'll need one of these," said the clerk, holding up a Bowie knife, a masterpiece of craftsmanship. The gleaming blade was nearly ten inches long and razor-sharp. The handle was six inches of carved deer antler. All in all a formidable weapon.

"Got me a pocket knife," said Deaton. "What would I need one of these for?"

"Sir, to protect yourself 'gainst Injuns and such."

"Got me a gun, too."

"It's only got five shots. What're you gonna do then? Rifle ain't gonna do no good in close. Long as you can stay on your feet, this ol' 'Arkansas Toothpick' will stand you in good stead. Lookee here, see how sharp it is?"

Deaton admired the knife in silence.

"And watch this," said the merchant. The man banged the blade against the counter and held it up to Deaton's ear. "Hear it hummin'?"

Deaton nodded. The merchant stepped to the door of the store and threw the knife across the street. "Now, you go over there and pick it up, and if she ain't still hummin', I'll give it to you."

The knife performed as promised and five minutes later MacKenzie Deaton stepped into the street with all he needed to protect himself from rain, wild beast, and savage Indian. The Bowie knife came in a buckskin sheath with a fringe on one side. The sheath was decorated with beads in some kind of Indian design and looked quite smart on Deaton's belt, though the entire rig looked more like a short sword than a long knife.

The sun was low on the horizon as Deaton set off to find lodgings for the night. He would have preferred to sleep on a steamboat, but, as he had not yet found one willing to transport him to the frontier, a hotel or boarding house would have to do. The only trouble was that lodgings were as hard to find as passage on a boat to Independence. Thus, the hour was late by the time Deaton found a room at the Missouri Hotel, at $1.00 per day, which was reasonable enough in spite of the abundance of cockroaches. He tried to write a few lines to his wife, but the urge to sleep was overpowering, and that duty, of necessity, had to be postponed.

# 14

The following morning, April 26, MacKenzie Deaton rose soon after daybreak. Twelve days had passed since he had left home. Breakfast would have to wait until after he found passage to Independence. No sense staying in St. Louis any longer than necessary. It was only 6:00 A.M. when Deaton got back to the levee. Two things surprised him: First, the number of steamboats had nearly doubled. This time he counted fifty-five. Second, in spite of the early hour, the massive throng seemed not to have dissipated at all since his arrival the previous afternoon. It was as if the whole of the human family was on the move, being channeled through this one city, all pressing forward toward that golden dream called California.

In fairly short order Deaton had engaged passage at $6.00 aboard the *St. Paul*, a steamer he judged to be of recent manufacture by the newness of the fixtures and a fresh coat of white paint.

The *St. Paul* backed away from the levee shortly before noon and headed north for the mouth of the Missouri River. The steamer was filled to overflowing with 250 tons of freight and more than a hundred passengers of every description: farmers, merchants, bankers, and even doctors. Rich and poor alike, they were all driven by the same motive, greed, though none were willing to say so. Instead, they talked of the great adventure, of "going to see the elephant." If anyone realized they were fools on a fool's errand, no one was going to admit it.

Wagons, horses, mules, tents, boxes, sacks and barrels crowded the decks of the boat. Every cabin was an arsenal of rifles, pistols, knives and hatchets. Sleeping space was at a premium. The early arrivals had beds, but the latecomers had to sleep on tables, bales, boxes and even the floor.

Before the *St. Paul* was even underway, poker games were going on in several locations. Deaton wondered what had become of the two cardsharps, Lang and Kelsey. He didn't have to wonder very long. Less than two hours out he saw them in action near the stern of the boat playing high stakes poker. As before, they played as partners, but pretended to not know each other. Five other men were in the game, and by nightfall two of them had been relieved of their entire stake. Deaton felt outraged that these two, Lang and Kelsey, could move around at will, fleecing the unsophisticated and the unwary. Then he had a foolish thought. He resolved to do something about it.

It was six days from St. Louis to Independence. The Missouri River presented a much different appearance than that of the Mississippi. The wooded banks and the greater number of bends in the river and the abundance of deer and geese and ducks, created an air of wildness that reminded the travelers of the real wilderness that lay before them. Deaton tried to pass the time by enjoying the scenery and reading a book he had picked up in St. Louis, but he found himself irresistibly drawn to the poker games. The mind-boggling amount of money changing hands served as a visual reminder of the potential wealth that lay at journey's end.

Two days out, Deaton found himself sitting near the poker game hosted by Lang and Kelsey that had been going on all day. Many players had come and gone. Only Lang and Kelsey had stayed on the whole time. When Deaton was beginning to think they had bladders made of iron, Kelsey stood up abruptly and announced, "I gotta go use the facilities."

As Kelsey passed MacKenzie Deaton, the gambler gave him a careful look. Deaton wondered if the gambler remembered him from the *Tempest*. A few minutes later Lang also excused himself. He paused next to Deaton and said, "Why don't you get in the game, friend. Can't make any money just watching."

Only three players were left. One of them said, "Yeah, c'mon. We can't play with just three."

Deaton looked in the direction Lang had gone. The gambler never looked back. By the time Lang and Kelsey returned, darkness had fallen and a lantern had been lit. The men were playing stud poker, and Deaton had just laid down the winning hand, three kings and a pair of sixes. Twelve dollars were in the pot. Including the three dollars and four bits he had lost on previous hands Deaton was now up eight-fifty. He was glad to see Lang and Kelsey back in the game.

The evening passed quickly. Two hours after sunset the moon, nearing its half-full phase, was also about to disappear below the horizon. The pilot put into shore and tied up for the night.

The game went on until only Lang, Kelsey, and MacKenzie Deaton were left. Deaton had nursed his stack to nearly thirty dollars. Lang and Kelsey relieved him of that in three quick hands.

"Guess that cleans y'out," said Kelsey, grinning.

Deaton leaned back, a frown of disgust on his face, and said nothing. It was quiet. Most of the passengers had gone to sleep. The clacking sounds of June bugs came from the woods, and the cold green light from hundreds of fireflies flickered on and off like some primeval Morse code. Deaton picked up his knapsack and set it on his lap. From it he removed his Bowie knife and laid it on the table. Then he took out his moneybag and dumped its contents, seven hundred and twenty dollars, in front of the two men.

"Gentlemen," said Deaton, "let's play cards."

Lang and Kelsey lit up like two little boys on Christmas morning. Not surprisingly, Deaton's luck abruptly changed. Every time Lang or Kelsey dealt, Deaton won. In only an hour he found himself more than three hundred dollars ahead.

"You got a lot of our money," said Lang. "What say we raise the stakes?"

"How much?"

"Five dollar ante, ten dollars to open and pot limit."

"Pot limit? What's that?"

"Let's say we all ante five dollars and I open for ten. That's twenty-five dollars in the pot. So now he can call my ten, making it thirty-five, and raise thirty-five. Now there's seventy dollars in the pot. And if you got a winner you can do the same thing. You understand all that?"

"I understand it," said Deaton. "But I ain't gonna play for that kind of money."

"What're you talkin' about?" said Kelsey. "You're the man's been winnin' all the money."

Deaton looked thoughtful. After a prolonged silence he pulled out his watch and held it up by the lantern. "Tell you what," he said. "It's late. I'll play, but only for another hour."

The two men smiled. That would be enough time to get the job done.

"But," he continued, "only for a one dollar ante and five dollars to open."

"Pot limit?" asked Lang.

"We'll see."

Lang shuffled the cards and dealt. In forty-five minutes Deaton had increased his winnings to more than five hundred dollars. The two gamblers feigned a grim look.

"C'mon," said Lang. "Give us a chance to get even. Five and ten, and pot limit. How 'bout it?"

"All right," said Deaton.

"How much time we got left?" asked Kelsey.

Deaton took out his watch and held it up to the lantern. "About twelve minutes."

"Let's play five card draw, jacks or better," said Lang as he started dealing the cards.

Deaton picked up his cards one at a time. First a nine. Then a king. Another nine. A third nine. And another nine. Four nines. A pat hand. And he hadn't even seen them make the switch.

"Open?" asked Lang.

"Not me," said Kelsey.

"Ten dollars," said Deaton, pushing a gold coin out onto the table.

"Call."

"Call."

"Cards?" asked Lang.

"Three."

"One."

"Dealer takes three."

The two gamblers made a show of looking at their cards. Deaton couldn't help smiling.

"Your bet," said Lang.

"Five dollars," said Deaton.

Lang and Kelsey looked at each other, startled. Then Lang quickly counted up the pot.

"I'll call your five and raise forty."

"That's forty-five to me and I'll raise a hundred and twenty-five," said Kelsey.

Deaton threw his cards face down onto the table. "This hand ain't worth that much," he said.

The two gamblers looked dumbstruck. Lang grabbed the discarded hand and turned it over. "Wait a minute," said Deaton. "You gotta pay to see those cards."

"We been payin', mister, and you've been cheatin' us," Lang raged through clenched teeth.

"Now, let's not stir up a tempest over a little card game," said Deaton.

"Tempest?" said Kelsey. "Now I remember. You came up the river on the *Tempest*."

The gamblers jumped to their feet, their hands going for their pockets, but Deaton was moving, too. Lang and Kelsey both froze when they saw the flashing blade of the "Arkansas toothpick."

"Hold it!" said Deaton. "You've been outsmarted fair and square and you know it. If there was any cheatin', it was you two that was doin' it. This is only pocket money to men like you, but I hope you've learned a lesson. Now back off!"

Lang and Kelsey sat down. They had lost, but they weren't beaten. Deaton could see it in their eyes. He knew he would have his hands full staying out of their way. Fortunately for Deaton, the commotion had brought the attention of others nearby. "What's goin' on over there?" a voice called out in the darkness. "Can't a fella get any sleep?"

"Just a friendly game of cards," said Kelsey. Then to MacKenzie Deaton he added in a voice just above a whisper, "Be seein' you...real soon."

"Can't wait," said Deaton, slipping his knife back into its sheath.

These were dangerous men. He thought of the farmer who had disappeared on the *Tempest*. Would they try the same thing with him? Maybe. Maybe not. All the same he planned to keep a wary eye on them.

# 15

Two days passed without further incident. MacKenzie surmised that when the *St. Paul* arrived at Independence, Lang and Kelsey would either continue to St. Joe or catch the next boat back to St. Louis. In either case this ugly affair would soon be behind him.

It was late afternoon, as the *St. Paul* steamed up the Missouri River. The sun was low on the horizon and appeared to be sinking right into the river, turning it into a ribbon of fire and gold stretching to the western horizon. The dazzling sight blinded the pilot, and the boat ran aground on a sandbar. Amidst cursing and swearing he reversed engines and tried several times to back off of the sandbar. The huge wheels churned the water into billows of brown and white foam, and the great boat shuddered and groaned in protest before the captain ordered the passengers to disembark. They waded the few yards to the riverbank and watched as lines were tied to the back of the boat to enable crew and passengers to assist in dislodging the *St. Paul.* MacKenzie Deaton thought it would be a good time to take care of his bodily needs and headed for the bushes. The riverbank was heavily wooded here and he didn't have to go far for privacy.

Finished, Deaton started back for the boat. As he stepped through some heavy brush he felt a sharp jolt and saw a bright flash before his eyes. He crashed backwards, landing on the ground in a sitting position. He tried to get up, but he was dizzy and disoriented. Deaton looked down. Blood was all over the front of his shirt. He had a salty taste in his mouth and his jaw hurt on the left side. He felt the inside of his cheek with his tongue. His upper teeth had opened a deep gash that felt like it went all the way through to the outside. Somebody was talking, but he couldn't understand what they were saying. He tried to look up, but his head just flopped backwards. Everything had a hazy look. He felt the same as he did the one time in his life that he got drunk.

Kelsey, hands shaking and his face a mask of blazing hatred, stood over the fallen man.

"Get up, y'dumb farmer. I'm gonna beat the hell out of you!"

Deaton shook his head trying to clear it. He knew he was in a tight spot. Somehow he had to get back to the boat. He rolled onto his hands and knees and tried to get up. Kelsey kicked him hard in the ribs. Deaton fell face down, gasping for breath. He waited several moments, assessing the situation. He tried once more. Kelsey kicked at him again. This time Deaton was ready. He intercepted the upraised foot and pushed it aside. Off balance, Kelsey went crashing to the ground. Deaton staggered to his feet, drawing his Bowie knife. He lurched toward Kelsey. He felt another sharp jolt against the back of his neck, just at the base of his skull. Deaton fell to the ground like a sack of potatoes, unconscious.

Myron Lang stood over MacKenzie Deaton looking smug and satisfied. He gently smacked the palm of his left hand with the blackjack he held in his right. It was a nasty little instrument, six ounces of lead encased in a leather pocket with a braided leather, flexible handle.

"Aw, what did you have to do that for?" whined Kelsey, getting to his feet. "I wanted to take 'im myself."

"We're partners, ain't we?" said Lang. "I knew you wouldn't want to keep all the fun to yourself. You can finish him off."

Lang kicked Deaton's Bowie knife over to Kelsey.

"Yeah," said Kelsey, cackling. "I'll do that."

Kelsey picked up the knife and knelt down astride Deaton's back. He grabbed a handful of the fallen man's hair and pulled his head back, exposing the throat. Kelsey giggled gleefully. Nothing was sweeter than revenge.

The night was dark and quiet, except for the crickets and the sound of flowing water. And other sounds: snoring and muffled conversations. MacKenzie Deaton hurt all over. He opened his eyes and tried to move. A groan escaped his lips. He heard sudden sounds of activity nearby.

"How're y'feelin'?" asked a voice in the darkness. A lantern was lit and Deaton could see the forms of three men hovering over him.

"I'm...I'm thirsty."

Hurried whispers, then gentle hands cradled his head and someone pressed a tin cup against his lips. Deaton felt very tired. He closed his eyes again and gave himself up to sleep.

The day was warm and the sky bright and clear. MacKenzie Deaton opened his eyes and looked around. He was on the *St. Paul* and she was churning upriver. He wondered what had happened, how he had gotten back on the boat.

"Well, look who's awake," said a cheerful voice.

Deaton sat up. He groaned. A throbbing pain across the back of his head from ear to ear was a graphic reminder of the incident in the woods. Where were Lang and Kelsey? And who were these three men looking at him so solicitously?

"Take it easy," said the cheerful voice. "You've had a rough time of it."

Deaton looked at the man. He was thirtyish, and had sandy blond hair and sparkling blue eyes. He was dressed as a common laborer and atop his head was a dark blue cap with a short bill and a full, rounded crown.

"Who are you?" asked Deaton.

"James Meade is the name. Originally of Dumphries in Scotland, but late of the Virginia commonwealth where I have been trying my hand at tobacco growing. And now, like you, on my way to the diggings."

"How did I get on the boat?" asked Deaton.

"Well, good sir, my two friends and I, Russell and Mr. Skinner, were walking in the woods when we happened upon you and your most serious predicament, as they say, just in the nick of time."

"What do you mean?"

"Well, it seems one of our fellow passengers was sitting astride your buttocks in the act of cutting your throat..."

"...with this," interjected a very large man with dark hair and a beard, brandishing MacKenzie's Bowie knife.

"That's my knife," said Deaton.

"Oh. Now that's really too bad," said the big man. "I had a real hankering for this beauty." The big man handed over the Bowie knife and said, "Rex Skinner. Pittsburgh, Pennsylvania."

"Then you saved my life."

"Aye," said Meade. "That we did. And there's no need to be thanking us. Just doing our Christian duty."

"What happened to..."

"...the other two men? The man bent on cutting your throat was not dissuaded by our most strenuous objections. In fact, I would say he had a genuine dislike for you. So we did what we had to do. I assure you, we gave the man a decent burial, certainly better than he deserved. As for the other gentleman, I think I have never seen a man run so fast."

"What happened to him?"

"Couldn't really say. As you can see we are under a full head of steam and the pilot promises Independence landing before noon tomorrow. We had to leave the blackguard behind. And that makes you a wealthy man."

"I don't understand," said Deaton.

"Aye, but you will," said Meade. "The pilot, as captain of this boat, has turned over the belongings of the late Mr. Kelsey to you as compensation for your injuries. The man was carrying a large amount of cash and, as far as can be determined, left no next-of-kin."

The Scotsman tossed a shabby looking carpetbag over to MacKenzie Deaton, who looked at the bag and then at the three men. "I don't know what to say."

"Open it," said Meade.

Deaton hesitated. Things were happening too fast.

"Go ahead," said Skinner. "It's yours now."

Deaton opened the bag and peeked inside. It contained two rolls of banknotes and a leather pouch, along with various and sundry items of personal belongings. He opened the pouch. It was dazzling. It was hundreds, maybe thousands of dollars in gold coin.

"Is this all?" he asked.

"My good fellow," said Meade, laughing, "how much more do you need?"

"It ain't a question of need. It's just...well, I don't want their money. And I don't need it. But I know someone who does." Deaton closed the carpetbag and pushed it aside. "Those men were thieves. They cheated at cards. This money belongs to them that was cheated. There ain't no way of findin' who they were, so the best thing I can do is help someone who really needs it."

"Would you still be going to California then?" asked Meade.

Deaton thought of his wife and children. He felt a momentary twinge of homesickness. "Yes, I'm going on."

"Good! Then would you be interested in joining us?"

"Joining you?"

"Aye!" said Meade. "You're traveling alone, are you not?"

"Yes, but I had hoped to join a company of emigrants at Independence."

"Aye, and so had we. But there's only three of us. We'll be needing a fourth man to go in with us on the purchase of a wagon. What do you say? Will you join us?"

Deaton looked at the three men. He had to join up with someone. Who better than someone who had saved his life? "Done," he said, and shook hands all around.

# 16

Independence was three miles from the upper landing on the Missouri River. The landing was at the bottom of a high bluff and went by the name of Wayne City, though there was no city to speak of.

MacKenzie Deaton and his three new companions hired a man to haul their baggage and started for the city on foot. It was a pleasant walk. From the top of the hill they had a good view of the river. Their course led them through rolling woodland, a welcome change from the steamboat with its constant swaying and the chugging and rumbling of the engines. It was midmorning and the temperature was moderate. The sun cast a kaleidoscope pattern of light and shadow through the trees. Birds were singing. The peaceful, tranquil setting was far removed from the violence of two days past.

Deaton's journey had proved to be more exciting than he had anticipated. His hurts were much improved, except for the bump on the back of his head. He hoped the remainder of his trip would be more mundane.

In little more than an hour the four men arrived at the city. Independence had been a typical frontier town before the electrifying cry of gold in California had transformed it, almost as if overnight. Founded in 1827, Independence was no stranger to transcontinental travel. Franklin, Missouri, had been the original eastern terminus of the Santa Fe Trail, but Independence enjoyed that distinction now. Traders had been hauling freight to Mexico since before the Mexican War and the acquisition of California. Settlers bound for Oregon found Independence to be a good starting point. So did MacKenzie Deaton and his friends.

The city was more chaotic than St. Louis had been. While the latter was an established city of some seventy thousand with a few thousand transient gold seekers, Independence was overwhelmed by the Californians, whose number surpassed the permanent population. It was an entrepreneur's dream.

The four travelers made their way to the town square. To the northeast was a spring where two men were filling water casks and loading them onto a wagon. To one side was a gambling house, surrounded by a great number of men trying to either get in or watch the activity through the open windows. Deaton couldn't help but think of his encounter with the riverboat gamblers. The sound of shouting drew their attention to the south side of the square where two men were engaged in a heated argument. Suddenly, one of the men drew a knife. A crashing blow from the fist of his opponent sent the man sprawling. He tried to get up, but the other man delivered a vicious kick to his rib cage. As quickly as the fight had started, it was over. The victor spat on the ground and walked away. The disturbance of the peace was barely noticed by most and not at all by some. Violence was simply a fact of life on the frontier, and this episode was of only minor significance.

The four gold seekers split up to take care of business: Meade to find lodgings, Russell to find a wagon train to join, Skinner to inquire about a wagon and team, and Deaton to perform an errand of compassion. MacKenzie Deaton had not felt comfortable having Kelsey's money. While he agreed he was entitled to some compensation for his injuries, he thought of Joshua and how the black man deserved compensation for his injuries. The man had no visible scars, but the injustice of slavery did more than scar the back. The separation of husband and wife, the sale of children; all of these left emotional scars, and, in some cases, wounds that would never heal. Deaton himself was surprised at his new attitude toward that southern institution, but he had changed in the past several days. This was more than just a trip to California. It was an education.

The banknotes Kelsey had left were issued by a St. Louis bank. Deaton used them to purchase a bank draft from a local bank at a premium of only 2 percent. His next stop was the post office, a little nine-by-seven room that was almost as busy as the gambling house. It took the better part of an hour to transact his business. As he left, he heard someone calling, "Mac! Mac! Is that you?"

MacKenzie Deaton turned to see who it was. Pushing his way through the crowd was Eli Bennett.

"Well, I'll be..." said Deaton. "I thought sure you'd be out on the prairie by now. How've y'been, Eli?"

"Fair to middlin' " said Bennett. "Reckon I should've been on my way to the gold fields, 'cept I lost my stake."

"You lost it? How?"

Bennett hung his head and nodded toward the gambling house.

"You lost it playing cards?"

"Yup. Got into it with a couple of fellas on the boat. They skinned me for most of it. When I got here I only had eatin' money left. So I tried to win enough to go on west. I had three kings and a pair of sixes. Thought sure I had a winnin' hand, but it wasn't good enough. Now I ain't got enough to get home even if I wasn't too ashamed to go. Been earnin' m'keep cleanin' out horse stalls. Lord, it's good to see you. Thought you was stayin' home. What changed your mind?"

"Can't really say, Eli. One day I just got a hankerin'. So here I am. How 'bout you? Y'still want to go to California?"

"Reckon I would, but I don't know how."

"Y'say you got skinned by two men on the boat? They wouldn't've been Kelsey and Lang, would they?"

"Yeah, that's them."

"Have I got a story to tell you!" said Deaton.

Deaton related his experiences on the riverboat, leaving out only the part about sending some of Kelsey's money to Joshua. Bennett just wouldn't understand. Deaton still had plenty of Kelsey's money. If anyone deserved some of it, Eli Bennett did. By the time Deaton went to meet his partners, the foursome was now five.


# 17


Meade had managed to find lodgings in the home of one W. H. Woodson, a gentleman in his early forties with two teenaged daughters. Mrs. Woodson had died of consumption in '46. Woodson had an itch to go to California, but since he was not one to shirk his family responsibilities, a boarding house was the only way he knew to cash in on the gold rush.

The Woodson home was a two-story, red brick house with a gabled roof. Not the typical boarding house. At least it hadn't been built for that purpose. Four chimneys, two on each side, vented the eight fireplaces that heated the house. A covered porch extended along the width of the house and a wooden stairway had been added to the outside to provide access to the second floor. Woodson had removed the interior stairs to provide more living space when he began taking in boarders, and had added a bedroom for himself on the back of the house. The previous occupants were in the process of moving out when James Meade had happened by.

Being a believer in the "bird in the hand" adage, he had rented the accommodations immediately rather than wait for his companions' approval. Deaton and his fellow travelers moved in right away, while Eli Bennett hurried to get his gear from the back room of the livery stable. He returned just in time for lunch.

The Woodson girls, Sarah, 19, and Esther, 17, cooked and served the meals, while their father worked as a wagon maker. Lunch this day was fresh-picked peas, fresh-baked bread hot from the oven with honey and butter, a smoked pork shoulder, and a large pitcher of milk. Dessert was a pie made from apples they had dried the previous October. Enjoying the meal with Deaton and his friends was the Woodsons' only other guest, a mountain man who introduced himself as Shadrach Jones.

Jones was a big man, about six feet and 250 pounds. He wore buckskin pants and a red plaid flannel shirt. His face was tanned and weathered, and his hair hadn't seen a pair of scissors in more than a year. He also sported a full beard, which he only grew during the winter months. His hair was brown and his beard reddish brown, except for two gray streaks, that angled down from the corners of his mouth.

Jones had an appetite that was as big as he was. He hunched over his plate with his left arm curled around it as he attacked the vittles. His right hand moved constantly as he conveyed the food from plate to mouth. When his plate was empty, he said, "C'n I have some more?" Which were the only words he spoke until he had polished off a second helping. Finished, Jones leaned back, belched loudly, and looked at the others, who had barely touched their food while they watched this eating machine in action.

"Wal now, that was purty good," said Jones, letting out another belch. "A man get's tired of his own cookin' after while. Too easy to forget what it's like havin' a woman around."

"I take it you are not married, sir," said Meade.

"Oh, I ain't never been, 'ficial-like, but I once had me a Injun bride. A real purty little gal. Twarn't many I could say that about. Most of them Injun squaws is downright ugly. Coyote ugly."

"Coyote ugly?"

"Yes, sir, coyote ugly."

"What's that?"

"Wal, there was the time a few years back, I was up at the rendezvous on Green River. We was awhoopin' an' ahollerin' an' havin' a grand ol' time. Long about sundown a bunch of them Flatheads rode into camp. Now you ain't seen ugly 'til you seen one of them Flathead Injuns. Wal, sir, we was all drinkin' an' havin' a real good time. It wasn't too long 'fore I was so drunk I didn't know who I was or where I was at. Woke up next mornin' with one of them Flathead squaws lyin' next to me. She was so ugly that if she'd been layin' on my arm I'd sooner chew it off than risk wakin' her by movin' it. Sorta like what a coyote caught in a trap does. That's coyote ugly."

Meade and the others laughed at the thought of the mountain man's predicament. "Tell me, Mr. Jones," said Meade, "did you, uh..."

"Who's to say? No tellin' what a feller's gonna do when he's got too much likker in 'im and ain't seen no civilization in nigh on to a year."

"Have you been in the fur business long?" asked Skinner.

"Came west right after Cap'n Bonneville done his explorin'. Trappin' is poor doin's, but it's a good life. Got no complaints."

"It must be frightfully lonely," said Meade.

"Wagh! It's a damn sight better'n pushin' a broom around a store! I go months on end without seein' another white man. If I get a hankerin' to see one, wal, I know where to find 'em."

"Seems like everyone is going west, Mr. Jones," said Meade. "What brings you east?"

The mountain man looked around, a twinkle in his eye, and said in a teasing voice, "Wanted to see me another white man." With that he laughed uproariously, while his audience managed only a chuckle or two.

The Woodson girls began clearing up the dinner table, seemingly oblivious to the conversation. Jones slouched in his chair, stretched his feet out, and belched again.

"You fellers headed for California?" he asked. The men murmured a response in the affirmative. "C'mon out on the porch and sit a spell."

"Thanks, Mr. Jones," said Meade, "but we have a lot of business to transact this afternoon."

"Reckon so," said Jones. "Got your outfit put together yet?"

"Actually, no," said Meade. "We only arrived this morning."

"Gonna pull with mules or oxen?"

"Ain't decided," said Deaton, looking at his companions. They nodded their agreement. "What about horses?"

"Wagh! Horses ain't no use! They'll give out 'fore y'get to the Black Hills, 'less y'tote some oats. Horses don't do good on grass. No sir, mules'd be my first choice. They're tough and durable, move a lot faster'n oxen. But they also cost a heap."

"How much?" asked Meade.

"Oh, hunnert dollars, and more if y'want the best. Now oxen is cheaper and they'll answer well to your purpose. I heerd someun's been sellin' oxen for forty dollars a yoke, but more likely they'll cost fifty dollars each. Keerful y'don't buy none of them Mexican steers.

Someun's been bringin' 'em up from Santa Fe. Most of 'em ain't never been in the yoke. Wild. You'll be spendin' most of your time tamin' 'em. Likely as not they'll tip your wagon once or twice. Don't buy from them Mexicans. Y'can't trust them greasers."

"Is there much danger from Indians?" asked Deaton.

Seeming not to hear the question, the mountain man rose from his chair and stretched, then patted his stomach. "Them's good fixin's, gals," he said to the Woodson girls. "Lookin' forward to supper."

The girls smiled and murmured a "Thank you." Their pa didn't hold with them being too friendly with boarders, so they tried to keep conversation to a minimum.

Jones removed a plug of chewing tobacco from his pocket, bit off a chunk and moved toward the door. The other diners rose and followed as if obeying some inaudible summons. The porch had no railing, only four pillars along the front to support its roof. Jones sat against one of the center pillars, his back to the steps with one knee raised and the other leg dangling from the porch. The others gathered around in silence, while he worked the chaw into a soft and juicy mass. When it was ready, he spat on the ground and resumed speaking. "Injuns is like white men. Some good, some bad."

"How can you tell the difference?" asked Meade.

"Wal, if one of them red niggers is liftin' your hair, you c'n be sure he's a bad 'un." Jones spat on the ground and laughed merrily. "Course you boys'll be travelin' with a large party. Jes keep your eyes skinned and don't get too far away from the wagons. Biggest problem you'll have is stealin'. Pawnees is the worst of the lot. They'll dig up a dead man and steal his clothes. Wagh! It's disgustin'."

"Would you be interested in advising us on our outfit?" asked Meade. "Provisions? Clothes?"

The mountain man chewed thoughtfully and spat on the ground again. "Could do," he said. "Most folks headin' west try totin' too much. Y'walkin' or ridin'?"

"None of us have a horse," said Meade.

"'Cept me," said Eli Bennett. "I got a horse."

"Them that plan on walkin' had best have two pair of shoes. Good shoes. Comfortable. Can't get far on sore feet. Take two of everthin' else, 'cept socks and drawers. Four pair cotton drawers and six pair woolen socks. Homespun trousers'll wear the best. Be sure'n get a broad-brimmed felt hat. Gotta keep the sun off your face. A burnt nose is hard to heal. For rain, a gutta percha poncho. Then a couple toothbrushes, a comb and two, three pounds of soap."

"What kind of mining tools do you recommend?" asked Deaton.

"Minin' tools? Wagh! Y'don't need no minin' tools! They's jes excess baggage. Only take what y'need to get to California. Y'can't eat minin' tools an' y'can't wear 'em. Leave 'em be!" Jones spat another load of tobacco juice before continuing. "An' speakin' of eatin', I hope you c'n cook! Ain't but one boardin' house twixt here an' California, at Fort Kearny, 'less y'have a mind t'go through the Mormon city at Great Salt Lake."

"I'm a pretty fair cook," said Russell. "But I'm not sure how much we should be taking."

"'Bout two hunnert pounds of flour for each man. Hunnert pounds of bacon, twenty pounds of coffee, an' ten pounds each of sugar an' salt. You'll need fruits an' vegetables. Don't buy none of them put up in tin canisters. Too heavy an' likely to go bad. Get 'em desiccated. They weigh next to nothin' an' keep for months. Sometimes it'll be too wet to make a fire, so take lotsa pilot bread. Y'might be able to get meat on the hoof, but don't count on it. I'd say take along pemmican, but y'can't find none around here."

"What, pray tell, is pemmican?" asked Meade.

"Injuns make it. They take strips of dried buffalo, beat it into a powder, put it in a leather bag, an' then pour in hot grease. You c'n eat it raw or make it into cakes an' cook it up."

The mountain man instructed MacKenzie Deaton and his friends for nearly two hours. When at last they departed for the town square, they felt like they were seasoned prairie travelers.


# 18


Getting into Independence was a lot easier than getting out. MacKenzie Deaton had expected his stay in the frontier town to last no more than a day or two. Like most of the would-be miners, he was ignorant of the logistics of getting to California. The key word in making a successful overland journey to the far west was "organization." Most men took the time and made careful preparations. Others were simply unwilling to put forth the effort, and they almost universally reaped the consequences of their folly.

Deaton and his friends spent the next few days looking for the best prices and trying to find an emigration company to join. They realized it would be foolish to go it alone. A trip across the continent required a cooperative effort, and security against Indians and other dangers came naturally from being in a large group. Most emigrant companies were joint stock ventures organized back home, though some trains did come together on the frontier. It was already late in the season and opportunities to join a wagon train were becoming fewer each day. Trains had been pulling out since early April and now, on May 5, the bulk of the emigration was already underway.

Late Saturday afternoon Russell and Skinner reported they had found a train to join. An organizational meeting was to be held that very evening in a grove of trees two miles east of Independence.

After dinner the five adventurers started walking to the meeting with Russell and Skinner leading the way. Shadrach Jones came along to offer advice, if necessary. The mountain man's appearance was much different from when they had first met him. He had shaved off his beard, explaining that most mountain men didn't wear beards and that he only grew his in the winter to keep his face warm. Now his face was two-toned, leathery brown on top and bone white on the bottom. All he needed was a haircut and a new suit of clothes and he would almost look like all the other men heading west.

It was dark by the time Deaton's group reached the encampment. Four wagons were arrayed in no particular order, and a few trees had been cut down, trimmed into logs and arranged into a square. A huge bonfire burned in the middle, illuminating the surrounding trees and sending a column of sparks rising into the darkness. In the shadows the on-and-off flicker of fireflies offered a cold, green counterpoint to the hot orange sparks of the fire. A bright glow on the eastern horizon announced the imminent rising of the nearly full moon. About fifty men stood around talking and smoking, and it being Saturday night was reason enough to be passing around a couple jugs of whiskey. Deaton's group joined in with the convivial atmosphere while waiting for the meeting to begin.

After some twenty minutes a man stepped forward and blew two notes on a bugle. All conversation ceased and the attention of everyone turned to the bugler. Another man stepped to the center and stood there for a moment, hands on his hips.

"Evening, gents," he said. "Looks like everyone who's coming is already here, so let's get started. My name's Baxter...Ben Baxter. A lot of you know who I am. For you newcomers, I'm captain of this company, least ways for the time being. We're eighteen men out of Plymouth, Indiana. As you can see, there ain't enough of us to make a decent train. Most of you are obviously in the same predicament. We propose to organize a train of at least twenty wagons. Those of you who decide to join up with us will be asked to pay one hundred dollars into the company treasury. You will have to supply your own wagon."

"Where do you get off making yourself captain?" asked one of the onlookers. "Seems to me that if we get twenty wagons, there'll be a lot more of us than there is of you."

"Someone had to take charge while we organized," explained Baxter, "but we anticipated an objection like this. I was elected captain for now, but our bylaws call for new elections after four weeks on the trail. If you've got any objections to the leadership, you can make 'em then. But first you gotta put your money down."

Baxter spent the next half hour explaining the organization of the company and the rules of the train. The company would be called the Plymouth Transportation and Mining Company. Officers would be a captain, a lieutenant, a secretary, a treasurer, and a chaplain. The men associated with each wagon would constitute a mess. Each mess would provide their own provisions and prepare their own meals. They would also elect one of their number to the company council, which would hear all disputes. Guards would be posted on the stock in two-hour shifts from nine at night until five in the morning. Each mess would take its turn in rotation. The camp would rise at five o'clock, eat breakfast and be under way by seven. Whenever practical, the company would refrain from traveling on Sunday. At journey's end the treasury would be divided equally among all members of the company. In the unfortunate case of any member's demise, his property would be auctioned off to the highest bidder and the proceeds forwarded to his next of kin when convenient.

MacKenzie Deaton and his associates found the proposal generally acceptable, and upon the advice of Shadrach Jones, they deposited their money with the treasurer and signed the articles of agreement, then started the long walk back to town.

Deaton felt a glow of excitement he could barely contain. His senses seemed more alive than they had ever been before. The others engaged in casual conversation, but he was content to merely listen and enjoy. He was keenly aware of the crickets and June bugs speaking their own special language. The moon was above the horizon now, bathing everything in a ghostly light. Deaton wanted to savor every moment and tuck it away in some unused recess of his memory, to bring it forth at some later date and relive it once again for his wife and children, his future grandchildren, and maybe just for himself. Beneath it all he was aware of the danger and hardship that lay ahead. But for now he was living the great adventure that most men only dreamed of.

# 19

Monday morning found MacKenzie Deaton and his friends eager to begin putting their outfit together. The Plymouth Transportation and Mining Company planned to leave for the West in a few days. The euphoria of Saturday night had now given way to a sense of urgency as they planned the day's activities around the breakfast table.

"First we should get the wagon," said Meade. "We can pack our provisions as we buy them."

"No, I disagree," said Deaton. "A wagon won't do us no good if we can't pull it. First we buy the animals."

There was a murmur of agreement.

"Well," replied Meade, gulping down some grits, "I hear the only animals available are wild. We'll have to break them to the yoke. Could bust up our wagon."

"Why don't we buy the wagon and use my horse to pull it out to the camp?" Suggested Eli Bennett. "We could then buy the animals, drive them out to the camp and break 'em at our leisure. When they're ready, we hitch 'em up and drive back into town to load up."

"I wonder what Mr. Jones thinks," said Deaton, looking around. "By the way, where is Mr. Jones this morning?"

"He's gone," said Sarah Woodson. The men looked up at her. Heretofore her presence had gone unnoticed as she went about her work. Now all eyes were on her. "Moved out this morning."

"That's a might sudden," said Skinner.

"I'll say," said Meade. "Did he say where he was off to?"

Sarah Woodson shook her head. The mountain man was gone, and Deaton felt a strange emptiness and a little bit irritated. He liked Shadrach Jones, and he didn't think it right that the man had gone off without saying good bye.

"Hello in the house!" called a voice.

It was Jones. Everyone got up and hurried outside. The old trapper sat astride his horse in full mountain man splendor. He wore buckskin from head to toe, decorated with fringes and Indian beads. His hair had been braided, and atop his head he wore an old floppy felt hat with an eagle feather. Trailing behind were two mules with fully loaded packsaddles. Strapped to his saddle was a Hawken rifle in a fringed buckskin case and tucked in his belt were two Colt's revolvers.

"Where y' off to?" asked Deaton.

"Bent's fort down on the Arkansas, then up to Cherry Creek."

"Why so soon?" asked Meade.

"Came to see a white man. Seen plenty, an' now it's time to go home."

Jones looked around at his audience, as if expecting a reaction. When he didn't get one, he continued, "It's cholera, boys. Never even heerd of it 'fore last week. Never been sick a day in my life. Ain't no reason to start now. Only been to a doctor once."

"What for?" asked Skinner.

"Broke my arm. Fell down a steep bank into a creek."

"While you was trappin'?" asked Bennett.

"Yup."

"Did it take long to get to a doctor?" asked Meade.

"Lemme see. I kinda lost count, but it must've been ten, 'leven days."

"Good heavens!" said Meade. "That must have hurt like the dickens!"

"I have been a sight more comfortable," Jones allowed. "But I've had a heap bigger hurt than that one."

Jones took out his pipe and a pouch of tobacco, and carefully packed it.

"I didn't know you smoked," said Meade.

"Gives me time to think," said Jones as he lit the pipe. "Let's see, where was I? Oh, yes. Once I was checkin' my trap lines and stopped to fill my pipe. Much to my chagrin I discovered I only had three matches an' the wind she was ablowin' sump'n fierce, so I hunkered down in a clump of scrub oak to light up. Tarnation if I didn't sit right smack on a bear trap! 'Tached itself right onto my hindquarters! Took off runnin' like the devil hisself was after me!"

"I suppose that would hurt worse than a broken arm," said Meade.

"Shor did, but I was hurt a dang sight more directly afterwards."

"When was that?" asked Russell.

"When I got to the end of the chain."

There were now smiles and chuckles all around. From the twinkle in Jones's eye it was impossible to tell if he was serious or just "funnin' " them. Meade stepped down from the porch and extended his hand.

"The best of luck to you, Mr. Jones. I had entertained the idea of asking you to join us, go to California with us."

"Wagh! Gold don't hold no interest for me. Trappin', huntin' an' fishin'..." The old trapper's voice became husky and he had a wistful look in his eyes. He had been a loner for so long, but now he had shared the company of decent, civilized men, and to his surprise he had found he liked it so much that he was considering making it more permanent. In his heart he knew it wasn't right, at least not for him. "...wal, thank you anyhow ...best be goin'."

Shadrach Jones turned the head of his big bay horse and started down the street. "Be keerful o'your topknot," he called out. There was a chorus of "goodbyes", but Jones never looked back.

The mountain man had good reason to be concerned about his health. Cholera was raging in Independence. Six deaths had been reported just over the weekend. The weather had been rainy of late, but wagon trains had been pulling out at a frantic pace in spite of the muddy road. It was never verbalized, but most emigrants had the strange notion they could somehow outrun the disease, never realizing that it was as futile as trying to outrun their shadows.

# 20

The Plymouth Transportation and Mining Company broke camp at 10:00 A.M. on Friday, May 11, 1849. Deaton's mess had moved out of the Woodson boarding house the same day Shadrach Jones started down the Santa Fe trail. They had spent the intervening days provisioning the mess and breaking the oxen.

Camp life was less agreeable than Deaton had expected. It was becoming less of an adventure and more like the hard work he had "enjoyed" at home. It rained a lot, and the weather turned chilly, but the time was well spent.

Each mess identified their wagon as belonging to the Plymouth company by painting the name on both sides of their wagon covers...except for a group of young men from Argos, Indiana, a very small farming community near Plymouth. They had proclaimed their independence and separate identity from their Plymouth associates by emblazoning the words "Argos Argonauts" on their wagon. It was a matter of community pride and the cause of much amusement among the company, but it was plain to see that Baxter was not enjoying it at all. He never missed an opportunity to offer his opinion that this was a disloyal act, even to the point of ordering the men from Argos to repaint their wagon cover. At first, they laughed at him, but it soon turned into a heated argument. By the time the week in camp had passed, some of the men were beginning to call Baxter, "King Ben", because of his autocratic manner.

One of the "Argos Argonauts" was a young man named Johnny Lloyd, a big, strapping fellow with brown curly hair. Not very bright, but he was a cheerful sort, always smiling, and liked to hunt and fish. Deaton got to know him while fishing on the creek that ran near the camp. In a couple hours they had caught several bass and Deaton had found a new friend.

By sunset of their first day on the trail the Plymouth company had passed through Independence and camped thirteen miles to the southwest along the Santa Fe Trail. The day's travel had been a monumental undertaking. The first four miles out of Independence had been quite hilly, and four days had not been enough time for Deaton's group to break in the oxen. Many others of the company were in the same fix. Teams of wild cattle were going in every direction, pitching and bellowing and trying to get loose. On one hill a wagon upset and the wagon tongue split. MacKenzie Deaton reckoned he had driven a team and plowed enough miles of furrows to get to California and half way back, but bull whacking was another matter. It was all he and the others could do just to keep the cattle moving in the right direction.

The campsite was on the edge of a good stand of trees and appeared to have seen a lot of use; litter everywhere and the remains of several campfires. Amongst the trees a fresh grave was a grim reminder of what would surely be the fate of many of their fellow emigrants. The men formed the wagons into a corral, unhitched the teams and drove them into the enclosure. Eli Bennett prepared dinner for his companions: bacon, beans, a strange brew he dared to call coffee, pilot bread, and some of last year's apples they had picked up at Independence earlier in the day. The men of Deaton's mess were exhausted and didn't bother to pitch their tents outside of the corral. They just wrapped up in their bedrolls and went to sleep.

Just before eleven someone awakened Deaton, shaking him violently. "Wake up, Deaton! Let's go!" said a voice from the darkness.

Deaton ached all over. He wasn't certain he could move even if he wanted. It was his turn on guard duty, so he drew upon some unknown reserve and forced himself to his feet. The night was cold and in the light of the waning moon he could see the mist of his own breath. He went to the wagon and felt around inside.

"What're y'doin'?" asked the voice.

"Gettin' my gun. I need it, don't I?"

"Sure, if you expect the animals will be shootin' at you. C'mon, let's go!"

Deaton found the gun. He felt the coldness of the steel for a moment, then put it back. He didn't want to be made out to be a fool.

As Deaton and his guide passed one of the tents, he could hear loud groans and the sounds of violent purging. Someone was in a lot of distress.

"What's wrong in there?" asked Deaton.

"Mr. Pearson. He's got the cholera."

Deaton shuddered. They were barely underway, probably not even into Kansas yet, and it had already started. Pearson was only a few years older than Deaton, and had a wife and five children. Deaton thought of his own family and wondered what they would do if he failed to return home.

Deaton shivered in the cold for two miserable hours. He certainly had no need for a gun, and in his opinion a guard was not needed either. A lantern had been lit at Pearson's tent and Deaton noticed a lot of comings and goings while he stood his watch. At 1:00 A.M. he was glad to crawl back into his blankets. He lay there for a long time trying to sleep, but he couldn't get the thought of poor Mr. Pearson out of his mind. While in a dreamlike state, somewhere between sleep and consciousness, a man came crawling up to Deaton and touched him on the shoulder.

"You awake, Mac?"

Deaton opened his eyes and looked at the man. Even in the darkness he could tell it was Johnny Lloyd.

"I'm awake, Johnny. What do you want?"

"Mr. Pearson's dyin', Mac. I'm scared."

Deaton put his hand on the young man's shoulder. "I know, Johnny. I know."

"I'd heard of the cholera, but I ain't never seen it before. What if I get it? Huh, Mac? There's a lotta things I still want to do in my life."

"Worryin' about it won't do no good," said Deaton. "Life is full of risks. Wouldn't be much fun without 'em."

Johnny Lloyd sat thinking for a while, leaning on one upraised knee. His voice trembled when at last he started to speak again. "I ain't never told no one this before, Mac."

"What's that?"

"Everybody knows I ain't married."

"You ain't the only one."

"Yeah, but I'm probably the only one that ain't never had a woman before."

Johnny Lloyd hung his head. Deaton wanted to laugh, but wisely decided against it.

"Do you think that's something to be ashamed of?" asked Deaton.

"Isn't it?"

"Course not. I never did either before I got married. Ain't no shame in that! Good lord, boy! What kinda crowd you been hangin' 'round, anyway?"

"Well, I been hearin' some of the men talk..."

"...and that's all it is, Johnny. Just talk. There's a time and a place for everything. When you got the right woman and the right time, you'll know it. Besides, there's more to life than that. Now go to bed and let's all get some sleep."

Johnny muttered a "thanks" and crawled away in the darkness.

Five o'clock came too soon to suit MacKenzie Deaton. Eli Bennett was up first, getting the fire going and starting breakfast. The air was cold and a heavy frost lay on the ground. Within the hour a group of men came by carrying shovels and the body of Mr. Pearson wrapped in a blanket. The men of Deaton's mess stood and removed their hats. By the time breakfast was over a new grave had been filled in the grove of trees.

The animals were turned out to graze before hitching up. There had been no time the night before. Consequently, the train did not get underway until almost nine o'clock.

The death of Mr. Pearson cast a pall of gloom over the company. As they traveled, the terrain changed from hills and trees to rolling prairie. It was beautiful, but no one seemed to notice. They had crossed the imaginary line between civilization and the Indian Territory. The road became much improved and by the time the wagons ceased rolling at the end of the day they had covered nearly twenty-five miles and camped at the Lone Elm campground.

Because the following day was Sunday, the company lay in camp all day. The men rested their sore muscles, and Deaton used the time to write a letter to his wife and bring his journal up to date.

On Monday the wagons rolled out of camp just past seven o'clock. By ten they came to a fork in the trail. To the left the trail continued west to Santa Fe. On the right was a small wooden signboard, hand lettered, that said simply, "Road to Oregon." This was the beginning of the Oregon Trail. At last, the road turned northwest toward the Platte River.

The wagon train had barely passed the junction when the sky turned dark ahead and the wind began to blow in strong gusts. Twenty minutes later rain began to fall and then hail. Amid thunder and lightning, Ben Baxter rode up and down the line ordering the wagons to be corralled. The animals were unhitched, but left yoked and driven into the corral. The wind blew too hard to set up tents, so the men sought cover from the rain any way they could.

The rain lasted a little more than two hours, though the wind continued to blow. While the company officers were trying to decide whether to push on, another wagon train came up the road. What had been a firm roadway earlier was now a quagmire. Oxen struggled to pull their loads while the bullwhackers had all they could do just to stay on their feet. The train of twenty-three wagons took more than half an hour to pass. Baxter passed the word to stay put. The emigrants of the Plymouth company spent a miserable day and night trying to get dry and keep warm. They had made only nine miles that day.

The weather cleared during the night and the temperature dropped into the forties. Deaton slept very little. He shunned the tent in favor of sleeping by the fire to keep it burning. Morning brought little relief from the collective misery. Before moving out, Deaton and the others in his mess rearranged the cargo in the wagon so that each man could take a turn sleeping while the wagon rolled. As council representative and the elected leader of the mess, James Meade took his turn first.

The road was only a little improved, making travel slow and difficult. The trail turned almost due north over a gently rolling prairie. MacKenzie Deaton would have appreciated the lush, luxuriant green grass of the prairie more if he had had a decent night's sleep. After five and a half miles the road turned again to the west and ascended a high bluff. At the top the emigrants were afforded a fine view of the countryside, and for the first time they saw the extent of the western migration. Behind them to the south and ahead of them to the west, as far as the eye could see, was an unbroken line of white wagon covers. To the north they got their first glimpse of the Kansas River. In spite of his fatigue, Deaton felt a sense of pride in his own part in this great endeavor.

Three more miles and the wagon train pulled off the road and camped. The time was only two in the afternoon, but the animals were exhausted, and the men in not much better condition.

Just before dawn a light rain began to fall. Not a storm, only enough to keep the road from drying out. The Plymouth company finally broke camp at ten o'clock. Travel was no better than the day before. After two miles they came to an insignificant stream called Little Wakarusa Creek. The approach to the ford was muddy. The first three wagons crossed with some difficulty, but the fourth wagon became stuck in the mire. A second team was brought up to help pull it free, but several tries failed to break the wagon loose.

A second wagon train came up to the ford, and when the pilot of the second train saw that no progress was being made, he led his company off the road to go around the Plymouth company wagons. At the ford the stuck wagon blocked the way. Enraged, the pilot of the second train began beating the oxen of the stuck wagon. The animals began bellowing, straining to get away from their tormentor. The driver of the stuck wagon, tried to intervene. "Are you crazy?" he shouted.

That only invited the pilot's attention. He began beating the man with his whip, forcing him backward, before resuming his abuse of the oxen. The men of both trains began moving toward the ford.

"Get 'em out of the way!" someone yelled.

The animals lunged forward. The wagon shuddered audibly, then with a loud crack the front axle broke and the wagon tipped part way over. This only increased the pilot's fury. He beat the oxen harder. They pulled again and the wagon tipped the rest of the way, dumping its contents into the creek.

"Get your guns!" someone shouted.

More than one hundred men from both wagon trains sprinted for their wagons. Guns were drawn. Some men looked angry. Most looked scared. A shot rang out and someone screamed in agony. Everyone looked for the source of the scream. Johnny Lloyd staggered a few paces from his wagon and collapsed. A rifle stuck out of the wagon, the barrel still smoking. He had grabbed the gun by the business end, and the hammer must have caught on something when he pulled it out.

The feud was instantly forgotten as the Plymouth emigrants hurried toward their fallen comrade. Deaton's concern for his friend turned quickly to anger.

"Where the hell's Baxter?" he demanded.

Across the creek Baxter sat on his horse by the lead wagon. Some of the men tended to Johnny Lloyd, while the others, men from both companies, righted the wagon, unloaded its contents and moved it out of the way. Baxter kept to his side of the creek, and the pilot of the second wagon train stood to one side by himself, his anger spent and his eyes downcast.

Johnny Lloyd lingered for two hours in great pain. He cried. He prayed. But at the end he was calm. The other members of his mess buried him beneath an elm tree.

After repairing the broken axle the wagons moved on. A deep sadness had settled over everyone. The mood was much different from when Mr. Pearson had died. Death on the trail was always tragic, but this death was for the silliest of reasons: anger over a short delay on a trip that would take almost five months. That morning Johnny Lloyd had been a happy young man, joking with his friends and excited about his future prospects in golden California. Now he was cold and in the ground, food for the worms.

The Plymouth company moved only another seven miles down

the trail to the east bank of the Wakarusa River before calling it quits for the day. A Shawnee Indian named Logan ran a small grocery near the river crossing and some members of the company couldn't wait to spend their money. Johnny Lloyd was gone, but life went on.

The date was May 16, 1849, and they were only five days out of Independence. The tragic events of these past few days did not bode well for the rest of their journey.

# 21

The campground on the east bank of the Wakarusa River was as dirty and littered as all the others. That alone would have ruined anyone's appetite. Deaton tried to eat, but he didn't feel hungry. He filled his plate and sat in his homemade camp chair, an interesting contraption made of two rectangular frames that locked together at right angles with a length of canvas running from top to bottom. The sun, low in the western sky, illuminated bands of cirrus clouds. Birds were singing and a gentle breeze shook the leaves on the trees.

Deaton should have been enjoying the early evening, but he couldn't. He looked at the concoction on his plate. It certainly wasn't what he had grown up on. None of the men could have been found guilty of being a cook, but Skinner was the worst. He had cooked up bacon, saleratus bread, boiled rice with gravy, and dried apples. The bread was black and nearly solid, not fit to eat. Even if it had been, Deaton was in no mood to eat it. He still seethed with anger at Baxter's lack of leadership back on Little Wakarusa Creek.

MacKenzie Deaton somehow managed to get the food down. By the time he finished his mood had improved. He tossed his tin plate on the ground and chuckled to himself.

"What's so funny?" asked Russell.

"I was just thinkin' how I've grown up to be my own pa," said Deaton.

"How's that?"

"My daddy used to tell me to eat everything on my plate 'cause it was good for me. I've been sittin' here tellin' myself the same thing: 'Go ahead and eat it, Mac. You gotta keep up your strength.' "

The men all laughed. All except Skinner. He jumped to his feet, an angry look on his face. "I ain't never said I was a cook!" He said.

"Diogenes, put out your lamp," said Meade. "Behold, an honest man."

Everyone laughed again, even those who had never heard the

story of Diogenes. Skinner went around behind the wagon and sat on the ground and sulked. Meade turned to Deaton. "I'm glad to see you are in a better mood, my friend. I noticed how you and Johnny had become friends."

"Well, life does go on," said Deaton. "And there's no helpin' Johnny now. But I intend on seein' that nothin' like that ever happens again."

"Nothing could have prevented that, Mac. The man made a mistake."

"I'm not talkin' about that. Johnny Lloyd never should've been reachin' for a gun in the first place. It's Baxter's fault."

"Why do you say that?" asked Meade.

"I suppose you didn't notice how Baxter stayed out of sight when the trouble started this morning."

"I did."

"Well, now, what've you got to say about that?"

"I hadn't given it much thought," said Meade.

"Well, I have. I think we need a new captain...someone with a spine. You're on the council. I want you to call a meeting to hear my grievance."

James Meade continued to chew some of his supper, then washed it down with coffee. He appeared to be deep in thought.

"I can't say I was very much impressed by Mr. Baxter's performance," said Meade. "But I'm not sure that we can blame him for Johnny's death. That's a very serious charge, Mac."

"I'm not accusing him of that," said Deaton. "I'm only saying he should've done something. Should've tried to stop the fight before it got that far."

"All right. I'll talk to Baxter. He has to call the council together... and if he won't, I will."

A huge bonfire drove back the darkness and gave some comfort from the chilled night air. Seventeen men, one from each wagon, comprised the council. Being camped on the prairie did not allow for a private meeting, so the entire company was present. As captain, Ben Baxter called the meeting to order.

"No need for formalities," he said. "It's been reported to me that someone has a grievance, so let's hear it."

Baxter sat down. Deaton was nervous, but determined. He rose slowly to his feet and stepped forward. The warmth of the fire felt good, but its brightness kept him from seeing many of the other men. His mouth was dry, making it hard to speak.

"We've been together almost two weeks," he said. "I know that ain't a long time, and most of us don't really know one another. But I joined this company with the idea that we was to all stick together.

In my way of thinkin' that includes the captain. Where were you this morning, Baxter, when there was trouble at the crossing?"

Everyone's attention shifted to Baxter, as he rose to face his accuser. "You know damn well where I was. What'd you expect me to do? Ride back across the creek? Then what?"

"As captain maybe you could've stopped the fight before Johnny Lloyd got killed," said Deaton. "I didn't know Johnny as well as some of you, but he was my friend and he didn't deserve to die. When it was time to do something, you just cowered on the other side of the creek. I don't call that leadership. I think we should elect a new captain. In fact, I demand it!"

"I don't care what you demand," said Baxter. "There'll be no elections till we've been on the trail for four weeks. You know the bylaws."

"Is that so?" said Deaton. "I'd like to hear what the council has to say about it. How do you men feel about what went on at the crossing today?"

"I say we vote on it," said Meade. "That's why we have a council."

"I don't suppose you're biased in any way?" said someone.

Meade jumped to his feet. "Whoever said that, come and say it to my face. I'll whip anyone who says I'm not a fair-minded man."

Like the sudden rising of the wind just before a storm, a torrent of angry comments was coming from every direction, some calling for a vote and others standing for the bylaws. Small groups of men were arguing heatedly. Baxter looked around the campfire at the storm of controversy that threatened to get out of control. He did the only thing possible under the circumstances. He stepped to the center of the group and raised both hands.

"All right! Quiet down!" he said.

The arguing slacked off almost immediately. When it was quiet enough, Baxter continued, "You members of the council who want a new captain go stand over by Mr. Deaton. The rest come stand by me."

When everyone had made their choice, the count was ten to seven in favor of Baxter, who turned triumphantly to Deaton and said, "Does that satisfy you?"

Deaton turned to the seven men who supported him and shook each man's hand, then walked back to his wagon. Frustration had now been added to his anger. He had not only lost the battle, he had also gained a bitter enemy.

## 22

The steep banks of the Wakarusa River made for a difficult crossing. The men set to work after breakfast and completed the task in three hours. The wagons moved out in a northerly direction for three miles before again turning west. The road was drying out, but it was still too soft, and the company made only twelve miles before calling it a day.

The following morning, Friday, the sky was clear and the sun was warm. A cool, refreshing breeze blew from the northwest, the best weather since leaving Independence. By three o'clock the Plymouth company had covered nineteen miles to the Papin ferry on the Kansas River. Two brothers operated the ferry, Joseph and Lewis Papin, half-breed Indians, who were making a fine living at one dollar per wagon. Two ferries were in operation, each a wooden platform mounted on three dugout canoes and capable of carrying two wagons apiece. Two companies of emigrants were waiting to cross, so Baxter ordered the company to corral the wagons, and set up camp.

Saturday was blustery; gusting winds and an occasional rain shower. The Plymouth company made only twelve miles after crossing the Kansas River. The next day being Sunday, the company laid by to rest. The sky was overcast with clouds ranging from silver white to dark gray, and a strong wind from the northwest made it difficult to keep the tents up. A heavy thunderstorm in the late afternoon forced most of the men into the wagons. Monday the road was wet and muddy, but the Plymouth company pressed on anyway. The wind had shifted to the east and blew so hard it became necessary to remove the wagon covers. On Tuesday the weather had moderated considerably, and by evening they were at the Red Vermillion crossing, a toll bridge operated by a chief of the Pottawatomie Indians.

Deaton was beginning to forget his anger at the death of the unfortunate Johnny Lloyd, but Baxter hadn't forgotten the affront to his leadership. He was a proud man and he resented the accusation that he was somehow responsible for Johnny Lloyd's death.

The campground at Red Vermillion was like all the others; litter everywhere. Cleaning up didn't mean much to the emigrants. Why should it? They never intended to come this way again. Good sanitation didn't exist. The common practice was to dig wells next to the campgrounds, shallow holes that filled with ground water. Because they also dug latrines nearby, contamination of the wells through seepage was inevitable.

Deaton's mess was located next to a small stand of trees along the river. After supper he and Eli Bennett sat down with their backs against the same tree and talked. Owing to the fact it was the night of the new moon, the only light came from the campfire. They talked a long time about home and California.

"Do you suppose we'll ever get there, Eli?" asked Deaton.

"Sure," said Bennett. "Why not?"

"I imagine Johnny Lloyd figured the same. What happened to him...could've been you or me."

"Reckon it could've," said Bennett.

"Twice I thought about turnin' back. Sometimes I think we're fools on a fool's errand. If we get to California, then what? Sure, there's probably gold in the diggin's, but that don't mean we're gonna get any of it."

The sounds of the camp were slowly dying and the noise of the crickets and June bugs grew louder. Bennett was beginning to feel Deaton's melancholy.

"Ain't never had much, Mac. You know that. Farmin's all I know, an' there ain't no money in that 'less y'own a whole passel of niggers. Since I lost Clara, ain't had no purpose in my life till now. If I'd had money so's Clara could've had proper doctorin', maybe I'd be home right now. Might never get rich, but I ain't intendin' to ever be poor again."

"Damn right, you ain't never gonna be rich...unless you learn to stay out of gambling halls. Where'd you be if I hadn't come along?"

Bennett looked over his shoulder at his longtime friend, stung by the remark. What could he say? It was true. Bennett got up and started for the wagon. "G'night," he said.

"Wait! Eli!" said Deaton, but Bennett did not look back. Deaton wanted to kick himself. He sat and brooded until the campfires all went out. Before retiring to his bedroll, he stopped for a drink from one of the wells dug by a previous wagon train. It tasted ghastly.

# 23

On the prairie the nighttime sky was like a river of diamonds on a background of black velvet. It was still dark, but the stars were starting to fade when Deaton awoke. Something was wrong. He never woke up before the bugle call at five o'clock. No one else was stirring. Deaton felt a queasiness in the pit of his stomach. He tried to ignore it, but it wouldn't go away. In a matter of only three or four minutes he was seized with gut-wrenching pain. Deaton rolled out of his blankets and struggled to his feet. He staggered a few steps toward the latrine and began vomiting. Luckily, he made it to the latrine before the diarrhea hit. In a few minutes more Deaton lay prostrated on the ground screaming in agony. In spite of the cold night air he sweat profusely. Worse than the physical pain was the mental anguish. MacKenzie Deaton knew he had the cholera.

The minutes seemed like hours. Deaton's body drew up into a fetal position as the pain intensified. His body fluids continued to gush out in great quantities. Slowly, he became aware of people standing, staring at him in the early light of dawn. The bugle must have sounded, but Deaton didn't recall hearing it. Someone came and covered his semi-nakedness with a blanket.

The noise level grew as the camp came to life. Breakfast was being prepared. The cattle were driven out to graze. Deaton was vaguely aware of someone kneeling next to him.

"Mac, how're y'makin' it?" asked Eli Bennett.

"Oh, god, it hurts, Eli. I'm dyin'. I ain't never gonna see Sarah and the kids again."

"You take it easy, y'hear? Doc Winter's mixin' up a potion that'll take care of you right smart."

"How's he doing?" asked James Meade.

Bennett looked up and shook his head. Deaton's skin was already taking on the bluish hue characteristic of cholera victims. It had been less than an hour since the disease had struck and already he had lost more than three quarts of body fluids. His legs were twitching and his sunken cheeks made his eyes appear to bulge. Doc Winter came up carrying a small crock, stirring something in it with a wooden spoon.

"Give 'im some of this," he said.

Bennett took the crock and looked into it. "What is it?" he asked.

"It's a mixture of whiskey and cayenne with a dose of laudanum."

Deaton gagged down as much of the concoction as he could. It was terrible.

After a time, Deaton heard the oxen being yoked. They were going to pull out. Leave him. He felt panicky. A horseman approached. Astride his horse Ben Baxter gazed down at Deaton, his face a look of silent contempt.

"We'll be movin' on now," he said to the other members of Deaton's mess. "You're welcome to stay here and take care of business. You can catch up later."

"Can't y'wait?" asked Bennett. "He needs tendin'."

"I'm sure you can handle it," said Baxter.

"Where's your heart, man?" asked Meade.

Baxter pretended not to hear. "Y'got a shovel? I can get you one if you need it."

Deaton tugged on Bennett's shirt. Bennett leaned closer.

"Got time to dig two graves?" asked Deaton. "Get me my gun. I'm gonna kill 'im."

"I can't let you do that, Mac. You're sick. You might miss. I'll do it."

Bennett got up and strode purposefully toward the wagon. Baxter thought he was going for a shovel. Meade looked at Bennett, too. The look on his face was unmistakable. Meade took after him at a dead run. He was too late. Bennett pulled a Colt's revolver from the wagon and turned, pointing it at Baxter. The captain saw the weapon. The color drained from his face. There was no escape.

"Don't do it, Eli," Meade pleaded as Bennett walked toward Baxter. "He's got friends. They'll hang you, lad. It ain't worth it."

"He's got it coming," said Bennett. He cocked the gun.

"I'm pleading with you. Think of your family."

"Ain't got one."

Bennett hesitated. Then he pulled the trigger. The gun discharged harmlessly over Baxter's head. Baxter dived from his horse and crawled as fast as he could under a wagon. Bennett laughed.

"Go on, run, you coward!" he yelled.

Meade closed his eyes, filled with relief. He put his arm around Bennett's shoulder and steered him back to the wagon.

"Come on, Eli. Put it away."

"You're right, James. He ain't worth it."

Bennett and the others watched the wagons pull out and cross the toll bridge. They were disgusted. If they didn't have money tied up in the Plymouth company, they'd join up with some other outfit. Bennett was glad to see them go. He needed time to calm down, and he wanted the chance to organize Deaton's personal things, so he could send them home to Sarah.

For two hours they waited as Deaton's condition worsened. The violent vomiting and diarrhea had stopped, but he had a vacant stare in his eyes and a soft gurgling sound in his throat. His fingernails were a deep blue. Meade, Russell and Skinner sat around on the ground staring at their feet. Silent. Waiting.

Three emigrant companies passed. They gave Deaton and his friends a wide berth. No one needed to tell them what was going on.

Bennett packed Deaton's things in his saddlebag. A slow, steady drizzle began to fall a little after nine o'clock. Bennett sat next to Deaton, holding a poncho over him to keep him dry. Meade and the others crawled under the wagon.

The rain let up around eleven o'clock. Meade crawled out from under the wagon and motioned for Bennett.

"Be back in a minute," said Bennett to Deaton. He covered his friend with the poncho and got up.

"Eli," said Meade, "it's getting late. No telling how long this will last. We'd like to move on. You understand. You have a horse. You could catch up fairly quickly."

Bennett looked at his friend and then at Meade. He knew it was the right thing. Deaton moaned and gurgled again.

"All right," said Bennett.

"I feel real bad about this," said Meade, "like we're running out on him."

"No need."

Meade turned to go, then stopped. "Of course before we go, we'll..."

"Yeah, thanks," said Bennett.

Russell and Skinner got the shovels while Meade looked for a good spot. He found a group of four graves down by the river. Half an hour later the grave was dug and they were ready to go. Meade stopped to say goodbye.

"We'll be leaving now," he said.

Bennett nodded, but didn't speak. In a few minutes they were gone, out of sight over the toll bridge. Bennett sat, head down, waiting for the end.

By two o'clock four more emigrant companies had passed. Deaton's condition was no better. Around four o'clock Deaton looked at Bennett and tried to speak. Bennett leaned close to hear.

"Water...drink..."

"I'll get you a drink from the well," said Bennett.

"No...the river..."

Bennett brought some river water in a cup and propped Deaton up to drink it. Deaton wanted more. He drank half a gallon in an hour. By six o'clock his color began to improve.

A wagon train came up the road and camped about fifty yards away. Owing to the fact that all of his provisions had departed with the wagon, Bennett approached the emigrant camp to try to buy some food.

"Hold it right there," said a man with a rifle.

"Hello," said Bennett. "My friend is sick..."

"We ain't blind. State your business."

"Our wagon went on without us, and we ain't got no food."

"You won't get no handouts here," said the man with the gun.

"I got money. We can pay."

"Y'got money, huh? Hold on a minute."

The man went back to the camp and relayed Bennett's offer to the other emigrants. A deal was struck at an exorbitant price and Bennett got his food. The avarice of the men disgusted Bennett, but circumstances left him no choice but to pay. He vowed never to turn down anyone who was in need.

Deaton was in no condition to eat, but he continued to consume large quantities of water. Bennett built a fire and lay down next to his friend. The night seemed longer than usual. Bennett slept fitfully, aware of every sound Deaton made.

In the morning Deaton was alert, but very weak. It didn't appear the grave would be needed after all. He was also hungry. Bennett refrained from eating so that Deaton could have the remainder of the food. Their immediate problem was food, but their long-term dilemma was Deaton's health. He was in no condition to travel yet, and with each passing hour the Plymouth company was getting farther away.

By afternoon Deaton was sitting up, but he looked terrible. His eyes were sunken with dark circles. He stared ahead as if in a trance. Bennett, on the other hand, was growing increasingly impatient. The Plymouth company was likely forty or fifty miles ahead. If Deaton were well enough to travel, it would still take three or four days to catch up.

"How're you feeling?" asked Bennett. "Will you be well enough to travel in the morning?"

"No. But you can go on without me if you want. I won't mind."

"Much as I'd like to be movin' on, I can't do that, Mac. Not just go off and leave you. You're in no condition to be left alone."

"I ain't goin' on with you," said Deaton. "It's time I was headin' for home."

An oppressive feeling came over Eli Bennett. He was choking on the smoke from his dreams going up in flames. If the weather held, they could get back to Independence in five days. But that was more than a hundred miles. The Plymouth company would keep moving, of course, leaving Bennett two hundred and fifty miles to the rear. It would take about four weeks to catch up. As a man of honor and integrity, he knew he had only one choice.

"What about your stake?" asked Bennett. "That's still in the wagon."

"Send it to me. I trust you."

"That's a heavy burden, Mac. You can count on me. But if you ain't comin', then I gotta see you get back to Independence."

Rising wind and an ominous rumble from the west announced the approach of a thunderstorm. They were going to get wet if Bennett didn't hurry. He found a spot on a gentle slope, spread the blankets and then covered them with ponchos. Using Deaton's Bowie knife, he dug a trench around the blankets to channel the runoff away. When the storm hit the two men were under cover and managed to stay reasonably warm and dry.

Two days later Bennett and Deaton started back down the trail. The weather was clear and stayed that way for two weeks. Deaton rode while Bennett walked. They made good progress, averaging more than thirty miles each day. Buying food was not a serious problem, and at a more reasonable price than Bennett had paid at the Red Vermillion, but their eastward progress was greeted with hoots of derision from passing emigrant trains. On the fifth day, May 30, they arrived at Independence, nineteen days after their first departure.

The town had taken on a whole new character. Most of the emigrants were by now on the road to California and the lowlifes who had come to fleece the suckers had departed for greener pastures. Independence was once again a small river town.

Bennett and Deaton put up for the night at Woodson's. The following morning Eli Bennett started again for California with provisions to last one month. Later that same day MacKenzie Deaton, older, wiser, and nearly broke, was on a steamer headed downriver. The big adventure was over.

# 24

Eli Bennett reached the Red Vermillion crossing in only four days. Twelve days had passed since the Plymouth company pulled out. Bennett pushed on to the Black Vermillion, then to the Independence crossing of the Big Blue. From there the trail led north to the junction with the St. Joe road and then up the valley of the Little Blue. After three days the road left the Little Blue and climbed a plateau leading to the Platte River valley.

The grass was sparse and the road sandy. Traffic had multiplied after the junction with the St. Joe road. A cloud of dust, kicked up by the seemingly endless line of wagons, extended from horizon to horizon. It coated everything. To avoid it, Bennett rode as far away from the road as safely possible. On his tenth day out of Independence he was on the Platte approaching Fort Kearny.

The terrain along the Platte was basically flat. The name "Fort Kearny" brought forth visions of earthworks, a log stockade with blockhouses and cannon. Thus, the reality of the prairie outpost was a major disappointment. Fort Kearny had been founded the previous year to provide assistance to emigrants as well as protection from the Pawnee. At the fort's inception emigration across the continent had been only a trickle compared to what was now underway.

Fort Kearny was less than adequate for its stated purpose. It was a loose collection of one-story buildings surrounding a parade ground. The storehouse was built of adobe, and two other buildings were made of timber obtained from the islands of the Platte. An additional six buildings were built entirely of sod except for the door and window frames. A sawmill powered by twelve mules, two temporary stables made of rails with canvas walls, and a scattering of tents constituted the remainder of the fort. The fort had no walls, no redoubt to defend against attack. The only artillery was two twelve-pounders. The garrison consisted of some 140 dragoons and eight officers. A hospital, being built out of sawed lumber, indicated this fort was more than a temporary facility.

The road passed only fifty yards on the north side of the fort, and less than a mile south of the river. It was going on three in the afternoon when Eli Bennett came riding up the trail. He was very tired. On the south side of the road was a wooden sign that read:

*Westbound emigrants are*
*Requested to register at*
*The post headquarters.*
*–by order of*
*The Commandant*

Bennett tied his horse in front of the post headquarters and went inside. A large number of emigrants were ahead of him, each waiting to be added to the growing record of the westward migration. The office was small, and a corporal was handling the registration, while a lieutenant was lounging at a desk looking out the window. The registry book lay open on a table in front of the corporal. The book was clothbound in sage green with a leather binding on the spine. When Bennett's turn came at the head of the line, the corporal barely looked up at him.

"Your name, sir?"

"Eli Bennett."

"How many in your party?"

"Just me."

The corporal scratched the information into the book with a

quill pen.

"Where are you from?"

"Greenwood, Mississippi."

"And your destination?"

"Sutter's fort."

The corporal completed the entry.

"Has the Plymouth company been through?" asked Bennett.

The corporal looked up at Bennett and frowned. Just then Colonel Bonneville, the post commander, entered the office. He approached the corporal who was paging back through the registry book. "Looks like the Plymouth company came through a week ago today," said the soldier.

"Good day, sir," said Col. Bonneville. "Did I hear you inquiring about the Plymouth company?"

"Yes, sir."

"Are you Eli Bennett?"

Surprised, Bennett said, "Why do you ask?"

"If your name is Eli Bennett, I have a letter for you."

"I am the man," said Bennett.

"Good. Come with me."

Bennett followed the officer out the door toward another building. It was a sod house, serving as the current officers quarters. The colonel went inside and returned with the letter. He handed it to Bennett, saying, "I'm Col. Bonneville, the commanding officer hereabouts. Your friends called on me last week. They didn't hold out much hope for your arrival, but left this letter for you in the event you should."

Bennett took the letter and opened it. It was from James Meade. It read:

*Ft. Kearny*
*June 2, 1849*
   *Dear Eli,*
      *It is with great hope but little expectation that I write this letter. Your delay in overtaking our caravan prompted me to borrow a horse and return to the Red Vermillion. To my great joy and even greater surprise I found the grave empty. I inquired at a nearby emigrant train and learned they had encountered you and Mac returning to Independence some few days earlier. They were of the opinion that you intended coming back after taking Mac to Independence. There is growing dissension in the company. Different factions have expressed a desire to split up and reorganize. Your money and property are safe in our hands. If you are unable to overtake us, I will devise some way to see you and Mac are justly compensated. If you should get to the diggings first,*

*save some rocks for us.*
        *Yours,*
        *James Meade*

Bennett folded the letter and stuffed it in his pocket. "Thank you," he said to the colonel. "I guess I'd best be movin' on."

"You won't be catching up with them today, Mr. Bennett. Stay and have some dinner first. We'll eat in a couple hours and you can stay the night."

"Thank you, colonel. I could use a good meal."

"Good for you!" said the colonel. "The food is really first rate. We take our meals with a Mormon family. They run a boarding house."

"Mormons?"

"They lost their stock across the river last year. The buffalo were moving north and overran their camp. When the buffalo had gone, so was their stock. Lucky for them the fort was under construction or their hair might be hanging from a pole in some Pawnee's lodge. Mr. Knowlton, he's the family head, has been helping run the sawmill. His wife and older daughters cook and wait table. It's been a very satisfactory arrangement I understand."

"Are you new at the fort?" asked Bennett.

"Been here a couple of weeks."

Colonel Bonneville took Bennett on a short tour of the fort. The highlight of the tour was the sutler's store. It was built in the style of the other buildings, with a dirt floor, and was stocked with a wide variety of supplies, some of it discarded by over-loaded emigrants, and all of it at reasonable prices.

At the appointed hour the officers of Fort Kearny gathered at the boarding house along with several emigrants, all paying customers, but more than the house could hold. The overflow sat at two long tables out front. Seating was on benches. Bennett went inside with the officers. As they sat down, a tall gaunt-looking man in his fifties came in and hung his hat on a hook by the door.

"Mr. Knowlton," said the Colonel, "come on over and meet my guest."

The man walked over to the table.

"This is our host, Sydney Knowlton," said Bonneville, then added, "and this is Eli Bennett."

"Pleased to meet you," said Bennett, rising and extending his hand.

Knowlton shook hands and nodded. "Headin' west?" he asked.

"Yes, I am. Got separated from my company and I'm tryin' to catch up."

"Would you be going through Great Salt Lake City?"

"Hadn't planned on it."

"Too bad. Been lookin' for someone to take a letter for me."

"Sorry."

During the meal, Bennett was also introduced to Knowlton's wife Harriet and twenty-year-old daughter Mary Ann. Bennett found the daughter very attractive. Her single status was of particular interest. The meal itself was a veritable feast: ham, fresh peas, coffee, milk, molasses, biscuits, pickles, bread and butter, and a large piece of apple pie for dessert.

After dinner, Bennett pitched his tent by the boarding house. Then he went to the sutler's store and bought a jug of whiskey. He had barely started on it when Sydney Knowlton joined him. By the time Bennett turned in he had received a thorough indoctrination in the Mormon faith.

# 25

Eli Bennett awakened to the sound of moving wagons in the morning, his head throbbing like the inside of a bass drum. The broken remains of the whiskey jug reminded him of his excesses of the previous evening. From the angle of the sun Bennett judged it to be well past nine o'clock. He groaned. He should have been ten miles down the road by now. Bennett crawled from his tent and set about packing his gear.

"Good morning," said a soft feminine voice.

Bennett looked around. It was the daughter of Sydney Knowlton. She was shaking out a tablecloth.

"Good morning, Miss Knowlton," said Bennett.

"Would you like breakfast?"

Bennett thought of the time. He really should be going, but traveling on an empty stomach would serve only to increase his misery. The girl walked over to Bennett, folding the tablecloth.

"We have fresh eggs and milk," said the girl.

"Mary Ann!"

Bennett and the girl looked at the house. Mrs. Knowlton was standing in the doorway looking stern.

"Come inside, girl," she said.

Mary Ann glanced at Bennett, then hurried into the house. Bennett ran his fingers through his hair. He realized how disheveled he must look; hair dirty and matted, no bath or shave since he left MacKenzie Deaton at Independence. He went up to the house and knocked. Mrs. Knowlton came to the door.

"What do you want?" she asked.

"Mrs. Knowlton, I'd like to clean up, have a bath and shave, and get something to eat before I move on."

"Are you sober?"

"Ma'am?"

"You was drinkin' last night, got my husband to sharin' that jug. I don't approve of liquor. It's against our religion and I don't like no one puttin' temptation in the way of my man. He's hardworking, a good husband and father, and I won't stand for it."

"I'm sorry, Mrs. Knowlton," said Bennett. "You can believe me when I say it won't happen again."

"You're leaving, huh?"

Bennett nodded. Mrs. Knowlton looked sternly at him for a moment. Then a slight twinkle appeared in her eye.

"C'mon inside," she said. "I'll heat you some water."

Forty-five minutes later Bennett sat down at the dinner table, clean shaven and minus about three layers of dirt. Mrs. Knowlton and her daughter came in carrying platters of food.

"My, my, I wouldn't recognize you," said Mrs. Knowlton.

"Well, I figured if my dirty black face didn't scare you two ladies last night it was because you had seen the elephant. A fella needs to look like a human being now and then, even out here on the prairie."

The ladies sat down at the table with Bennett. Cleaned up, he was actually quite handsome. He and Mary Ann kept exchanging glances, which didn't go unnoticed by her mother. Mrs. Knowlton was beginning to warm to Bennett, and he suspected she was actually encouraging him. There was something very attractive about this family, a wholesomeness that belied all the stories he had heard about Mormons.

"You're the first Mormons I've ever met," said Bennett. "You're not at all what I expected."

"And just what did you expect?" asked Mrs. Knowlton.

"Dunno. I was surprised to hear that you was Christians. Mr. Knowlton told me a lot about your religion. Y'know, it had a familiar ring to it, like I had heard it all before."

"I'm not surprised," said Mrs. Knowlton. "The Savior said that He was the good shepherd and that His sheep would know His voice. It was His Spirit testifying to you."

"Well, I dunno about that, but it's given me a lot to think about."

"Are you going through Salt Lake City?" asked Mary Ann.

"That depends. I've gotta catch up to my wagon train first. I dunno which route they intended on takin'."

"We're going on to Salt Lake City in a few weeks," said Mrs.

Knowlton. "It would be nice to see you again."

"I don't think so," said Bennett. "I'm going to the gold fields."

The Knowlton ladies looked genuinely disappointed. Bennett felt a little disappointed himself, but he had an obligation to fulfill. The conversation digressed into small talk while Bennett finished his meal. By eleven o'clock he was packed and mounted on his horse. Mary Ann and her mother came out to say goodbye.

"Mrs. Knowlton, Miss Knowlton, thanks for your hospitality," said Bennett.

"Will you write to us when you get to California?" asked Mrs. Knowlton. "I'd like to know that you arrived there safely."

"Yes, ma'am, but where will you be?"

"Just write in care of the postmaster at Great Salt Lake City. We'll get it."

"I'll do that, ma'am. Goodbye."

Bennett tipped his hat, turned his horse and headed west. Ahead and behind were long columns of wagons and huge clouds of dust. He passed two emigrant trains the first hour. Now Bennett had a new problem. Across the Platte was another line of wagons heading west. How was he to know whether or not the Plymouth company had crossed the river? It was unlikely, but how would he know? They were too far away to read anything written on the wagon covers. He pressed on, pushing his horse as much as he dared.

The miles ticked slowly by, five to seven every hour. The sun beat down from a cloudless, blue sky. Sweat beads on Bennett's face joined together as drops, then ran together in streaks. Dust coated his clothing and caked to his face.

The hours turned into days. Bennett passed the lower ford at the junction of the North Platte and South Platte, then the middle ford. He passed several trains, inquiring at each if they knew anything of the Plymouth company. The answer was always no.

After four days Bennett had covered 167 miles from Fort Kearny to the upper ford, or California crossing, of the South Platte, arriving about five o'clock in the afternoon. The South Platte was only three feet deep, but the current was swift. The river was nearly half a mile wide. Crossing was difficult owing to the sandy bottom. Animals had to keep moving or they would sink into the shifting sand. Bennett spurred his horse into the water, angling first downstream to the middle, then upstream to the far shore. In fifteen minutes he was across. An emigrant company was camped on the north bank. Bennett stopped to ask if he could camp with them and if they had heard of the Plymouth company. The answer to both questions was yes. This wagon train had been in camp since the previous day to rest their animals and repair two wagons that had upset while fording the South Platte. The Plymouth company had crossed in the morning.

Bennett was excited. They were only one day ahead of him. The desire to find his friends urged him on, but with only two hours of daylight remaining, it wasn't wise to be traveling when the wagons were not rolling. This was Brule Sioux country, and, though they weren't particularly hostile as a group, a lone rider at dusk might be too tempting to pass up. Bennett made camp and fixed his supper of jerky and pilot bread. He was confident that in 24 hours he would be back in camp with the Plymouth company. More than three weeks had passed since he had watched them roll out across the Red Vermillion.

As soon as it was light enough in the morning to see his way, Bennett was in the saddle. Breakfast was a luxury he would have to forego. Most wagon trains took two hours to get on the road. In that amount of time Bennett expected to cover at least seven or eight miles.

The road led up California Hill, a steep incline that started less than a mile from the north bank of the South Platte River. The trail then meandered some fourteen miles along ridgelines and rolling hills. Shortly after ten o'clock Bennett arrived at Ash Hollow, a box canyon opening onto the North Platte.

Ash Hollow was so named because of the ash trees growing along the stream that drained the canyon into the North Platte. Westbound travelers faced the steepest descent between the Missouri River and the Sierra Nevada Mountains. Bennett judged it to be about 300 feet to the bottom. At the base of the hill were the abandoned wrecks of four wagons. They had been stripped of their contents and usable parts. Ash Hollow was like a deep bowl at this point, about a mile across, that opened into a canyon that zigzagged three miles to the North Platte.

Bennett picked his way on foot carefully leading his horse to the bottom of the hill, then turned north. Forty minutes later he came upon a wagon train camped at a spring. It was the Plymouth company. A feeling of relief and satisfaction surged through Bennett. He urged his mount to an easy gallop.

Bennett's approach drew little notice until he was recognized, then there was a considerable stir in the camp. Several men started walking in his direction, among them Ben Baxter, carrying a shotgun. Bennett stopped a few yards short.

"What do you want?" asked Baxter in a low, menacing voice.

"You know what I want. I own stock in this company," said Bennett.

"Not anymore, you don't."

Bennett looked around the camp "Where's Meade...Russell and Skinner?"

"They ain't with us no more. Broke down a few days after we left Fort Kearny. We left 'em. They was nothin' but trouble anyhow. I'm glad to be rid of 'em. And you ain't welcome here neither. So you can just keep movin'."

Bennett shifted in his saddle, looking over the faces of the men. It didn't appear that many of the men shared Baxter's hostility. He decided to take a chance.

"I don't want no trouble with you, Baxter," said Bennett. "But I got a right to water from the spring and I intend on havin' a bite to eat before I go, 'less you plan on murderin' me in front of all these witnesses."

Baxter looked sullenly at Bennett a few moments. "Help yourself, and then git!" he said.

"One more thing," said Bennett.

"What's that?"

"I bought into this company back in the States. I ain't leavin' without my money."

"Well, it looks like you're gonna have to," said Baxter, sarcastically. "I gave your share to your friends when we left 'em."

"And Mr. Deaton's?"

Baxter lowered his head and looked away in disgust. "His, too," he said, then turned and walked away.

Bennett was invited to eat with one of the messes and he eagerly accepted. He hungered more for information than for food. They dined on fresh bread, bacon, beans, boiled rice and coffee. The cuisine was at least familiar, if not improved. Bennett squatted by the campfire and ate. Joe Hamilton, a merchant from Indiana, came and sat next to him.

"We heard Mr. Deaton pulled through," said Hamilton.

"He did."

"Turned around, huh?"

"He's a married man," said Bennett. "Two kids. I reckon he'd seen the elephant. What're y'all still doin' here anyhow?"

"Two wagons upset coming down the hill. Baxter said we should lay in here for a day or two for repairs and to recruit the animals."

"I see," said Bennett. "What happened after you left Fort Kearny? How come y'all didn't stop for Meade and them?"

"Baxter said no. There's been bad blood between him and your mess ever since Deaton tried to lay the blame on him when Johnny Lloyd got shot."

"So you left them all alone out there?"

"No, sir," said Hamilton. "Another company was camped close by. I believe Meade joined up with them."

"Where'd they go?" asked Bennett.

"Can't say," said Hamilton. "They must've crossed at the lower crossing. If they'd come our way you'd have seen 'em, and we would've, too."

"How'd they break down?"

"Busted tongue."

Bennett was seething inside. Baxter was making it a habit of deserting people in distress. He was convinced that Baxter would have left them even if they had been alone. He thanked Hamilton and the others for the meal, then mounted his horse and rode out of camp. After half a mile he reached the North Platte. The Ash Hollow route joined here with the road from the lower crossing. Bennett wondered: right or left? Turn east and backtrack to the lower crossing, or turn left and head west toward Fort Laramie? He thought it over for a few minutes then turned east. Even if they were ahead of him, he could turn around and catch them in a few days.

On Friday, June 22, Eli Bennett rode into Fort Laramie. He had traveled two days eastward on the North Platte before he turned around. He had met a lot of people, but none of them had seen James Meade. He had seen all of the famous Oregon Trail landmarks, Jail Rock, Courthouse Rock and Chimney Rock, but they made little impression on him. He never mentioned them in his journal or wrote home about them. He was running out of time and provisions. And he was worried. Since Fort Kearny, the trail had made several branches. It crossed the South Platte at three different places. At Scott's Bluff it split, one route going through Mitchell Pass and the other through Robidoux Pass. He could have passed Meade without knowing it.

Like Fort Kearny, a register was kept at Fort Laramie. Bennett learned that Meade had passed the fort on the 19th and the Plymouth company had passed on the 20th. It was likely he would catch Meade within four or five days, if he pushed his horse harder.

Bennett left Fort Laramie in the early afternoon. Less than an hour later he found James Meade. On a gentle slope about thirty yards south of the trail was a fresh grave. The marker read:

*James Meade*
*D. June 20, 1849*
*Cholera*

# 26

Fort Bridger was even less deserving of the title "Fort" than had been Fort Kearny. More accurately, it was a trading post, the commercial descendant of the mountain man rendezvous held yearly in various locations where the trappers and traders met to conduct business and engage in general hell raising. The fort consisted of eight log houses and a picket enclosure ten feet high that served as a corral. Several Indian lodges were in the vicinity.

Mountain man Jim Bridger and his partner Louis Vasquez had built the trading post in 1843 along river bottomland. The third and most famous of Bridger's forts, it was like an oasis in a barren wilderness, and an ideal location to deal in the emigrant trade. The fur business was dying just as the settling of the West was about to move into high gear. Bridger described it thusly, "The fort is a beautiful location on Black's Fork of Green River, receiving fine, fresh water from the snow on the Uintah range. The streams are alive with mountain trout. It passes the fort in several channels, each lined with trees, kept alive by the moisture of the soil."

After finding the grave of James Meade, Eli Bennett had still entertained the hope of catching up to Russell and Skinner. West of Fort Laramie the road had become a maze of trails as succeeding wagon trains had to search increasingly farther from the main road for adequate forage and water for their animals. Four days out of Laramie Bennett's horse drank some bad water. By the time he knew the water was alkali, it was too late. The animal swelled up and died. For the next three weeks Bennett had walked west, begging food from emigrant trains along the way. Footsore and desperate, Eli Bennett came trudging up to Fort Bridger on July 18, 1849.

Bennett approached one of the three emigrant companies camped near the fort, a party from New York, and asked for help. They laughed him to scorn and sent him on his way. At the second wagon train Bennett approached a man with his back turned, hunched over a campfire stirring a pot. After several moments and the man had not turned around, Bennett cleared his throat. The man gave Bennett a sideways glance.

"Looking for something?" he asked.

"I was hoping to get something to eat."

The man removed the spoon from the pot, blew on it a couple

times, then put it in his own mouth.

"Pretty good," he said, reaching for a wooden bowl. He filled the bowl and, turning around, handed it to Bennett.

"What's the matter?" asked the man. "Never seen an Indian before?"

Bennett's look of surprise turned to embarrassment. "I'm sorry," he said. "I've never seen an Indian wearing white man's clothes before."

The man laughed and extended his hand. "I'm George Keys. A Cherokee. One of the 'civilized tribes'."

Bennett shook the man's hand and looked around the camp. As a small boy he had heard of Indians that were relocated from the southeastern states to a place west of Arkansas called the Indian Nations.

"Are all of you Cherokees?" asked Bennett.

"No. We have several whites traveling with us. Not only do we wear the white man's clothes, we live in white man's houses, farm the land, and we also have the white man's vices. We want to get rich. We're going to the gold fields in California. Are you traveling alone?"

Bennett related his experiences to the Indian as he downed a bowl of corn meal mush, a bowl of bacon and beans, and half a loaf of bread. Keys was suitably impressed with Bennett's grit.

"Why didn't you turn back?" asked Keys.

"Many a time I asked myself that question," said Bennett. "I don't know. I s'pose it's for Mac. I owe 'im. Then, I never did fancy myself a quitter."

"You walking to California all by yourself?" asked Keys.

"Can't go back. Can't stay here. Thought I might winter in Salt Lake City. Get me a job and earn me a stake, so I can go on to California next year. Met a Mormon family back at Fort Kearny. You know, the Knowltons. They run the boarding house."

"Sorry. We didn't come that way. We came by Bent's Fort and Pueblo. It's very much shorter. We're going through the Mormon city. You're welcome to come along."

"What about your friends?"

"It's no concern of theirs," said Keys. "You'll be traveling with me."

"Thank you, sir," said Bennett. "You are a true southern gentleman."

"I hardly think so," said Keys, shaking his head and smiling. "But we Cherokees know what it is like to be strangers in a strange land. It is our custom to be hospitable. Do you need a blanket?"

"Reckon I do. Sure am tired."

Though only four in the afternoon, Bennett found a shady spot, spread the blanket and slept till morning.

The company of Cherokees pulled out of Fort Bridger shortly after daybreak on July 19, 1849. The road to Salt Lake City, just more than a hundred miles away, became increasingly difficult. The trail went over the mountains and down Echo Canyon to the Weber River. On their fourth day out of Bridger, they left the Weber River and followed the route pioneered by the ill-fated Donner party three years before. The road was a narrow track with many short turns through dense bushes and trees that went south for eight miles, crossing Kanyon Creek thirteen times. Eli Bennett was sure that if this stretch of road were left untraveled for five years, all trace of it would disappear. The Cherokees camped five miles below the head of Kanyon Creek on the east side, near where the road crossed over for the last time and turned up a narrow side canyon.

In the morning the wagon train crossed Kanyon Creek and began the ascent up Big Mountain. By midmorning they had traveled four miles and reached the summit of Big Mountain Pass. Before them lay a breathtaking view. The road descended a steep canyon. In the distance, beyond two mountain ridges lay the valley of the Great Salt Lake. They paused for a few minutes to enjoy the view, then chain-locked the rear wheels of their wagons and began the descent.

About a mile below the summit the road crossed a rickety, makeshift bridge over a deep ravine. After another five miles the road turned northwest and zigzagged for a mile to the top of another ridge, then descended into Emigration Canyon. The daylight was fading when they passed out of the canyon onto a bench and then down onto the valley floor. They traversed Great Salt Lake City along its southern limit and camped on the east bank of the Jordan River.

The following morning Bennett awoke to the sound of nine rounds of artillery being fired, accompanied by the playing of martial music from a brass band. The entire camp was astir, curious about what the commotion was all about. Musicians were being driven around the city in two carriages, taking turns playing as they went. Bennett and George Keys ate a quick breakfast and then hurried to find the cause of this great excitement.

They found the city in the midst of a great celebration. A large crowd had congregated at the public square, upon which was situated a spacious bowery more than one hundred feet long. A large American flag, 65 feet in length, flapped in the breeze atop a 100-foot flagpole.

"What's all the ruckus about?" Bennett asked one of the bystanders.

"Pioneer day celebration," the man said. "Been two years since we settled this valley."

The date was Tuesday, July 24, 1849, the second anniversary of Brigham Young's entrance into the Salt Lake Valley. The first party of Mormon pioneers had arrived two days ahead of him, but apparently they were not officially there until the arrival of the Prophet.

Next came a salute by six guns, followed by the ringing of the Nauvoo bell, saved from the Mormon temple in Nauvoo, Illinois, and transported across the plains.

The playing of the brass bands kept up for some time. At nine o'clock a procession started from President Brigham Young's house to the bowery. Leading the way was the Prophet himself, followed by the two bands and a host of others, including twelve bishops carrying the flags of their respective wards, and two groups, one of young men and the other of young women, all dressed in white. Next came twenty-four horsemen mounted on silver grays, each bearing a staff flying the stars and stripes, and each flag bore the legend "Liberty and Truth."

The young men and women sang a hymn as they marched, and the roar of cannon and rifle fire could be heard from the public square, along with the continuous ringing of the Nauvoo bell.

Enthusiastic cheers greeted the Prophet as he arrived at the bowery. Everyone rose to their feet. Then, as if by some unseen signal, the voice of thousands of people became one as they shouted in unison, "Hosanna! Hosanna! Hosanna to God and the Lamb!" Brigham Young proceeded to the speakers' platform and took his place. One of the young men then came forward and presented to him the Declaration of Independence and the Constitution. President Young then rose to speak.

"My dear brethren and sisters, like the children of Israel, we have crossed the wilderness to escape the persecutions of our enemies. We have laid the foundation of a great city and raised the ensign of the Lord in the tops of the mountains for all the world to look to for their salvation. Indeed, we have fulfilled the prophecy and made the desert blossom as a rose. Here we shall gather the Lord's chosen people from the ends of the earth and establish Zion.

"Two years ago a small band of brave and hardy pioneers planted the seeds of liberty and justice in this valley, and now today you see the fruits of their labors. It has not been an easy task. We have endured hardship and the temptation of the gold fields. But our task is not fulfilled. Our journey is not ended. Our enemies are not through with us. Lucifer, that great destroyer, has been held in check for a season, but in due time, he shall come forth again to deceive and torment. Our enemies were content to leave us alone in the wilderness, for verily, who could prosper in this place? The day will come when they shall see what we have wrought in this valley, and their hearts will be stirred up once more by hatred and greed. Once more they will seek to kill the prophets. I say, let them come! This time we shall be ready, for the Lord will make of us a mighty people, and who can fight against the Lord?

"Now let us thank God for the blessings of freedom. We invite all visitors to our city to join in, to partake of our fellowship and share in our spirit of thankfulness for this great land, the United States of America. Brother Isaac Delaney will lead us in prayer, and then, let the celebration begin."

Bennett took part in the festivities with enthusiasm. His brief visit with the Knowltons at Fort Kearny had prepared him a little for this experience, but he was still overwhelmed by the warmth of the people. He thought back to his experience at Independence and the tightfistedness of many of his fellow travelers between Fort Laramie and Fort Bridger. Circumstances had forced him to come to Salt Lake City, or so he had first thought. Now he wondered if he had not been guided to this place.

Following the program, dinner was served. Two hundred California emigrants joined the more than six thousand residents of the city. The supply of food was plentiful and included fruits and vegetables that most of the travelers had not seen since leaving their homes in the States.

Bennett and George Keys sat together. Sharing the same table was Orson Thomas and his family. Keys was the subject of close scrutiny by those around him. Most had not seen a "civilized" Indian before. The Thomases took great pains to acquaint George Keys with the history of the Lamanites contained in the Book of Mormon, telling him that the American Indians were descendants of the Lamanites, and how great blessings were promised to those of his race, who would accept the gospel and be baptized into the Mormon church. Keys listened politely, not wishing to offend his hosts, but the only blessings he was interested in were to be found in the gold fields of California, not in some book.

Meanwhile, Bennett was trying to make a good impression on Diana Thomas, Orson's nineteen year-old daughter. He did this by ignoring her completely. Instead, he made conversation with her mother. Knowing that the greatest obstacle any suitor faced was the girl's mother, he decided to plough that field first. Not that he intended to be a suitor, for after all he only planned to stay the winter and then go on to California in the spring. But as long as he was going to be around for awhile, he might as well try to make it a pleasant experience.

"Where are you from?" asked Mrs. Thomas.

"Greenwood, Mississippi, ma'am," said Bennett.

"Oh, a southerner! I should have known by your accent. We're from Ohio. Have you ever been to Ohio?"

"Never been there, ma'am, but I have thought I would someday like to pay a visit."

"We hear there are thousands of emigrants on their way to California," said Mrs. Thomas. "But we don't get many of them here."

"I hadn't planned on it myself, ma'am."

Bennett then related his experiences on the trail. Mrs. Thomas was especially interested in his visit with the Knowltons and was happy that he knew as much as he did about the Mormons. When he finished his story, she turned to her husband at the other end of the table. "Orson, this nice young man will be staying here until next spring. He says he likes it here and is hoping to find work and a place to stay."

"Is that so? What's your trade, young man?"

"I'm a farmer, sir," said Bennett.

"Good, good. There's plenty of work around here. I'll talk to some of my friends. I'm sure we can find you a place to stay. There's always room for one more."

When the Cherokees pulled out the following morning, Bennett bade a sad farewell to his friend George Keys. Without his help Bennett might not have made it this far.

Orson Thomas was right. There was plenty of work. Bennett found himself so busy that more than a week passed before he had time to sit down and write a letter to MacKenzie Deaton. He was anxious to tell his friend that he was well and still hoping to find Russell and Skinner and make an accounting of the money that had been left in their trust.

# 27

Nothing about the few wispy clouds suggested any relief from the heat of the merciless, summer sun. The air was still and oppressive. The only sound was the rhythmic squeak of the rocking chair on the front porch. It hadn't rained in more than two weeks, and with the temperature above one hundred degrees it wasn't a good day for working in the fields. MacKenzie Deaton didn't feel much like working anyway. He only wanted to sit in the shade of the porch sipping cool drinks. Not that he was sick or anything like that. In fact he had recovered fully from his bout with cholera. No, Deaton was suffering from melancholy...and he was discouraged. Not about the aborted trek to California, though he did worry about Eli Bennett. Deaton was glad to be back home with his wife and kids. He wondered why he had ever left.

The door swung open and Sarah came out on the porch. "Ain't y'workin' this afternoon?" she asked.

"Too hot, Sarah."

Sarah came and stood behind her man. She placed her hands on his shoulders and gently kneaded them, pressing deep with her thumbs. Several moments passed as she gently tried to massage MacKenzie's cares away.

"This is good land," said Deaton, a hint of sadness in his voice. "Maybe I shouldn't't've give up."

Sarah rested her cheek on the top of MacKenzie's head. "I'm just glad you're home," she said.

A few minutes later a carriage turned up the lane, trailing a cloud of dust. It was Sam Tyler, sooner than Deaton had expected.

"Afternoon MacKenzie, Mrs. Deaton," said Tyler after he had stopped his carriage.

"Good afternoon, sir," said Deaton.

"I heard you were back. Kinda thought you'd stop by and talk things over."

"Been too busy, Tyler. Should've known better'n to leave with all the work that needs doin' around this place."

"It's a hot day, Mr. Tyler," said Sarah. "Why don't you come up on the porch and sit a spell? I'll bring you out a cool drink."

"Thank you, ma'am."

Tyler climbed down from his carriage and joined Deaton on the porch. Deaton rocked slowly in his chair and fanned himself.

"Expectin' a good crop this year?" asked Tyler.

"Looks that way."

"D'you think it'll bring enough to pay off your note?"

"Y'don't waste no time, do you, Tyler?"

"This ain't no social visit, MacKenzie. We have a business arrangement, and it doesn't appear you'll be able to fulfill your obligation."

"You knew the risks. You risked your money and I risked my life."

"It seems you still have your life," said Tyler. "Where's my money?"

"I almost lost my life," said Deaton sharply.

"And you're gonna lose your farm," said Tyler.

"The note ain't due for two years, Tyler. I'll have to listen to you then, but I ain't gotta listen to you now."

"I don't want to wait two years. In two years I can have it by having the sheriff serve papers. Sell it to me now and I'll give you a fair price. You can make a new start somewhere else."

"What's the big hurry?"

"The last thing I need is a farm, MacKenzie."

"Then why do you want to buy mine?"

"Because I've got a buyer," said Tyler. "I can make a little profit now, or maybe a lot of profit later. Trouble is, I don't know what the market will be like in two years."

"I don't wanna leave this place," said Deaton.

"I understand your feelings," said Tyler. "Were I in your place I wouldn't want to leave either. But think it over. You can sell it to me now or you can give it to me later."

Tyler's argument made sense. Sarah returned with the drinks and conversation turned to more mundane topics. In a while Sam Tyler was gone, leaving MacKenzie and Sarah to consider his offer.

# 28

By early August the California emigration had mostly come and gone. Not a soul among them had not heard of the Donner tragedy of 1846. The latecomers were not as lighthearted as their predecessors. Time was their enemy, and they behaved as if being chased by a shadow, keenly aware of any sign of a change in the weather.

It was a well known fact in Salt Lake City that large amounts of hard goods had been dumped on the prairie to lighten overloaded wagons. The latecomers were even more prolific in this activity. Nothing was unworthy of being sacrificed if it could hasten their journey by a couple of days or even one. It didn't take long for someone in Salt Lake to figure out that more wealth lay next to the emigrant road than was to be had in California.

Isaac Delaney's marriage had restored purpose to his life. Harriet could not fill the void in his heart left by the passing of his dear Molly. She knew that. But she had set out to carve a place in his affections that would be hers alone. She was secure in the knowledge that he loved her as much as she did him, and that the children were not his and hers, but rather theirs. Together with John and Elizabeth and Samantha, they were a family. When the child she was carrying was born in December, the bond between them would at last be complete.

Harriet liked to watch her husband work. She sat quietly, rocking on the porch as he made sure the wagon was fit for travel. He packed enough provisions for six weeks. He hoped to be back in less time. When at last Delaney was ready, Harriet came down from the porch to say goodbye.

"Be careful, Isaac. Don't take chances."

Delaney placed his hands on her shoulders and looked into her eyes. "You needn't worry, my dear," he said. "I'll be thinking about you all the time I'm gone."

"I'm glad you found someone to go with you," said Harriet.

"So am I. Morley Townsend is a good man, and I hear he's bringing at least one more with him. I shouldn't think we'll have much trouble. There's a lot of goods out there. I don't intend on passing up my opportunity twice. If all goes well, we'll soon be making a fine living."

Isaac and Harriet embraced, their lips met and lingered for a while. Then Delaney was in the wagon and driving up the road toward the east bench and the mouth of Emigration Canyon. Harriet wiped away a tear.

For Eli Bennett the California dream was over. Dead forever. There would be no renewal of the journey in the spring. Diana Thomas had seen to that.

"Take good care of my girl," said Orson Thomas.

Bennett shook the elder man's hand. He had come west seeking gold and had found something far more precious. His instruction in the Mormon faith by the Knowltons was only a beginning. Now he had embraced it wholeheartedly and in the process had gained a wife.

"No need to concern yourself about that one bit, Brother Thomas. Y'all been real good to me. Now I'm gonna take real good care of her."

Mrs. Thomas stepped forward and hugged Bennett. She wanted to say something, but she couldn't. She was crying, completely overcome with emotion.

Bennett helped his new bride into the wagon. They waved a cheery farewell to family and friends, then Bennett snapped the reins and the horses began to move, carrying them to their new home.

Summer had passed and then the harvest season. The winter was mild, a time that MacKenzie Deaton would normally spend hunting and repairing farm implements, getting ready for the next growing season. Instead, he spent the time traveling, looking for a new opportunity.

When spring came there were new faces on the farm. A stranger was plowing Deaton's fields, reaping their annual harvest of rocks.

On a fine morning in April 1850, MacKenzie and Sarah Deaton loaded their family and belongings into a wagon and started down the lane to the main road. Sarah, Joel Oliver, and Laura Jean were all crying. Deaton's face was grim. It was almost a year to the day that he had set out for California with such high hopes. What rash foolishness! Whoever said "The love of money is the root of all evil" would have no trouble convincing MacKenzie Deaton. The decision to go to California was the great turning point in his life. It had brought him to financial ruin and would influence every aspect of his future existence.

Sarah and the children looked back as the farm faded in the distance, but not Deaton. Like his friend Eli Bennett, he knew that he must push forward and put the past behind him. He set his mind on Arkansas, their new home, and a new beginning.

# 29

*DESERET NEWS — July 27, 1850*
*"Brethren of Great Salt Lake City and vicinity who are full of faith and good works, who have been blessed with means, who want more means and are willing to labor and toil to obtain those means, are informed by the Presidency of the Church, that a colony is wanted at Little Salt Lake, Iron County, this fall. That fifty or more good effective men, with teams and wagons, provisions and clothing are wanted for one year."*

*DESERET NEWS — October 27, 1850*
*"Wanting one hundred men ready to start on the first day of December, with five hundred bushels of seed wheat, thirty thousand pounds of breadstuff, or three hundred pounds to each person, thirty-four plows, seventeen set drag teeth, one ax, spade shovel, and hoe to each man. One millwright, five carpenters and joiners, two blacksmiths, two shoemakers and one surveyor, each with tools. Four top and pit sawyers, with saws; one stone cutter, two stone masons; grain and grass scythes, sickles and pitch forks, fifty each; one gun and two hundred pounds of ammunition to each man; fifty horses, twenty-five pair of holster pistols. One gunsmith, one cow to two beef cattle, potatoes and seed of the ball, radish, beets, squash and garden seeds of all kinds, also Henry Miller with his threshing machine next year."*

The call for families to colonize the southern part of the territory had been noised abroad for several months by the time Isaac Delaney was sent for by the Prophet on November 13, 1850. A move to the south was the farthest thing from Delaney's mind as he approached the President's door. After all, Brigham Young was his friend. He would never ask Delaney to relocate his family so soon. He knocked and was immediately admitted into the President's office.

"Brother Isaac!" said the Prophet, rising and extending his hand. "I'm glad you could come. Please sit down."

Delaney took a seat, crossed his legs, and hung his hat on his knee. He knew this wasn't a social visit, but he seemed almost detached. He had a pleasant, relaxed look on his face. "What's your pleasure, Brother Brigham?"

"Isaac, I've been hearing good things about you. I hear your business is prosperous and your family is growing."

"That's right. Two children in the last two years "

"Do you believe the Lord has blessed you?"

Delaney thought of his dear Molly. How she would have loved to see this valley and enjoy the fruits of Delaney's labor. Then he thought of Harriet. Had Molly lived, they may never have met, and probably never married. For a moment Delaney was confused as he considered the love he felt for both of his wives.

"Yes," he finally said, "I believe I see the lord's hand in my life. Two years ago you promised that my faith would be rewarded, and indeed it has."

"I have a new challenge for you."

*He's going to ask me to take another wife.*

"You used to be a carpenter. Are you still good at it?"

"I still try my hand at it now and then."

"The Lord was a carpenter."

"I know that."

"But when the time came, he put away his tools and turned his attention to the ministry..."

*He's going to call me on a mission. I won't go. I can't go. Not now.*

"...I feel impressed to call you on a mission..."

*I knew it.*

"...to Iron County."

"Iron County!"

"Yes, brother Isaac. Surely you've heard about it by now."

"Yes, but I never thought that I..."

"Isaac, you know I wouldn't ask you if I didn't think it was the right thing. Besides, I am not the one who calls you, but rather the Lord. I am but the instrument of His will."

Delaney hung his head and stroked his chin. This was totally unexpected. There must be something he could say, something to persuade the prophet to change his mind.

"I hear that Ezra Clark was called, but he was released from the call by giving four hundred bushels of wheat."

"Yes, that's true," said Brigham.

"Well, sir, I am a man of means..."

"I know that, Isaac. The Lord has given you much... and now it's time to give some of it back."

"How much do you want?"

"Just you...and your family."

"I don't understand. There are other carpenters."

"The Lord doesn't want another carpenter. The Lord wants you."

Isaac Delaney thought of the promises Brigham Young had made to him two years before. It was true. He had been blessed. He thought of Harriet and the children. He thought of the hardship they had endured. Slowly, a realization began to take shape in his mind. It wasn't the goal that brought happiness, but rather the striving for that goal. Southern Utah would bring new opportunities, which in turn would bring new happiness to his life. With tears in his eyes he looked up at the prophet.

"I'll go, brother Brigham" said Delaney. "I'll go."

Provo was the appointed place of rendezvous for the company of pioneers who were to colonize Iron County. For over a week the people came to that place, and finally, on Sunday, December 15, 1850, a meeting of the company was called to order by the Apostle George A. Smith.

"This is the first time we have seen each other's faces. Those who have obeyed this call have done it by the voice of the Presidency. I have been appointed to gather and lead out this company to the place of our destination. I would expect the saints to play their part well. I hope our ears will not be saluted with swearing or the taking of the name of God in vain. We want no gambling. We are going to gather the saints and build the kingdom of God. We should act as though we are on a mission to preach the gospel. The Sabbath day should be observed in all cases.

"We shall try and move every day, if we do not go but a few miles, it will be better to change camp. I will prophesy that if we work with our heart and mind, we shall perform our mission and return in safety. I hope that every person will remember to call upon the Lord at the close of the day, and in the morning pray to the god of heaven.

"We are going into Indian country. We should have about 120

men and it is necessary for every man to get his arms ready for service and be ready at a minute's warning. We will try to keep together at all times, lest we be tithed by the Indians.

"Remember that we are the citizens of Iron County and do not want a mean man to settle in that country. I bless you in the name of the Lord. Now, let us pray."

The Apostle bowed his head and offered up a fervent prayer in behalf of the assembled Saints, that they might come through in safety and be rewarded according to their faith and works.

The following day the company pulled out from their encampment on the Provo River. The roads were bad and the weather cold and blustery. A blanket of snow covered the ground. By the end of the week they had crossed the divide into Juab Valley. By Christmas, they had reached the Sevier River.

It was not a Sunday picnic or a stroll across the prairie in the summer, but was a very arduous trek. Nevertheless, the people were cheerful. A sense of purpose permeated the entire company; not an ordinary company of emigrants, but a handpicked group of artisans and craftsman, trained in all the arts and skills in the factories and shops of Europe.

By January 10 the party had crested the last ridge and had their first glimpse of the broad valley that would be their new home. Men fired off their guns and Jacob Hoffheins saluted the occasion by setting off three charges from the Old Sow cannon, a brass six-pounder they had brought along to put the fear of God in the local Indians.

When they finally reached their camp on the site of the future town of Parowan, the Apostle George A. Smith called them all together to offer up a prayer of thanksgiving. Reverently, they knelt in the snow.

"Our Father in Heaven, we thank thee for thy protecting care that has been over us. And we ask thee to be with us here in this beautiful valley. Lead us and guide us in the way that thou would have us go. Help us to be faithful and diligent, that we may be successful in our efforts to build up this part of thy vineyard. Be with us and protect us at all times we pray, in the name of Jesus. Amen."

Isaac Delaney rose to his feet and gathered his family around him. They had left a comfortable home for this wilderness. Now Delaney knew what the Saints must have felt when they first entered the Salt Lake Valley. He was excited about the future, for at last he had caught the vision. He had not left Zion. He had brought it with him.

Isaac Delaney. MacKenzie Deaton. Eli Bennett. Three men

separated by miles and circumstances, yet united in a common bond. A beam of sunlight reflecting off a piece of yellow metal beneath a few inches of running water had changed their lives forever and set them all on a course that would eventually join their separate lives in a common destiny.

# The Second Time Around

# 30

Joel Deaton awoke with a start. The dim light coming through his bedroom window was too bright for moonlight. Then he remembered. It was Sunday afternoon. The weather was still cold and gloomy and Joel had been sick for the better part of a week. Reverend Claiburn had been by earlier to inquire about his health. Joel was improved, but his illness had left him with a wrung out feeling. After lunch he had lain down for a nap. Something had awakened him. He wondered what. Then he heard shouting from another part of the house. His mother and father were arguing.

Joel got out of bed and went to his bedroom door, opened it, and peered out. He saw his father take down his rifle from its place above the front door and go out, slamming the door behind him. Joel's mother was sitting at the dining table, her head buried in her arms, crying. Joel quietly closed his door and got back in bed.

After dinner Joel went out to the barn to do some work in preparation for the spring plowing. He repaired some harness and sharpened the plow. About ten o'clock MacKenzie Deaton came driving up in the wagon.

"Joel! What y'all doin' up so late, boy?"

"Got work to do, Pa."

"Ain't no call for doin' that, son. It's Sunday. You ain't s'posed to be workin' on Sunday."

"I ain't been pullin' my share of the load around here, Pa. I figured I'd get things ready for the plowin'."

Deaton tried to get down from the wagon, but in doing so he fell flat on his face. He was so drunk he could barely stand up. Joel went to his father and tried to help him get up. Deaton jerked his arm away.

"Leave me be, Joel!" said Deaton. "I can get up by myself. Now you go on to bed, y'hear?"

Joel looked at his father. This wasn't like him. MacKenzie Deaton was not a drinking man. The argument between his parents must have been more serious than Joel had first thought. He turned and started for the house. Behind him he heard Deaton grunting as he tried to get to his feet.

Inside, Joel lit a candle and went to his room. He got down the journal his mother had given him for Christmas and began to write:

*January 11, 1857—Sunday...*

# 31

The Deaton farm was a mile east of Carrollton, Arkansas, a crossroads community near the southern end of the Ozarks, an ancient plateau that had eroded into what some would call mountains, ranging up to 2500 feet. In the reddish soil it was possible to eke out a modest living as a farmer and perhaps Deaton should have been content. But the image of California had been rattling around in his brain for eight years, and now it was a constant buzz.

Two days after the big argument between his parents, Joel Deaton was up early doing his chores. It felt good to have his strength back. He had done a little work the day before, mostly of necessity, since his father had been gone all day on a trip to Boone County. Shortly after sunrise MacKenzie Deaton came out of the house. The temperature was so cold his breath was visible, but he was not wearing a coat. Ignoring Joel, he set right to work feeding and watering the stock. In no time he had worked up a good sweat. Twenty minutes later he stopped what he was doing and came over to Joel.

"D'you wanna talk, son?" asked Deaton.

"What about?"

"I reckon you heard your mama and me arguing the other night."

"Yes sir, I did."

"I reckon you'd like to know what it was all about."

"Don't know. You never asked me before. I don't reckon you'd want to be tellin' me now."

"We've lived here a long time, Joel. 'Bout eight years now. I don't s'pose you remember the time I went off to California..."

"Sure I do, Pa," said Joel. "That's why we lost the farm."

Deaton looked a little uneasy. He hesitated, looking around, trying to choose the right words. Over at the house he could see that Sarah was up fixing breakfast.

"Life has never been the same since we left Mississippi," said Deaton. "There ain't no future for us here, Joel. Your mama wants to just stay put, but I can't do it. I still want to go to California."

"You reckon things'll be better in California?"

"I don't know, son. I only know they'll never get no better here."

"I don't want to leave this place, Pa."

"I know that, Joel, but I gotta see the elephant before I die."

"What does that mean?" asked Joel. "They got elephants in California?"

Deaton shook his head and smiled. "No, son, it's just an old story. Someone who does somethin' he ain't never done before, and had a lotta trouble doin' it, is said to have seen the elephant."

"I don't understand, Pa."

"Well, there was this old farmer who had heard about elephants, but he had never seen one. In fact, he doubted if there really was such an animal. One day he heard that the circus was coming to town and they had elephants. Well, he loaded up his wagon with produce to sell in town and set off for the market. Along the way he came upon the circus parade, and when his horses saw the elephants they set to snortin' and soon bolted. Well, his wagon overturned, was all busted up, ruined his produce and darn near killed him. On his way home he ran into one of his friends who had heard about his bad luck. When the friend gave his regrets, the farmer said, 'I don't give a hang! I have seen the elephant!' Emigrants headin' west ain't never done nothin' like that before. By the time they've seen Indians, buffalo, and their friends dyin' of the cholera, when they've seen enough to know it ain't no circus or Sunday picnic, then they have seen the elephant."

"You got the cholera, didn't you?" said Joel.

"Well, that's true," said Deaton, "but I didn't see the elephant. Just caught a whiff of his stinkin' breath."

Deaton told his son about a man named Alexander Fancher who had returned from California in late October. It was his second trip across the continent. His older brother, John Fancher had moved his family to California in 1849. During Alexander Fancher's first visit to see his brother, John had sold him on the idea of moving his own family west. Alexander Fancher was a born leader and highly respected by his friends and neighbors. He spent considerable effort convincing friends and relatives that a better life awaited them in the "Golden State", and soon more than a dozen families wanted to go along. On behalf of several families in Boone and Carroll counties he had taken an option to buy more than three thousand acres of prime farmland on his second trip. With the coming of spring, Fancher, his family and friends were heading west.

MacKenzie Deaton felt like a Young man again. He still had the California fever and there was only one cure for it.

# 32

*March 23, 1857* The grass was wet with dew and only a few stars were visible overhead in a sky that changed from dark in the west to pale blue on the eastern horizon. The air was alive with the sounds of birds greeting the dawn. A smell of smoke from the fireplace filled the air as Sarah Deaton fixed breakfast for the last time in the house that she had once thought would be her home forever.

Only thirty-five, but already a few gray hairs, Sarah Deaton had lived a very hard life. The daughter of a tenant farmer, she had married a farmer when she was only eighteen, right after her family had moved from North Carolina. She had endured four pregnancies. Joel Oliver was her firstborn. He was now in his sixteenth year. The second child was stillborn, another boy. Next came Laura Jean. Her birth was the cause of much excitement among the Deaton clan. Most Deaton children were male. A little girl Deaton...well, she certainly had a lot of aunts and uncles coming to see her, some of whom older brother Joel had never seen before.

After the move to Arkansas another child, Jesse, was born in 1851. Jesse was a brown-eyed little towhead. He had a determination in the way he walked and he always had an easy smile that could quickly change to a mischievous grin. He loved to tease and he was not afraid of anything. He drowned in the creek before his fourth birthday. Sarah never got over the loss of her little Jesse. It affected every aspect of her life. Having another child was out of the question. On the frontier every birth was a potential tragedy. It simply wasn't worth the risk.

Now, MacKenzie Deaton had persuaded his wife to risk everything. He had sold his farm and thrown in with the Fancher wagon train. Rumor had it that the money and property of the emigrants were worth more than $70,000. Deaton was the "poor man" of the company. In fact, he had been forced to hire on as a drover for the large stock herd. Deaton figured he would've had to work if he stayed home, so he saw no reason why he couldn't work in exchange for his outfit and the chance to emigrate to California.

The sun was high, midmorning, when the Fancher train appeared on the eastern horizon. It had started soon after daybreak from Beller Stand and moved along the military road toward Carrollton. The first indication of its coming was a thin cloud of dust in the distance. The caravan was in sight for several minutes before it could be heard. The pounding hooves, the creaking of wagons and the bellowing of animals grew louder as the train drew nearer. The sight inspired excitement in the Deaton family. About a thousand head of cattle, several hundred horses, about twenty wagons and some carriages for the ladies to ride. Some of the men rode horses, but everyone else would walk the 2500 miles to California. The wagons were for hauling goods, not people.

As the wagon train passed by, Captain Fancher was in the front on horseback. Tall, slim, and of dark complexion, Alexander Fancher had an almost regal bearing as he sat astride his horse. He doffed his hat to the Deaton family and spoke a greeting that went unheard above the noise. The Deatons fell in at the rear of the train. Sarah and the children walked along side the wagon and MacKenzie Deaton was the bullwhacker, walking along side the oxen. Their extra animals were herded in with all the others.

At the end of the train, the Deatons would eat dust all the way to California, but the hardships of the trail ahead were of little concern. Just as spring makes everything fresh, the lives of the Deatons were being renewed by the great adventure that lay ahead of them.

# 33

Travelers taking the northern route, from St. Joseph or Independence, Missouri, usually had to wait until early May for the Plains to dry out and the grass to green up. Those wishing an earlier start came down the Mississippi and up the Arkansas River to Fort Smith where they bought their outfit and then set out overland west into Texas or north into Kansas Territory. This gave them the advantage of less competition for water and good grass for their cattle.

The consequence of driving such a large herd dictated an early start by the Fancher party, to take the northern route to avoid the desert heat and to insure they would cross the Sierra Nevada mountains before the first snows of winter. In only a few days they had left the white man's civilization and crossed into the Indian Nations.

Westward expansion, the "manifest destiny" of the white man, created unyielding pressure for the American Indians. They fought against it, but, in the long run, sheer numbers and the ability to produce firearms and other manufactured goods gave the white man the upper hand.

As the white man moved west, the natural result was the displacement of the original inhabitants. Those who would not move were exterminated. In the early 1800's, through a series of treaties, the Cherokee, Chickasaw, Choctaw, Creek, and Seminole Indians were uprooted and moved to an area west of Arkansas that was called "The Indian Nations." No one thought to learn the opinion of the Indians already inhabiting the area, so by 1824 when hostilities between the Osage Indians of eastern Indian Territory and the Cherokee Indians of western Arkansas became critical, the U.S. Army moved west and established a new outpost at a site on the Grand River three miles north of its confluence with the Arkansas River in the Cherokee Nation.

Fort Gibson, as it was called, became a crossroads of sorts as the Army built roads to connect the various forts in the area. The fort was the first major stopping place for the Fancher wagon train. The word had gone out to friends and relatives telling them of the westward trek, and so the Fancher train lay by for several days before pushing on to California, waiting to rendezvous with others who wished to come along.

The fort was originally a stockade built of vertical logs, but by 1857 had become more like a settlement. Indians were no longer a threat and a profusion of buildings, including a hotel and a trading post, had sprung up in the vicinity. The hotel was barely worthy of the name, but the trading post offered a wide variety of wares for the emigrants to purchase.

The next day after their arrival, MacKenzie and Joel Deaton visited the trading post to buy a few articles Deaton thought might be necessary for the months on the trail. As he reached for his purse Joel tugged on his elbow.

"Look at that, Pa," said Joel.

Deaton looked at the shelf on the wall behind the counter. An oblong box was propped up at an angle. In it was a shiny new Navy Colt. Deaton looked at his son and then back at the revolver. "Let's have a look at that Colt," he said to the trader.

The gun was handed over and Joel took it in his hands and turned it every which way. It was beautiful, not a mark on it. Joel lovingly caressed the long barrel. He cocked it part way and rotated the cylinder.

"Do you want it?" asked Deaton.

Joel's eyes turned to his father. With a hopeful look, he nodded his head.

"Do you know how to use it?"

"I can learn," said Joel.

"It takes a man to handle one of those."

"Well, Pa, I ain't gettin' no younger."

"I reckon not. Well, I s'pose if you're old enough to want one, you're old enough to have it."

Deaton paid the trader, and he and Joel left the store. The next few days at Fort Gibson were spent teaching Joel how to load and fire the weapon safely. Deaton hadn't forgotten Johnny Lloyd and how his careless handling of firearms had cost him his life.

After three days, the Fancher train, along with the new arrivals from Ohio, Illinois, and southern Arkansas, pulled out from Fort Gibson along the same road George Keys and his fellow Cherokees had taken in 1849. The trail led north from the ford of the Neosho River through the different Indian towns to the confluence of the Verdigris River and its tributary, the Caney. None of these travelers had previously seen many Indians, and they found it strange to see them living in houses and dressing just like white men.

The emigrants forded the Verdigris River and drove on into Kansas through country that alternated between beautiful prairie and heavy timber. MacKenzie Deaton was amazed. What a difference eight years had made! What had been strictly Indian land was now Kansas Territory, open to settlement by the white man. Farms and towns appeared with increasing regularity.

The wagon train pushed forward at a slow but steady pace, herding more than a thousand head of cattle. Frequent spring rains turned the road into mire. Each day the drovers started the herd out two hours ahead of the wagons. By midday the wagons usually caught up and then went on ahead, so the ladies wouldn't have to eat the dust kicked up by the cattle.

On April 26, they reached the Santa Fe Trail at a point on Turkey Creek. To the east, sixty-seven miles, was Council Grove, the last real town on the trail before New Mexico. To the west, their journey took them into the Great American Desert. The wilderness was a land of great distances. The sun and heat were almost unbearable, the wind and dust blew almost constantly, and the threat of Indian attack was always present, especially so in the ten years since the war with Mexico.

MacKenzie Deaton felt a twinge of disappointment that they were not continuing north to the Oregon Trail. He dearly wanted to see the sights described by Eli Bennett in the many letters he had received over the years. But Deaton would see new sights and tell Bennett all about them as soon as he got to Utah. Nothing would stop him this time. He was determined to see the elephant or die in the attempt!

A few miles west of their junction with the Santa Fe Trail the Fancher party stopped for the night at a spring. Just before dark a group of some twenty men on horseback trailing pack mules came up the road and stopped at the camp. Captain Fancher and many of the others went to meet them. MacKenzie Deaton tagged along out of curiosity.

The horsemen were a hard-looking lot. They were dirty and had a greasy appearance. They were all strangers to razors except two young men who didn't look old enough to shave.

"Evenin', boys," said Captain Fancher. "What can I do for you?"

One of the men urged his horse a few steps forward. He was a rather placid looking man, as if there was nothing at all on his mind. He wore a big slouch hat and a large chaw of tobacco bulged in his cheek. Tobacco juice had stained his lips and a brown streak ran from his mouth down into his beard. The man leaned forward, his left forearm resting on the saddle horn.

"Evenin', friend. I'm Bill Jones. We'd be lookin' for an outfit to join up with."

"Well, boys," said Fancher, "We're driving a pretty big herd. Kinda slows us down a lot. I don't reckon you'd want to be slowed down by us."

"Reckon we would," said Jones as he spat a big load of tobacco juice on the ground. "Had a run in with a band of Pawnee 'bout twenty miles back. Lost a man. He was run through by a Pawnee spear, but we got the red nigger that done it. Got a few of his friends, too."

"Sorry to hear that," said Fancher. "Certainly, you're welcome to join us. Where're y'all from?"

"Caldwell County, Missouri," said Jones. "Call ourselves the Missouri Wildcats. Thank you for your hospitality. We'll try not to be a bother."

The Missourians picked a spot nearby and set up tents. In a few minutes the Fancher camp settled back into its normal routine.

True to their word, the Missourians were not a bother. They camped alone and traveled separate from the wagon train, but they were always close. After three days the wagon train passed a small shanty on Cow Creek, where a man was doing business, selling whiskey at exorbitant prices. The Missourians disappeared for a few hours, but caught up with the train at their evening camp, drunk, but well behaved. Nevertheless, their proximity gave MacKenzie Deaton a creepy feeling, as if a dark cloud loomed on the horizon, always the threat of a storm.

# 34

The Santa Fe Trail was as hard and smooth as a city street, and right next to it the marks of civilization were seen everywhere. Mile after mile, the Fancher company was never out of sight of broken up wagons and discarded equipment. Tons of scrap iron, the refuse of more than thirty years of freighting activity. Off the road the land was still primitive. In every direction the prairie was tinted with the color of wild roses, morning glories, and large yellow flowers in the midst of a carpet of green grass that the wind caused to ripple like waves in the ocean. Wildlife abounded: deer, wild turkeys, antelope, and buffalo, and here and there a prairie dog town, the little fellows chattering away as the party of emigrants slowly passed by.

The wisdom, or lack of it, of joining forces with the Missourians became clear as the Fancher train was nooning near Pawnee Rock on May 2. Several women and teenaged girls worked in pairs, gathering buffalo chips, one holding up her apron by the bottom corners while the other tossed in the chips. Both jobs were disagreeable, the one having to continually bend over and handle the chips, and the other having to carry the growing weight of the load. The scarcity of timber required the use of buffalo chips as fuel. They were plentiful, considering the enormous number of buffalo roaming the plains, and needed only to be gathered. They burned hot and answered well to the purpose, though almost everyone commented on the unusual flavor imparted to meat cooked on a spit.

Suddenly, two of the women screamed and dropped their collection of "firewood" and started running for the wagon corral. In seconds a general panic spread among the ladies. Coming in from the southwest was a large number of Kiowa Indians, some on horseback, but most were on foot. They numbered nearly two hundred, men, women, and children. The men on horseback, their faces painted red, black, and yellow, galloped toward the circled wagons.

"Keep your guns and knives handy, men!" yelled Captain Fancher. "Don't shoot unless you have to."

The Indian horsemen stopped short of the wagons and began speaking loudly while making sweeping gestures with their hands. They were armed with an assortment of guns and bows and arrows, but none of the weapons were being displayed in a threatening manner. Complicating the situation was the fact that no one with the wagon train spoke or understood the Kiowa language.

In a few minutes the rest of the Kiowas had reached the wagons and the two parties stood facing each other. The Indians enjoyed superior numbers, but the emigrants had more firepower. A standoff.

"I don't think they mean us no harm," said Deaton.

"Well, now, I wouldn't bet m'hair on it," said Bill Jones.

"What do you think, Mr. Deaton?" said Fancher. "Do you know what they want?"

MacKenzie Deaton was embarrassed that his meager experience of eight years past should put him in the position of being looked to for advice. One of the Indians, who appeared to be the leader, made hand gestures, as if eating. Meanwhile, two of the bucks advanced to the wagons and started to rummage through one. It was the wagon of John Baker.

"Look here, you savages," said Baker, moving to stop their trespass, "this is my wagon. Get your filthy hands off of it."

One of the Indians placed both hands on the old man's shoulders and pushed him away, all the time jabbering in his strange tongue. Baker's son, Abel, rushed in with a revolver in his hand, pressing it against the Indian's body. At the same instant the entire mass of Indians surged forward, seemingly bent on looting the wagons.

"Stop it right there!" MacKenzie Deaton shouted. It was a moment frozen in time. All eyes were on MacKenzie Deaton, waiting. Mac wasn't sure exactly what he was going to do next, but he remembered the incident long past when Johnny Lloyd lost his life at the Little Wakarusa crossing because no one wanted to take action. The Indians were growing more excited.

"Now, y'all just listen to me," said Deaton. "Fire one shot and a lotta people are gonna get killed. These people are just hungry. If we feed 'em, they'll likely as not go away. I know some of you've got canned goods. Well, break 'em out and let's get these people fed."

When the Indians saw that they were going to be fed without having to fight for it, they backed off a few paces and waited. A couple hours later, after a simple meal of canned meat and pilot bread, the Kiowas began to move out to the north.

Bill Jones came over to MacKenzie Deaton, glaring at him contemptuously as he said, "You're a damn fool, Deaton. We could've whupped them Injuns. World'd be a better place without 'em."

"Well, it's true, Mr. Jones. Some people are just takin' up valuable space on this planet. And I may be a fool, it's true. I've been called worse, but there weren't nobody killed neither...not even you."

Deaton turned and walked back to his wagon. He reasoned it was best to not be seen arguing with a fool, lest people not be able to tell the difference.

# 35

The weather continued clear and fine, and the road was good as the miles piled up behind the wagon train. By the 10th of May they had passed the ruins of Fort Mann, abandoned by the Army a few years before and destroyed to prevent it from falling into the hands of the Indians.

It was midmorning, and the wagon train was a few miles west of the Arkansas crossing, the beginning of the Cimarron Cutoff of the Santa Fe Trail that branched to the southwest. Above the constant noise of the cattle and wagons the rumble of thunder could be heard. Captain Fancher was on his horse near the head of the procession, when Charlie Mitchell rode up.

"What d'you make of it, Cap'n Fancher? There ain't a cloud in the sky."

It was true. It hadn't rained in more than three weeks. Perhaps a storm was brewing out of sight over the range of sand hills that lay in front of them.

"Strange weather, I'd say," replied Fancher. "Never heard thunder without lightnin', let alone without clouds."

Everyone was looking toward the western horizon for the source of the sound. In a few seconds the ground began to shake.

"Earthquake!" someone yelled.

The animals in the herd and those pulling the wagons began to bellow from fear. It was one of the women who first noticed the dark mass on the southern horizon. It quivered and rippled like the waters of a flash flood as it grew ever larger where the land met the sky. A wispy cloud of dust hung over it. The emigrants had all heard of it, but none had ever seen it before. It was magnificent!

MacKenzie Deaton held his wife close, a look of utter amazement on his face. "My god...buffalo! There must be thousands of them!"

The closer they came, the louder the thunder and the more the ground shook. From east to west, as far as the eye could see, the shaggy beasts were bearing down on the hapless wagon train, bound for their summer grazing grounds in the northern plains.

"Quickly!" yelled Captain Fancher, riding up and down the line of wagons. "Corral the wagons!"

The bullwhackers started the wagons moving again. The first wagon pulled to the left and the second to the right. The others followed suit, alternating into two lines, each making an arc until the two lead wagons had come back together. The front wheels of each wagon came up next to the rear wheels of the wagon in front of it, with the wagon tongues on the outside of the circle. The teams were unhitched and driven into the corral. The people took refuge in the wagons and under them.

Fortunately, the Arkansas River separated the emigrants from the buffalo. The water wasn't very deep, but it slowed the buffalo down enough so that they passed the wagon corral without overrunning it.

Nearly an hour went by, and then the buffalo were gone. The destruction was unimaginable. Not a blade of grass was still standing. The stock inside the corral milled about uneasily. Fancher mounted his horse and rode around the outside of the wagons, calling everyone to a meeting.

"Friends," said Fancher, when they had all come together. "We've been mighty lucky today. I've heard of wagon trains losing all their stock to a buffalo stampede. We'd be in a hell of a fix if we didn't have animals to pull our wagons. We'd likely die out here. The critters are probably still a little skittish, so I think we'd better noon here until they've all calmed down. I'll send a couple riders ahead to see if the main herd is all right."

The people began setting up camp. Plenty of buffalo chips were available, but these were all too fresh to use in a fire. Water would be a problem. The river was nearly half a mile away. Some folks made a meal from jerky and dried fruit and leftover bread from their most recent encampment, while others found a place in the shade of their wagon and took a nap.

About two hours later the alarm went out again. This time a band of twenty to twenty-five Cheyenne came riding up from the same direction the buffalo had come. They were well armed, but not painted for war. Something that sounded like greetings were called out as they passed, and a few minutes later they had disappeared over a rise to the north. Apparently they were a hunting party on the trail of the buffalo herd. Hunting buffalo would have been a good source of fresh meat for the emigrants, but no one was very enthusiastic after their recent, harrowing experience.

# 36

The Fancher company continued moving up the Arkansas River for the next several days until they reached "The Big Timbers", a grove of cottonwoods, the first substantial stand of trees west of Council Grove, that extended a distance of about 45 miles on the north side of the Arkansas. The Cheyenne, Arapaho, and Kiowa used it as winter camping grounds. Now, with plenty of firewood and, on the south side of the river, excellent grass for the herd, they could take some time to rest and recruit their animals. In only two days they would be at Bent's new fort.

Deaton remembered hearing of Bent's fort back in '49 while at Independence, and it brought back memories of Shadrach Jones, the mountain man. Mac hadn't thought of that colorful character in years, but now he wondered what had become of him.

One of the first traders to head down the Santa Fe Trail was William Becknell, who departed Franklin, Missouri, on September 1, 1821, with five men and goods-laden pack animals. They did a brisk business with the New Mexicans, and Becknell returned from Santa Fe with $180,000 in gold and silver, and $10,000 in furs, which represented a 600 percent profit on his trade goods.

Two brothers, Charles and William Bent, had grown up in St. Louis amid stories of mountain men and fur trapping on the upper Missouri River. Those tales of wealth and adventure lured the brothers into the fur trade, where, after spending several years and with little to show for it, they returned to St. Louis. Charles was 30 and William 20, when their attention turned toward Mexico and the huge profits in the Santa Fe trade.

William Bent built a small wooden stockade in southern Colorado and began trading with the Indians, and soon had a considerable following among the Cheyenne and Arapaho. His brother Charles convinced him that a larger, permanent fort on the Santa Fe Trail was necessary for the expansion of trade with the Indians, mountain men, and westward emigrants.

The Bents built their fort in a strategic location on the north bank of the Arkansas River, the border then between the United States and Mexico. Mexican labor from Taos constructed the fort of adobe, the cheapest material available and able to stand up well in the dry climate. William Bent named it Fort William, after himself, but the traders called it Bent's fort.

The Bents dominated trade on the Santa Fe Trail with their fort until its destruction in 1849. In August of that year William Bent, discouraged by the growing hostility from the Indians who had previously been his friends, abandoned the fort for good.

So many Indians were camped around Bent's new fort, it looked like it was under siege. This fort had been built by William Bent in 1854 about thirty miles farther east down the Arkansas River from the old one after his brother Charles had been murdered by Mexicans during the war with Mexico. Scattered among the Indians were a few mountain men with their squaws. MacKenzie Deaton didn't see a familiar face, but he thought he would inquire whether any of the mountain men knew the whereabouts of Shadrach Jones.

"Joel," he said to his son, "Want to meet a mountain man?"

"Sure do."

"C'mon."

The mountain men were approachable, especially when a wagon train stopped. It was an opportunity to trade. Goods, news, and stories. Accordingly, Joel and MacKenzie Deaton found three standing together, engaged in conversation.

The three mountain men certainly looked the part. Each man was full-bearded, their faces burned a deep bronze by the sun, and clad in buckskins. One man, the tallest, wore an old slouch hat with the brim in front pinned back to the crown with what appeared to be a peg of polished bone or antler of some kind. He was smoking a long-stemmed pipe and looked to be listening thoughtfully to the conversation of his two companions.

"Good day, gentlemen," said Deaton.

"Gentlemen?" said one of the mountain men. They all laughed. "Either you're sellin' somethin' or you've been away from the society of real gentlemen too long to remember what one looks like." They all laughed again.

"I ain't sellin' nothin'," said Deaton. "And I treat all men as gentlemen 'til they've proved me wrong."

"Well spoken, friend," said the man with the pipe. "Happy t'make your acquaintance. Headed for California?"

"Yes, sir, we are."

"Lotta that goin' 'round," said the second man.

"Too much," said the other.

"Pay them no mind," said the man with a pipe. "Too much sun," he added with a wink.

"I'm used to it," said Deaton. "Once knew a man named Shadrach Jones. Ever hear of 'im?"

The three men reacted the same. Smiles all around. Each man

allowed that he had known Mr. Jones at one time or another.

"Any idea where he is now?"

"Couldn't say for sure," said the man with the pipe. "The days of the rendezvous are long past. Big country out here. Haven't seen 'im for years."

"I hear he went under back in '55, during the trouble with the Sioux up at Ash Hollow on the Platte," said one of the other two.

"Yup," said the third man, "his hair's probably hangin' from a pole in some Injun lodge right now."

"Went under?" said Deaton.

"Dead."

"Oh," said Deaton, sadly. "Are you sure?"

"Nothin's sure about somethin' like that," said the man with the pipe, "Less'n y'see it happen, and then y'can't be too sure. Some men are just too damned ornery t'die."

"Know 'im well?" asked one of the others.

"No," said Deaton. "Just shared a few meals with him a long time ago."

MacKenzie and Joel walked back to their wagon. Mac didn't know why he should feel sad about the prospect of Shadrach Jones being dead, but he did, and it would be several days until he had put it out of his mind.

Two days later, on May 20, the emigrants passed the ruins of Bent's old fort. It was the place Shadrach Jones had been bound for when he left Independence in 1849. Bent and his family abandoned it the same year and it was destroyed, either by William Bent himself or by the Indians. Bent never would say.

The mountain branch of the Santa Fe Trail crossed the Arkansas River here, but the Fancher train was following the river on the north side to Pueblo where the road turned north. Being late in the day, they camped by the old fort, and after dinner several of the people visited the ruins, many of whose adobe walls were still standing. The walls were covered with names and messages left by prairie travelers for those coming behind. The fort looked sad and forlorn, dead and broken, the same as the dreams that had driven Deaton toward California in '49.

Deaton was staring wistfully at the ruins, reliving those days of the gold rush, when a commotion nearby caught his attention. Peter Huff was standing in the center of a small group of people, holding his right wrist with the other hand and shaking it. Rummaging around in the debris, he had thrust in his hand and had been bitten by a tarantula.

The wagon train moved on in the morning. Peter Huff's wife

had treated his wound, but his hand had swollen so badly he was unable to do even the lightest chores. In a few days it became infected. Blood poisoning set in and before the end of the month Peter Huff was dead, leaving a widow and five children.

# 37

Rounding up the cattle before dark was a daily chore and for weeks Joel had sought the opportunity. Now he wasn't so sure that "opportunity" was the correct term. It was hard work, taking most of an hour. Though the sun was low in the sky, the temperature was still in the nineties, though only early June. The junction of Cherry Creek and the South Platte lay only a couple of days ahead.

Joel's energy was pretty well spent by the time the gathered herd was being driven toward the camp. Faint wisps of smoke from the cook fires could be seen in the distance. The fact that the fuel for those fires was buffalo chips didn't matter anymore, not after two months on the trail. All Joel could think of was a hot meal and the comfortable embrace of his bedroll. There would likely be music and singing and other activities, but the only thing this pioneer wanted was to dismount and work out the kinks. Having walked most of the way from Arkansas, Joel's posterior had been unprepared for its extended reacquaintance with a saddle.

Joel's horse belonged to the Mitchells. It was a good mount, easy to handle. Following the herd, the horse fell into a steady rhythmic stride. Soon, Joel was feeling drowsy. He forgot the shooting pain in his buttocks. Maybe he wouldn't eat. Maybe he would just drop into his bedroll and sleep.

The pounding of hooves on the dry prairie soil roused Joel from his reverie. In a cloud of dust Charlie Mitchell reined his horse to a halt next to the boy. Mitchell was twenty-five, but looked older. Maybe it was the weathered look of his skin from living outdoors in the blazing sun. In any event, he looked even older now. A fine coating of dust had been added to his features. His forehead was beaded with sweat, and here and there a rivulet of perspiration streaked down his face, looking like a stream in the desert. Joel wondered how he looked to Charlie.

"We're missing one," said Mitchell. "Alonzo says he saw the critter go over that rise."

Joel turned in the saddle and looked over his shoulder in the direction Mitchell was pointing. The effort made him remember how badly he wanted to get off this horse. Joel groaned audibly.

Charlie Mitchell couldn't let an opportunity like this pass him by.

"Tell you what, Joel," he said, with a twinkle in his eye, "you go fetch 'im and I'll let you come help us again."

No look of dismay or any other indication betrayed Joel's thoughts. He looked Charlie straight in the eye. The older man tried hard, but he couldn't stifle a grin. Joel turned the horse's head to the right and nudged it sharply with his heels. Joel had a determined set to his jaw. He'd show 'em. He could trail cattle as well as any man...and better than some.

In a few minutes Joel reached the rise and halted. The ground dropped sharply in front of him about twenty feet down to a dry creek bed, up a couple of feet, then leveled out in a broad plain some two hundred yards wide before rising again into gently rolling hills. The stray animal was nowhere in sight.

Joel looked for an easy place to descend, but could see none. So, with a shrug he booted his mount over the precipice and started down. Near the bottom his horse lost its footing, and in the ensuing scramble Joel covered the final few yards on the seat of his pants. Ignoring the new assault on his backside and cursing the horse, Joel regained his feet and ran after the animal. The horse was probably glad to be free of its burden. At least it didn't seem ready to stand still. Joel caught up with the animal, settled it down, and prepared to remount. With saddle horn in his left hand and his left foot in the stirrup, Joel began to swing into the saddle when something caught his eye.

Not fifty yards distant was the stray animal...being butchered by two Indians. It was strung up by its horns in a willow tree, and Joel surmised that's why he hadn't seen it from above. One of the Indians was looking at Joel. He nudged the other one, pointing at Joel and speaking loudly in his own tongue. Joel didn't need a translation. He knew he was in big trouble.

Joel quickly mounted his horse and took off at a gallop. He looked over his shoulder only once. Whooping and hollering, the half-naked savages were astride their horses and gaining on him.

Desperately, Joel sought an easier way back up the slope. The pounding of hooves grew louder behind him. He hunched his shoulders, expecting at any moment an arrow in the back. The Indians were so close now he could hear the snorting of their horses. *This is it*, he thought. He would never see his family again.

Joel felt a stinging blow to his right shoulder as one of the Indians galloped past him. Joel looked up, startled. Instead of a bow in the young buck's hand, he carried a multicolored stick with a pair of feathers dangling from it. The Indian's arms were widespread and his head thrown back as he uttered a loud, high-pitched cry. The young warrior had "counted coup" on his enemy. Another sharp rap and the second Indian galloped by, bellowing his own victory cry.

Joel was completely confused. No one had told him of the Indian custom of touching the enemy with a "coup stick" to prove one's bravery. The boy reined his horse to a stop. The two Indians were circling around to have another go at it. Joel had one shot in his rifle and five in the Navy Colt tucked into his belt. But he was a terrible shot even under the best of circumstances. He wheeled his horse around and took off again. He wished he hadn't. Attracted by the commotion, more Indians were coming from the opposite direction.

Indians at his front and rear, the steep slope to his right, Joel turned his mount in the only direction left. His heart sank. More Indians blocked his last avenue of escape. Resistance was futile. He stopped and waited. He prayed it would be over quickly.

The Indians surrounded the would-be cowhand. Joel looked searchingly into their faces, trying to find some sign of compassion. He tried his best not to betray the fear that was clawing at his insides. Joel counted eight, most likely Sioux, or maybe Arapaho or Southern Cheyenne. They were all young, handsome men, not much older than Joel. Their naturally dark skin had been burned a deep bronze by the sun. They wore only breechclouts and moccasins. Some were ornamented with strings of bone and animal teeth, and other such trinkets. Some wore feathers in their long black hair that hung loosely about their shoulders. The Indian who had first counted coup on Joel drew up next to him and began talking loudly to the others, probably boasting of his brave deed. Then he reached for Joel's rifle. Instinctively, Joel grabbed hold of it, but the Indian tore it from his grasp and waved it in the air above his head, shouting once again his victory cry. The others responded with yips and cries of their own. The second Indian who had counted coup then approached and claimed his prize: the Navy Colt that had been given to Joel by his father.

The first Indian then began slowly circling the boy, making a speech to the others. Not being conversant with Sioux or any other Indian language, Joel did not know the young buck was degrading his manhood, calling him a woman for offering no resistance. Several times the others laughed. Finally, the Indian stopped and stared contemptuously at the white boy. Joel smiled wanly. Suddenly, the brave slapped him hard on the face with the back of his hand, the ultimate display of contempt.

The Indians closed in around Joel. He felt a sudden sharp pain in his left thigh. One of them had stabbed him with the point of a lance. Before Joel could react, another had grabbed him by the collar and dragged him from his horse. In an instant they were all whooping and hollering. Joel was being poked and prodded from all sides. Any second, he expected a fatal thrust, but it never came. As if by some signal, the Indians ceased their assault and rode away, the Mitchell horse in tow.

Joel was too shocked to realize his good fortune. He sat there on the ground wanting so much to cry. He had failed in his duty. He had been humiliated. But he was alive. The wound in his thigh was bleeding freely. He knew he had to get help or bleed to death.

Slowly, Joel crawled up the slope, then staggered off toward the camp nearly a mile away. The sun was low on the horizon. It would be dark by the time he got there. If he got there.

# 38

Hatless and dirty, Joel Deaton stumbled on. The pain in his thigh throbbed in rhythm with his heartbeat. His left calf was beginning to cramp. He wanted to just fall down and rest for awhile. He glanced back at the rise and saw he had covered less than a hundred yards. He turned and pushed on.

After a few more agonizing steps, Joel saw a rider coming. The rider didn't seem to be in much of a hurry. Joel decided to stand and wait. In a few minutes Charlie Mitchell's horse trotted up to the boy.

"Now ain't you a sight," said Mitchell. "Where's my horse?"

Joel hung his head. "I was set upon by Indians. They took the horse."

Charlie's jaw clenched down tight as he looked off in the direction of the rise. He spurred his horse, but instantly pulled back on the reins. The horse did a stutter step, not knowing whether to go or stay. Mitchell had the same problem. His gaze shifted between Joel and the horizon. Finally, he extended his hand to the injured boy.

"C'mon. Get aboard."

It took only six minutes to get back to camp. It seemed longer to Joel. When they were within shouting distance, Mitchell began hallooing and waving his hat. Nearly everyone in the camp came to see what the ruckus was all about. Charlie Mitchell halted next to the gathering crowd.

"Indians! Joel's been hurt! They took my horse!"

Eager hands gently helped the injured boy from the horse and carefully laid him on the ground. Sarah Deaton pushed through the throng and knelt next to Joel. She looked concerned, but not panicky.

"Are you hurt bad?" she asked.

"Just my leg," said Joel. "One of them Indians poked me with something. Mama, it hurts real bad!"

"Where's the doctor?" Someone asked.

"I am coming," said a heavily accented voice.

Gerhard Schnitzler was a German immigrant. He had studied medicine in Leipzig and practiced several years before succumbing to the lure of opportunity in America. Fat and fortyish, he did not present a very appealing appearance. He did not possess the manners and gentility one usually expected of the medical profession. He wore a thick beard and glasses, and his face was pockmarked. The doctor was cursed with a chronic case of flatulence, and when not traveling seemed to always be eating. When at last he stood over Joel he looked around and asked, "Anybody have a knife?"

"What are you gonna do?" asked Joel, his eyes wide with fear.

"Don't worry. I will only cut your pants. I have to see how badly you are hurt."

Someone gave the doctor a knife. He split the pant leg and probed in the wound. Joel threw his head back and clenched his teeth as hard as he could.

"It is not serious. But we have to stop the bleeding. I will need a hot iron and some whiskey. Do you drink, boy?"

Joel shook his head. Mama didn't hold with drinking.

"Well, today you gonna get drunk for the first time."

Joel closed his eyes. He couldn't bear to look at the people. The pain of his humiliation felt worse than his leg. But he couldn't shut out the voices.

"Anybody for going with me?" asked Charlie Mitchell. "I'd like to get my horse back."

Bill Jones, leader of the Missouri Wildcats, smiled broadly at the invitation. "What d'you say, boys? Huntin' Injuns'd be more sport'n huntin' buffalo."

There were shouts of agreement and the Missourians rushed to get their guns and horses. Some of the others lifted Joel and carried him to one of the campfires where an iron was being heated. A jug was produced and the fiery liquid had to be forced down the boy's throat.

Captain Fancher made his way to where Charlie Mitchell stood waiting for the Missourians. "I don't like to tell you this, Charlie, but you'll never see that horse again. Them Indians are long gone."

"It ain't the horse so much, Cap'n, it's that saddle. I paid more for it than I did for the horse."

Fancher shook his head. "Forget it. You're just spittin' in the wind."

The Missourians were coming, so Charlie Mitchell mounted his horse. He looked down at Fancher. "Gotta try, Cap'n Fancher. There ain't no use for a man who won't try."

"Just be careful. There ain't no moon tonight."

Fancher watched the search party ride off. He was more than a little worried. Losing a horse was one thing. He didn't want to lose any people.

At the Deaton tent Joel was getting quite drunk. But he wasn't drunk enough. Six men held him down while Schnitzler applied the glowing iron. The boy struggled and screamed before he fainted. The men turned their heads away, sickened by the smell of burning flesh.

The doctor packed the wound with axle grease, a mixture of tar and animal fat, then wrapped the leg with clean strips of cloth.

"He will sleep now," said Schnitzler. "But he cannot walk or ride for several days."

"Thank you, Doctor," said Sarah Deaton. "We'll take care of him."

The people began returning to their own tents. It was nearly dark, and dawn came very early at this time of year. Captain Fancher stopped on the way to his tent to inquire about Joel's condition.

"The boy will be all right," said MacKenzie Deaton. "But it looks like we'll have to stay behind."

"What for?"

"Joel can't walk or ride and there's no room for him in the wagon."

"Nonsense! We'll find some room for him somewhere. We can't leave you folks out here all alone."

"We would be so grateful," said Sarah Deaton.

"Don't worry about it," said Fancher. "I'll take care of it. Y'all just get some sleep."

Near midnight Mitchell and the others rode wearily into camp. They had the same number of horses they had left with.

# 39

By July 4, the Fancher train had left the plains and turned west toward Fort Bridger on the same road pioneered by the Cherokee Indians in 1849. They were at the North Platte, but many miles south of the established road to California. They were traveling in a valley so broad it didn't look like a valley. Mountains could be seen in every direction, but they were so far away it was like looking at a picture. In spite of the lateness of the season, many of the mountains were still capped with a gleaming, tantalizing blanket of snow.

Captain Fancher had found a place for Joel Deaton with the recently widowed Mrs. Huff and her sixteen year-old daughter Cordelia. They proved to be excellent nurses. Joel's leg healed nicely, but they were unable to do anything to heal his wounded spirit.

Joel sat against a wagon wheel sopping up the last bit of gravy with a chunk of fresh-baked bread, when he noticed Charlie Mitchell heading in his direction. Since the loss of Charlie's horse, back on the plains, Joel had been inconsolable. He felt guilty for what had happened and acted accordingly, generally moping around and avoiding eye contact with anyone but his family and the Huffs. Joel assumed his best sulking pose: shoulders slumped, a frown on his face, and his eyes downcast. It didn't have a noticeable effect on Charlie Mitchell.

A pair of dusty boots stopped a couple of feet in front of Joel. He just stared at them. Mitchell wanted to reach out to the boy and give him some encouragement, but he didn't want to play along with Joel's sullen behavior. So, he just stood and waited. Joel continued to stare at the ground. With each passing moment he felt more uncomfortable. Why didn't this intruder just get the hell out of here? Finally, he couldn't stand it anymore. His eyes turned upward as far as they could go, then he slowly lifted his head. Charlie Mitchell was looking at him with a pleasant grin.

"How's your leg, Joel? I saw you walking and it looks like you're gettin' around okay."

Joel averted his eyes. "Well," he said slowly, "it's all healed up, but it'll never be the same no more."

"Count your blessings, boy. That leg could have just as easily been taken off. Why, I saw a feller who got his arm crushed when a wagon fell on him while changing a wheel. The doctor wanted to take it off, but the man wouldn't let him. By the time he agreed to have it off, his arm stunk real bad from the infection. Well, the doctor cut it off all right, but it was too late. Poor feller died next day from blood poison."

Joel looked at his leg and shuddered. There wasn't much in life for a man with only one leg.

"You through eatin'?" asked Mitchell.

"Yes, sir."

"Get your gear, then. I want you to help mind the herd till midnight."

"You do?" said Joel, sounding surprised.

"Well sure! If you think you're just gonna ride in the back of a wagon feelin' sorry for yourself all the way to California, you better think again."

"I'm not feelin' sorry for myself!" Joel protested.

"Oh? Well, you do a right good imitation of it."

"Well, you're wrong. It's just...well, I didn't think no one would trust me after losin' that horse."

Charlie Mitchell squatted down in front of the boy and picked up a twig lying on the ground. He turned it over and over in his hands. He spoke in a quiet, sincere voice.

"Let me tell you something, Joel. Part of growin' up and bein' a man is ownin' up to your responsibilities. You do something wrong, you make it right. You break something, you fix it. Some things just can't be helped."

"I'll buy you a new horse."

"I ain't worried about the horse. There's not a man among us who could've kept them Indians from stealing' that horse."

"But I didn't even try to stop them. They took my gun. And...they laughed at me."

Mitchell shook his head. "Joel, do you work? Do you help your daddy?"

"I sure do," said Joel indignantly.

"Suppose you'd put up a fight. Them Indians would've killed you sure as sun up. If we'd had to bury you back on the plains, how would you help your ma and pa? Joel, you did the only thing you could. Why, any fool can get himself killed. It takes a man to get out of a tight spot like that."

"I was just lucky."

"Well, there ain't no denyin' that," said Mitchell. "But you *are* alive. And well. And you have responsibilities. So get your gear and let's get going before I have to kick your backside."

Joel didn't have much to say as he got ready for the first watch, but secretly he was pleased. It felt good to be trusted again.

From his vantage point on a fairly large rock Joel could see the camp slowly going to sleep. Campfires were dying and most of the people were already wrapped in their bedrolls, out in the open or in their tents. The western sky was fading rapidly from a brilliant orange streaked with gold and gray. The sun had been down for half an hour. The moon, a thin silver crescent poised just above the mountains, would soon follow. The herd was milling around quietly and Joel was thankful that it was midsummer. The hot summer sun had driven the buffalo herds far to the north and the Indians had followed. So there was little threat to the livestock, at least in this part of the country. Joel just had to be sure that none wandered off.

Summer temperatures in the mountains could vary as much as fifty degrees between day and night. Joel was beginning to wish he had worn a coat. He considered going back to the wagon, but decided against it. The moon was disappearing in the west when he heard a rustling sound in the prairie grass.

A chill shook the boy's body. He was unable to determine whether it was from the cool night air or because of memories of his experience with the Indians. Joel pulled out his father's revolver and strained to see the source of the noise. Coming through the sagebrush from the direction of the camp was what appeared to be a human form.

"Joel, where are you?" called a feminine voice.

A feeling of relief surged through the boy. "I'm over here on the big rock, Delia."

Cordelia Huff followed the sound of Joel's voice. Joel slid down off the rock to meet her.

"How are you tonight?" asked the young girl.

"Just tryin' to stay awake. The herd's pretty quiet."

"You didn't wear a coat. Aren't you cold?"

"It ain't so bad," Joel lied. "Besides, I'm only gonna be out here till midnight."

"I brought you a blanket. In case you get cold."

The blanket was draped over Delia's folded arms. She handed it to Joel.

"Thanks."

The two teenagers stood looking at each other. Talking had been easy for them while Delia had helped to nurse Joel when his leg was hurt. But other people had always been around then. Now they both felt a little shy.

"Do you want to sit up on the rock with me?" Joel blurted out. "We could talk for awhile."

"We can talk down here," replied Delia.

Joel didn't have an answer for that, at least not one that would make sense. "Well," he stammered, "I'd like to sit up there."

The girl looked over her shoulder toward the camp. "I suppose it wouldn't hurt. But only for a little while."

Joel smiled. "C'mon, I'll help you up."

He took her by the elbow and helped her up the face of the huge chunk of sandstone. It was not a difficult climb.

"What a beautiful sight," said Delia. "All the tents and wagons. It's like a little city all alone in the wilderness. Does it always look like this?"

"I reckon so, but I can't say for sure. Never did no guard duty at night before."

"Listen," said Delia.

Joel listened for awhile. "I don't hear nothin', 'cept the cattle movin' about."

"That's what I mean. It's so noisy and dusty during the day, but so quiet and peaceful at night."

Delia leaned back on her elbows and looked up at the heavens. "Look at the stars. You can almost reach out and touch them," she said.

As Joel leaned back to look at the sky his hand brushed against Delia's. Instantly, he drew his hand away as if it had touched a hot stove. Out of the corner of his eye he looked at the girl, trying to deduce what she was thinking. Delia just kept looking at the sky.

"It's like the eyes of God and his angels," she said. "looking down at us, watching over us. They look just the same as they do back home in Arkansas. Maybe Grandma or Uncle Paul or one of my friends is looking at the stars right now. How I wish I could tell them all is well with us! I can almost see them under the same sky without a thought of keeping guard over their homes."

Joel did not share her awe of the nighttime sky. His mind was on weightier matters. He let his hand brush against hers. Delia seemed to take no notice. In spite of the chill, Joel was sweating. He placed his trembling hand over hers. Nothing happened. He didn't see it, but Delia was looking at him out of the corner of her eye. She felt a queasiness in the pit of her stomach. Joel was almost afraid to breathe. Their shoulders touched, lightly at first, then they were practically leaning against one another. Slowly, they turned and looked into each other's eyes. Suddenly they both looked away as if embarrassed. But inevitably they turned their heads back. Hesitatingly, they moved closer together. Delia's eyes were downcast. They were each leaning on one elbow. Joel touched her on her shoulder with his free hand and gave a gentle tug. Delia raised her head, eyes closed. Their lips touched. They embraced. The kiss was gentle and lingering. Someone shuddered, maybe both of them. They couldn't tell. Finally, they separated.

Joel leaned back and looked at the sky. If he had known about adrenalin, he would know what was making his heart pound. Delia was sitting up with her arms wrapped around her knees and her head resting on top of them as she looked at Joel.

"What are you thinking?" she asked.

"I ain't never kissed a girl before," said Joel.

"It doesn't matter."

"Ain't never felt this way about someone neither."

"Neither have I."

Delia slipped to a reclining position facing Joel. Joel turned toward her and placed his hand on her cheek.

"I'll never forget this night as long as I live," said Delia. Joel kissed her gently. "I love you, Joel. I would do anything for you. Do you know what I mean? Anything."

They embraced again, pressing tightly against one another. It was as if they couldn't get close enough. They wanted this moment to last forever. There was a desperateness about their embrace. Their breathing quickened.

"Delia!"

"Oh, my gosh!" whispered Delia, sitting up. "It's my mother."

"Cordelia!"

"Yes, Mother!"

"It's time you were in bed, girl."

"Coming!"

Delia turned to Joel, kissed him quickly on the cheek, then slid down to the ground. She took a step and stopped. She turned back for a moment.

"Good night," she said, and then she was gone, running through the grass.

Joel's relief was half an hour late, but he didn't care. He wouldn't sleep much this night anyway.

Joel was up at first light. The enchantment of the night before had turned into the reality of the trail. The stock needed to be driven to water, firewood gathered, and meals cooked. Joel found himself unable to concentrate on anything but Delia. The Huff wagon was on the other side of camp. No matter what he was doing, Joel found himself looking in that direction, hoping to get a glimpse of her.

The sky had become overcast during the night and the temperature had dropped. Everyone knew that it meant a storm was likely. As this was a good campsite, Captain Fancher decided to lay by for awhile to see how severe the storm would be. With nothing important to do, Joel wandered over to the Huff wagon. He found Delia sitting on a camp stool mending the wagon cover.

"Good morning," said Joel.

Delia stood up, looking a little bit flustered. She dropped her eyes and turned away. Just then her mother came around from the back of the wagon and walked up to Joel. She stood facing him, hands on hips.

"Joel?"

"Yes, ma'am?"

"I don't know what happened last night and I ain't saying anything did. I only let Delia take a blanket out to you because it was cold. She was gone longer than I thought proper. With her pa gone it's left me with a heavy burden. You're nigh on to bein' a man and there's a proper way for young folks to meet. I ain't ready to be no grandma just yet, if you understand my meaning."

Joel looked at Delia. She was blushing.

"I'm afraid I don't know what you're referring to, Mrs. Huff," said Joel.

"Joel, I think you're either a fool or a liar. You tell me which." Now it was Joel's turn to look flustered. He hung his head and said nothing. "It's as I thought," said Mrs. Huff. "Don't come around anymore, Joel. Delia isn't old enough for this kind of shenanigans."

Joel looked at Delia. She had tears in her eyes. Then he looked at Mrs. Huff. She had been like a mother to him while his leg was on the mend. He couldn't believe this was happening. He had never been in love before. Why couldn't Mrs. Huff understand? But of course she did. And that was why she was doing the only thing any prudent parent could do. To protect the chickens from the fox, first you have to keep the fox out of the chicken coop.

# The Gathering Storm

# 40

An ill wind knows no season. Abraham Smoot had first heard the rumor of impending trouble from Feramorz Little at Fort Laramie while traveling east with the June mail for the YX Company, the express company owned by Brigham Young. Farther along the trail he had encountered troops and supply trains. Inquiries about their purpose and destination were to no avail. At Independence Smoot had learned from William H. Russell, owner of a freighting company, that the supplies were headed for Salt Lake City with an army to follow. Brigham Young had been deposed as territorial governor. A new governor, judges, and other federal officials were to be escorted by an army to Utah to subject the Mormons to the will of the federal government.

Smoot was baffled at first, and then became infuriated. How could this be? The Saints were snuggled safely in their mountain fastness...or so they thought. The persecutions of Kirtland, Nauvoo, and Missouri were a fading memory. In the ten years since their arrival in the Great Salt Lake Valley the Saints had built a marvelous city in the desert. Indeed, the biblical prophecy had been fulfilled; the desert had blossomed as a rose. Abraham Smoot himself was a pioneer of 1847, having led an emigrant train of 139 people, and was now the mayor of Salt Lake City. Newcomers were arriving in large numbers each summer.

Though they had left society behind, surely the Saints must have known it couldn't be permanent. They had taken something no one wanted and had turned it into an oasis. Converts came as a flood, while gentiles in the guise of entrepreneurs and federal bureaucrats arrived as a trickle. Their numbers were small, but their role was as the serpent in the garden of Eden.

In 1854, W. W. Drummond, a federal judge, had arrived in Utah, and the troubles between Mormon and Gentile began to escalate. The gentiles, Drummond included, looked upon the Mormon practice of plural marriage as an immoral institution. Drummond, on the other hand, practiced the middleclass standard of morality: he had left behind in the States, some said deserted, a wife and children, and had brought along his mistress.

Drummond had resigned in March 1857, and in his letter of resignation to President Buchanan, he charged the Mormons with open rebellion against the federal government, murder, destruction of federal court records, and abusing the rights of emigrants in the local courts. Because the local court officials were also priesthood leaders in the Mormon church, in the eyes of outsiders Utah courts were merely church courts.

So now President Buchanan was sending an army to put down the "Mormon rebellion." Abraham Smoot was the bearer of this disturbing news. On his own authority he was closing the freight stations and driving the stock back to Utah.

Orrin Porter Rockwell was one of the earliest converts to Mormonism, having been baptized by the Prophet himself before the church was even organized. In fact, he was a distant cousin of Joseph Smith. There was no limit to his love and loyalty for Joseph. Porter Rockwell would have killed for the Prophet. Some said he did.

The man enjoyed a fierce reputation. To hear some of the stories one would have expected Porter Rockwell to look and act like a fire-breathing giant. He was of only average height and of stocky build, though not fat. He had a full, coal black beard, and waist-length hair that he kept braided and tucked up under his hat. The Prophet had promised that, like Samson, if Porter Rockwell did not cut his hair, he would be protected from his enemies. He followed that injunction to his dying day, with one exception. In 1855 he had chanced upon the widow of Don Carlos Smith, the Prophet's brother, in California. She was recovering from typhoid fever, in consequence of which her hair had fallen out. Having no money to help the poor woman, he cut his hair and had it fashioned into a wig to hide her baldness.

Looking unlike the desperado he was portrayed to be, Porter Rockwell could easily pass among the gentiles by simply using another name. His most striking feature, his eyes, were gray, and so intense, one could not gaze upon them for very long without feeling a strong urge to look somewhere else.

About a hundred miles east of Fort Laramie Smoot came upon Porter Rockwell, headed east with the July mail. Rockwell was trying to better the record time of fifteen days, an average of eighty miles a day, set only a month earlier. Smoot and his party were lucky if they made one fourth that distance each day. Driving cattle was slow, tedious work.

Rockwell was driving the mail coach like a one-man Pony Express, but he slowed down when he recognized the people in the approaching party.

"Afternoon, Smoot," said Rockwell after he had stopped the coach. "Thought you was haulin' the mail. What're y'doin' with all them animals?"

"I have terrible news, Brother Rockwell, simply terrible."

Porter Rockwell stared at the man impassively. Abraham Smoot waited for some reaction. Rockwell just shifted in his seat on the mail coach and spat on the ground. "Well, get on with it," he finally said.

"We have lost the mail contract."

"Nothin' earthshakin' 'bout that. There'll be others."

"That's only the beginning," said Smoot. "President Buchanan is sending an army against us. They intend to subjugate us or drive us from our homes."

"Do tell? Now, how'd you find this out?"

"I've seen troops on the move and large freight shipments, enough for a long campaign. When I questioned Russell, he confirmed my fears. So I have closed down all the freight stations, and I'm driving the stock back to Salt Lake. I would advise you to come with us."

Suggestion was about the strongest form of persuasion one could use on Porter Rockwell. He was a dangerous man and was always heavily armed. Once he had been arrested and was found to have several knives and enough firepower on his person to fire 71 rounds without reloading.

"Can't do it, Smoot. Gotta get the mail through."

"You'll need relief teams," said Smoot. "We have all the animals with us."

Rockwell looked around as if surveying the landscape. He wasn't sure of what to do in spite of the logic of Smoot's argument. Just then Judson Stoddard, who was accompanying Smoot, came riding up. "Howdy do, Porter," he said. "Guess you heard the news?"

"I have."

"Then you'll be coming home with us?"

Rockwell looked at the mail sacks and shrugged. "Reckon I will. Let the government tote their own mail. We can drop it off at Fort Laramie."

"Good for you, Brother Rockwell," said Smoot. "We'll be needing you. You're a good man with a team."

Porter Rockwell joined the others for the return trip to Salt Lake City. The pace was considerably less than Rockwell would have preferred. By the time they reached Fort Laramie, Porter Rockwell had had enough.

Late in the afternoon of July 18, 1857, a wagon bearing Rockwell, Smoot and Stoddard thundered out the gates of the fort, headed for Salt Lake City.

# 41

July 24, 1857, would mark the tenth anniversary of the arrival of the Mormon pioneers in Utah. The first party of emigrants had arrived on the 22nd day of July, 1847, but the Mormons celebrated the 24th as Pioneer Day, because that was the date Brigham Young had arrived. It was also an important date for Eli Bennett, for it marked the eighth anniversary of his arrival in the Salt Lake Valley, an event that had changed his life forever.

This year the festivities were to be held in Big Cottonwood Canyon, several miles southeast of Salt Lake City. A road had first been hacked up the narrow defile for the purpose of gathering timber and building a sawmill. Over the years the road had been improved, but it was still a tortuous trek for the nearly three thousand celebrants.

Preparations had been going on for days. The women of the city had baked hundreds of loaves of bread, cakes and pies of every description, and had put up gallons of serviceberry preserves. Two crews of workmen had gone up the canyon to Silver Lake to prepare for the celebration. They gathered and cut fire wood, and dug fire pits for cooking. Then they cut down trees to build three spacious boweries for the people to gather and eat in the shade.

On the morning of the 22nd Eli Bennett loaded Diana and the children into their wagon and started for the rendezvous at the mouth of Big Cottonwood Canyon. They were among the first to arrive since their farm was only a couple of miles southwest of the canyon near the settlement called Union, which they had moved to only the summer before.

Union had been settled in early 1849 because it was an area abundant with water, grass, wood, and clay. In 1853 and 1854 a fort, a rectangular structure, was built on ten acres of land donated by Jehu Cox a mile and a half northwest of the original settlement to provide protection from forays by the Ute Indians. The wall was made of rock and adobe bricks with clay for the mortar, and was six feet wide at the bottom, two feet wide at the top, and twelve feet high. The walls enclosed twenty-three houses and a building that served as school, church, and amusement hall.

Eli Bennett built his house outside the fort to the east along the creek. He was a forty-niner. He had stared death in the face on the gold rush trail. A few scruffy Ute warriors were of little concern for him.

It was an all-day trek to the encampment at Silver Lake at the head of the canyon. The main body of Saints arrived in a caravan of some 500 vehicles at the rendezvous at the mouth of Big Cottonwood Canyon after more than four hours travel from Salt Lake. The narrow passageway between the hills had the appearance of a tent city. In the open space at the center of the camp a martial band greeted the revelers with a variety of tunes. Bennett found a good spot to camp and set up his tent.

After awhile, word went quickly through the camp that President Brigham Young was approaching. The prophet's usual practice was to arrive late at any gathering, so that more of his loyal followers would have opportunity to greet him. As his buggy came in sight up the dusty road the band poured forth its brass blare of welcome, men and boys waved their hats, the women and girls waved sunbonnets, and everyone rose to their feet and cheered. The Mormon prophet tipped his hat to the crowd and smiled. His carriage stopped at the camping place previously prepared for his use. President Young alighted and, after shaking a few hands, disappeared into his tent. The rest of the camp quickly went back to what they had been doing: children playing, women fixing meals, and the men gathering in small groups to talk.

At sunset a bugle sounded. Regardless of what they were doing, everyone moved to the open square. Hats were doffed as young and old knelt reverently in the grass while those previously appointed to the task offered up fervent prayers on behalf of the assembled multitude. For Eli Bennett it was one of the most spiritual experiences of his life. Here in the shadow of the everlasting hills he had found peace and happiness. The evening breeze blowing out of the canyon gently touched his face, while the boiling sound of Big Cottonwood Creek filled his ears. He lovingly took his wife's hand in his as tears of joy coursed down his cheeks.

The evening service over, the Saints retired to their wagons and tents. The western sky was a brilliant tapestry of gold and orange hues. Surely God was smiling on their accomplishments. The silver crescent of the new moon slipped behind the Oquirrh Mountains on the west side of the Great Salt Lake Valley. Soon the encampment was enclosed in the silence of the mountains, except for the crickets singing their cheerful song.

# 42

The setting sun meant Porter Rockwell and his companions would have to stop for the night. The moon had been new the night they left Fort Laramie and now it was barely half way to its first quarter. The road was dangerous enough in broad daylight. The dim light of the Milky Way would be of no help.

Ft. Bridger lay a little more than an hour behind them. Smoot and Stoddard had wanted to stop there, but not Rockwell. He was not one for sitting around when work needed to be done. Besides, he intended to sleep in his own bed the following night with the warm companionship of his wife, not on the hard ground somewhere in the Wasatch Mountains.

"We'll stop at the springs six miles west of Bridger," he had said. "It's a mighty fine campground, good water and grass for the horses."

Just as it was becoming too dark to drive, a roaring bonfire came into view.

"We're in luck, boys," said Rockwell. "Maybe we can get a hot meal tonight."

Five minutes later they pulled up to the Fancher wagon train. A man carrying a rifle in the ready position stepped out of the shadows as Porter Rockwell drew the team of horses to a halt.

"Evenin' boys," he said.

"Good evening, sir," said Smoot. "Do you mind if we camp here?"

"Just the three of you?"

"That's right."

"Where y'headed?"

"Salt Lake City."

"Travelin' kinda light, ain't you?"

"We live there," said Smoot.

"Uh, huh. Then you'd be Mormons," said the man. "Well, I ain't got no prejudices. Find you a spot."

"Thank you," said Smoot.

Rockwell maneuvered the wagon to a favorable spot and started unhitching the team. As was his custom, he quietly assessed the situation. This was a good-sized wagon train, more than forty wagons and a few carriages. The number of cattle enclosed in the corral must have been six or seven hundred head. The bonfire was at the eastern opening of the corral, and around the outside perimeter of the circled wagons were several cooking fires as well as a large number of tents. Most folks paid the three strangers no mind, except for a group of about a dozen men lying about the bonfire. A jug was being passed around among them. Rockwell stroked his bearded chin, wondering how he might get a slug of that stuff.

A crashing sound behind him caused Rockwell to reach instinctively for a gun. In the flickering of the orange light from the fire he saw the image of a boy driving a young steer ahead of him with a switch he had cut from a birch tree.

"Evening, sir," said Joel Deaton as he passed the bearded man.

"Good evening to you, son," said Rockwell.

Joel shuddered involuntarily. Something about this man gave him the willies.

One of the men by the fire went over by the sentry and spoke to him quietly. After a moment's conversation he returned to the others and said a few words. Then he turned to the three newcomers. Smoot was spreading out his bedroll.

"Hey!" said the man.

Smoot, Stoddard, and Rockwell looked at the man, but continued working.

"I said, 'Hey!' "

"We heard you," said Rockwell in a voice almost like a growl.

"Why don't you boys just move on outa here? We ain't got no use for Mormons. We run trash like you outa Missouri once before. We sure as hell ain't gonna sleep in the same camp with you."

"Then you must be plannin' on staying up all night," said Rockwell. "Or movin' on."

"You're the ones that'll be movin' on."

"Now see here," said Smoot. "We've come a long way and we're tired. You know we can't travel in the dark. We'll stay right here."

"C'mon, let's go," said Stoddard, tugging on Smoot's sleeve.

Smoot jerked his arm away. "We're staying," he said firmly.

Stoddard moved close to Smoot, his back to the Missourians, and spoke in a voice only Smoot could hear. "It ain't worth it. We got more important business to attend to."

"I'm not running from this border trash," said Smoot.

"Let 'em stay, Cal," called out one of the Missourians. "Just make sure they stay downwind. Wouldn't want to spook the herd."

The comment was greeted with raucous laughter. The liquor made the Missourians bolder than was prudent.

"Why, there's never been a more infamous imposter than old Joe Smith," said Ned Willesen, sneering. He pulled out a pistol and held it up for all to see. "This here's the gun that put that blackleg in the ground where he belongs. And it ain't through with Mormons yet."

Porter Rockwell tensed when he saw the gun drawn. They were likely only doing this for sport, but he noted the jug and remembered all the crazy things he had seen men do when they had too much liquor.

Willesen held the gun up to his ear and pretended to listen. He nodded and said, "It says, 'Where's old Brig? Got a message for 'im.' "

"What's the message, Ned?" asked a Missourian.

Willesen listened again. "It says, 'Bang! Yer dead!' "

As the Missourians laughed heartily, Rufus Pierce looked up at the man coming around the back of the wagon. He walked with a limp, one leg being shorter than the other because of a broken leg improperly set when only a boy.

"Wheat!" said Rockwell.

Pierce's grin dissolved into a look of distress. Even in the dim light one could see the color had gone out of his face. He cursed himself for not recognizing the man sooner. "Wheat" was Porter Rockwell's war cry. He had long believed it was his divine mission to "separate the wheat from the tares." He had a revolver in each hand and his pockets bulged with two Paterson Colt pocket pistols. In the bed of the wagon lay a shotgun, both barrels loaded with buckshot.

Willie Sharp had seen the guns, too, and his right hand was moving toward his own pistol when Pierce grasped his wrist and whispered hoarsely, "That's Porter Rockwell!"

"Who?"

"Porter Rockwell! The man who shot Governor Boggs!"

Sharp had only been seven years old when an unknown assassin had fired a load of buckshot through a window at the former Missouri governor in 1842. Two of the pellets had lodged in his brain and, though the doctors had given him up for dead, he eventually recovered.

Governor Lilburn W. Boggs had issued an order in 1838 that the Mormons were to be either exterminated or driven from the state. Though it was never proved, it was widely believed that Porter Rockwell was the governor's assailant. He never actually denied the crime. Instead, his simple defense, logical to those who knew him well, was that had he done the deed Boggs would be dead. Because Rockwell had been the bodyguard of Joseph Smith, the Mormon prophet, it was rumored that Smith had ordered the assassination. Rockwell denied it. Nevertheless, because of it he had acquired the nickname, "The Destroying Angel," a name he detested.

Willie Sharp strained to pull his hand from Pierce's grip. "What're you scared of?" he asked.

"I hear he's kilt more'n a hundert men," replied Pierce. "Some of 'em just for the fun of it."

"There's more'n twenty of us," said Sharp. "We c'n take 'im."

"Some of us'll die," said Pierce. "You might be one of 'em."

The expression on Porter Rockwell's face gave no indication of his mood. His gray eyes seemed to penetrate each man as they darted back and forth, coolly searching for any hint of danger. His voice was quiet and calm as he spoke.

"Gentlemen, I take exception to your kind of talk."

Every face in the group of Missourians was turned toward Rockwell, some blank, some grinning, some hostile. Pierce rose suddenly to his feet. Instantly, the hammers clicked back on Rockwell's two Colts. Everyone froze. Some of the men looked like they wanted to make a move, but no one wanted to be first.

"I don't want no part of this," said Pierce.

Rockwell's eyes did not rest on Pierce, but kept moving. "All right," he said slowly. "Just step aside."

"You're Porter Rockwell, ain't you?" said Pierce.

"I am."

The mood of the Missourians changed instantly. They fell silent and their hostile expressions disappeared. The tension was electrifying. Rockwell knew he was outgunned and didn't want to shoot unless he had to, and the Missourians were too scared to take action.

"What's the trouble here?" asked Captain Fancher, approaching the group carefully.

"Just a case of bad manners," said Rockwell. "If the boys here will just get up and walk slowly to the other end of the camp, we'll be on our way. Hitch up the team, Stoddard."

"That sounds like a good idea, men," said Fancher. "How about it?"

"It don't matter none," said Bill Jones. "We hear the army's comin' to clean out the whole rascally lot. I only hope they get here in time for us t'see it. I'd like to pop some of 'em myself. Let's go boys."

One by one the group rose and retreated. Captain Fancher stepped up to the three Mormons, shaking his head sadly. "I'm sorry we can't offer you the hospitality of our camp. I regret allowing those men to join us, but they're here and some of the people have become good friends with them. I hope you understand."

Rockwell released the hammers on his Colts and placed them in the wagon with his other gear. "Sure do, Cap'n. Be seein' you in Salt Lake."

Fancher frowned and started toward his tent. In a few minutes Rockwell, Stoddard, and Smoot were on the trail again. Now they would have more to report than the coming of an army.

# 43

Porter Rockwell didn't need a clock. A multitude of cues invaded his senses, telling him a new day was about to begin. Birds began to sing. The sky was dark, but the stars had lost some of their luster. A gentle breeze began to blow. While the others slept, Rockwell hitched the horses to the wagon, then went to the spring to fill the water keg. By the time he returned, the stars were fading. Smoot and Stoddard had awakened and were loading their few belongings into the wagon. They could leave anytime. They didn't need a cook fire. They were subsisting on dried beef, dried fruit, and pilot bread. Rockwell set the keg into the wagon and climbed onto the wagon seat.

"Home cookin' tonight," he said. Then he gave a whistle, snapped the reins, and they were off. Several miles behind them the Fancher train was just coming to life. Ahead of them...

Eli Bennett rolled over and groaned. In '49 he had grown used to sleeping on the ground as he came west, but that had been an everyday affair. Doing it on an occasional family outing increased his appreciation of a good civilized bed. No position was comfortable. As in "The Princess and the Pea", he felt the presence of every rock, twig, and pebble in the vicinity. He would have welcomed a few moments more in the arms of Morpheus, but the sound of the bugle to rouse the camp at last put an end to his torture.

Diana seemed oblivious to the discomforts of camping, and of course the children didn't mind at all. To them this was just a great adventure. Their mother was already up preparing breakfast by the time their father made his appearance at the entrance to the tent. Bennett stood up and stretched and made a sound like an animal in agony.

After breakfast the wagons pulled out of camp in no apparent order, except that Brigham Young went first. He didn't demand to be first or even ask it. The people loved and revered this modern-day Moses, and no one would dream of making the Prophet eat their dust.

In a way, this trek to the mountains was a miniature version of the first emigration. It was fitting to commemorate it in this manner. The throng of wagons and carriages was so great that more than two hours passed before the last vehicle left camp. The long steady climb up the canyon, amidst crags and pine-covered hills took the people up through the windings of "The Stairs", and then higher still. The people laughed and talked and sang. Sometimes they got out and walked awhile or stopped to rest along the cool, rushing stream. Little girls picked wildflowers. Boys threw rocks into the creek.

For twenty miles and most of the day they climbed the steep road, passing along the way three sawmills and the cabins that housed the workers and their families. At last the grade lessened, and then, topping a slight rise, the travelers saw the object of their journey, a bowl-shaped valley with a silvery lake on its western rim. The encircling mountains were dressed in the emerald green of tall, straight pines, and their summits were topped with a light dusting of snow. The lake reflected the entire scene right up to the fluffy clouds and deep blue sky. Sheer granite cliffs towered above the lake on its southern shore. Lodged in deep clefts were heavy patches of snow that never saw direct sunlight and thus never completely melted.

A massive granite rock marked the entrance of the camp on the north side of the lake. Nearby grew three stately pines from which was suspended a large flag bearing the motto, "Clear the Way", with an all seeing eye in the oval of the upper margin, above two clasped hands, under which were the words, "Blessings Follow Sacrifices" inscribed on a scroll. A representation of the first pioneer company crossing the North Platte on rafts filled the center of the flag. Below was another inscription, "The Pioneers of 1847 at the Upper Crossing of the Platte, in Pursuit of the Valleys of the Mountains."

Near the northwest corner of the camp stood another tall pine, from which flew the Stars and Stripes, billowing and dancing on the breeze. Another banner nearby bore the representation of a bundle of sticks bound together with strong cords, and the inscription, "The Constitution of the United States. Equal Rights! Woe to the Violators!"

In the center of the camp stood the three boweries and the tents of Brigham Young and his counselor Heber C. Kimball. From the front of the central bowery hung three great banners, the first having an American flag rising from a great rock and the inscription below, "The Constitution of the United States! The Mormons will Defend the Rock! Who Can Prevail Against It?" The second banner showed a lion with one paw upon a rock. Above the lion were the words, "Utah Courage," and below, "The Spirit of '76 is not Dead." On the third banner was a lamb lying quietly beside a fierce lion. The legend printed below read, "Peace Reigns Here."

At the same moment an army of 2,500 men were marching

against this people on the word of an adulterer. What stranger happening upon this scene could believe the Saints to be anything but loyal citizens of the United States?

The remainder of the afternoon was spent setting up tents and putting the camp in order. Swings had been built for the children, as well as rafts for the lake. Men were detailed to take charge of the swings and rafts to guard against accidents.

As the evening hour grew late the people gathered in and near the central bowery. A mournful trumpet began playing the notes of the pioneer hymn they all knew so well. The assembled multitude had no need for a conductor as they spontaneously joined in singing:

*Come, come ye Saints, no toil nor labor fear,*
*But with joy wend your way;*
*Though hard to you this journey may appear,*
*Grace shall be as your day.*
*'Tis better far for us to strive,*
*Our useless care from us to drive.*
*Do this, and joy your hearts will swell—*
*All is well! All is well!*

*Why should we mourn or think our lot is hard?*
*'Tis not so; all is right!*
*Why should we think to earn a great reward,*
*If we now shun the fight?*
*Gird up your loins, fresh courage take,*
*Our God will never us forsake;*
*And soon we'll have this tale to tell—*
*All is well! All is well!*

*We'll find the place which God for us prepared,*
*Far away in the West;*
*Where none shall come to hurt or make afraid;*
*There the Saints will be blessed.*
*We'll make the air with music ring,*
*Shout praises to our God and King;*
*Above the rest these words we'll tell—*
*All is well! All is well!*

*And should we die before our journey's through,*
*Happy day! All is well!*
*We then are free from toil and sorrow too;*
*With the just we shall dwell.*
*But if our lives are spared again*

*To see the Saints their rest obtain,*
*O, how we'll make this chorus swell—*
*All is well! All is well!*

The song had a marvelous effect on the assembled Saints. It made their hearts as one. Eli Bennett felt it. He looked at his wife Diana and their five children. He thought of how he had come west seeking wealth and how he had found something of far greater worth. All the gold in California couldn't buy what Bennett had, joy and real happiness in his religion.

"Look, Eli," said Diana. "The Prophet is going to speak."

All eyes were on Brigham Young as he rose and stepped to the front of the raised platform. The people fell silent.

"We unite, my friends and brothers and sisters, in gratitude to that Father who has permitted us to enjoy this festive occasion. Tomorrow morning at seven o'clock the bugle will call you here to morning devotions. We wish those who have small children to watch over them carefully, that the cry will not go forth that this, that or the other child is lost. I also wish to give a word of caution to all who may visit this lake or the ones in the hidden vales above us. I would rather have stayed at home than to have it said that a child had been lost, or any person drowned through visiting this place.

"Ten years ago, our first week in the valley, a boy of tender years wandered away from his family and was found drowned in City Creek. How bitter was the pain and anguish of his parents! Now suppose a child of yours should be lost in the woods and could not be found. Suppose you should lose a sister, or daughter, or a companion on this lake. You would always think of your visit to Big Cottonwood Canyon with bitter regret. A circumstance of this kind would mar the peace of everyone. I wish the sisters and children to keep away from these rafts, unless they have someone in their company capable of taking care of them. If they know enough to do as they should, they will listen to this counsel.

"Here are swings and boweries prepared for your enjoyment. Here are most beautiful groves, meandering streams, and lovely sheets of water, amid the towering peaks of the Wasatch Mountains. Here are the stupendous works of the God of Nature, though all do not appreciate His wisdom manifested in His works, but are tempted to recklessness through the buoyant feelings of youth and health, and without caution are liable to run into danger.

"Some, if they had the power, would be on the other side of those lofty peaks in ten minutes, instead of calmly meditating upon the wonderful works of God and His kind providence that has watched over us and provided for us, more especially in the last fifteen years of our history. I could sit here for a month and reflect on the mercies of our God, and humble myself in thankfulness because of His favors to myself and to all this great people.

"What do you think the Prophet Joseph Smith and his brother Hyrum, the Patriarch, would have given to have seen this day in the flesh, and to have been here instead of being taken to Carthage like lambs to their slaughter and butchered by their enemies? We are hid up in the Lord's secret chambers, according to His promise, where none can molest us or make us afraid.

"Here is a good floor which we have prepared expressly for your enjoyment, there are two other boweries for the mothers and their children, and here are three bands forming a great orchestra to provide music tomorrow for dancing. Tonight, before we have our evening prayers, we are pleased to hear from the orchestra, 'Overture to Tancreda.'"

The band on the platform opposite the Prophet's began to play the theme from the opera by Rossini. The beautiful notes reverberated gently from the surrounding peaks giving the piece a second life. Even the trees seemed to sway in rhythm with the music. And then it was over.

All heads bowed reverently as the President's Counselor, Heber C. Kimball, stepped forward to offer the evening prayer. When he had finished, the people dispersed, some to their beds, others for a quiet walk by the lake, while others gathered to talk. High above, the eastern peaks were painted a fiery orange by the last rays of the setting sun.

But all was not well. The wagon driven by Porter Rockwell thundered out of Emigration Canyon, past the massive rock formation over which the Donner party had pulled their wagons in 1846 rather than hack their way through heavy brush to reach the valley. Another couple of miles across bench land, down the hill and they were on the valley floor. It was dark when they pulled up to the residence of Brigham Young. There were no lights, but that did not deter Porter Rockwell. He went to the door and pounded with his fist, then stepped back and looked up, expecting to see a light come on. When none did, he repeated his action twice more.

"It appears no one is home," said Smoot from the wagon.

Rockwell just grunted and walked back to the others. He climbed aboard and snapped the reins. The wagon moved off down the street. Rockwell turned south on East Temple Street.

"Where're you going?" asked Smoot.

"We're s'posed to be haulin' mail, ain't we? Gonna get the postmaster out of bed."

Nearly every house they passed was dark. When they got to the postmaster's house, Rockwell pounded on its door, this time with favorable results. A head stuck out from an upstairs window.

"Who is it?" asked Judge Elias Smith.

"Porter Rockwell."

"Be right down."

A minute later the door opened and Smith admitted the three men to his living room. "I thought you were out on the Platte, Brother Rockwell. Did something happen to the mail?"

"We had more important business," said Smoot. "We have been to the Governor's house and find him not at home."

"He's gone," said Smith. "Gone up Big Cottonwood Canyon for the Pioneer Day celebration. Whole town's gone. Now, what's this business more important than delivering the mail?"

Smoot spent several minutes detailing the charges Drummond had made against the church, the loss of the mail contract, and the army headed toward Utah.

When Smoot had finished, Smith sat with his head bowed, staring at the floor. "So it starts again," he said.

Elias Smith remembered the persecutions. He had thought that was all behind them. "You men be over here at six o'clock in the morning. We'll have a good breakfast first, then we'll all go up the canyon. This news is too important to wait for Brother Brigham's return."

# 44

"That one's a horse's head," said Mary Bennett.

"Could be," said her father, "but I think it looks more like a mule."

"Oh, Daddy!" said the young girl, jumping onto Eli as he lay in the grass. "A mule looks just like a horse!"

Bennett tickled his daughter and she rolled over in the grass giggling. Mary was his firstborn, only seven years old. In another year she would be baptized. Bennett enjoyed times like this with his family, watching clouds drift by. He was totally caught up in the moment and didn't hear the horses until they were upon him.

Shunning the trail, Porter Rockwell and his companions had taken a shortcut through the meadow. They didn't see Bennett and his daughter lying in the deep grass until it was almost too late. Porter Rockwell wheeled his big bay horse to the left at the last moment, his companions quickly following his lead.

The pounding hooves startled Eli and Mary. Before they could move, the riders were past them. Bennett sat up and watched the horsemen galloping toward Brigham Young's tent. He easily recognized the lead rider. Everyone knew Porter Rockwell. But why was he in such a hurry?

It was just past noon and the festivities were in full swing. Most everyone noticed the arrival of the riders. Activities continued, but rumors and speculation began immediately. The urgency of the horsemen was obvious. The people's mood changed noticeably. Bennett took his daughter by the hand and started walking toward Brigham Young's tent. If he was going to be almost run over, he wanted to know the reason why.

Porter Rockwell reined his horse to a halt in front of the Governor's tent and dismounted. He didn't wait for the others. He just swept everyone out of his way, including the church President's Life Guard. If anyone in the territory could come and go as he pleased, it was Porter Rockwell. The Prophet stepped forward to greet him, hand extended.

"Porter! Brother Rockwell! Good to see you, but I thought..."

"Bad news, Brother Brigham. We've been punishing horses for five days to get here."

Smoot, Stoddard, and Smith dismounted and came to the tent. The men exchanged handshakes and greetings with the Prophet, then all retired to the interior of his tent.

"Brethren," said Brigham, "I am troubled by your appearance and the distress I see in your faces. You have come a long way and I would suppose very quickly. Pray tell, what is this bad news you bring me?"

"The postmaster at Independence refused to turn over the mail," said Smoot. "I am informed that our contract has been canceled."

"I feared this would happen," said Brigham. "Rumors to that effect have been reaching our ears since February."

"That's not all," Smoot continued. "Drummond has filled the ears of President Buchanan with lies. He is sending an army of twenty-five hundred men against us. Several supply trains are already on the way. They say General Harney is to command the expedition."

The name Drummond filled the Prophet with disgust. "Drummond! He comes amongst us as a federal judge living openly with his mistress, then chastises the Saints for living the principle of plural marriage."

"We should've sent him over the rim of the basin before he had a chance to work his mischief," said Rockwell.

"Murder ill-befits us, Porter," said the Prophet. "Drummond will someday receive his due. But now, General Harney. Isn't he the one who battled the Sioux at Ash Hollow?"

"I believe he is."

The name Harney filled Brigham Young with great concern. General Harney would be a formidable opponent. Only two years before, he had led a force against the Brule Sioux in the Battle of Ash Hollow and slaughtered them, man, woman, and child. Very few of the tribe had escaped his wrath.

"I suppose he intends to deal with us in the same manner," said Young.

The Prophet looked as if the sins of the world had been placed upon his shoulders, but only for a moment. His initial emotions were replaced by righteous indignation and a cool determination to see that justice be done. He stood at the entrance to the tent, his back to the others, seemingly drawing strength from the surrounding mountains. He motioned to a member of his entourage. "See that these brethren are fed and their horses cared for. Then gather all of the leading brethren you can find."

When Young turned back, his voice almost thundered. "No! They will not drive us out again! They will not steal the fruits of our labor as they did at Nauvoo! They slaughtered the Prophet Joseph and his brother and they drove us into the wilderness! We turned the other cheek then...but this time we fight for our freedom!"

The Prophet fell silent for a few moments, then said, "What do you think, Brother Rockwell? You're a military man. How soon can they bring an army against us?"

"Troops could be here in sixty days or less," said Rockwell, "but an army ain't no good without supplies. Passed one company of dragoons that was mostly barefoot, so I reckon they won't be here before the supply trains. Maybe before winter, maybe not. We'll have trouble before then anyhow. Passed a company of Missourians just this side of Bridger. A sorrier lot you have never seen. They know about the army coming and they think they've got some old scores to settle, but then I reckon so have we."

Brigham Young stepped to the entrance of his tent once more and looked silently at his surroundings. The mountains were a natural fortress. Then his gaze fell on Eli Bennett standing a few yards away. He smiled at the man and nodded, then turned back inside his tent.

"Brethren, get yourselves a hot meal, then come sit in council with us."

Outside the tent Bennett approached a member of the Prophet's Life Guard. "What's the commotion all about?" he asked.

"Can't say. But I'm sure you'll hear about it when everybody else does."

Bennett watched the four messengers leave the Governor's tent. Then, after a few moments, he left too.

"Then we are in agreement, brethren," said Brigham Young. "The Nauvoo Legion will harass the army, destroy their supply trains, anything to slow them up and keep them out of the territory before snow closes the mountain passes. Elder Smith, a most important assignment falls to you."

"I am ready, Brother Brigham," said George A. Smith.

"You're the best man for this job, George, since you pioneered the southern settlements in '51," said Young. "The people know you and trust you. Take a few good men and visit those people. Be sure they know we're not looking for a fight, but we won't run from one either. Tell them to store up their food and supplies, and not to give in to the temptation of selling to emigrant companies passing through the territory. Give 'em hellfire and damnation, George. You're good at that. Well, that about covers it. We'll tell the people tonight."

The men rose from their seats and exited the tent.

The meeting at Brigham Young's tent had lasted late into the afternoon. Few people failed to notice what was going on. When the meeting was over, the grimfaced participants scattered to their families. People were curious, but the Saints knew better than to ask questions. Everyone just went about having a good time.

Near sunset the bugle sounded, calling the Saints to evening prayers. Brigham Young, Heber C. Kimball, and General Daniel H. Wells sat on the platform with other church dignitaries. When the Saints had gathered, General Wells stepped to the front of the platform and addressed the people as the Prophet had instructed him.

"Brethren and sisters, I feel there has been a good spirit with us here today. It rejoices and makes glad my heart to see that righteousness predominates here in the midst of the Saints of the living God. Ten years ago we came here to the valleys of the mountains to establish peace and righteousness here upon the earth. We have come here because the Lord wanted us and all His people to form a nucleus where his chosen ones could rally round and build up a kingdom. We came here stripped of everything, as the poor among men. We can now lift up our hearts and rejoice in God who has wrought out His salvation, temporal as well as spiritual.

"Now it appears to have fallen to my lot to report on the news brought to us by the messengers who arrived at midday. When we were driven from Nauvoo, the disposition of our enemies was to destroy every vestige of the Holy Priesthood from the face of the earth. That disposition still exists in the hearts of a great many people. Our enemies have persuaded President Buchanan, through lies and deceptions, to usurp our right to self-government. A new governor, new judges, and other officials are now on their way to Utah. To enforce our subjection to their will, President Buchanan is sending an army of twenty-five hundred men.

"We have resolved today in council to resist this threat to our liberty. We are all familiar with what armies can do. We remember the Carthage Greys, charged with protecting the lives of the Prophet Joseph Smith and his brother Hyrum. No! We will not quietly submit, either to be treacherously murdered, as was Brother Joseph by the Carthage Greys after meekly surrendering himself, or to see an armed force, steeped in prejudice and hatred, and sustained by the sentiment of hostility prevalent throughout the nation, turned loose to work its will upon a disarmed and helpless community.

"In the days and weeks to come we will prepare against the day when we are forced to defend our homes. We will use every resource to convince the Government of its error, that we seek only to live in peace and have the opportunity to live our religion.

"Let us then, my brethren and sisters, take comfort in the knowledge that God lives. He rules in heaven and presides over his covenant people here upon the earth. To that degree of righteousness we attain, He will hide us up and protect us from the evil designs of our enemies. The Lord and one good man, we are told, are a great majority. How much stronger then are we when we stand together in living the great principles revealed to us in this, the Dispensation of the Fullness of Time. That we may do so and preserve ourselves in integrity before high heaven, and be united together as the heart and voice of one man, is my prayer in the name of Jesus Christ. Amen."

A trickle of voices soon grew to a torrent of conversation. The rumors had been confirmed. It was like a dream. It seemed so unreal. How could this be happening? The Saints had lived in peace for ten years. They had left their enemies behind. Why could they not just be left alone?

Brother Wells raised both his hands as a signal to the people and in a moment all were silent. The church leader then bowed his head and offered a fervent prayer on behalf of all those present. At the conclusion, some retired to their tents and wagons to solemnly meditate upon what they had just heard, while others, the major part, engaged in the dance and concluding festivities of the celebration. In spite of what should have been tidings of gloom, filling the people's hearts with fear and apprehension, not a soul was daunted. Songs were sung, and mirth and merriment reigned supreme. At daybreak on the 25th the campground began to be vacated, and before another sun had set the people had all returned to their homes.

During the next ten days, as the Fancher wagon train slowly plodded toward Salt Lake City, the Mormon capital was a maelstrom of activity. Councils were held and plans were laid. On August 1st word was sent to all units of the Nauvoo Legion, the territory's militia, that an army was approaching.

# 45

*August 3, 1857* The Fancher company had been on the trail for more than four months.

"Get 'em moving!" yelled Charlie Mitchell.

Joel Deaton and the other drovers began yelling and whistling at the herd. In a few minutes the animals were on the move up the steep hill out of Little Dell. The road to the top of the pass called Little Mountain was a little over a mile and fairly straight, making only a few slight turns. The cattle didn't follow the road, but spread out over the landscape. Soon the entire hillside seemed to be alive and moving. The sun had not yet peeked over Big Mountain to the east, but there was plenty of light. The camp was awake and getting ready to follow the herd.

Joel rode at the back of the herd. Mitchell wanted it that way because it was safer. Once the herd was moving he rode over to Joel's position.

"Everything okay?" asked Mitchell.

Joel blushed a little. He believed Charlie had never really forgiven him for losing that horse back on the prairie. "Just fine," he said.

"C'mon, Joel! Buck up! Salt Lake City is on the other side of this mountain. Think of it! A real city! Houses and stores, maybe even a boarding house where we can get a real meal."

"I reckon."

"What's the matter Joel? What's troubling you?"

Joel stopped and shifted in the saddle so he could look back at the camp. Cordelia was probably up. He couldn't see her. In fact, he hadn't seen much of her the past month. Mrs. Huff had seen to that. Her mother's instinct had been right. The chemistry had been right between her daughter and Joel Deaton. Charlie Mitchell stopped and looked in the same direction as Joel.

"Better forget about her," he said. "I don't think her mama believes you're an appropriate suitor."

Joel blushed. He hadn't realized his feelings for Cordelia were so obvious. That was the trouble with wagon trains. It was like a big family, no privacy. If someone on one side of the camp sneezed, someone at the other side said, "Bless you!" What did they expect? He wasn't a kid anymore. In a few more years he would be expected to marry and start a family.

"It ain't fair," Joel muttered.

"Hell, Joel! There's other girls."

"Not for me."

"You'll see. A year from now you won't even remember what she looks like."

Images of Cordelia, walking along the trail, singing while she worked, floated into Joel's conscious mind. He laughed.

"You're almost right," said the boy.

"How's that?"

"A year from now I won't remember what *you* look like."

Joel kicked his mount in the flanks and moved away. He had had enough of this conversation.

Nearly an hour later Joel reached the summit of Little Mountain pass. Before him lay a winding, heavily wooded canyon. Several miles to the west was the Great Salt Lake Valley. He couldn't see the city, or even the lake further on. He was tempted to climb the slope on the north that was Little Mountain. It would be a relatively easy climb for a horse, the terrain was favorable, but Joel didn't want to be seen as negligent to his duty by leaving the herd.

The descent into Emigration Canyon was shorter and steeper than the other side, though not as steep as the trail down from Big Mountain. It was harder now to herd the cattle. Too many had a tendency to wander off in the thick brush and small side canyons.

By noon the herd was out of the canyon and the wagons had caught up. The city was so close now the temptation to push on was on everybody's mind. The Missourians did just that, since they were all mounted and had only pack animals. Joel hoped the separation would be permanent. He didn't really like them. They were crude and arrogant. Captain Fancher, on the other hand, was a man with good sense. An hour or two delay wouldn't matter. He ordered the company to noon just north of the wagon road, so the people could get a warm meal.

By midafternoon the wagon train reached the city. They passed along the southern edge of the town, nine blocks south of the public square, and camped about a half mile east of the Jordan River. Once the camp was set up, Captain Fancher called all the men of the company together.

"Gentlemen, I know it's been a long time since anyone of us has been in a city of any size and I know you're all anxious to get going.

We're gonna be here a couple days to reprovision and recruit the teams, so there ain't no hurry. We can't all go at once. Someone needs to mind the herd. I think it best to keep to our usual rotation." Fancher took out his ledger book and opened it. "First watch will be John Stevenson, Peter Hamilton, Josiah Miller, Richard Wilson, and Solomon Wood. Second watch will be George Baker, Robert Fancher, John Prewett, David Beller, and Joel Mitchell. Third watch will be Charles Mitchell, Jesse Dunlap, William Cameron, Joel Deaton, and William Prewett. Except for the first watch, you're all free to go."

Joel turned to his father and asked, "Can I go into town, Pa?"

"What's your hurry, son?" said MacKenzie Deaton. "It'll still be there tomorrow."

"Hey, Joel!" yelled Charlie Mitchell. "Let's go to town, boy!"

Joel looked at his father for an answer. Deaton started walking back to their wagon. Over his shoulder he said, "Be back before dark."

Joel threw his hat in the air and let out a whoop. A grinning Charlie Mitchell motioned to his young friend and they started for the horses. Twenty minutes later they were ambling down Salt Lake City's main thoroughfare astride two of Mitchell's best mounts. People stared at them.

"What's wrong, Charlie?"

"Don't know. Everyone's sure giving us a hard look."

As they came up to the Townsend Hotel, Joel noticed a man walking along the sidewalk carrying a tin pail.

"Hey, Charlie," said Joel, "ain't that Willie Sharp walkin' down the street?"

Mitchell looked at the man, a Missourian. "Staggerin's more like it. Yeah, that's Willie all right. Didn't waste no time gettin' drunk."

Willie Sharp saw them and stopped. He leaned toward them as if trying to get a better look and squinted at them through bleary eyes. "Hey, Mitchell! What y'doin'? Want a drink?" he held up the tin pail.

Mitchell nudged his horse in the Missourian's direction. "H'lo, Willie. What're you drinkin'?"

"Valley Tan."

"Any good?"

"How do I look?"

"Drunker'n a skunk."

"Well, there y'have it!"

"Where'd you get it?"

"Kimball's store. But y'gotta ask for it. They keep it in a back room. Dollar a quart. C'mon up and have a drink with us. Bring the kid."

Mitchell looked at Joel. "Wanna go up?" he asked.

Joel shrugged. "Never had no liquor before. 'Cept for medicinal purposes."

"Gotta start sometime, boy. You said you ain't a kid no more."

"C'mon," said Willie.

Joel gritted his teeth and nodded. Half an hour later he was in a fine spirit, and half an hour after that he was in a state of total stupor.

The next morning he awoke in his family's tent. He felt like every animal in the herd had walked over him, and his mouth was dry and had an awful taste. His tongue felt like it had been dragged on the ground all the way from Arkansas. Joel tried to rise, but immediately fell back. The attempt caused a painful throbbing in his head and everything seemed to swirl. His father noticed him stirring and came over to the tent.

"Joel!"

"Yes, Pa," he said weakly.

"Get up and get some food in your belly. We're going."

Joel looked around. No one else was getting ready for the camp to move.

"It's just you and me, son."

"I can't, Pa. I think I'm sick."

Deaton came over and squatted down by his son. "You ain't sick, Joel. You're hung over. Your ma's fit to be tied. I ain't exactly tickled myself. I thought Charlie Mitchell had more sense. Everybody in the camp is talkin' about it. Mrs. Huff said she's been right about you."

Joel closed his eyes and groaned. Any chance he might have had to overcome Mrs. Huff's objections to his seeing Cordelia had gone right out the window.

The very thought of food sent waves of nausea sweeping through Joel's insides, but he managed to force down some bacon and gravy over broken pieces of bread. His mother served up his food, but her pointed silence said more than any scolding could have. He had gotten drunk. And he had no idea what he had done while in that condition. He had probably missed his turn watching the herd. He ached within. Now they would have one more thing to talk about, and a few more bricks had been added to his load of guilt.

# 46

The two things Eli Bennett missed from back home in

Mississippi were trees and plenty of rainfall. Trees were not a big problem. He could always visit them if he had a mind to ride up one of the canyons. However, rainfall was scarce, and crops still had to be watered. Digging irrigation ditches was hot, back-breaking work. Though still early August, the temperature still rose into the nineties.

Bennett was getting ready to open another ten acres to cultivation. He had already built a head gate next to Little Cottonwood Creek and an irrigation ditch, lined with rocks. He had worked all morning to connect it together by digging a channel from the head gate to the creek. Less than three feet remained when he stopped for lunch.

Bennett sat down against the head gate and waited for Diana to arrive with his meal. The only available shade was his hat, so he tried to make the most of it. He had brought a melon with him in the morning, and it was cooling in the stream. Bennett was giving serious consideration to joining it when he saw two riders approaching. He didn't pay too much attention to them until he saw they were coming straight for him. He felt a mild sense of irritation when he realized that neither one of them was his wife.

"There he is," said Deaton to his son.

Bennett looked at the two riders with curiosity. It was a man and a boy. He wondered what they wanted.

"Ready for lunch, Eli?" asked MacKenzie Deaton.

Bennett got to his feet. He knew the voice and he knew the face, but nothing was registering. He looked dumbstruck.

"Well?" said Deaton. "You look like a man who has seen the elephant. Are you hungry or ain't you? Your wife asked us to bring your lunch."

"Well, I'll...Mac...MacKenzie Deaton...it's really you."

"One and the same," said Deaton, alighting from his horse. "This here's my boy, Joel. You remember him."

"Joel. All growed up now. And Mac. How in the world did you find me?"

The two old friends shook hands warmly. More than eight years had passed since they had last seen each other, but in only a few minutes it seemed just like yesterday. Diana had packed enough lunch for all of them and they spent the next two hours sharing memories and filling in the blanks for one another.

"Tell me about this new religion of yours," said Deaton.

"It's wonderful," said Bennett. "It's made a new man of me. Remember how I lost my stake playing cards in Independence? That could never happen to me again. I would never take a chance like that with my family's future. Of course, if I'd been a Mormon back then I never would've started for California in the first place. Gold don't hold no interest for me no more. Like the scriptures say, I'm laying up treasures for myself in heaven. For where your treasure lies, there shall your heart be also."

"I see you got some kids," said Deaton.

"You bet. Now there's my real treasure. Mary, she's my oldest, I'm gonna baptize her next spring."

"*You're* gonna baptize her?"

"You bet. Every worthy male can hold the priesthood. I do. I'm a high priest in the church."

"You? You sure ain't the Eli I remember."

"Thanks. I hope not."

"How come you're gonna wait till next year to baptize her? She looks old enough to me."

"She won't be eight till then," said Bennett. "The Lord has set eight years old as the age of accountability. All children are born innocent. They ain't responsible for their sins until they're that old."

"I can't think of much sinnin' a seven year old could do," said Joel with a snicker.

"But I can think of some sinnin' that was done by a sixteen year old," said his father. Joel blushed. He wished he hadn't butted in. Deaton continued, "You sound pretty confident, Eli."

"Well, certainly no man knows for sure how he'll fare on Judgment Day, but I've got a pretty good idea how things'll come out. I live a good clean life, I'm honest in my dealings, I've got no moral problems, and I've never shed innocent blood."

"I hear Mormons have more than one wife," said Deaton. "How does that square with the Ten Commandments? Havin' more'n one wife is against the law, if nothin' else."

"The Lord gives commandments," said Bennett. "Men make laws. In our day God has commanded that we are to care for the widow and the orphan. No woman is to be without the protection of a husband. No woman is to be deprived of the joy of motherhood. I have only one wife, but if the Lord commanded, I would take another."

"And what's this innocent blood you're talkin' 'bout?"

"Remember back on the Red Vermillion? The captain of the Plymouth company? What was his name?"

"I know who you mean," said Deaton. "Who could forget? But I ain't thought of him in years, and his name don't come immediately to mind."

"I almost killed that man, Mac. Could've done, but I didn't. He was a man ruled by his feelings of self-importance, a petty tyrant who would leave a sick man for dead rather than minister to him in his hour of need. I think men like him are just takin' up space. Killing him, it's not as if it would've been the shedding of innocent blood, that one could've gone either way. But it wouldn't have been like taking the life of a child who had not reached the age of accountability, either. They're innocent blood.

"Now, you take a man who's stealin' your livelihood, or molestin' your women, or who seeks to take your life. It ain't no crime to shed his blood. In some instances it's the best thing that could be done for them, for some sins can only be forgiven by spilling the blood of the sinner."

Deaton felt a shiver go through his body. Eli Bennett was talking of taking someone's life as casually as swatting flies. "Eli, have you ever killed a man?"

Bennett looked squarely at his old friend. "I have never shed innocent blood," he said, firmly.

It was not a satisfactory answer, but MacKenzie Deaton was sure that it was the only answer he was likely to get. The conversation turned to more mundane topics and before long the afternoon had slipped by.

"Do you think you'll ever come this way again?" asked Bennett.

"Who's to say?" said Deaton. "If you'd asked me a year ago if I was going to California, I'm sure I would've told you no. But, here I am."

"You're right, Mac. Tomorrow is promised to no one. But if you ever do stray in this direction, y'all come by and see us again. God go with you, Brother, and y'all be careful now, y'hear?"

The two friends embraced, and MacKenzie and Joel Deaton mounted their horses and started back to town. Deaton was pleased. At last he had laid to rest that particular ghost that had haunted him for years.

MacKenzie Deaton noticed something different about the camp from when they had left it in the morning. For one thing, some new wagons were in the camp, and some others were gone. For another, the Missourians had returned. Joel thought it likely they had worn out their welcome in town, especially if they had been repeating the remarks they had said about Mormons while camped near Fort Bridger a few days back.

MacKenzie and Joel stopped at the Mitchell wagon to return the horses. Charlie Mitchell came out of his tent.

"It's late," said Mitchell. "I was beginning to think you'd got lost."

"No need to worry 'bout us," said Deaton.

"There's been some big doin's while you was gone. Lotta people are upset. 'Specially Cap'n Fancher."

MacKenzie Deaton looked at the Missourians and nodded in their direction. "Have they been stirrin' things up again?"

"Nah, nothin' like that," said Mitchell. "One of the Mormon leaders came by today and warned us that we would be facing the same danger the Donners did back in '46 if we was to take the Humboldt route. It's late in the season and the herd is slowin' us down. Cap'n Fancher thought it over and decided to take us south. It's farther and it'll take at least six weeks longer to get there, but everybody pretty well agrees that it's the prudent thing to do. 'Cept there's one bunch that says they're fed up and want to take the northern trail. Henry Scott and some of the others are joining up with another train and are headin' out in the morning. You comin' with us or goin' with them?"

"We ain't in no hurry," said Deaton. "If Captain Fancher thinks it's safer goin' south, that's good enough for me."

# 47

On the morning of August 7, 1857, the Fancher train began the pull south toward the Utah Valley. Some of the people had grumbled about the delay, but Alexander Fancher had argued that the trail from Fort Bridger had been hard on the draught animals, particularly the pull over Big and Little Mountains. They needed to recruit the animals and it would save time in the long run.

The Mormons had built a good road from Salt Lake City to the settlements south. The first day's journey brought the Fancher train to the south bank of Little Cottonwood Creek. A beautiful place to camp. The creek ran through a wide depression that would have been called a ravine had it been narrow. A good stand of trees offered shade from the summer sun, and plenty of good grass and water for the animals.

Deaton set up his tent by the creek. While Sarah fixed supper, he and Joel went down to soak their tired feet in the cool water. MacKenzie Deaton sat staring in the creek for a long time.

"What's on your mind, Pa?" asked Joel.

"Just thinkin' about Eli. Wonderin' if I'll ever see him again. He lives on this creek. We went through so much together. I thought I'd feel real good about seein' 'im again."

"Don't you?"

"I don't know. He's so different now. He had a good head on his shoulders. And he had grit. There ain't a man alive I would've trusted more'n Eli Bennett. He done some foolish things back then." Deaton picked up a pebble and threw it into the creek. "Hell, we both did. But I'm the same man I was then. Only a little older now. Eli looks the same. His voice sounds the same. But he don't talk like the Eli Bennett I knew. Probably don't think the same neither. I thought I would've been happy to see 'im, and at first I was. But now...I don't know."

"People change, Pa. Why, I bet you don't think I'm the same as I was when you went away in '49."

Deaton looked at his son and grinned. "No, you're the same ornery kid as you were back then. Only bigger and y'get into bigger trouble."

"Aw, Pa! Ain't y'ever gonna let me forget that?"

"Some day, I reckon, but now I'm havin' too much fun with you to let it go just yet."

"Dinner's ready!" Sarah Deaton called out.

Deaton pulled his feet out of the creek and wiggled his toes. He looked around the camp. He saw the Missourians camped to the southwest against a hillside.

"Now why do you suppose they came with us?" Deaton wondered out loud.

"Who's that?" asked Joel.

"That Missouri trash. They could make a lot better time on the Humboldt with the other group. It don't figure."

"I heard one of 'em say they weren't in no hurry to get out of Utah. Said they was gonna hoorah every Mormon they could find before they left the territory."

Deaton just shook his head. If he'd known the Missourians would be coming south, he would have taken the other trail. Maybe the Fancher company would get lucky and the Missourians would push on. If not, there was going to be trouble for sure.


# 48

The day was hot, well into the nineties. The temperatures hadn't backed off much since they peaked in July, but the weather was of little concern to William Aiden. True, it was because of the heat that he was now climbing to the divide between the two peaks just east of Provo, but his only care was that he had the entire day to indulge in the passion of his life, sketching the beauty of his surroundings. Though hot in the valley, the temperature was no more than 75 in the mountains.

Aiden had packed a lunch and left before daybreak. The climb to the divide between the two peaks was difficult, but a trail of sorts began at that point. It meandered along the north side of the divide for a short distance until it came to a broad meadow of grass and quaking aspens that bridged the gap between the two mountains. Another path turned south and then back west, ascending toward the southern peak. Part way to the top Aiden came to a small spring flowing from the rocks, forming a shallow pool. The water was icy cold and delicious. Further up the trail, he came upon an outcropping of rock that stuck out over the divide. He climbed out onto it and sat down. It afforded him a spectacular view of the western half of Utah Valley.

William Aiden was an artist from Tennessee, barely into his twenties. He had come west in the spring of the year for his first big adventure, to sketch the western people and landscape. From a poor, but sturdy, family, he had decided to stay in Utah for awhile because of his previous association with Mormons. His parents had boarded Mormon missionaries for a time. Though they found their guests to be respectable, they had no desire to become members of the Mormon faith.

Aiden earned his way as a painter and doing odd jobs, though he would have preferred working as a painter of pictures rather than houses. He was well-liked for an outsider, and on the whole he had enjoyed his stay in Provo, but now was anxious to move on.

It was a beautiful day, hardly a cloud in the sky. Aiden's perch on the rock was favorable, because he would be in the shade until midafternoon. A gentle breeze rustled through the quaking aspens.

Soon, Aiden was completely absorbed in his sketching. He didn't hear the approach of the two Ute Indians until they were almost upon him. The sounds of nature were all around him and he had grown quite used to them, and so something unusual must have attracted his attention. Aiden turned in their direction and saw the two men peering at him through a clump of scrub oak. Though armed, they didn't appear particularly dangerous.

Aiden looked around for some avenue of escape and saw none. To get off the rock and back on the trail, he would have to get past them. He slowly reached into his knapsack and found the handle of the Colt's revolver given to him by his uncle before he left home. He cocked it, but left it in its hiding place. There was only one thing to do, so he did it. He continued sketching.

When Aiden looked up again, he found the Indians had moved closer. Deciding they were only curious, he turned to face them squarely and motioned for them to join him. The two Indians smiled broadly and stepped out of the scrub oak. They were a sorry looking pair. Dirty, stringy, black hair hung down to their shoulders and they were dressed in tattered castoffs from the local whites.

"Come, sit with me," said Aiden, motioning with his hand. The Indians didn't understand the words, but they did come and squat down beside him.

"Do you like pictures?" he asked.

Aiden held up his sketchbook, and one of the Indians took it from him, and leafed through the book while he and the other Indian talked to each other excitedly. Suddenly, they stopped talking and looked at Aiden. One of the men handed back the sketch book and spoke some words, pointing first to himself and then to the book.

"Ah," said Aiden slowly as he began to understand what the Indian was trying to say, "You would like me to draw your picture."

Aiden pointed to the Indian and then made drawing motions with his hand. The Indian smiled and nodded.

Aiden opened his sketchbook again and began to draw a portrait of the young man. He filled it in with trees, mountains and wildlife. When he had finished, he tore it from the book and handed it to the Indian. Both he and his companion were delighted. The second Indian indicated that he wanted his picture done, too, and that one was soon finished and handed over. Then Aiden got them to sit for a portrait of them both. When he was finished, he showed it to them, but closed the sketchbook and put it away. The two Indians looked a bit disappointed, but seemed to understand that he wanted to keep it for himself. After some friendly gestures, the two Ute braves moved off through the trees and were quickly out of sight.

Aiden gathered up his things and started back down the trail. The hour was late and he wanted to get home before dark. When he reached the end of the divide, the trail led around a large rock and turned north before starting down the slope. Aiden stopped because of the arresting view that lay before him. Twenty miles to the north, where the Salt Lake road came over the point-of- the-mountain, was a squiggly white line and something that shifted and moved like a swarm of ants. Wagons and a large herd. The first southbound emigrant wagon train of the season. Aiden smiled broadly. Now, at last, he could go on to California. They would probably be at Provo by tomorrow night. With any luck he could be in Los Angeles by the end of September.

The Fancher company accepted William Aiden without reservation when they discovered that he was not a Mormon. He didn't have an outfit to speak of, only his art supplies, clothes and other personal belongings, an old roan mare, and about $400 in cash. Like people everywhere, the Fancher party was downright friendly to anyone who had cash money.

The journey south contrasted sharply with what the emigrants had experienced thus far. The prairie had been a lonely, desolate place. Utah territory, by comparison, was teeming with activity. The wagon train was constantly being passed by travelers, mostly Mormons, but also Ute Indians. The Indians were usually in small bands, poorly armed and shabbily dressed. Not at all the noble savages depicted by the imaginative storytellers who published in the East.

# 49

Cedar City was all abuzz on Sunday, August 15, 1857. The Apostle George A. Smith was visiting the settlement and was to address the Saints at the afternoon church services. He had left Provo for the southern settlements on August 4, carrying military orders from General Daniel H. Wells. His mission: to organize the militia and prepare the Saints for war. At Parowan, where he maintained a home, Elder Smith had delivered the orders to Colonel William H. Dame, commander of the Iron Military District. After a week's sojourn there, he had joined Col. Dame and his staff as they began a tour of the southern portion of the Military District to complete the organization of the regiment, inspect the troops, and give them instructions. Their first stop was at Cedar City.

Among the worshipers were Isaac Delaney and his two families. He had been a man of means in Salt Lake City, and, as the advertisement in the Deseret News had promised, he had gotten more means. Not in the ordinary sense, for there was still little cash money to be had, but he had acquired some land and another family. John, now nineteen, was looked upon with great favor among the young ladies in the southern territory, while Elizabeth and Samantha were in that awkward age, about to enter puberty. Harriet had borne Isaac seven children in the eight years of their marriage. In 1854 he had taken another wife, Kathleen, but their union had not yet been blessed with any offspring.

The day was hot and an overflow crowd filled the meeting house. All the windows were open, as well as the door, and most of the people were fanning themselves.

As leader of the first colonization effort, Elder Smith was loved and respected by the southern Saints. When his turn came to speak, Elder Smith stepped to the pulpit and waited. He was a stout man, with harsh features that gave the impression he was a rather stern character. All eyes were on him. Slowly, he looked through the room. Whenever he saw a familiar face, he nodded and the hint of a smile appeared at the corners of his mouth. Finally, he cleared his throat and spoke.

"Brothers, sisters, my good friends, I am nearly overcome with emotion to be here among you again. It is always a blessing to gather with the Saints anywhere, but there is, and will always be, a special place in my heart for you good people who accepted the call seven years ago to establish the Iron Mission and bring the gospel to our Lamanite brethren. President Young and the other leading brethren in the church are pleased with the great progress you have made..."

The Apostle's speech continued for more than thirty minutes in much the same vein, touching on various topics before he arrived at the purpose for his southern excursion.

"...Express riders have been to all the settlements and I am sure there is no one amongst us who does not know of the army approaching our borders. For years we were driven by our enemies. We were deprived of our homes and property. When we sought redress from those sworn to protect us, we received only the back of their hands. Is there anyone here who has forgotten Haun's Mill?"

A murmur of "no" swept through the crowd. Everyone present knew of the Haun's Mill massacre. Some had friends or relatives who died in the slaughter.

"Or Carthage Jail?"

"No" again, but louder.

"Perhaps in the days to come, many of our brethren will be called upon to make the same sacrifice as Joseph and Hyrum. We know about armies. The Carthage Greys were pledged by Governor Ford to protect the Prophet, but instead of giving shelter, they gave him death. It is not an army that comes against us, but an armed mob."

The Apostle loosened his collar and mopped the sweat from his face with a large handkerchief. He paused, as if to catch his breath, then started again.

"In the days and weeks to come we must prepare and be vigilant. For years the gentiles have come among us. They humbly ask to buy provisions and then mock our laws and insult our religion. From this day forward treat all strangers with suspicion. Find safe places in the mountains to which you can resort if it becomes necessary to abandon your homes. Store up your grain and produce. Do not feed it to your cattle or sell it to your enemies. Nevertheless, succor the needy. Make friends of your enemies...but be wary of treachery.

"Now, I have seen the boys drilling in Parowan and I am sure that they will make do in a scrape if it comes to that. All must be made ready. You sisters mend clothing, make quilts and put up food. You brethren must be as the Nephites of old." Elder Smith opened the Book of Mormon that lay upon the pulpit. "When the Nephites were threatened, that great general Moroni rent his coat and took a piece of it and wrote upon it the Title of Liberty and fastened it upon a pole and to the people he said: 'Surely God shall not suffer that we, who are despised because we take upon us the name of Christ, shall be trodden down and destroyed.' And further, as if speaking to us: 'Behold, whosoever will maintain this title upon the land, let them come forth in the strength of the Lord, and enter into a covenant that they will maintain their rights, and their religion, that the Lord God may bless them.' Let it be so with us." A chorus of "amens" echoed through the meeting hall.

The Apostle closed the Book of Mormon and opened the Bible that also lay upon the pulpit. "We have always sought to live in peace with our neighbors. Their response has been mobbings, arson, and murder. In ancient days the Lord spoke these words through the prophet Joel, and I say them now again in His Holy Name: 'Proclaim ye this among the Gentiles; Prepare for war, wake up the mighty men, let all the men of war draw near; let them come up: Beat your plowshares into swords, and your pruning hooks into spears: let the weak say, I am strong'." Elder Smith was like a lion. He slammed the Bible down and struck a dramatic pose, his right hand in the air, the index finger accenting each word. "We will not be driven again!" he roared.

Women wept and men trembled.

When the meeting was over some of the people left for their homes, but most stood around outside in small groups talking about many things, but foremost in the conversations was the speech they had just heard. The spirit of their religion burned brightly within the bosoms of many. They would be steadfast in defense of their freedom. No more would they be driven by their enemies.

# 50

The weather continued hot and dry. Every few miles, wherever a stream of any size came out of the mountains, was another Mormon settlement. Payson. Salt Creek. Cedar Springs.

As the wagons pulled through each settlement the local people stopped whatever they were doing and stared at the strangers. And not from curiosity, either. The faces seemed to emit a restrained hostility. Even the Missourians were cowed by the Mormons' attitude. That is, until they reached Buttermilk Fort on the 17th of August.

Perhaps the first white men to see Pauvan Valley were Father Escalante and his men when they came from Santa Fe in 1776 looking for a route to Monterey, California. It was just another place in the wilderness until President Millard Fillmore appointed Brigham Young governor of the Utah territory in September 1850. Since the territory encompassed an area covering all of Utah and Nevada, and parts of Wyoming, Colorado, New Mexico, Arizona, and southern California, the new governor was directed to locate a capital city somewhere near the geographical center of the territory.

Brigham Young and a party of officials came south in October 1851. They stopped for awhile at Cedar Springs, a favorite camping place for travelers, but moved on to Chalk Creek and camped. All the requirements for a settlement were present. With little ceremony and no permanent residents, the town of Fillmore was born.

By the summer of 1855 the town had grown sufficiently to permit further colonization. Ten families were called to move six miles north and start a new settlement on Pioneer Creek. Within a year the venture failed for lack of an adequate water supply. The settlers moved a few miles farther north to Cedar Springs and tried again.

Buttermilk Fort was the nickname for the settlement at Cedar Springs, so named by emigrants because of the refreshing buttermilk available from a local farmer. Near midday the Fancher train came through Round Valley Pass. Cedar Springs was just ahead. The wagons rumbled slowly down out of the hills and spread out in a loose array east of the fort.

Tents were set up to give some respite from the hot sun, and the ladies were soon preparing meals over open campfires. In the meantime Joel, Charlie Mitchell, and Bill Aiden rode over to the fort.

Joel Deaton and William Aiden had become good friends in the days since they had left Provo. They were close to the same age and came from similar backgrounds. Joel was intrigued by the drawings of people Aiden had met. It didn't take much prompting for him to do a portrait of the Deaton family. It was a good likeness and was received with appreciation.

Cedar Springs looked more like a military installation than like a pioneer settlement. The fort was built of adobe and logs, 75 by 150 feet, with a large opening at each end where heavy doors were to be hung, but hadn't been because the Indians were not as great a threat as first supposed. The fort was a number of small houses built side-by-side in two rows with the outside walls of the houses forming the walls of the fort. A thirty-foot courtyard separated the two rows of houses. Several large fields in the vicinity were under cultivation.

The fort looked almost deserted as the three men approached. A few children peered shyly from the gateway. Joel and his friends rode up and stopped.

"Howdy," said Mitchell. The children turned and ran. "Well now, don't that beat all."

"I don't understand this," said Bill Aiden. "I've lived among these people for months and they've always been friendly to me."

"Howdy, boys!" called out Rufus Pierce as he rode up. "Where is everybody?"

Joel and Charlie looked at each other. Neither of them really cared very much for the Missouri bunch. Before they could answer his inquiry, a woman came walking out of one of the houses, drying her hands on her apron. Joel thought she might have been pretty when she was younger, but the pioneer life had taken its inevitable toll. Her hair was tied back in a bun and her face had a very tired look. She looked at the men for a moment, then turned to go back inside.

"Hey! Wait a minute!" yelled Rufus Pierce. "Where y'all goin'?"

The woman stopped, but didn't turn around. She looked a little flustered. Pierce moved forward on his horse until he was right beside the woman. "Hey, now, we're just lookin' for a little hospitality...or don't you folks know what that is?"

"C'mon, Pierce. Leave her alone," said Charlie Mitchell. Just then Richard Johnson, the leader of the small community came walking up from the far end of the fort. "What's going on here? Are these men bothering you, Fanny?"

"No problem, mister," said Mitchell. "We were just wondering about some buttermilk. We were told in Salt Lake that we could get some here."

"Ain't got none for sale," said Johnson.

"How 'bout some whiskey?" asked Pierce. "Or some valley tan? Y'got some of that?"

"We don't have none of that either. We don't hold with drinking."

Rufus threw his head back and laughed, showing his mouth full of rotten teeth. "Hey! They don't hold with drinkin' in Salt Lake neither, but they sure know how to sell it."

"Well, you won't find none of it here," said Johnson.

Pierce leaned forward, his left arm resting on his saddle horn. "Well, then, how about some women? Y'got plenty of them, ain't you?"

"That's enough, Pierce," said Mitchell.

"Mind your own business, Mitchell!" said Pierce. "What about it, Mister? Y'got some good lookin' gals around here, or are they all as ugly as this one?"

Johnson's face turned red. There were four of them, though only one appeared to be belligerent. "Look here, sir, this woman is my wife!"

"Well, is she your number one wife, or number two, or maybe even three? Just how many wives you got, mister? I hear you boys say it's a religious principle, but you an' me, we know what it really is. Kinda like havin' your own private whorehouse, ain't it?"

Richard Johnson charged toward Pierce, his fists clenched. Hardly moving, Pierce whipped the pistol from his belt and stuck it in Johnson's face. "That's far enough!"

Johnson stopped, his face changing rapidly from red to white. Charlie Mitchell advanced, drawing his own pistol. Pierce didn't perceive any danger. The Fancher company had put up with the doings of the Missourians since they joined up on the Santa Fe Trail. Pierce had no reason to think things had changed. But they had. The arrogant grin on Pierce's face turned sheepish when he felt the muzzle of Charlie Mitchell's pistol pressing against his head behind the ear.

"Pierce, I'd blow your brains out if you had any," said Mitchell. "Now hand it over!"

The Missourian looked at Charlie Mitchell out of the corner of one eye. He was afraid to turn his head. Meekly, he handed over his gun.

"Now get back to the wagons before I decide to leave you here to take your punishment!"

Rufus Pierce swung his horse around and took off at a gallop.

"Sorry, mister," said Mitchell. "He ain't one of us. Let's go boys."

Charlie, Joel, and Bill headed back for the wagon train. Mitchell's words had fallen on deaf ears. The disclaimer had not impressed Richard Johnson. He saw little distinction between Pierce and the others. They were all gentiles. Outsiders. The enemy.

Back at the camp Mitchell rode up to the Missourians. Pierce had already spilled his guts, judging by the looks on their faces. Mitchell threw Pierce's gun on the ground and turned away. Talking would do no good. Not with this crowd. Many miles still lay ahead. Charlie Mitchell had made a bitter enemy. He hoped there would be no more trouble before they got to California, but he knew he had to be prepared. If Charlie Mitchell had known what awaited him and the others in the southern end of the territory, he would have given no thought at all to Rufus Pierce.

# 51

*August 25, 1857* The sun was only a memory, suggested by the orange glow on the western horizon. Silas Smith, bone-weary after traveling forty miles since leaving Beaver that morning, was having trouble seeing the road. The crescent of the moon, hanging low in the sky and still two days short of its first quarter, was of little help in discerning the road north. Asleep in the back of the wagon were his cousin George A. Smith, Jacob Hamblin, Philo T. Farnsworth, and Elisha Hoops. Thales Haskell was following behind, driving the baggage wagon. They were out of the mountains now, and had passed the jumbled lava formation that signified they were near their destination for the day, Corn Creek.

The Apostle George A. Smith's tour of the southern settlements had taken him from Parowan to Cedar City and Hamilton's Fort, thence to New Harmony and Washington, arriving there on August 18. Next stop was Santa Clara, or Clara, as the locals called it, the farthest most outpost of Mormondom within the territory.

As Elder Smith and his companions had journeyed northward on their return to Parowan, they encountered a band of Indians under Chief Jackson a few miles below Mountain Meadows, and at his invitation had dinner with them. The following morning they continued through Mountain Meadows, and stopped for the night at Pinto. At Cedar City they were caught in the rain and a flood that poured from Coal Creek Canyon, but pushed on, finally arriving back at Parowan after an arduous journey of 185 miles in only seven days. Having rested for two days at Parowan, Elder Smith was now on his way back to Salt Lake City to report his findings to the Prophet.

Corn Creek had not yet been settled by the whites, but the local Indians, under Chief Kanosh, had a thriving corngrowing farm in the vicinity, hence the name of the stream.

Near ten o'clock, the Smith party reached the campground by a spring that flowed into the creek. Silas Smith skillfully guided the wagon through the creek and stopped on the north side. On the other side the night guards of the Fancher train had watched their arrival with interest.

"We're there," Silas called out to the others.

His announcement was met with some groans, but few comments by the others. One by one they alighted from the wagon, stretching and yawning, and began setting up their camp. The weather was good, so each man laid out only his bedroll. No need to set up the tents. Two of the men gathered firewood, while the others turned out the stock to feed and got out some provisions for their evening meal. Soon the fire was blazing and the smell of food was being carried on the breeze to the Fancher camp, some 100 yards south.

Though he had eaten a full meal for supper, the aroma of food cooking at the other camp was getting to Joel Deaton. He was on guard duty and he didn't get off for probably another two hours. He wished he could get a taste of whatever it was that smelled so good.

"How long have they been there, Joel?"

Startled, Joel turned to see Captain Fancher approaching in the darkness.

" 'Bout ten or fifteen minutes, I reckon."

"Which direction did they come from?"

"South."

"Guess I'll go over and have a talk. D'you wanna come along?"

"Sure do," said Joel, smiling.

They had only gone a few steps toward the other camp when Dr. Schnitzler called out to them. "Wait for me. I am coming, too."

Dr. Schnitzler had been on the other guard post. Captain Fancher frowned. He didn't know why the doctor would want to come along, but then he couldn't think of a reason why he shouldn't.

Being late in the season, the creek was nearly dry. It couldn't be more than two or three inches deep. As they waded it, Joel appreciated the fact that he wouldn't have much trouble with soggy boots in the morning.

The glow from the campfire emphasized the haggard look of the men of the Smith party. They had the faraway look of total fatigue in their eyes. Little in the way of conversation passed between them as they ate their supper. They barely noticed the arrival of Captain Fancher and his two companions. "Good evening," he said. "Fancher's my name. We're camped over on the other side of the creek."

"You're welcome here, sir," said the Mormon Apostle. "I'm George Smith. This here's my cousin Silas, Jacob Hamblin, Bishop Farnsworth, Elisha Hoops, and Thales Haskell. Would you like something to eat?"

"Thank you, sir, but no, we've all had our supper," said Fancher.

Joel grimaced at the missed opportunity. He said nothing himself, but his stomach growled its displeasure. "Could do with some information, though," Fancher added.

"Of course," said Elder Smith. "It's a bit chilly tonight. You and your friends have a seat by the fire and warm yourselves."

Fancher squatted down, his arms wrapped around his knees, while Joel and the doctor sat cross-legged by the fire. Joel had brought his rifle along and it was lying across his lap, the business end pointed at Jacob Hamblin.

Hamblin was the epitome of the rugged frontiersman, tall and lanky, and dressed in buckskin pants and shirt. "Hey, there, boy," he said to Joel, "don't you know nothin' about guns? I'd take it kindly if you'd not point it in my direction."

"Oh, sorry," said Joel.

Joel looked around at the travelers. The one calling himself Smith seemed friendly enough, but the others had a kind of wary look about them.

"How can we be of service?" asked Elder Smith.

"We noticed you come in from the south," said Fancher. "Thought maybe you could tell us the lay of the land. Our teams are jaded. We've been here five, six days recruitin' 'em. I was hoping you could direct us to a good campground. You know, good grass and water, before we get to the desert. We've been on the road for nearly five months. Longer than we'd expected. We were gonna take the northern trail from Salt Lake City, but it's so late and we didn't want to take a chance with the snow. It's been a tough ol' road, but by god we'll get to California yet."

The Apostle looked at Fancher for what seemed a long time, as if studying him. He didn't think much of people who used the Lord's name in casual conversation.

"Well, sir, I have a home in Parowan, though I don't get down there as much as I'd like. Brother Hamblin lives down on the Santa Clara and he'd know as much or more than any of us about the good camping places."

Smith turned toward Hamblin, but he was gone. He had finished his meal and had left the campfire.

"Brother Jacob," Smith called, "talk to this gentleman. He would like some directions."

Fancher left the fire and the attention turned to Joel and the doctor.

"Where're you folks from?" asked Silas Smith.

"I...well, most of us are from Arkansas," said Joel. "We picked up a few others along the way. Illinois, Indiana, Missouri."

Joel seemed to detect a tenseness in his listeners when he mentioned Missouri, but in a moment the tension was gone.

"And you, sir?" said Silas Smith to the doctor.

"Germany. But now I am coming from Pennsylvania," said Dr. Schnitzler in his heavy accent.

"It's been a long time since I come across the plains," said Elisha Hoops. "Is it still a rough trip?"

Schnitzler laughed. "I tell you, it is not like Germany. We have all the time hot weather. Lotsa dust. No water. No grass. The oxen are very weak. We better find some good place to rest soon or we in a lotta trouble."

"Still a lot of cholera on the plains?" asked Hoops.

"Oh, ya, to be sure. I have seen a lotta that disease."

George Smith's eyes showed more than passing interest. "What about the soldiers?" he asked. "Much cholera among the soldiers?"

"Oh, no, I don't think so."

"Too bad."

"We've had a bit of cholera in our camp," said Joel.

"How did you handle it?" asked Elder Smith.

"I take good care of them," said Schnitzler. "When they are sick with cholera, I give capsicum and camphor and opium and brandy. It don't always cure them, but at least they are feeling happy before they die."

"Are you a doctor, sir?" asked George Smith.

"Oh, I have been at one time, but no more. Now I am becoming big landowner in California."

Just then Captain Fancher returned from talking with Jacob Hamblin. "C'mon Joel, Doctor, let's get back to the wagons. Mr. Smith, gentlemen, thank you for your hospitality."

In a few moments they were across the creek and had disappeared in the darkness. They walked nearly half way in silence.

"How did it go?" asked Joel, finally.

"We're in luck," said Fancher. "Mr. Hamblin has a ranch at a place called Mountain Meadows. He says there's plenty of grass and water. It's a valley about a mile wide and five miles long and it's all grass. We spend a few days there and we'll be ready for the desert."

The desert. Joel thought of the terrain they had already traversed. If the desert was worse than this, it must be a pretty bad place.

Following their usual routine, the drovers from the emigrant camp ate a quick breakfast on the morning of August 26, and moved the herd out on the road south more than an hour before Smith and his companions awoke. Jacob Hamblin was awake first. He started a fire with the extra firewood gathered the night before. The other camp was already bustling with activity. By the time Hamblin's friends were awake he noticed a delegation approaching from across the creek, Dr. Schnitzler and Bill Jones, leader of the Missouri Wildcats.

"Mornin', gents," said Jones. "Sorry to trouble you so early, but we got us a dead ox over there and we was wonderin' if you could help us out. D'you think the Indians'd want it?"

"I'm sure they would," said Thales Haskell. "If you didn't want 'em to have it, they'd probably steal it."

"I think the Indians are better fed than that," said Silas Smith. "Why don't you dress it out and pack it with you? It'd keep 'til noon. Make a fine feast for your party."

"Well, now, we don't have no time to fool with it," said Jones. "We thought we might get the best deal possible from the Injuns hereabouts, seein' as how they's the ones that killed it."

"Killed it?" said Hamblin.

"Yeah, it was shot with an arrow the first night we was here. Doc Schnitzler here tended to it, but it died last night. We don't figure to let 'em have it for nothin'."

"If it's cash money you're after, well, they ain't got none," said Hamblin. "Maybe you could get some buckskins or trade goods out of 'em. They ain't got much of anything else, 'cept maybe corn."

"We already traded for plenty of corn, thank you," said Jones. "Buckskins, huh? Not a fair price, but...we'll strike an even bargain."

"I think I will make a gift of this ox," said the doctor, smiling. Not being conversant with the German language, the men of the Smith party failed to see the double meaning of the doctor's comment, that 'gift' was the German word for poison.

Jones and the doctor returned to their camp while the Smith party loaded their wagons. Elisha Hoops kept stealing glances in the direction of the other train. He couldn't put his finger on it, but something about the way Jones had asked about the ox had created suspicion in his mind that the emigrants were up to no good.

By the time the Smith party was finally ready to leave, the emigrant company had broken camp and had moved nearly a quarter of a mile south. Philo Farnsworth was at the reins of the passenger wagon and Thales Haskell was once again aboard the baggage wagon. The conversation was light and George Smith was entertaining his traveling companions with a story while they were waiting to get started.

Elisha Hoops was the last man to get into the wagon. Hoops climbed into the rear and sat down with his back to the side, but he kept looking in the direction of the dead ox. As the wagon started to move, he saw the doctor a short distance off to one side of the ox tying his horse in the brush by the side of some willows. The doctor walked up to the ox, took out a dagger from his pocket and stuck it into the carcass. The blade of the knife glinted in the sunlight. He stuck the animal three times, at the joint of the shoulder and at the hip and toward the back.

Suddenly the Smith wagon lurched forward and one of the lead horses reared up.

"Whoa!" called out Farnsworth.

The horses were all pulling in separate directions. Hoops jumped out of the wagon and ran around to the front. He grabbed the harness and settled the horses down.

"What's the problem?" asked Farnsworth.

"Hames strap's come undone."

The harness was old and worn. The strap that held up the neck yoke had broken away from the ring that held everything together and the trace on one side had fallen to the ground.

"Gonna take long?" asked Farnsworth.

"I don't know," said Hoops. "I'll see if I can tie it together."

Hoops' task was complicated by the fact that he was trying to keep an eye on the German doctor at the same time. The doctor reached into his pocket and extracted a small, half-ounce vile of clear glass. He removed the cap and poured a clear liquid into the three incisions he had made.

After several minutes Elisha Hoops had managed to get everything back together by carefully tying it with some string he had in his pocket. Just then three Indians came up to where the doctor was standing by the ox. Hoops got back into the wagon and it began to roll. He looked back at the doctor and the Indians. They appeared to be bargaining. After some minutes the Indians gave the doctor two buckskins. He mounted his horse and rode off in the direction of the emigrant train, which was now nearly out of sight, while the Indians set about skinning the dead animal.

Hoops stewed over what he had seen for nearly half an hour. In the meantime the distance between the two parties had grown to more than three miles.

"Did anybody see what that man did to the ox?" asked Silas Smith.

Some of the party turned and looked back.

"Couldn't tell for sure," said Farnsworth. "I thought he might be pointing out the meat to them Indians."

"I saw him stick that ox with his knife and pour something in from a bottle before the Indians came up," said Hoops. "Then he traded the ox to 'em for a couple of buckskins."

George Smith turned and looked in the direction of the dead ox. He pondered for a long time. Could any man be so low as to poison that ox? If he had, repercussions would surely follow. That would be all right, he thought, as long as the local people were not affected.

Soon they were out of sight of the emigrants and the conversation turned to other things. The incident with the ox was not forgotten, but many days would pass before they would speak of it again.

# 52

*August 29, 1857* The Mormons had done a good job of road building since their arrival in 1847. Previously, the road to California had only been a trace in the wilderness traveled by trappers, Indians, and even John C. Fremont. Now it was a good wagon road, marked with milestones and fingerposts to show the distance between settlements. It had been a tough haul over the mountains from Corn Creek, but shortly after breaking camp on Saturday morning the town of Beaver came into view as the Fancher company descended from the hills.

Robert Kershaw had been watching the approaching wagons for some time before they halted in front of his house in the lower part of town. He took out his watch and noted the time: not quite 10 o'clock. It was a good-sized train, and the first emigrant company he had seen this year. He counted 31 wagons, drawn principally by ox teams, two or three yoke to the wagon. He guessed the loose stock numbered maybe three hundred head or more, horses, mules, and cattle. He made a mental note that the people appeared to him to be families, men, women and children, middle aged and old people, not at all like the vicious enemies they had been represented to be.

Captain Fancher rode right up to where Kershaw was standing. He took off his hat and wiped the headband with a handkerchief and then his forehead.

"Good morning," he said. "Gonna be another hot one today."

"Could use some rain," allowed Kershaw.

"Noticed your fine garden. I see you have peas, potatoes, melons and onions. We'll buy all you can spare."

Kershaw took out his own handkerchief and wiped the back of his neck. The heat he was feeling wasn't from the weather, but from the talk he had heard a few days earlier. He could use the hard cash, but orders were orders.

"Well, sir, normally I would be happy to oblige," said Kershaw. "But Elder George A. Smith, one of the leaders of our church, was by here a few days back, and he has forbidden us to sell our produce. We are to store it against hard times that are coming this winter."

Fancher shifted uneasily in his saddle. "So that's how it is. We met this man back at Corn Creek. He seemed friendly enough. He said nothing about an embargo. Even gave us directions on where to find good grass and water. Surely, you must have misunderstood his meaning."

"Well, if I did, I ain't the only one."

Fancher wanted to keep talking, try to persuade the man to sell some of his vegetables, but thought better of it. The teams were badly in need of a rest, so he decided to set up camp first and then try again.

"Where's a good place to camp around here?"

"Other side of town," said Kershaw. "There's a creek."

Fancher bid goodbye to the man and returned to the train. The emigrants proceeded through town on the main street and camped about half a mile beyond Beaver on the other side of a little stream called Spring Creek.

Their passing was noted with interest by the citizens of Beaver, who had heard of the wagon train several days before. Its arrival brought back to mind the letter that had been read in Sunday meeting. The army was coming and trading with the emigrants was forbidden. Many of the people were determined to follow counsel, and resolved to keep as far away from the emigrants as possible. However, a goodly number of the townspeople didn't share that sentiment. Within an hour of their arrival, the Fancher company was receiving visitors.

Bill Aiden had become really thick with Joel Deaton and Charlie Mitchell since they left Provo. Joel and Bill were helping Mitchell stake out his horses when the citizens of Beaver began to arrive at the camp.

"I don't figure it," said Joel. "The Mormons have been treatin' us like dirt since we left Salt Lake. This bunch seems downright friendly."

"I told you they were good people," said Bill Aiden. "Always treated me square."

"I think we're gonna see a different attitude from here on," said Mitchell.

"How's that?" asked Joel.

"In case you didn't notice, most of the trouble has come from the Missouri bunch. They hate the Mormons and I think the Mormons hate them. Since we left Buttermilk Fort them boys've been keepin' to themselves. They don't want no trouble with us. Seems the only thing they understand is a loaded gun, and there's a lot more of us than there is of them."

"I think the Captain should've told 'em to head out a long time ago," said Joel.

"Can't fault your thinkin' on that," said Mitchell. "But you know the cap'n. He ain't one to turn his back on someone in need, and there ain't no question, they need us and they know it."

After giving the matter considerable thought, Robert Kershaw had come to the camp, too, toting a sack over his shoulder. Before he could approach anyone in the emigrant company, Seth Dodge stepped in front of him, barring his path. Dodge had come to the camp acting as policeman, walking around and intimidating the people from trading with the emigrants.

"What y'got in the sack, Brother Kershaw," he asked.

"I reckon that ain't none of your business."

"I'll make it my business when people go against the counsel of the brethren. You were at the meetin'. Them that trade with the emigrants will be cut off."

"I ain't willing to be cut off. I only came down here to gain information."

"What about?"

"That ain't none of your business either."

"Well, you just put your sack down if you don't want it reported that you were tradin' with the emigrants."

Kershaw gave in. He looked around at the crowd. No one seemed to be trading with the emigrants except for one man, John Morgan, who was trading a cheese for a bed quilt. As Kershaw was leaving, he could see Morgan being harassed by Seth Dodge. There would be hell to pay, if Dodge had anything to say about it.

On Sunday, more people came to the camp to talk, but not to trade. It was not exactly as Charlie Mitchell had predicted. True, the people did seem friendly, but subdued. Things were not going to get better. And they were going to get worse.

At about two o'clock the emigrant company broke camp and headed south. Captain Fancher was angered by the duplicity. A smiling countenance and the back of their hand. He couldn't get out of the Territory soon enough.

# 53

*August 31, 1857* The Fancher wagon train rolled up to the closed gates of Parowan late in the afternoon. In spite of their late start the day before, they had made about fourteen miles, stopping only for dinner and again when it was too dark to go on. They started again early in the morning, and after covering another sixteen miles to Parowan everyone was nearing exhaustion.

Like many of the outlying settlements, Parowan was a walled city, built in such a manner to protect against Indian depredations, though in most cases the gates were rarely, if ever, closed. No sentry was visible on the city wall, as if the townspeople had all gone away and locked the door behind them.

Captain Fancher rode up to the gate and called out, "Hello in the fort!" After waiting for a reply, Fancher tried again. "Can you open the gates?"

Bill Jones rode up and stopped alongside Fancher. "What've I been tellin' you? Now d'you know why we run 'em out of Missouri?"

"Mr. Jones," said Fancher, "I was predisposed to think you and your men were the cause of all our problems since we entered the territory, because frankly you're a pain in the ass. But now I'm not so sure anymore. I say damn them! Damn them all!"

Fancher turned his horse around and stood up in the stirrups. "Take 'em around! They ain't gonna let us come through!"

Wearily, Fancher led the company around the town to join up with the road south, which exited on the southeast side of the town and then took a southwesterly direction against the mountains and up a large swell known locally as Summit. In spite of their fatigue, Fancher was determined to put as much distance between them and Parowan as possible. He was a patient man, but they had now pushed him beyond his limit.

The emigrants camped at Summit Creek at about seven o'clock in the evening. Very little in the way of conversation had passed between Captain Fancher and William Aiden since he joined the company in Provo, so he was surprised when the young man sought him out.

"Captain Fancher, I'll be taking my leave of you for a spell. Back home in Tennessee my folks made the acquaintance of some Mormon missionaries. They lived with us for a while. They were fine people. I'm embarrassed to say that one of those young men lives in Parowan. He's written to us. My folks wanted me to look him up when I got here, so I'm going back."

"Young man, you're free to come and go as you please, but I think you're making a big mistake. These people will not receive you. You'd be better off to stay here."

"Sorry, Cap'n," said the young artist, spurring his horse. "I'll catch up as soon as I can."

Forty minutes later, William Aiden rode up to the gates of Parowan, which were now standing open. If anyone had noticed his approach, they must not have thought he was connected with the

Fancher company or perhaps they would have closed the gates again. He hailed the first person he saw on the public square and asked directions to the house of William Laney. A few minutes later he was knocking on the door.

A woman opened to him. "Is this where William Laney lives?" he asked.

"Who are you?" she replied.

"I'm Bill Aiden...from Tennessee."

"Oh, dear! You're with the emigrant train. Oh, dear!"

"Yes, ma'am..."

The woman started to close the door. From inside a male voice called out, "Who's at the door?"

In a moment the man appeared. He looked surprised and then happy. "Bill! Bill Aiden! Come on in!" He grasped the young man's hand firmly. "Got a letter from your folks awhile back. They said you'd be comin' this way, but by gosh, I never thought you'd really come."

The dinner hour had passed, but food was brought out and Bill Aiden had his first sit down meal in more than three weeks. They talked of old times until well after dark. In the morning Aiden was on his way back to the wagon train with a sack of fresh onions slung across his saddle. If he had known the grief that sack of onions would cause William Laney, he would certainly not have taken them. A short time later Laney was called out by some of the local men, and beaten senseless for trading with the enemy.

# Into The Net

# 54

*September 1, 1857* For the most part the citizens of Cedar City were recent converts to the Mormon faith, filled with zeal and enthusiasm because of the recent reformation within the church. They enjoyed a peaceful, yet tenuous, relationship with the local Indians, and they wanted to preserve it. They had been told of the approaching wagon train and the past difficulties the Fancher company had experienced during their journey south. Even though an army was coming against them from the States, an air of uneasy calm rested over the community. They had reported to Elder George A. Smith on his recent visit that they were ready to protect their religious liberty. If the government wanted to fight, they would be happy to oblige.

For their part, the emigrants had grown weary of the insolent treatment they had received over the past few weeks. They needed supplies. They expected to buy supplies. And they resented that the supplies had not been forthcoming. In the midst of this volatile, charged atmosphere, the wagons of the Fancher party arrived on that afternoon.

The founders of Cedar City understood the real meaning of hardship. On November 11, 1851, a small party of 35, mostly men and a few of their wives, had set up a camp in the cove of a knoll their second day out from Parowan. Their "city" was formed by setting the wagon boxes on the ground facing south in an east to west line. Each wagon was fronted on the south side by a semicircle of dirt and brush, higher than a man's head, to provide shelter from the wind, a place to build a fire for heating and cooking, and a semblance of privacy. These crude habitations were their homes for the first six months. These early pioneers had a twofold mission: to bring the gospel to the Indians and to produce iron. On September 30, 1852, they poured the first iron west of the Mississippi.

During the next three and one half years two forts were built. The first, a few rods southwest of the wagon box camp, and, the second, newer fort directly southwest of the old fort when the population of the community outgrew the original facility. In May of 1855, another city was laid out about a mile southeast when Brigham Young advised the Cedar City Saints to get to higher ground after three years of flooding. And now, two years later, the new city was beginning to grow, though many of the townspeople still lived in the new fort, which was already beginning to be called the "old fort", just as the old fort was now known as the "old, old fort."

Captain Alexander Fancher halted the wagons on the site of the original old fort, now torn down, and with a party of men rode into the new fort to try to do a little business. Except for some wheat they purchased from a man named Jackson, they were greeted with the same somber look and a shake of the head.

Fancher was furious. When he returned to the wagons, he gave instructions to move the company through the fort and on the road west three miles to the far side of the community fields. Meanwhile, he and three others rode over to the mill to get a grist done of the wheat he had just bought.

The miller was full of the faith and, though willing to grind the wheat Fancher had brought, refused to sell any flour.

"I'm sorry, mister," he said, "but I can't sell you what ain't mine. This grain belongs to someone else."

"Sorry?" exclaimed Fancher, pulling his revolver. "Why you sorry son-of-a-bitch, I'm buyin' 200 pounds of that flour. You can name your price, but by god you're sellin' it to me."

Fancher was backed up by three of the Missouri men. Normally, he didn't care for their company, but he had wanted the toughest, meanest men available. The miller decided not to make an issue of it. He ground the wheat and accepted payment.

By the time Fancher and his men got to the camp west of town, John M. Higbee, town marshal and counselor in the Cedar stake presidency of the Mormon church, had been notified of the incident at the mill. Because it was late, he decided to ride out early in the morning.

Higbee took two men with him in case he had to make an arrest. When he arrived at their camp, the emigrants were casually lying around as if they were in no real hurry to move on, as if they hadn't a care in the world. They had knocked down fences, turning their stock loose into the grain fields, and had used the fence rails for firewood.

"I'd like to speak to the head man," Higbee announced.

A crowd quickly grew around Higbee and his men. Fancher stepped forward. A few days ago he would have extended his hand in friendship, but no longer.

"I'm in charge here," he said. "State your business, then get out."

Higbee's face flushed with anger. "I'm John Higbee, the town marshal. It's been reported to me that you and some of your men took flour from the grist mill at the point of a gun."

"We paid a fair price," said Fancher.

"It's also been reported that your people have been swearing in the town and disturbing the peace. Some even came to the house of President Haight last night, drunk, demanding that he come out. I want all those people to come forward and accept judgment for their crimes. Pay the appropriate fine."

Captain Fancher laughed at Higbee. Soon, everyone was laughing. Joel and Charlie Mitchell were standing off to one side.

"Is this guy crazy?" asked Mitchell. "Does he think he can just walk in here like this and arrest someone?"

"I don't know, Charlie. I heard some of those Missourians went into town last night and caused trouble."

"I know, Joel, and I ain't defending that bunch. But these people have given us a rough time the past few weeks."

"Mr. Higbee," said Fancher, "We've been abused by your people ever since we came into the territory and we ain't takin' it no more."

"That ain't the way I heard it," said Higbee.

"We know about the army coming here from the east," said Fancher. "Met a few of 'em while crossin' the plains. Well, I'll tell you what. We've got us a fine herd of cattle here. We're gonna fatten 'em up so's we can feed the army we're gonna bring from California to clean out this nest of vipers. I hope to go back to Salt Lake and hang Brigham Young myself. So, Mr. Higbee, I'd advise you to get on out of here, before someone gets hurt."

Higbee's hand moved to the grip of the revolver tucked in his belt. Instantly, several guns were drawn by the emigrants. The clackity sound of hammers being drawn filled the air. Higbee felt a hot flash go through his body. Beads of sweat formed on his forehead and his mouth felt dry.

"All right," said Higbee, moving his hand away from his gun. "I ain't no fool."

Higbee carefully turned his horse, and he and his two companions rode back to Cedar. Forty-five minutes later, when he reported to President Isaac C. Haight, he was still quivering with rage.

# 55

*September 3, 1857* Thursday morning the Fancher company moved out, confident that they at last had put their troubles behind them. The road to California led west out of Cedar City, through

Pinto, Mountain Meadows, Santa Clara, and then onto the desert. An express rider passed them around nine o'clock and took the road south to New Harmony. He was carrying a message to John D. Lee, the Indian agent, the man who had the most influence with the Indians in the southern part of the Territory.

Philip Klingensmith came out of his house northeast of the public square in the fort and walked south along the street toward the community store. Down below the fort wall, close by the old school, he saw John Higbee and Isaac Haight engaged in conversation. Haight was the President of the Cedar City Stake of Zion, and the highest man in the Mormon priesthood in that vicinity, and second only to William H. Dame in all of Southern Utah. As Lieutenant Colonel, he was also second to Dame in the command of the Iron Military District. When Haight saw Klingensmith, he motioned for him to join them.

"Good morning, Bishop Klingensmith," said Haight. "I was hoping I'd see you today. We've been talking again about the emigrant company that passed through here yesterday."

"I've heard the charges against them, Brother Haight, and I've given the matter much thought since we talked yesterday," said Klingensmith. "For my part I would like to see this people go through unmolested."

Higbee was beside himself. He could not disguise his feelings of anger and disgust.

"Bishop, I don't think..." he began.

Haight silenced the man with a wave of his hand. He looked hard at Higbee as he pulled a letter from his pocket and held it up for Klingensmith to see.

"You may go with Mr. White over to Pinto Creek with a letter and tell the people there that these people shall go through, and try and pacify the Indians...for that people to go through."

Just then Joel White came up the street. "You sent for me?" asked White.

"Yes, I did," said Haight. "I would like you to take an express letter over to Pinto Creek. The letter is for Brother Robinson, the head man there. He is to pacify the Indians and let the emigrant company pass by unmolested."

"I will go over with you," said Klingensmith.

White looked at each man in turn. He had not been in town the day the emigrants passed through, but he had heard of the disturbance. He believed the offenders should be punished for their misdeeds, but he, as always, was willing to follow the counsel of the leading brethren.

"All right," said White. "I'll take the letter."

After White and Klingensmith departed, Higbee turned to Haight and asked, "What was that all about? I thought we had agreed to send them over the rim of the basin."

"And we shall," said Haight. "But it's not wise to include everyone in our plan just yet. If Bishop Klingensmith wants them to go through, it's all right for him to think that. He doesn't know what's in the letter but what we tell him. He'll come around when the time is right."

White and Klingensmith saddled their horses and started for Pinto in the afternoon. As they neared the lower end of the big field, about two and a half miles from town, they saw John D. Lee driving up in a wagon with his Indian boy Clem at his side. Lee reined his horses to a halt and spoke to the two men.

"Where're you going?" said Lee.

"We're carrying a message to Pinto," said White. "We're to see that the emigrant train goes through unmolested."

"I see. What are the feelings of the people about it?"

"The same," said White. "My orders are to pacify the Indians and see that they go through unharmed."

Lee looked grim. "I have something to say in that matter," he said, "and I will see to it."

White and Klingensmith made no reply. Lee drove on for Cedar City. The two messengers looked at each other.

"What do you suppose he meant by that?" asked White.

"I couldn't tell you," replied Klingensmith.

They looked back at Lee, then spurred their horses toward Pinto. They wanted to get there before dark if they could.

# 56

Lee entered the gates of the fort and stopped at the house of Isaac Haight. Haight was not there, so Lee continued through the fort and out the east gate toward the new town, where Haight had built a new home.

When Lee reached the new city, he met Haight on the public square of the town. Haight saw Lee and hailed him.

"Got your message," said Lee. "Came as soon as I could. What do you want with me?"

"I need to have a long talk with you, Brother Lee."

"What about?"

"It's a private matter. Particular business you might say."

Haight climbed aboard Lee's wagon and they drove over to Haight's new home, the first brick house built in southern Utah and a veritable palace by pioneer standards. They had a little supper and afterwards Sister Haight tucked Lee's Indian boy Clem into bed.

The two men took some blankets and went over to the iron works to spend the night, so that they could talk in private. At the iron works they spread out their bedrolls and got comfortable.

"Brother Lee, I'm sure you remember the counsel we received from Elder Smith last month. We are charged with protecting the southern territory from our enemies, whoever they might be."

Lee nodded.

"The train of emigrants I mentioned in the express I sent are a rough and abusive set of men. While traveling through the territory, they have been very abusive to our people. They have insulted and outraged our women. The abuses they have heaped upon the people during their trip from Provo to Cedar City, have been constant and shameful. They have burned fences and destroyed growing crops. I have heard that they poisoned some springs. People and stock that drank of the water have become sick, and some have died from the effects of poison. Why, one of them even proclaimed that he had the very pistol with which the Prophet Joseph Smith was murdered, and threatened to kill Brigham Young and all of the Apostles. While they were here in Cedar City, they said they have friends in Utah who would hang Brigham Young by the neck until he was dead before snow fell again in the territory. They also said that an army was coming from the East and they were going to return from California with soldiers as soon as possible and would then desolate the land and kill every damned Mormon, man, woman and child, that they could find in Utah. They violated our ordinances, and when officers tried to arrest them, they were driven off at gunpoint. They camped by the big field and burned a lot of the fencing. Now there is nothing to protect the crops from the herds of stock in the surrounding country. I heard they gave poisoned meat to the Indians at Corn Creek, and that their chief, Kanosh, is on the trail of the emigrants, and will soon attack them."

"These are serious charges," said Lee. "These people should be dealt with according to the law. They should not be allowed to transgress and then go their way. How many are they?"

"About a hundred I would say. Maybe more, maybe less. Unless something is done to prevent it, the emigrants will carry out their threats and rob the smaller settlements in the south. If they bring troops back from California, we're all liable to be butchered. I have counseled with the leading brethren today and it was decided to arm the Indians, give them provisions and ammunition, and send them after the emigrants, and have the Indians give them a brush, and if they killed part or all of them, so much the better."

"Brother Haight, who is your authority for acting in this way?" asked Lee.

"It is the will of all in authority. The emigrants have no pass from anyone to go through the country, and they are liable to be killed as common enemies, for the country is at war now. No man has a right to go through this country without a written pass. I met in council with Colonel Dame this morning and everyone agreed to let the Indians get at the emigrant train and use them up if they can."

"Brother Haight, I don't think you called me in to just tell me what is going to happen to those emigrants. What is it you want me to do?"

"Your orders are to go home to New Harmony, and send Carl Shirts to the Indians in the South. He is to notify them that the Mormons and Indians are at war with the 'Mericats' and bring all the southern Indians up. When there are sufficient Indians to make a successful attack on the emigrants, we will have them attack the train when they reach the junction of Mogatsu Creek and the Santa Clara. I have also sent Bishop Klingensmith and Joel White with a letter over toward Pinto to stir up the Indians and force them to attack the emigrants."

"I met them as I was coming into town today," said Lee. "That's not what they told me."

"It's not important for them to know our plans just yet," said Haight. "They will know when the time comes."

"Have you talked to Nephi Johnson, yet?" asked Lee. "He speaks the Indian language well."

"Not yet."

"He could be of great use to you," said Lee. "You could send him to stir up all the other Indians he can find. With a large enough force we'll give the emigrants a good fight."

"That's good counsel, Brother Lee. I'll send for him in the morning."

Several moments of silence passed. Lee was not opposed to a good scrap, particularly when it involved defending his religion. He had no doubt these were bad people, but encouraging the Indians to attack whites might turn out to be a mistake. What if the Indians, having tasted blood, turned on the local settlers, he reasoned. The only defense some of the settlements relied on was the goodwill they had established with the Indians.

"The more I think of it, the more I am troubled that we must rely upon the Indians to do our fighting," said Lee.

"These are the orders that have been agreed upon by the council, and it is in accordance with the feelings of the entire people," replied Haight.

"Wouldn't it be better to first send to President Young for instructions and find out what he thinks about the matter?"

"No," said Haight. "That is unnecessary. We are acting by orders. Some of the Indians are now on the warpath, and all of them must be sent out. All must go, so as to make the thing a success. It is intended that the Indians shall kill the emigrants. No white men are to be involved. If this thing is ever questioned, it shall be laid at their door and not at ours."

"You know what the Indians are," Lee protested. "They will kill all the party, women and children, as well as the men, and you know we are sworn not to shed innocent blood."

"Oh hell!" said Haight. "There will not be one drop of innocent blood shed, if every one of the damned pack are killed. They are the worst lot of outlaws and ruffians that I ever saw in my life."

The two men looked at each other in the darkness. Lee felt very uneasy. He wondered how high in authority this decision had been made. He remembered the visit of Elder George A. Smith in August. "Suppose an emigrant train should come along through this southern country," Smith had asked, "making threats against our people. Would they be permitted to go their way, or would the brethren pitch into them and give them a good drubbing?"

There must be some support for this action, Lee reasoned, for the brethren leading the people in the south would not dare to undertake such an action on their own.

"I expect you to carry out your orders," said Haight.

Lee understood the underlying meaning of that statement. The word and command of Isaac C. Haight were the law in Cedar City, and Lee believed that disobedience of his orders meant certain death. And, right or wrong, no Saint was permitted to question them. Lee had no wish to disobey, for he believed that his superiors in the Church were the mouthpieces of Heaven, and that it was an act of godliness to obey any and all orders given by them without asking any questions. Nevertheless, Lee was troubled. He wished that he could hear the counsel of Brigham Young. What would the prophet think of all this?

Their conversation at an end, Lee and Haight rolled up in their blankets and went to sleep.

Haight and Lee returned to Haight's house in the morning and had breakfast. As Lee got ready to start for home, Haight said to him, "Go, Brother Lee, and see that the instructions of those in authority are obeyed, and as you are dutiful in this, so shall your reward be in the kingdom of God, for God will bless those who willingly obey counsel, and make all things fit for the people in these last days."

Lee was impressed by all he had heard. He thanked Haight for his hospitality, and then he and Clem set out for home.

# 57

*September 4, 1857* Richard Robinson had read the letter from Isaac Haight the previous evening and put it away without sharing its contents. His orders were to gather the Indians and instruct them about the wagon train. As missionary to the Indians, he was the man they looked to as speaking for the Mormons. They were to have a free hand against the emigrants, to take all the cattle and other goods once the job was done. They were to gather at Pinto and wait for John D. Lee, who would direct them in how to mount the attack in the most effective manner. Finally, Robinson was told to discuss the plan with no one, not even the men who had brought the message.

About the time Lee started for home on Friday morning, Klingensmith and White were leaving Robinson's home. They had only gone a short distance when they came upon the Fancher train pulling up a long hill. Little conversation was exchanged as they passed.

Joel Deaton had seen the two riders. They rode by as if they hadn't seen the emigrant company. They must be Mormons, he thought. They had no gear except their horses and saddles, so they couldn't be going very far, and the only people in these parts were Mormons. He didn't care who they were. Like the others in the wagon train, he was tired of the treatment they had received the past few weeks. It didn't matter much anymore. In another three or four weeks they would be in Los Angeles and he would soon forget these unhappy experiences.

The day was sunny and clear, and Joel was on foot. He only got to ride one of Charlie Mitchell's horses when he was driving the herd, so he was enjoying the scenery as he trudged along. It was beautiful. If not for the hostility of the Mormons, he would be content to stay right here. The road was easy and led through narrow canyons, with plenty of timber and an abundance of water in the mountain streams and springs. A gentle breeze carried the smell of sagebrush, which was now in bloom, topped with a fringe that looked like a covering of yellow dust. Scattered everywhere were plants with bright purple flowers that Joel took to be thistles. It was wonderful to be alive and young enough to enjoy it. Three wagons ahead he could see Delia Huff. Joel shook his head. If only her mother could understand his feelings.

Before John D. Lee reached the New Harmony cutoff at Round Meadows, he came up alongside a large band of Indians under Moquetas and Big Bill, two Cedar City Chiefs. They were in their war paint, and fully equipped for battle. They spoke to Lee in the Indian language saying they had had a big talk with Haight and Higbee, and had received orders from them to follow up the emigrants and kill them all, and take their property as the spoil of their enemies. They demanded that Lee go with them and command their forces.

"No, I cannot go with you," said Lee. "I have orders from Haight, the big Captain, to send other Indians on the warpath to help kill the emigrants. I will go and do that. You must go where the emigrants are and camp until the other Indians come. I will meet you when all the Indians have come and lead you in battle."

The Indians appeared to be satisfied, but they needed assurance that Lee would come, so they asked him to send his little Indian boy, Clem, with them. Lee thought it over and finally consented to let the Indians take Clem with them. Not understanding what was happening the boy begged Lee not to leave him behind. With tears in his eyes, Lee embraced the boy and did his best to reassure him. As the Indians rode off with their hostage, the boy kept looking back. Lee wiped away his tears and climbed aboard the wagon. He gave a whistle and started for home again. What an ugly affair this was turning out to be.

About seven miles from Cedar, Klingensmith and White met Ira Allen. They stopped and exchanged greetings.

"Have you heard about the emigrant train?" asked Allen. Klingensmith and White allowed as they had, but declined to state the nature of their errand. "Well, the doom of the emigrants is sealed, the die has been cast, the doom fixed for their destruction. John D. Lee has orders from headquarters at Parowan to take men and stir up the Indians to attack the emigrants and destroy them."

White and Klingensmith looked at each other, but said nothing. Neither was particularly disturbed by the news, but they were both surprised that such a turnabout had come so soon. After some more small talk the riders went their separate ways.

At New Harmony, Lee began preparations for his expedition. He relayed the orders to his son-in-law, Carl Shirts. Lee didn't know how long his business would take, but he intended to be prepared for a long siege, if necessary, so he packed enough provisions for several days. He expected to leave by Sunday.

Late in the afternoon, the Fancher company came down out of the hills into the northern end of the Mountain Meadows. It was a beautiful valley, a sea of grass, rippling in the gentle summer breeze and fed by a multitude of springs. The valley was shaped roughly like a figure 8, about three miles wide in the northern and southern ends, but narrowed to about a mile in the middle where the slight ridge called the Rim of the Basin divided the waters of the Great Basin from the Colorado drainage. The mountains surrounding the valley were merely low, rounded hills, rising only a thousand feet above the valley floor and topped with juniper, sage, and scrub oak.

Near a spring at the northern end of the meadows was Jacob Hamblin's ranch. Hamblin had not yet returned from his trip to Salt Lake City, and had left the ranch in the charge of David Tullis and Samuel Knight.

Knight was from the settlement on the Santa Clara. He had brought his pregnant wife to the Mountain Meadows for relief from the summer heat. They were living in a wagon box at the side of Hamblin's house.

It was to Tullis and Knight that Alexander Fancher presented himself as the emigrant train rolled past the ranch.

"Is there water ahead?" he asked.

"Yes," said Tullis. "There's lots of water ahead."

"I was told by a man named Hamblin of a place called Mountain Meadows where we could recruit our stock before crossing the desert."

"This is it," said Knight.

Fancher looked around at the scene. He could see a large spring nearby and two Indian boys dressed in white man's clothing tending a herd. This would not be a good place to stop.

"Can you direct us to the best camping spot?" he asked. "We'll be stopping for a few days to rest up."

Knight walked over to the man and stood facing south.

"Follow the road south about three or four miles," he said, pointing. "When you get to where the road goes over a considerable hill, turn right instead, and go about half a mile to the spring. Directly west of the spring is a ridge. On the other side is a good meadow where you can graze your animals."

Fancher thanked the men and returned to the train. In another two hours they were setting up camp on the north side of the spring. It was a good camp site. The ground was soft and overgrown with a good stand of wire grass that covered several hundred acres. The spring drained into a narrow, shallow ravine that led into a canyon to the southwest. It was a peaceful, pastoral setting. The emigrants settled in for a long weekend of rest and relaxation.

# 58

*Sunday, September 6, 1857* A chain of circumstances had been forged, starting many years before. The Fancher party, the Missouri Wildcats, the Mormon leaders of southern Utah. Their separate destinies brought them together to act out a drama that none of them would have dreamed possible only a few days before. As in a Greek tragedy, the stage was set and all the players were beginning to take their places.

A strong force of Indians was gathered at Pinto, awaiting the arrival of John D. Lee to lead them against the emigrant wagon train. Orders delivered to Samuel Knight at Hamblin's ranch directed him to go south to the area around Clara to instruct the Indians to arm themselves and prepare to attack the emigrants. In a day or two, after the Arkansas company had vacated the Mountain Meadows, the Indians would pitch into them and punish them for all their perceived offenses during their stay in the territory.

Washington City was a city in name only. It consisted of about fifty families camped in wagons and tents on the sandy banks of the Virgin River, surrounded by desert. The people had set up an irrigation system, a marvel of engineering, considering their circumstances. Five hundred acres were under cultivation in corn, cotton, and grapes. The environment was harsh, but tolerable because of the faith and discipline of the people.

Only seven men were in the party of militia that left Washington when Carl Shirts arrived with the call-to-arms. Among their number were Harrison Pearce and his son Jim. The Pearce's had lived in Payson until late summer. The Fancher train had passed through four days before they themselves started south to their new home in Washington. The Fancher company had traveled slowly because their oxen were poor and because of their large herd. The Pearce's had quickly overtaken the emigrant company. Not much had passed between them, but Jim Pearce remembered speaking to some of the teenagers in the party.

Jim Pearce was only fourteen years old, and proud to be considered old enough to join the expedition to the Mountain

Meadows. Most of the company had guns along. Not owning one, Jim had to borrow one from a neighbor. Like some of the others, he wasn't really clear about their intended mission. They had heard a report of a wagon train passing through that had been causing trouble. He was taking the gun with him only because the others were. He certainly hoped he wouldn't have to use it.

On the way to Mountain Meadows, Jim kept silent, knowing that the opinions of a fourteen year-old boy were not welcome in adult conversation. He listened as all the rumors about the Fancher company were repeated in lurid detail: that they had been in the mob that had persecuted the Saints in the States, and poisoned springs and committed other outrages against the people during their trek through the territory, that they were going to raise an army of a thousand men in California, and return and exterminate the Mormons. The most provocative rumor was that some of them claimed they had helped to kill Joseph Smith.

There was wild talk amongst the men. Some talked of going to arrest the offenders among the emigrants. Others wanted to kill them all. Jim Pearce feared that what had started as a youthful adventure was taking shape as a nightmare.

Under the date of September 6, 1857, Rachel Lee inscribed in her diary ...*Bro J. D. Lee went on an expedition south Sunday...*

John D. Lee had ridden south out of New Harmony with a small group of Indians at about two o'clock in the afternoon. They took the trail over the mountains to the Meadows, a distance of only twelve miles. To have taken the wagon road would have involved a trip of between forty and fifty miles. Lee wanted to be finished with the nasty business as soon as possible.

At Mountain Meadows, the Fancher company was getting ready to pull out in the morning. The day before, Saturday, two men had been sent into the pines to make pine tar for axle grease, and had not returned. Sunday morning, Joel and Charlie Mitchell had gone to round up cattle that had strayed, with the added responsibility of looking for the men sent to make pine tar. They stopped to water their horses at Hamblin's ranch, and their reception gave no indication of what was afoot. They were anxious to get the job done. On Monday they would leave their troubles behind and start the long haul across the desert.

"They drove us out to starve. When we pled for mercy, Haun's Mill was our answer, and when we asked for bread they gave us a stone." President Isaac C. Haight's oratorical skills were in fine form at Sunday services in Cedar City. It was a fiery, militaristic sermon. "We left the confines of civilization and came far into the wilderness where we could worship God according to the dictates of our own conscience without annoyance to our neighbors. We resolved that if they would leave us alone, we would never trouble them. But the Gentiles will not leave us alone. They have followed us and hounded us. They come among us asking us to trade with them, and, in the name of humanity, to feed them. All of these we have done and now they are sending an army to exterminate us. So far as I am concerned, I have been driven from my home for the last time. I am prepared to feed to the gentiles the same bread they fed us. God being my helper, I will give the last ounce of strength and, if need be, my last drop of blood in defense of Zion."

Haight was a longtime member of the Mormon church, suffering through the persecutions at Nauvoo, where he had been a policeman and bodyguard of the Prophet Joseph Smith. He had led a pioneer company across the plains. Greatly respected by the people and always diligent in carrying out his assignments in the church, he had endured plenty over the years. Now it was time to pay back for all the wrongs and injustices.

At the conclusion of church services, the Stake Presidency and High Council gathered for their regular Sunday meeting. The main order of business was the punishment of the Arkansas emigrants for their transgressions against the community. Isaac Haight intended to gain ecclesiastical approval for the course of action decided at the military council at Parowan on Thursday morning. Seven men were present besides Haight: John M. Higbee, Ira Allen, Wesley Willis, Robert Wiley, and Bishop Philip Klingensmith and his two counselors, James Whitaker Sr. And John Morris.

The first to speak was President Haight. "Brethren, we are all aware of the grave situation that confronts us. Our lives, our homes, our religious liberty are in great danger. For ten years we have lived at peace in this territory. Now, with an army at our borders, our enemies come among us and think to mistreat us with impunity. The emigrant company, which passed through our city a few days ago, has broken our laws, abused our people, and have threatened to bring an army from California to exterminate us. The military council has met and our intention is to destroy that company before they can bring death and destruction down on our heads."

Isaac Haight spoke for several minutes, laying out the reasons for the intended action. As was the custom at council meetings, each man was allowed to speak in turn, to state his mind on the matters at hand. As counselor in the Stake Presidency, John Higbee spoke next.

"I have been to the emigrant camp upon complaint against their conduct at the mill. They knocked down fences and burned the rails. They turned their stock loose into the fields. When I sought to bring them to justice, I was driven off at gunpoint. I see no other choice than to cause the destruction of that company."

Higbee went on for several minutes in a similar vein and when he had made an end of speaking, Philip Klingensmith rose to his feet. He knew the seriousness of opposing the leading brethren, and he would follow counsel when a final decision had been made, but his interpretation of sustaining his leaders was not that he should blindly obey without question, but that he should support them with the best advice he was capable of giving.

"President Haight," began Klingensmith, "this matter weighs heavily upon my mind. I'm sure there are many good and logical reasons for taking this action. My concern is that if this thing should take place, what would be the consequences of such a thing? Will we someday be called to account for this? What effect will it have on us? Our families? Our community? I don't believe the reasons stated give sufficient cause for destroying the emigrants. I cannot speak in favor of it."

Ira Allen spoke next. He expressed his willingness to follow the orders of the military and ecclesiastical leaders. As Allen was speaking, Laban Morrill of Johnson's Fort entered the room and took a seat. He listened for a few moments, then leaned over to the man next to him and inquired about the preceding discussion. Morrill did not wait for his turn to speak.

"Pardon me for interrupting, Brother Allen, but I find these measures to be too extreme. Why not simply send out the militia and place the guilty parties under arrest?"

"They refused to submit to arrest a few days ago," said Higbee. "If they were to resist, some of our people might lose their lives."

"Besides," added Ira Allen, "there is no place to hold them and there is barely enough food for the townspeople, let alone sufficient to feed the emigrants."

What had started as an orderly discussion quickly turned into a passionate debate. Although the consensus was in favor of the destruction of the emigrants, Klingensmith and his two counselors stated their opposition to the proposal in the strongest of terms. Suddenly, Isaac Haight jumped up and walked out of the room.

"Just a minute," said Higbee to the others as he got up.

Outside, Haight stood fuming. Higbee came and stood by him, but said nothing.

"I hadn't expected this," said Haight. "If only one man was opposed, I could deal with that, but there are too many."

"Come back inside," said Higbee. "We'll work something out."

Inside, Laban Morrill was on his feet, pacing as he spoke. He seemed to be highly agitated.

"It matters not that the Indians are to do the dirty work," he said. "Even if I thought this was the best course of action, the Indians cannot be trusted to remain silent. I will never countenance such a course of action and I think it folly to proceed without obtaining approval of the presiding authorities in Salt Lake City."

Some who had spoken in favor of attacking the wagon train, though silently opposed to it, seized upon this suggestion. President Haight saw the tide had turned, and finally a vote was taken on the proposition to stay the planned attack upon the emigrants and to send a dispatch rider to Brigham Young as soon as possible. The motion was carried unanimously.

Near Pinto the Indians were still waiting for John D. Lee to appear. One of the chiefs, Moquetas, had fallen asleep near the fire as the potatoes and corn were roasting for the evening meal. He slept fitfully. He dreamed he saw himself approaching a pool of cool, clear water. He dropped to his knees and, cupping his hands, he dipped them into the water for a drink. Raising his hands, he saw they were filled with blood.

Startled right out of his sleep, the chief rose to his feet and began shouting to the assembled warriors. He had received a sign. No need to wait for the white man to lead them. The emigrants had been delivered into their hands. They must march for Mountain Meadows at once.

# 59

*Monday, September 7, 1857* Only two days past its full phase, the moon hung low on the western horizon and the stars in the eastern sky were beginning to fade as the first fires of the day were being lit in the Fancher camp. Joel lay sleeping next to the Deaton wagon. He and Charlie Mitchell had put in a hard day's work before returning to the camp around midnight. MacKenzie Deaton was up already, tending the fire on the north side of the camp. The elevation was around 5700 feet and, though still summer, the nighttime temperatures sometimes dropped into the forties. The fire toasted Deaton on one side as he froze on the other. About fifty yards south, near the spring, Rufus Pierce of the Missouri party was tending the other fire.

All of the remaining Missourians were up and standing

around the fire. Twelve of their number had left in a huff Saturday morning after an argument about not wanting to be slowed down on the desert by the wagon train. The fuss had raised a few eyebrows, but the Arkansas contingent didn't really care what the Missourians did.

The sound of a single rifle shot drew MacKenzie Deaton's attention. A woman began to scream as she dropped to her knees beside one of the children. Another shot and Rufus Pierce fell dead by the campfire. Several more shots came from the ravine that drained the spring south of the camp. Screaming and shouting amidst the gunfire, the people ran for cover. Deaton had taken only a few steps, shouting for Joel to wake up, when a rifle ball tore through his left shoulder and lodged against the shoulder blade. He dropped like a sack of potatoes, writhing in pain.

As Deaton struggled to crawl to the wagon, he heard a new sound. Dozens of voices shrieked Indian war cries as the Paiute Indians charged from the ridge west of the camp.

"Pa! Pa! Are you all right?" shouted Joel. He took his father's good arm and helped him to the wagon.

"Get your gun, Joel! Protect your Ma!"

Throughout the camp revolvers had been drawn and Kentucky rifles were fetched from the wagons. The emigrants laid down a deadly, accurate return fire. Several of the Indians fell wounded, and the rest began to retreat. The element of surprise had been lost.

Lee had arrived at Mountain Meadows on Sunday afternoon, and had set up camp while he looked the situation over. The plan was for Lee to wait until the wagon train pulled out, then fetch the Indians from Pinto and attack the emigrants while they were on the move. Lee was terribly upset by the early arrival of the Paiutes. He had tried to dissuade them from the attack, to wait until the wagon train reached the appointed place for the ambush, but the Indians were not to be denied. Their chief had been given a sign.

During the night the Indians had moved into position in the valley behind the west ridge. A small group had been sent down toward Mogatsu Creek Canyon and then crept back up the small ravine toward the spring. An overly anxious warrior had fired before anyone else was ready and the sporadic beginning had allowed the emigrants to get their guns and return fire before the full-scale attack could be mounted.

Lee's part in the attack had been to kill the herdsmen of the emigrant party, since he did not wish to be seen at the slaughter of the main camp. He had come upon one of the herdsmen sleeping. He shot at the man, but the cap burst without firing the charge in the chamber. The man awoke and ran for cover at the main camp. By now the attack was underway and the herdsman had to run through a hail of bullets. He never made it to safety.

As the Indians retreated, Captain Fancher moved among the wagons, assessing the damage and giving directions. A few men were posted to watch for a second attack, while most of the others heaved the loosely arranged wagons into a tight corral. The wheels of adjacent wagons were chained together. The two men detailed to guard the herd were missing and presumed captured at best, but probably dead. A trench four feet deep, five feet wide, and twenty feet long was dug in the center of the corral so the people could take cover. Holes were dug and the wheels of the wagons were lowered into them. The wagon covers were removed so the defenders could see what they were shooting at. Finally, the dirt from the excavations was packed under the wagons, so the Indians could not shoot under them.

In the corral, confusion had been replaced with order. Seven were dead and seventeen were wounded. Their situation was serious, but not impossible. Water would be a problem, because the spring was more than thirty yards from the corral and they had no way of knowing how many Indians might be hiding in the ravine.

The Indian camp was complete chaos. The Mormons had promised that God would protect them and now two or three of their number were dead and several wounded. They were howling mad. Some were already calling for a war on all the whites. Lee was having a terrible time trying to restrain them. He pointed out how hot the battle had been for him, that he had risked his life in the fray. One bullet had torn a hole in his shirt and another had cut the front of his pants and a third had pierced his hat, cutting the hair on the side of his head. Gradually, he began to regain control of the situation.

On the western ridge, several Indians had taken up positions behind the rocks and kept the emigrants pinned down by firing occasional shots into the corral. At first the emigrants returned shot for shot, but after a couple hours they only fired at targets they could see.

The Indians were not good military tacticians. They had never conducted a siege before, but it didn't matter. The emigrants weren't going anywhere because their ox teams were in enemy hands. Only a few horses that had been staked out in camp were available to them. For now, the emigrants could only wait and hope.

It had taken considerable time for Isaac Haight to prepare the letter to Brigham Young and get another letter from Col. Dame authorizing the bearer to requisition horses along the way to Salt Lake City. In the meantime, he had written another letter to Lee, ordering him to stay the action against the emigrants until he received further orders. Haight was in a quandary. He wished to see the emigrants destroyed, but in spite of his position as Stake President, he deemed it unwise to defy the council.

In the middle of the afternoon Haight summoned James Haslam to carry the dispatch to Salt Lake City and Joseph Clewes to take the message to Lee. By four o'clock Haslam had saddled his Spanish horse, a blazed-face bay Mustang that had been brought back from California by the Mormon Battalion, and was galloping along the road toward Parowan.

By late afternoon Lee had persuaded the Indians to let him go south for reinforcements. Obviously, the Indians on the field could not get the job done. About ten miles south of Mountain Meadows, at dusk, Lee saw a rider coming, leading a large group of men. It was Samuel Knight, some white men, and about a hundred Indians.

"Brother Knight," said Lee, "it's good to see you. What are you about?"

"Been down to Clara delivering orders that came in yesterday. Where're you headed?"

"I needed to get away. The Indians are very excited. I believe they would've killed me if I had stuck around any longer. They have made a muddle of it. They couldn't wait. Attacked this morning at first light. I was drawn into it myself. Look at this."

Lee showed Knight the bullet holes in his clothing. At Lee's suggestion, Knight and his party made camp for the night, but the Indians rushed on to join their friends at the camp on the Meadows.

The men gathered around the campfire to hear Lee's report. Lee was glad to see among the group his son-in-law, Carl Shirts. Some he recognized, others he didn't. Besides Knight, there was Oscar Hamblin, William Young, Harrison Pearce, James Pearce, John W. Clark, William Slade Sr., James Matthews, Dudley Leavitt, William Hawley, William Slade, Jr., George Adair, and John Hawley.

Lee told all that had taken place at the Meadows, but none of the men were surprised in the least. They all seemed to know that the attack was to be made. Eventually, the conversation turned to other topics, and the men broke up into smaller groups.

Far to the north James Haslam was still urging his horse along the road toward Beaver. At Parowan he had only paused to answer inquiries regarding his mission and then, without even dismounting, had ridden out the gates of the town.

Shortly after nine o'clock Haslam rode into Beaver and stopped at the house of Bishop Philo T. Farnsworth. He showed the note from Col. Dame. Farnsworth, only recently returned from his escort of George A. Smith, went immediately to fetch a fresh horse from Edward Thompson. Haslam ate a hasty supper, and by the time he had finished, the horse was saddled and ready to go. Though stiff and tired, Haslam was driven on by the knowledge that lives depended on his speed. He mounted the Pinto and rode out of the little village, urging the animal on as fast as he dared toward Fillmore.

# 60

*Tuesday, September 8, 1857* Haslam rode all night, picking his way in the waning moonlight through the foothills and mountain passes. Daylight was fast approaching on Tuesday morning, when he was stopped by a band of Paiute Indians between Cedar Ridge and Corn Creek. They were armed and their faces painted for war. Though their manner was threatening, making Haslam more than a little nervous, when they learned he was a Mormon, they seemed less disposed to kill him.

The Indians inquired about his business and Haslam told them he was on his way to see the "big captain" Brigham Young. He told them they were not to kill the emigrants, but they replied they were mad and they were going to kill them before Haslam could return. They repeated the stories about the poisoned ox at Corn Creek and then told of another wagon train camped at Beaver and how an Indian had been shot by these emigrants. Now they were on their way to make war on all of the emigrants. Once again Haslam warned them of interfering with the wagon trains, and then galloped on toward Fillmore.

The Pinto was barely able to move as Haslam entered the territorial capital Tuesday morning. Fillmore was mostly still sleeping and Haslam wished he was, too. He was only 32, strong and vigorous, but he was beginning to feel as if he had been carrying the load instead of the horse. He inquired of a man chopping wood and was directed to the house of Bishop Seymour Brunson.

At the bishop's house Haslam's knock was answered by a woman who looked tired and careworn, aged beyond her years by a life of work and privation.

"I'm James Haslam. Is the bishop here?"

"He's gone hunting."

Haslam's eyes darted around the property, looking for a barn or stable. "I need a fresh horse," he said.

"Don't have one," said the bishop's wife.

Haslam pulled Col. Dame's requisition order from his pocket and stuck it in the woman's face. "Here. I think you'd better read this."

Sister Brunson read the letter and handed it back. "It don't make no difference. We still ain't got a horse."

Haslam turned away. He was angry and frustrated, but he didn't want the woman to think it was because of her. He was only half way to Salt Lake. He thought of the people whose lives depended on the success of his mission.

"You might as well come on in and get some breakfast," said Sister Brunson. "Then you can get some sleep, too. I'll wake you when my husband gets back."

Dr. Schnitzler had probed MacKenzie Deaton's wound and extracted the ball, but he was in great pain. The laudanum had dulled his senses, but not completely. Deaton was also thirsty. During the night a party of men had tried to fetch water from the spring, only thirty yards away, but were driven back by Indians who were guarding it.

Captain Fancher called a meeting of all able bodied men. They gathered on the west side of the corral, so they could have cover from the Indians occupying the west ridge.

"I'll be honest with you," said Fancher. "It doesn't look good." He looked in the direction of MacKenzie Deaton, lying on the ground. "Some more of our people are going to die before this is over. We don't have teams to pull our wagons, and it'd be too slow anyway. We only got a few horses, so we can't make a run for it...at least all of us can't."

"What do you mean by that?" asked John Baker, an older gentleman who was called "Captain", though he had no authority in the emigrant company.

"I mean maybe someone...someone who is daring...might be able to ride for help."

Bill Jones, the man from Caldwell County, Missouri, was slowly stroking the edge of his Bowie knife on a small whetstone.

"And just where do you propose this daring someone would go for help?" he asked, cynically. "You know how we've been treated by the Mormons. They ain't gonna help."

"He's right," said John Prewett.

"I disagree," said Bill Aiden. "I know these people. They feel the whole world is persecuting them because of their religion. They always treated me kindly. They're just afraid."

"They got good reason to be afraid," said Bill Jones. "We drove 'em out of Missouri. Just didn't drive 'em far enough, that's all."

"I see no reason why we should put anyone at risk," said Captain John Baker. "We ain't the only ones traveling this road. There's bound to be someone come along sooner or later."

"It's the 'later' I'm worried about," said Fancher. "Some of the wounded will die, if we don't get help."

"We got food enough to hold out for weeks," said Jones.

"What about water? We need water," said Joel Deaton.

"Shut your mouth, kid," said Jones. "You ain't got nuthin' t'say I wanna hear."

"The boy's right," said Fancher. "Water is the one thing we can't do without...and we don't have any."

"Well, what I was gonna say," said Jones, "is that if we can get some water from the spring...not a lot, mind you... don't wanna get no one killed...but enough to hold out for a few days, me and some of the boys could take these horses and go for help in California."

Fancher looked at the man, unable to mask his feelings. "Do you really think I believe you'd come back?"

Jones' face flushed. He opened his mouth to speak, but thought better of it.

"I think we should stay right here," said Fancher. "The Indians haven't found the mark once since the initial attack. We have food and we'll get water somehow. If we kill enough of them, maybe they'll give up and leave. All right, all those in favor?"

By a show of hands the emigrants decided to stay put. They were safe for now, but in their hearts everyone knew they couldn't hold out for very long.

Lee and the others came on to Mountain Meadows early Tuesday morning. The road came up a narrow canyon and turned sharply northeast over a considerable hill. Half a mile to the west they could see the emigrant corral when they reached the bottom of the hill. It was an appalling sight. The Indians had killed a number of the emigrants' horses, and about sixty or seventy head of cattle were lying dead on the Meadows, which the Indians had killed for spite and revenge. The number of Indians had increased in Lee's absence. At least three hundred and maybe as many as four hundred.

Knight went on to Hamblin's ranch, while Lee and the others turned up a small hollow to the east and made camp by a spring. Lee ordered two of the men to round up one of the longhorns belonging to the emigrants. When the men returned, they slaughtered the critter and butchered it.

While the meal was cooking, Lee climbed to the top of a small hill a few hundred yards to the east of the corral for a closer look. He lay on his stomach and watched. A few Indians were around, but they ignored Lee. They knew who he was. Lee was safely out of range of the emigrants' Kentucky rifles, but the distance was also too great to see what was going on. Lee felt a twinge of conscience. He had never really been red hot for this undertaking. Now he wished he could find some way to get out of it.

After two days of having virtually nothing to eat, Jim Pearce ate with abandon. He never ate this good at home. And so he quickly made a pig of himself.

The hearty meal finished, Lee called the men together in council. "Brethren, I've had a look at the emigrant camp and they are in a pretty bad fix. I think they have been punished enough by the Indians and it's time to call them off."

"What about the orders we got from Cedar?" asked Oscar Hamblin.

"I know what you're thinking," said Lee. "Orders is orders and we're bound to obey. But I think they've paid for their crimes. Several have been killed by the Indians. If we let them go their way, they'll think twice about sending an army back from California. As far as orders is concerned, I think we can prevail upon President Haight to reconsider. If he does, we'll need reinforcements to persuade the Paiutes to withdraw."

After some more discussion, the decision was made. George Adair would ride to Cedar to inform Haight of the situation and seek relief for the emigrants. Lee walked with Adair to his horse.

"Tell Haight," said Lee, "for my sake, for the people's sake, for God's sake, send me help to protect and save these emigrants, and pacify the Indians."

The messenger started for Cedar City at about 2:00 P.M., expecting to get there late in the evening. Lee figured help would not arrive before late Wednesday or early Thursday. He prayed it would not be too late.

While Lee tried to quiet and pacify the Indians by telling them that he had sent to Haight, the Big Captain, for orders, the militia separated into two groups, the Washington men camping farther uphill and closer to the spring than the others. The Indians appeared satisfied by what Lee said, and expressed confidence that Haight would send word to kill all the 'Mericats', a corruption of the English words 'American' and 'emigrant', which the Indians used to describe all non-Mormons.

James Haslam groaned. He hurt in places where he had never

felt pain before. Slowly, he came to his senses and opened his eyes. He didn't recognize the strange room. Suddenly, he remembered where he was. From the angle of the sunlight coming in through the window, he knew it was late in the day. This was terrible! He lurched to his feet and staggered to the door and looked outside.

Sister Brunson was hanging out the washing. "The day is nearly gone," Haslam said angrily. "Why didn't you wake me?"

"Still ain't got a horse."

"The bishop is still out hunting?"

"Oh, he'll be back by dark. Always is."

The bishop's wife got some dinner for Haslam, then he went outside. He was too filled with anxiety to just sit. He checked on the horse he had ridden from Beaver. That animal wouldn't carry him another five miles. He'd just have to wait. Meanwhile, he explored the town.

Like most of the original Utah settlements, Fillmore had started out as a fort. This one had walls ten feet high that enclosed a large acreage. The front wall was made of cobblestones, while the rest were of adobe and rocks. Chalk Creek entered the fort on the east and exited to the northwest.

At dusk the bishop and several other men came riding into town. Haslam hurried to the bishop's house and showed him his requisition order. The bishop offered his own horse. Saddles were exchanged and Haslam was on his way again.

After only a few miles the horse began to falter, but Haslam pushed on. Buttermilk Fort was just ahead. He could get a fresh mount there.

He was wrong. No fresh horses were to be had at Buttermilk Fort. A messenger was sent back to Fillmore to get a better horse. Haslam threw his saddle on the ground and used it as a pillow. He cursed himself for not turning back as soon as he realized the horse was jaded.

"I don't understand," said Isaac Haight. "Didn't Brother Lee receive my express?"

"I didn't see one," said George Adair.

"This is terrible," said Haight. "I sent word to Lee to pacify the Indians until further orders could be had from higher authority."

"When was it sent?"

"Yesterday. Yesterday afternoon."

"The Indians attacked at dawn yesterday," said Adair.

"I see," said Haight, stroking his bearded chin. "Well, it's late. You may eat supper here, and stay the night if you wish."

Adair accepted Haight's offer of supper and a bed. The stake president didn't want to trust a message to an express rider, so he saddled his horse and set off for Col. Dame's house in Parowan. The two men conferred far into the night, planning a response to the situation at Mountain Meadows.

At three o'clock in the morning the messenger returned from Fillmore with another horse for Haslam. It looked fresh enough to ride, but so had the other one. He put his saddle on it and rode out of the settlement and into the hills that separated him from his next stop, Nephi.

# 61

*Wednesday, September 9, 1857* Shooting pains stabbed along the inside of Haslam's thighs, the skin raw. His lower extremities, from the knees down, were numb. He felt every jolt as the horse loped along the road. The sun was up, illuminating Mt. Nebo and the surrounding peaks. It was nearly seven o'clock in the morning and Haslam was keenly aware he was several hours behind the schedule he had set for himself. At Nephi he changed horses, got breakfast, and thirty minutes later he was back in the saddle.

The road from Nephi north stayed close to the mountains on the east. In less than two hours Haslam rode to the top of the swell that marked the southern edge of Utah Valley. Before him, glistening in the midmorning sun, was Utah Lake. Beyond the northern shore of the lake, he could see the Jordan Narrows, where the Jordan River flowed from Utah Lake on its journey to the Great Salt Lake. Haslam knew he would be lucky to reach Salt Lake City by the following morning.

Haight rode back to Cedar City with the orders he had received from Col. Dame, and sent for John Higbee.

"I've been to Parowan," said Haight. "Here are the orders for Major Lee."

Higbee took the document and read it:

*Compromise with Indians if possible by letting them take all the stock and go to their homes and let the company alone, but on no conditions you are not to precipitate a war with Indians while there is an army marching against our people.*

*As Indian Farmer and a Major in the Legion, I trust you will have influence enough to restrain Indians and save the company. If not possible, save women and children at all hazards. Hoping you will be*

*able to carry out the above orders in helping to make peace between the two parties.*
>        *By Wm. H. Dame Col.*
>        *Commanding Iron Military District*

"As usual, Col. Dame has managed to cover his own tracks," said Haight. "I'd like you to deliver these orders to Major Lee as soon as possible. That should make him happy."

Higbee folded the paper and put it in his pocket. He took a step toward the door and stopped. "There's something you might want to think about," said Higbee.

"What's that?"

"Col. Dame left us a lot of room to maneuver, if you take my meaning."

"I don't follow you."

"He said to pacify the Indians, if possible. Suppose it ain't possible?"

A look of understanding came into Haight's eyes. He looked thoughtful as he stroked his beard.

"I see," he finally said. "You may also call out the militia, Major Higbee. It'll take more than just a few men to pacify the Indians."

Isaac Delaney was hard at work in his carpentry shop. Since the day he heard Elder Smith's sermon, he had paid little attention to the talk of war. He knew most folks would rather talk about it than do anything about it. Oh, he had heard the rumors about the emigrants, all right, but he didn't see them as much of a threat.

Delaney was busy building an exterior door for one of the houses up in the new city when the message came. President Haight wanted to see him down on the public square in the old fort.

Joel White had heard nothing of the emigrant train since his return from Pinto. He was busy in the field hauling wheat when he noticed a rider approaching. It was John Higbee. He motioned to White, who went over to see what he wanted.

"Brother White, things have not gone well at Mountain Meadows. We have received an express from Brother Lee that the Indians have killed some of the emigrants and got the rest in a bad fix. The militia is being called out. Get your company's baggage wagon and report to the public square in the old fort."

"Didn't do no good to take that letter over, huh?"

"Doesn't look like it," said Higbee, as he turned his horse and rode away.

The militia was organized in companies of ten men. Each company had a baggage wagon kept by one of the men. When anything came up, the men knew right where to go. White went home as soon as he could, got his wagon loaded up, and went up to the square in the city.

Ezra Curtis, a lieutenant in the militia, brought the orders to Samuel Pollock.

"Remember the emigrant train that came through here last week?" he asked. "Well, the Indians have got 'em surrounded and just about wiped 'em out."

"We gonna help 'em?" asked Pollock.

"Looks like. We're sending a posse of militia out there right away to try and save the balance and bury the dead. We're assembling down on the square at the old fort. Bring a pick and shovel, and a spade if you got one, as well as a gun. Come as soon as you're ready."

John Bradshaw earned his living farming and making bricks. He had lived in Cedar City since the fall of 1852. He had heard of the Arkansas emigrant train coming before they arrived, but had given them little thought except that he had noticed a few of them that went out to get grinding done at the mill as they passed through. He was surprised when orders came to muster up. The Indians had killed the emigrants off, he was told, and the militia was to go out to bury them.

Isaac Delaney reported as ordered, along with his son John. They walked to the gathering in front of Col. Pugmire's house on the square. Isaac carried his rifle on one shoulder, a shovel on the other, and a Colt's revolver tucked in his belt. John was leading a horse with a shovel and rifle strapped to the saddle.

Delaney saw several wagons with men in them. The sun had just gone down, and even though it was getting dark, Isaac could recognize several of the men in the group: Jimmy Williamson, an old Scot, John Higbee, William C. Stewart, David Stoddard, Ezra Curtis, Robert Wiley of the High Council, William Bateman, Thomas Cartwright, and Samuel Pollock. Joel White was just driving up in his baggage wagon. Delaney couldn't recognize any others in the waning light.

White drove around to the rear of the wagons that were ahead and began loading in some baggage that was waiting for him there. Just then John Bradshaw came up, carrying a shovel on his shoulder. Isaac Haight was speaking to the assembled men.

"If it hadn't been for some old fools tampering with the Indians, they would have been dead and in their graves by this time. Never mind," he said, "they have only got further into the net."

Haight noticed Bradshaw standing on the edge of the group. "How do you come to carry just a spade?"

"I was told the emigrants were killed by the Indians," said Bradshaw.

"All right. But where's your gun?"

"I didn't know that a gun was wanted to bury the dead."

"Bradshaw, you're a damned fool. You don't understand things."

"How's that?"

"You don't know what's going on here, do you? You don't know beans about it. If you did, you'd've brought your gun."

"Even if I had brought it," said Bradshaw, defensively, "I don't have any ammunition for it."

Haight looked disgusted with the man. "You can go home. I have no further use for you."

The militia loaded up and pulled out. Except for the leaders, no one had a clear understanding of their purpose. Haight's speech only confused the issue. Some thought they were on a mission of mercy, while others believed they were to see the emigrants didn't get away.

Joel White had only one man with him in his wagon, Jimmy Williamson. Some of the wagons carried mostly baggage, and some carried mostly men. A few men rode horses. The distance to the Meadows was almost forty miles, and there would be no moonlight to show the way until around midnight.

The sound of gunfire from the west side of the valley roused the men in the militia camp at Mountain Meadows. The Indians had renewed the attack just before the sun set. They kept up a steady crossfire from the west ridge and the ravine by the spring. They had built miniature parapets of stones on top of the ridge so they could shoot without exposing themselves to return fire. Behind the ridge, the Indians' best archers were lofting arrows into the air that fell in the middle of the circled wagons.

John D. Lee, William Young, and John Mangum ran across the northern end of the wire grass meadow to the backside of the west ridge, their purpose to get the Indians to stop the attack. The Indians were so excited they fired a volley at Lee and his companions. When Lee got to them, he spoke to them as best he could in the Indian tongue. He told them the Great Spirit would be mad at them if they killed the women and children. An emotional man, tears came to Lee's eyes as he sought to induce the Indians to break off the attack.

When the Indians saw the tears, they laughed at him and called him "Yaw Guts," a derogatory expression in the Indian language meaning "cry baby." Lee's entreaties were to no avail. After a time Oscar Hamblin, an excellent interpreter, came over from the militia camp and was able to convince the Indians to stop the attack.

Inside the wagon corral the people had rushed to the side of the wagons for shelter from the arrows. The emigrants were returning fire, but hitting nothing. After about half an hour, the shooting stopped as suddenly as it had begun. It was too dark for either side to see the other.

Distraught, Lee headed back to the militia camp. He realized his influence with the Indians was less than he had previously thought. The emigrants were in greater danger than ever.

Back at camp Lee noticed a man rolled up in a blanket, moaning. "What's wrong with him," asked Lee.

"That's my boy, Jim," said Harrison Pearce. "Ate too much beef and got himself a case of the botts."

"Too bad. We need every man we've got."

Captain Fancher called another council.

"We've gotta have water!" said William Cameron. "I've got five kids and they're sufferin'."

"Ammunition's gettin' low," said Abel Baker.

"All right, all right," said Fancher, holding up his hands. "It's plain to see we're gonna have to take action."

"My offer still stands," said Bill Jones. "A couple of riders and good horses...we could be in California in just a few days."

"I think we should ask the Mormons for help," said Aiden.

"You'll get no help from them," said Dick Wilson.

"That's right," added Bill Jones. "D'you think the people up at the ranch don't know what's goin' on down here? They heard the shootin', they had to. If any help was comin' it'd be here by now."

"I have a friend in Parowan," said Aiden. "He'll help us. I know he will. They won't turn on one of their own."

"I think Aiden's right," said Fancher. "It's dark. A couple of riders could slip out before the moon comes up and be there before morning."

"And just who might these riders be?" asked Jones.

"We could draw lots," said Fancher.

"No!" said Jones. "One of my men has gotta go along."

"I'm open to suggestions," said Fancher.

There was a moment's hesitation. "Of course, I'll have to go," said Bill Aiden.

"Like I said," added Jones, "One of us has gotta go, too, so it's gonna be me."

Captain John Baker cleared his throat. Everyone looked in his direction. "My boy, Abel, is a good horseman. If he's willing, I'll send him."

"There, you see?" said Jones. "Now everybody's represented."

"I'm not opposed," said Fancher. "Let's vote on it."

The motion carried unanimously. A light was struck in the trench and a letter written. It was signed by every man in the company. Three horses were saddled, and each man was given some food and armed with two revolvers and a rifle.

The faint glow in the sky from the west side of the ridge and the singing and chants of the Indians gave the emigrants hope that the riders could get away undetected. To the east they saw two campfires about a mile away up a hollow. They didn't know it was the Iron County militia. Aiden, Baker, and Jones, led their horses out of the corral and walked slowly and silently to the northeast. A small hill was about two hundred yards to their right and the rocky ridge was to their left. Each man carried a revolver in his hand.

In about ten minutes they had come to a rise in the ground. On the other side of it they were out of sight of the corral. They mounted their horses and started out at a walk. A few minutes later, when they could no longer hear the Indians, they spurred their horses to a faster pace.

As the miles accumulated slowly, Haslam was falling further behind schedule. Payson. Provo. American Fork. Well after dark, Haslam reached the Jordan Narrows. Exhausted and in a dreamlike state, he allowed the horse to drift. He was making little progress at all.

The trail through the mountains to Cedar City was hard to follow in the darkness. It would likely take all night to get there. The moon, in its last quarter, had just risen and provided some illumination, but not enough to satisfy Aiden. He was anxious to get to Parowan and safety.

Little conversation passed among the three men. Aiden's thoughts were about the several months he had spent in Utah. It had been the best time of his life. He had done a lot of sketching and painting, but more important he had made a lot of new friends. This one fact caused him the most distress. How could a people so full of love and kindness also demonstrate so much hostility?

Nearly two hours after they had slipped out of the wagon corral, Aiden, Baker, and Jones crested a hill and saw the glow of a campfire through the trees. The three riders drew up side-by-side and stopped.

"What d'you think?" asked Baker.

"I don't know," said Aiden. "We only come about six or eight miles. I doubt it's any of the local people. What's your feeling on it?"

"Could be Indians," offered Baker.

"Not likely," said Jones. "They'd be camped back at Mountain Meadows."

Aiden's eyes swept the horizon. Hills as far as he could see in the dim light. "It'll take too long to go around," he said.

"Then let's just go right on down and see who it is," said Jones.

"Too dangerous," said Aiden. "If we couldn't trust the people back at the ranch, I don't want to trust these strangers, either. We'll have to go down and try to find a way around."

"I'm game," said Baker.

"Okay, let's do it," said Aiden, booting his horse to a slow walk. He knew they had no real choice. He felt like a little kid again, taking the shortcut through the cemetery, coming home from the Halloween party. Sure, there were no ghosts or goblins, but he still had a knot in his stomach.

Bill Stewart was sitting on the ground, half-asleep. He didn't know why he was doing sentry duty anyhow. But this was the militia and the leaders liked to play at being soldiers. They had been on the road for hours and had stopped and camped on the east side of Ritchie Spring to rest and water the horses.

Stewart heard a noise and looked up. The three horsemen were almost upon him. In the dark he couldn't see who they were, so he decided to get up and play the sentry in case it was some of the leading brethren.

For their part Aiden, Baker, and Jones were approaching the campsite warily. Nice and easy. They could see a number of men in the moonlight, some asleep and others talking, a couple of uncovered wagons, some horses, and a few mules staked out nearby.

Aiden stopped on the west side of the spring and the other two came up on either side of him. Pointing to the right, he said quietly, "Let's water the horses and go around. We don't know these folks, and we can't be too careful."

Suddenly, Stewart stepped out of the darkness. "Who's there?" he demanded. "State your business!"

Aiden and his two companions were startled. It was more than fifty yards to the camp, but from the looks of things the challenge had been heard. Some men were coming in their direction. It was time for some fast talking.

"Howdy. I'm Bill Aiden...from Tennessee. We're with an emigrant company stopping at Mountain Meadows. We're in a terrible fix. Indians have been attacking us for three days running. Must be three, four hundred of 'em."

Stewart squinted in the darkness, looking at each man in turn. To Jones he cried out, "I know you! You're in a bigger fix than you realize. You're one of 'em who killed widow Evans' chickens and then threatened to shoot her."

Stewart raised his rifle. Aiden urged his horse forward, his hand in the air. "Wait!"

Bill Aiden was only two to three paces away when Stewart fired. He saw the bright flash of the muzzle and felt himself being hurled backwards.

Aiden landed in a heap on his back, his mind reeling. Above him he could see the stars through the trees. He knew he had been shot, but he couldn't believe it. He struggled to get up. He felt a terrible burning in his gut where the .58 cal. Slug had ripped apart flesh and organs.

Baker and Jones were stunned. They turned their horses around to flee. Baker hesitated. He wanted to help his fallen companion, but his survival instinct took over. He heard shouting and the sound of men running. Joel White and Benjamin Arthur were the first men on the scene. While Stewart was reloading his gun as fast as he could, White fired at Baker and Jones. Abel Baker cried out in pain and tumbled from his horse.

"Got 'im!" yelled White.

Baker got back on his feet. The bullet had passed between his body and his left arm, ripping through his clothing and glancing off his ribs. Raising his left hand to grasp the saddle caused unbearable pain. "Help me!" he yelled at Jones.

"C'mon!"

"I can't!"

Bill Jones jumped from his horse. He grabbed Baker by the collar and the seat of his pants and heaved him onto the horse's back. "Let's go!" he said, mounting his own horse.

"What about Aiden?"

"There ain't no helping him!"

Amidst the sound of gunfire and bullets whining past them, Jones and Baker rode off into the darkness, west toward the Mountain Meadows. Both of them now knew the horrible truth that everyone had suspected, but that no one had wanted to give voice to: they were completely alone. Their cries for help would only fall on merciless ears.

John Higbee was about the only man among the militiamen who wasn't holding a gun. He was also the only one who was calm in the midst of chaos. The others were firing wildly into the darkness in the direction Baker and Jones had gone.

"All right!" shouted Higbee. "That's enough!"

The men stopped shooting. Higbee went over to where Bill Aiden lay on the ground. The fallen man was still alive.

"Who did this?" asked Higbee.

"I did, John."

Stewart couldn't see Higbee's face in the dark. Had he been able to, he wouldn't have been so quick to claim responsibility. Higbee turned to the militia and addressed them all.

"I don't know how this happened. We weren't supposed to get involved. The Paiutes were supposed to take care of business, but they made a mess of it, and there was a change in plans. We were sent out to help these people, not kill 'em. There's bound to be trouble over this." Higbee paused to let his words sink in. "All right, let's move on out of here."

Bill Aiden lay thinking about home and family, and all the things he had planned to do. His eyes darted around at the militiamen. In the darkness he couldn't see their faces or detect any sign of compassion. No one came to his aid. He was conscious of the pain and that his feet felt cold. In a few minutes he lost consciousness from loss of blood. And then, while Higbee and the others set about loading up, William Aiden, the young artist from Tennessee, gasped twice, shuddered, and died.

Getting back into the wagon corral was almost as hard as getting out of it. Jones and Baker crept up to the wagons, leading the horses. They had managed to make it back without being seen by the Indians. In the corral, David Beller was on guard at the north opening of the circled wagons. He saw the dark shapes approaching. He waited until they were almost upon him. "Hold it right there! If you move, you're a dead man!"

"It's me, Bill Jones."

"Come ahead," said Beller.

Alexander Fancher was roused from his sleep first, then others, hearing the commotion, got up from their beds too. "Where's Aiden?" asked Fancher.

"We was ambushed," said Jones. "Aiden's dead."

"Indians?"

"Whites."

Fancher turned and moved away a few paces. He needed to think.

"What're we gonna do, Cap'n?" asked someone in the darkness.

"I don't care what anyone else's gonna do," said Jones. "I brought Baker back. Now I'm headin' for California."

"We have no other choice, do we?" said Fancher, turning around.

"Nope."

Fancher looked at the quarter moon just overhead and guessed the time. "It'll be getting light in a few hours. We'd better get things ready."

Another council was held. With only four fresh horses, Jones demanded that he be allowed to go. Someone suggested drawing lots, but Fancher asked for volunteers. No one said it, but many of the men realized that these messengers would have the best chance for survival.

As owner of two of the horses, Charlie Mitchell said he'd like to go, but, since he had a wife and child, his younger brother Lawson would go instead. MacKenzie Deaton had been listening to the proceedings. When no one else spoke up, he did.

"My boy Joel is young and hardy. He'll bear up on the ride better than most older men."

"I don't want no kid along," said Jones.

"It's not up to you," said Fancher. "How about it, Joel? Do you want to go?"

Joel looked at his parents. He was unsure. His father wanted him to go, so he must have a good reason for it. MacKenzie Deaton motioned for his son to come closer.

"Joel," he said, "we're in a real bad fix. We might not get out of it. Someone has to preserve our family name, our heritage. Laura Jean's too young. I'm hurt. Your ma can't go. So that just leaves you. I want you to go and I want you to take my journal for safekeeping. If things don't work out, I want to be remembered."

"All right," said Joel. "I'll do it."

No one else volunteered, so lots were drawn. Dick Wilson was the one chosen.

Food was brought out and the horses saddled. They took no water. Those left behind would need it, while Joel and the others would be able to find water along the way.

The four men led their horses out of the corral on foot. They had gone less than a hundred yards when a shot was fired in their direction. They quickly mounted their horses and headed for the mouth of Mogatsu Creek Canyon. A few more shots, and then silence.

The terrain descended rapidly. Joel Deaton and the others were making good time. Jones was in the lead, then Lawson Mitchell, then Joel, and then Wilson bringing up the rear. They were just at the southern end of Mogatsu Creek Canyon when Mitchell suddenly cried out. Joel looked up and saw the young man flying through the air as his horse tumbled to the ground.

"What's up?" said Jones.

Everyone stopped and dismounted. Joel ran over to Mitchell.

"You all right, Lawson?"

Mitchell was on his hands and knees. "Damned horse must've stepped in a hole. Banged up my ribs some, but I think I'm okay."

The horse was back on its feet. Wilson caught it and brought it back.

"It's no good," said Mitchell, after he had checked the animal over. "This horse'll never carry me."

"We'd best cut 'im loose then," said Jones. "Hide the saddle. We don't want 'em to know we're ridin' double. If you're hurt, you'd better ride alone. Two of us will double up."

"That'll wear down a horse mighty quick," said Mitchell.

"We'll take turns," said Jones.

Lawson Mitchell took Joel's horse and Joel rode behind Wilson. They rode on in the darkness, but more carefully now.

# 62

*Thursday, September 10, 1857* The sun was well up above the peaks of the Wasatch range when James Haslam reached Willow Creek. It was less than twenty miles to Salt Lake City. He wanted to urge his horse to a greater pace, but the animal was almost as tired as he was. Only another three or four hours.

The militia stopped at Pinto Creek and got some breakfast at daylight. An informal council was held about the killing at Ritchie Spring.

"I don't see how we have a choice," said Joel White. "Killing that man was a big mistake, but how can we let 'em go now?"

"I was sent out to bury the dead and save the rest," said Samuel Pollock. "I won't lift a hand against the emigrants unless I am ordered to do it. And I'm not sure I will even then."

The discussion continued for several minutes. Only a few men were willing to offer an opinion. In the end they decided that John Higbee, as senior officer, would ride back to Cedar to inform the authorities and get further instructions. Higbee looked again at the order to save the emigrants, signed on Wednesday by Col. Dame. He wouldn't be needing it after all. He folded it and put it away.

In spite of their agreement to wait until orders were received from Haight, the Indians had made a determined attack on the train about daylight. The emigrants were still effective with their Kentucky rifles. The Clara Indians had one brave killed and three wounded, which was enough for them. They left for home driving a large number of cattle with them.

Lee climbed the small hill two hundred yards east of the wagon corral. He was bolder now, standing upright. At that distance he didn't expect anyone to recognize he was a white man. After awhile he saw two men leave the corral and run to the spring with buckets. They quickly filled them with water, and ran back. Bullets flew around them thick and fast, but they got into the corral safely. Lee shook his head in wonderment. He admired their grit.

Lee went back to the militia camp, got breakfast, and then lay down for a nap. Later, when the reinforcements didn't come, he got up to go have another look. He wasn't very good at waiting.

"Where're y'going, Brother Lee?" asked John Mangum.

"I think I'll cross over the valley and go up on the other side on the hills to the west of the corral and take a closer look at the situation."

As Lee was crossing the valley, he heard shouting from the wagons. He figured they must have seen him, because they ran up a white flag in the middle of their corral. Then two little boys from the camp came out as if they were looking for Lee. Lee hid in the brush. He wanted to avoid contact with the emigrants until he had heard from Haight. After some time the boys gave up and turned back toward the wagons.

As Lee continued on to the west side of the rocky ridge, he was met by several Indians asking for ammunition with which to kill the boys.

"No!" said Lee in the Indian tongue. "You must not hurt them! I will kill the first one of you who tries!"

Lee opened his coat and showed them the revolver tucked in his belt. Coolly, he glared at each of the Indians. Sullenly, they turned and rejoined the other Indians up on the ridge.

Joel found a shady place by some scrub oak and sat down. The sun had not yet reached its zenith, but it had already begun to cook his brains. In contrast, the night air had been quite cool when they left the lofty environs of Mountain Meadows. Ahead lay ninety miles of desert to cross. If it was this hot now, Joel wondered, how would they make it across the desert. He tried to make himself comfortable by stretching out full-length. It was of little use. His backside felt like he had spent the past few hours straddling a picket fence rather than a horse. He was beginning to regard the animal as a mortal enemy instead of the means of his deliverance.

Joel was overcome by exhaustion and a sense of melancholy. The others must have felt the same way. Their conversations were brief and subdued, then ceased altogether. Each seemed to turn inward as they sprawled on the thick, coarse grass. Except for Bill Jones. He kept scanning the horizon with his field glasses, searching for any sign of pursuit.

When the horses had drunk their fill at the spring, they began drifting slowly around, grazing on the sparse grass. It was a scene of peace and tranquility, unlike their former situation. Joel succumbed easily to the lure of sleep and soon his mind was tormented with vivid images of Mountain Meadows.

Joel didn't know what had roused him from his sleep. As he awoke, his eyes focused on his three companions. Lawson Mitchell was looking intently with the field glasses in the direction they had recently come. The other two men were crouched behind him. Dick Wilson reached for the field glasses.

"Let me have a look," he said.

The transfer of the instrument from one man to the other was more a taking than a giving. Wilson studied the situation for several moments.

"Well?" said Mitchell. "Is it them?"

"Can't say for sure."

"Gimme that!" said Jones, tearing the field glasses from Wilson's hands. Jones raised the instrument to his eyes for another look. "Yeah. It's them all right."

"How many?" asked Mitchell.

"Thirty, forty, mostly Injuns. Two or three whites."

"Damn!" said Wilson.

"They seen us yet?" asked Mitchell.

"Not likely," said Jones. "Too far away."

"Maybe we c'n hide out," offered Joel.

Jones dismissed the suggestion with a glance at the boy, then turned to the others. "We'd best be goin'."

Quickly, the men rounded up the horses and packed their gear. Mitchell took hold of a stirrup and tried to raise himself up. He cried out in pain.

"Sorry, boys. You're gonna have to help me get on board this critter."

Wilson and Jones helped him up while Joel mounted the horse Jones had been riding. When Mitchell was securely situated, Jones slapped the horse's rump and let out a whoop. The horse sprang into motion, almost spilling its rider, then galloped off down the trail.

Wilson swung into the saddle he and Joel had shared for the last twenty miles, and said, "C'mon! Let's go!" He rode off after Lawson Mitchell.

Jones just stood looking at Joel. "That's my horse you're sittin' on, boy."

"But, Mitchell's on mine!"

"Don't none of these horses belong to you, boy."

Joel's face reddened with anger and fear. Of course, Jones was right, but this was a life or death situation.

"We got some hard ridin' to do, boy. Two of us on one horse won't get far. Ain't no use in both of us gettin' kilt. Now, are y'gettin' off by yourself or am I gonna have to help you?"

Joel looked at Jones, pleading with his eyes. Jones just shook his head slowly. Joel looked down the trail, then suddenly spurred his horse. But it was too late. Jones had hold of Joel and the reins. The horse reared and Joel tumbled to the ground. With some difficulty, Jones mounted the now skittish animal and looked down at the boy.

"You wanted to hide out," he said. "Here's your chance, boy."

Without another word, Jones turned the horse and spurred it to a gallop. In moments he was out of sight around a bend in the trail.

It had grown quite still at Mountain Meadows. Though the Indians were careful not to show themselves, the emigrants knew they were there. Toward the northern end of the west ridge was an outcropping of rock with a small clump of scrub oak growing on it. A natural seat was formed by the rock, so Lee sat down on it. He could watch the corral quite comfortably, yet be safe from any firing from the emigrants. He stayed on the west side of the valley for about two hours, looking down into the wagon corral, contemplating the suffering of the unfortunate emigrant company. Were it possible, he would turn back the clock a few days and see them safely on their way. Even though people made things happen, he also knew that the human participants are often molded by the events. The situation was well beyond his control, and had been ever since the Indians were brought in. He had warned Isaac Haight of the possible consequences, and now it was obvious a heavy price would be extracted. He didn't see how it could be avoided.

Lee was still deep in thought when he saw two men leave the corral and go outside to cut some wood. The Indians kept up a steady fire on them, but they paid no attention to danger, but kept working until finished, and then went back into camp. Worn down with trouble and grief, Lee got up and wearily made his way around the wire grass meadow to the militia camp to wait for word from Cedar City.

Haslam had been pacing back and forth for several minutes when the door to the President's office opened. The imposing figure of Brigham Young stood framed in the doorway. "I understand you have an express for me, Brother...?"

"Haslam, sir."

"Come in, Brother Haslam."

Haslam followed Brigham Young into his office. A half dozen other men were present. Haslam recognized John Taylor, the Apostle, and Daniel H. Wells, Counselor to Brigham Young and commanding general of the Nauvoo Legion. As a group, they showed no interest in him, carrying on quiet conversations among themselves.

"Let's see this important message," said the Prophet.

Haslam took the letter from inside his coat and handed it over. Brigham Young slipped on his glasses and read the dispatch. When he had finished, he turned his attention to the express rider. "Have you read this?"

"I am familiar with its contents," said Haslam. "Some of the leading brethren in the south want to send the emigrants over the rim of the basin, to use them up."

"What is your opinion?"

"I will follow the counsel of my leaders."

"As you should, Brother Haslam," said the Prophet. "It will take some time to compose a response. How long have you been on the road?"

"Since Monday afternoon."

"You had better go and lie down and take a little sleep. Can you stand the trip back?"

"I am your servant, sir."

"Very good, Brother Haslam," said the Prophet. Brigham Young took out his watch and looked at it. "Come back at one o'clock. I will have a message for you to carry back."

After Haslam left, Brigham Young sat down and read the message a second time, aloud. When he had finished, he looked around the room at the others. No one spoke.

"Brethren," said Brigham, finally, "this unfortunate turn of events in the south threatens to undermine our efforts to reach an accord with the army. President Isaac Haight has put the Indians onto an emigrant company at the Mountain Meadows. He reports the emigrants are of the lowest sort and have caused much trouble during their passage through our settlements. A fortnight ago I would have bid our Lamanite brethren Godspeed in their errand of destruction, but the visit of Captain Van Vliet persuades me that we must pursue another course. We must convince our enemies that we are like a wounded bear, powerful and dangerous if pushed into a corner, but ever willing to live in peace if left alone. Brother Haight proposes to call out the militia to assist the Indians in their purpose. I can think of nothing that would do more to impede our cause than our involvement in the destruction of a company of emigrants. On the other hand, if we could assist the emigrants to safely complete their journey, it could accrue to our benefit. It would be noised abroad amongst the gentiles that we are a peaceful people. Therefore, I propose that we counsel our brethren in the south to assist the emigrants and mollify the Indians if possible. Now, I would be interested in hearing your thoughts on the matter."

The discussion was short. It was generally agreed that every effort should be made to convince the southern leaders that the danger was not so serious as previously supposed. A clerk was summoned and the reply to President Haight was prepared.

The militia descended the long hill into the north end of Mountain Meadows and stopped at Jacob Hamblin's ranch to water their teams. Samuel Pollock wasn't very familiar with the area, but he knew some of the people. Three or four hands, he supposed, were working at the ranch. He spotted David Tullis and went over to chat. They exchanged pleasantries and then their conversation turned to the situation at the south end of the Meadows.

"How long has this been going on?" asked Pollock.

"I first heard shooting on Monday morning and several times since. When the wind's blowing, I can't hear anything."

"What's it like down there?"

"I ain't been down there yet," said Tullis, "and I'd just as soon not. I hear the Indians have killed several and the emigrants have got in a few licks of their own. Their stock is scattered everywhere. We have our hands full trying to keep our stock separate from theirs. Lee's been trying to get the Indians to take some of the stock and leave. Are you men here to help out?"

"I don't know why we're here," said Pollock. "When we left Cedar, we were told we were coming out to help the emigrants and bury the dead. Some of 'em got out of camp last night and headed for Cedar. One of 'em was shot by Stewart at Ritchie Spring."

"Was he killed?"

"Yep."

Tullis shook his head. "Now what?"

"I don't know," said Pollock. "Some of these boys seem bent on throwin' in with the Indians. Higbee has gone back to Cedar for orders. We're gonna report to Major Lee and then wait and see what happens next."

The conversation drifted off into other matters and soon the wagons were rolling again. About noon the men from Cedar City passed up within a mile of the emigrant corral and stopped at the spring where the southern militiamen were waiting.

Lee walked out to greet them. He was pleased to see they were outfitted well, adequate provisions, tools, spades, shovels and picks in the wagons, and most everybody was well armed. Several of the newcomers were men he knew.

In all, more than thirty men were now in the field. They had been drilled, but they were not really soldiers. They had no uniforms. Military discipline and courtesy were almost nonexistent. They were "militia" in the true sense of the word: citizen soldiers.

These men had little to say. After the incident of the previous evening, most of the men knew why they were there. Lee asked if they had brought new orders, but they had none and no one was anxious to relate the happening at Ritchie Spring.

Along with some of the men, Lee moved his camp from the little hollow to another site about four hundred yards farther north on a hill near another spring. The new camp was out of sight of the emigrants, beyond two hills, a large one and a smaller one closer to the corral. Some of the men lay down to sleep in the shade, while the more curious went up onto the smaller hill just east of the corral to look things over.

Indians were everywhere, firing from five or six points around the corral. Sometimes the only evidence of their location was the cloud of smoke as they fired from concealment in the brush.

With time on their hands, part of the militia started taking shots at the emigrants' wagons as if their fate had already been decided. When questioned by Lee they said they were doing it to keep in practice and to help pass off the time. One man fixed up a seat under the shade of a tree where he continued to load and shoot until he got tired. Lee was discouraged by the attitudes displayed, but kept his thoughts to himself and prayed that orders would soon come.

Col. William Dame was just sitting down to his noonday meal. The events of the past several days were heavy on his mind, especially the business out at the Meadows. The decision to send an express to Salt Lake had been the right choice. Haslam would be back soon, and the whole affair would no longer be Dame's responsibility.

Dame looked around the table at his family. All faces were turned toward him, waiting expectantly. Dame bowed his head and the others followed suit.

"Our eternal Father in Heaven, we humbly bow our heads in gratitude for this food which Thou hast provided for our needs..."

A sudden pounding on the door caused everyone to look up. Dame looked at the door, at his family, and then bowed his head again.

"...we ask Thy blessing upon this food that it might strengthen and nourish our bodies..."

The pounding was louder and more insistent.

"...that we might be better able to carry out the work of building

Thy Kingdom here on earth. Guide us with Thy Spirit and grant us those blessings which Thou seest we stand in need of, we pray in the name of our Lord and Savior, Jesus Christ. Amen."

Dame pushed his chair away from the table and went to the door and opened it. Outside were Isaac Haight and John Higbee, dusty, sweaty, and looking very distraught. Dame felt a hot flash go through his own body.

"Isaac, John, what is the matter?"

"Brother Dame," said Haight, "we have serious trouble. We gotta talk."

Dame eyed Haight and Higbee, then turned and looked at his family. He turned back to the two men and said, "We're just eating. I'll not turn my family out. We'll eat first and then we can talk. You're welcome to join us."

Haight and Higbee looked at each other, exasperated. They took off their hats and entered the house.

When the meal was over, Col. Dame excused his family. "Well, brethren, what's the trouble?"

Haight looked at Higbee and nodded.

"Bill Stewart killed one of the emigrants last night," said Higbee.

Dame almost jumped up from his chair. "Why did he do that? I thought we agreed to rescue them from the Indians."

"I know," said Higbee. "I ordered out some of the militia yesterday, about a dozen or so. Stewart was one of 'em. We were stopping at Ritchie Spring last night. Somehow, three of the emigrants got away and were heading for Cedar when they came upon our camp. Stewart and Joel White were posted as night guards. They challenged 'em. When Stewart heard who they were, he shot one of 'em."

"What happened to the other two?"

"They got away. One of 'em might've been wounded."

Dame lowered his head and groaned. "Oh, my God, this is the worst possible news."

"How are we going to handle this?" asked Haight.

Col. Dame rose from his chair and looked at the two men. He walked around the table looking at the floor, his jaw set and his lips pressed tightly together. He paced for several moments, then stopped at his writing table and opened the drawer. He shuffled through some papers, took out the patriarchal blessing he had received only three years before, and read it as he often did when confronted with difficult decisions.

Certain words and phrases caught his attention, "The spirit of inspiration shall rest upon thee...thou shalt understand things which are in the future...Thou shalt be called to act at the head of a portion of thy brethren and of the Lamanites in the redemption of Zion and the avenging of the blood of the Prophets upon them that dwell in the earth. The angel of vengeance shall be with thee, shall nerve and strengthen thee. Like unto Moroni, no power shall be able to stand before thee until thou hast accomplished thy work."

Dame put the paper away, went to the window and looked out. His children were playing in the yard, running and laughing. He watched for several moments, then turned to face his two guests.

"Everyone old enough to tell the tale must die," said Dame with finality.

Haight and Higbee exchanged glances.

"What do you mean?" asked Higbee.

"I mean the Indians can't get the job done, so the militia will have to do it."

Higbee sat with his head hanging down, forearms on his knees. He had blown hot and cold on this matter over the past few days. Now he was no longer sure this was the right thing to do. "Do you realize what you're asking? This is murder."

"This is war," said Dame.

"I don't care what you call it," said Higbee. "I'm against it."

"You were willing to let the Indians do it," said Dame.

"That is another matter."

"Is it?"

"Yes," said Higbee. "The Indians just have to wait them out. When they get thirsty enough, they'll come out."

"Jim Haslam should be back in a day or two," said Haight. "Perhaps we should wait and see what Brother Brigham has to say."

"Suppose he says we are to aid the emigrants?" asked Dame. "What then?"

"I don't see how we can go against counsel," said Haight.

"That is precisely why we can't wait," said Dame. "If these people are allowed to carry word to California that we are in league with the Indians, that we are responsible for the deaths of several of their number, we all might hang. Haun's Mill will seem like a Sunday ride in the country."

The logic of Dame's argument was inescapable. Higbee just sat there with a stupid look on his face.

"I'm sure President Young will endorse our actions," said Dame.

"So am I," said Haight.

"And if he doesn't," Dame continued, "then we can blame it on the Indians. And if we do it now, no one can accuse us of disobeying counsel."

"Are you sure this is what you want to do?" asked Higbee. "There are children. We'd be shedding innocent blood."

"I think we can overcome that difficulty," said Haight.

Higbee let out a sigh. "All right, Brother Haight, if you've got a plan, let's hear it."

At one o'clock James Haslam returned to the church offices. Brigham Young was waiting with the letter in hand.

"Here is the reply, Brother Haslam. Go with all speed, spare no horseflesh. The emigrants must not be meddled with, if it takes all Iron County to prevent it. They must go free and unmolested. Go now and God be with you."

Haslam took the letter and pinned it inside his coat. A minute later he was astride a fresh horse, galloping through the streets of Salt Lake City.

By three o'clock the plan was worked out and Haight had prepared a written order. "Give this to Brother Lee," he said to Higbee.

"Suppose he refuses."

"He won't," said Haight. "Brother Lee always accepts counsel from his superiors."

"But what if he does?" said Higbee.

"Tell him that if he obeys this order, his calling and election shall be made sure," said Haight. "His place in the celestial kingdom will be guaranteed if he proves worthy of this sacred obligation."

Higbee folded the piece of paper and stuffed it in his coat.

"It's time to be going," said Col. Dame, as he showed them to the door. "See that this order is carried out no later than tomorrow."

The men shook hands and departed. The first stop would be Cedar, where more of the militia would be called out, and then to Mountain Meadows.

Arriving back at Cedar, Haight sent Dan MacFarlane to get Philip Klingensmith. The Bishop came as quickly as he could and met Haight behind his house by the Iron works.

"Bishop," said Haight, "they haven't got along as they anticipated at Mountain Meadows. When the news came in to me for reinforcements, I immediately went over to Parowan and there got further orders what to do. I have orders from Colonel Dame that we are to decoy the emigrants out and to spare nothing but the small children that cannot tell the tale."

Klingensmith was shocked. The council had agreed to withhold any action until hearing from Brigham Young. "Have we heard from Salt Lake yet."

"There is no time for that. Stewart has killed one of the emigrants at Ritchie Spring and two others got away. We must take action immediately. Go down to the old town and report to Higbee. We're sending more men."

Philip Klingensmith was passing Ira Allen's house when he saw John Higbee, Ira Allen and Charley Hopkins in the front yard.

"President Haight sent me to find you, Brother Higbee," said Klingensmith. "How can I be of service?"

"You are ordered out armed and equipped as the law directs to go to the Mountain Meadows," Higbee replied.

Klingensmith went and fitted up, got his horse and gun and ammunition. As before, the men gathered at the square. Klingensmith, Hopkins, and Higbee rode out on horses, while John Willis drove a wagon filled with men, and Sam McMurdy drove a baggage wagon. This trip would not be a mission of mercy.

# 63

*Thursday night* Time was critical. Higbee pushed the men and animals, stopping only to water the horses. They struck Mountain Meadows near Hamblin's ranch past midnight. They watered their horses and then continued on to Lee's camp at the southern end of the valley. The camp was roused by the arrival of more troops. Higbee immediately sought Lee out. Higbee, Lee, Charley Hopkins, Ira Allen, Robert Wiley, and Philip Klingensmith, all church or civil leaders, along with a few other militiamen, moved off to one side about ten rods up in the mouth of a little wash. Lee gave his report of the happenings and the current situation on the field. He stated that the emigrant train had strong fortifications, that he knew of no possible chance to get them out. When Lee had finished, he asked Higbee if he had brought any orders.

"Orders is from me to you," said Higbee, "that they are to be decoyed out and disarmed and got out in any manner, the best way you can. It is the orders of the President that all the emigrants must be put out of the way. President Haight has counseled with Colonel Dame, and has had orders from him to put all of the emigrants out of the way. None who are old enough to talk are to be spared."

Higbee then launched into a discourse on all the misdeeds of the emigrants, that they were enemies of the church, that they had no authority to pass through the Territory during this time of emergency, and that if they were to go to California and raise an army, the lives of all the southern Saints would be in jeopardy. He argued that the only safety for the people was in the utter destruction of the whole rascally lot.

"God will have to change my heart before I could consent to such a wicked thing as the wholesale killing of these people," said Lee. "It is even more wicked to kill the women and children."

"I will hear no more of this," said Higbee. "You are resisting authority. I was told you would accept counsel."

Higbee turned to the others and continued, "Brother Lee is afraid of shedding innocent blood. Why, brethren, there is not a drop of innocent blood in that entire camp of Gentile outlaws. They are a set of cutthroats, robbers and assassins. They are a part of the people who drove the Saints from Missouri, and who aided to shed the blood of our Prophets, Joseph and Hyrum, and it is our orders from all in authority, to get the emigrants from their stronghold, and help the Indians kill them."

"I knew the Prophet Joseph Smith," said Lee. "He told us never to betray anyone. We can't get the emigrants out of their corral unless we use treachery, and I am opposed to that."

"These are the orders of President Isaac C. Haight to us, and Haight got his orders from Colonel Dame at Parowan," said Higbee.

"We are of one mind in this matter," said Charley Hopkins. "We have been sent by the Council at Cedar City to the Meadows to give counsel and direct the disposal of this company of emigrants."

"I know this is difficult for Brother Lee," said Philip Klingensmith. "Perhaps if we joined in prayer to seek the mind and will of the Lord..."

"A good suggestion," said Higbee.

The men then knelt down in a prayer circle, their elbows touching, as the Bishop led them in prayer, invoking the Spirit of God to direct them how to act in the matter. The prayer concluded, the men stood up and Lee started to walk away.

"Here are the orders," said Higbee, and handed Lee the paper from Haight.

Lee moved closer to the campfire so he could see in the darkness. The orders were as Higbee had said and were signed by Haight, as commander of the troops at Cedar City. As Lee read it, his hands began to tremble. He hadn't wanted to believe it, but now it was unmistakably confirmed. He dropped the paper on the ground, saying, "I cannot do this."

His head bowed, Lee walked away a few paces and knelt in prayer to ask God to overrule the decision. After several moments, Lee felt a hand on his shoulder. He looked up and saw Charley Hopkins.

"John," he said, "I understand your feelings. This is a terrible thing, but it is all right under the circumstances. The brethren in the Priesthood are all united in this and it would not be well for you to oppose them."

"It's true," said Lee, "I have enemies who would rejoice in my destruction, but the Lord must change my heart before I could ever do such an act willingly."

"Let's go back to the others," said Hopkins, "and talk some more."

Once again the council knelt in prayer, this time each man in turn prayed aloud for divine guidance.

After prayer Major Higbee said, "I have the evidence of God's approval of our mission. It is God's will that we carry out our instructions to the letter."

"My God!" said Lee. "This is more than I can do. I must and do refuse to take part in this matter."

"Brother Lee," said Higbee, "I am ordered by President Haight to inform you that you shall receive a crown of Celestial glory for your faithfulness, and your eternal joy shall be complete."

Lee was wavering. He wanted desperately to save the emigrants, but he totally believed in the sealing power of the Priesthood and that those who held the keys had the authority to bestow such blessings.

"Suppose we give the Indians all the stock of the emigrants, except sufficient to haul their wagons, and let them go," said Lee, desperately.

"The Indians already have all the stock," said someone in the darkness.

Robert Wiley had remained silent throughout, but now he felt moved to give voice to his feelings, "Brethren, we have been sent here to perform a duty. It is a duty that we owe to God and to our Church and people. The orders of those in authority are that all the emigrants must die. Our leaders speak with inspired tongues, and their orders come from the God of Heaven. We have no right to question what they have commanded us to do. It is our duty to obey. If we wished to act as some of our weak-kneed brethren desire us to do, it would be impossible. The thing has gone too far to allow us to stop now. The emigrants know that we have aided the Indians, and if we let them go they will bring certain destruction upon us. It is a fact that on Wednesday night, three of the emigrants got out of camp and started back to Cedar City for assistance to withstand the Indian attacks. They had reached Ritchie Spring when they met Bill Stewart, Joel White and Benjamin Arthur, three of our brethren from Cedar City. The men stated their business to the brethren, and as their horses were drinking at the Spring, Brother Stewart, feeling unusually full of zeal for the glory of God and upbuilding of the

Kingdom of God on earth, shot and killed one of the emigrants, a young man by the name of Aiden. When Aiden fell from his horse, Joel White shot and wounded one of the other Gentiles. But he unfortunately got away, and returned to his camp and reported that the Mormons were helping the Indians in all that they were doing against the emigrants. Now the emigrants will report these facts in California if we let them go. We must kill them all, and our orders are to get them out by treachery if no other thing can be done to get them into our power."

And so it went, far into the night.

From a distance Dudley Leavitt would have looked like a statue of some war hero in a public park. He had sat motionless on his horse for nearly three hours and he didn't much like it, except for the fact it took him away from the Meadows for a while. As the heat of the day had been blistering, so was the cold of the night air numbing to his senses. He was bundled up as warm as he could get and half asleep. From his vantage point on a hill to the southwest, he could have seen most of the Meadows if it were daylight. As a picket Leavitt wasn't worth much and he knew it, but the Iron County militia was supposed to be a military outfit, so picket duty was a sop to those military geniuses who were in charge of this operation. Perhaps if he had been more alert he would have at least heard and maybe even seen the shadowy figure coming up the canyon, but his thoughts were elsewhere for the moment.

Joel spotted the sentry as soon as he came around the hill. The moon, in its last quarter, that had lighted his way for several miles was on its way down, but still silhouetted the sentry against the western sky. The Meadows had to be near, he reasoned, if a sentry was posted. Joel had hurried as fast as he dared in spite of the painful abrasions he suffered on his knees and forearms when Jones threw him from the horse, but it appeared he would fall short of his goal. The stars in the east were beginning to fade, and the chorus of birds heralding the coming day was echoing from the surrounding hills.

Joel realized it would be light before he could get safely back into camp. He looked around for a good hiding place. A narrow draw opened eastward from the canyon, so he took it. He came upon a trail that climbed up to a ridge and in a few minutes he was there. The sagebrush and scrub oak were too sparse to offer adequate cover and the sky was growing brighter. Joel looked around. To the north was a high hill, maybe two hundred feet up, and at the top were trees and a heavier growth of scrub oak. Joel didn't hesitate. It was his only option.

He was breathing hard by the time he reached the top and, in spite of the cold, he was drenched in sweat. At least he was out of sight of the sentry. It was a good thing. The sky was now gray and only a few stars were faintly visible in the west. Mountains seemed to be all around except to the north. Perhaps it was the Mountain Meadows down below. Joel made his way in that direction, carefully winding along through the sage and oak brush. He wanted to see if the camp was below. Maybe he could make a dash for safety.

Suddenly, Joel heard a rustling in the brush, and then an Indian stood up in front of him, not four feet away. He didn't appear to be particularly menacing. His hair was long and greasy-looking, and his clothing was a hodgepodge of buckskin and castoffs from local whites. His face was expressionless and in his hand was a fairly new rifle, though he was not pointing it in a threatening manner. Joel wondered how he had come to own such a fine-looking weapon. In the surprise of the moment Joel noticed a lot of things about the Indian. Most of all he noticed the smell. The aroma was like that of a wet dog.

The Indian spoke in a language Joel had never heard before. Some English words were mixed in, such as "Mormon" and "big captain." The Indian stopped talking and waited as if he expected Joel to speak. Then he pointed at Joel and spoke one word, "Mormon?"

Of course! The emigrants were in the circled wagons. A white man in the hills would have to be a Mormon. Joel nodded. The Indian smiled, then gestured for Joel to follow as he turned and started toward the crest of the hill. Joel had no choice but to follow.

*This isn't any good at all,* thought Joel, looking around. What should he do? It was only a matter of time before this savage found out who he really was. It appeared that no one else was nearby. He would have to act fast.

Joel felt a phantom pain in his right thigh and remembered the Indian lance that had been jabbed into his leg back on the prairie only three months ago. Joel looked at the Indian again. Time was running out. He had to decide quickly. His heart was pounding, his knees felt weak, and his throat was dry.

An outside force seemed to take control of the boy's body. Joel felt as if he were in a dream, observing his own actions, yet participating. As if in slow motion, his left hand reached for the Indian's head, while his right hand pulled his hunting knife from his belt. It would be like finishing off a wounded deer. The blade swung in a sideways, sweeping arc as Joel's left hand grabbed the Indian by the hair, jerking him backwards. Before the Indian could cry out, the blade was buried in the side of his neck, slashing the carotid artery and blocking the windpipe.

The Indian broke free of Joel's grasp and, dropping his rifle, staggered a few steps forward before turning around. The life force was pouring from his wound and down the front of his clothing. The Indian had a stupid look on his face as he tried to understand what was happening to him. His right hand reached up and touched the handle of the knife. Moving his lips, trying to speak, he dropped to his knees, then fell forward on his face.

Joel felt sick. He had never killed a man before. Though he knew he had no choice, still he felt remorse. Joel approached the apparently lifeless form very carefully. There was one way to tell for sure if the Indian was dead. He walked around behind him and with all the force he could muster, Joel kicked him squarely between the legs. The Indian didn't move.

Joel knelt astride the body and removed his knife from the dead man's neck. Then he dragged the body as far as he could into the scrub oak. To finish the job of concealment, he piled rocks on the corpse and scattered sand over the blood stains on the ground.

When he was finished, Joel took the Indian's rifle and ammunition, and crept to the crest of the hill, and burrowed his way through the dense brush. His hands were scratched, as was his face. The sun was not yet up, but he was rewarded with a fine view of the Mountain Meadows. Just below and maybe three hundred yards away was the circle of wagons. There was no way he could reach them. The brush on the hillside was too thick to run through. He would be spotted before he got halfway down.

Dozens of Indians were positioned on the rocky ridge to the west of the corral. Others were on the small hill about two hundred yards east of the corral. Joel saw some movement and realized Indians were also hiding in the brush below him on the same hill. The fear of discovery grew almost to panic proportions.

Looking for someplace to flee, Joel scanned the surrounding terrain. There! To the east! White men! Two larger hills lay beyond the little one on the east side of the wagon corral, the east most being the higher of the two. He saw two camps of white men, one on the north side of the large hill and the other on the south side, up a narrow hollow...and Indians were in the northern camp! Joel felt a deep loathing. He could hardly wait until dark to slip back into camp. But that was a long time away and he had slept little in the past two days. In spite of the discomfort of his hiding place, in moments he was sound asleep.

# The Angel of Vengeance
# Shall Be With Thee

# 64

*Friday, September 11, 1857*

"I am satisfied that it is the will of all of the leading brethren in the Priesthood," said John D. Lee to the council.

Lee had finally decided to be obedient to the wishes of those in authority and had laid his personal convictions aside and accepted as inevitable the destruction of the emigrant company. What choice did he have? He believed his superiors were inspired men who could not go wrong in any matter relating to the Church or the duty of its members.

The council finally broke up at daylight. All the horses except five were turned out on the range. Two of the five horses were for Ira Allen and Bill Stewart to overtake anyone who might try to escape, one for Nephi Johnson as liaison with the Indians, one for Major Higbee as field commander, and one for Dan MacFarlane to act as adjutant to carry orders from one part of the field to another. The men at Lee's camp then sat down to a hearty breakfast, the only meal they were to have until evening.

Soon after breakfast Major Higbee sent for the two Indian interpreters, Carl Shirts and Nephi Johnson. "You will go with Brother Lee to inform the Indians of the plan of operations, and to place the Indians in ambush, so that they will not be seen by the emigrants."

Lee and the two interpreters went to the Indian camp and explained the plan and detailed the role of the Indians. Runners were sent out to all the Indians surrounding the corral and in only a few minutes not a single Indian was in the vicinity. Now it would be easier to convince the emigrants that the Mormons were acting in good faith and had indeed persuaded the Indians to call off their siege.

The militia from Cedar moved out south a quarter of a mile to the camp of the southern troops up in the hollow. Major Higbee then called all the people to order, and directed Lee to explain the whole plan to them. The men gathered around in a loose formation with Lee in the middle.

"I think you all know why we are here," said Lee. "These people have broken our law, defied authority, and terrorized our people. Some of you came here thinking to rescue them from the Indians, but the situation has changed. For our own protection it is the decision of the council that the emigrant company be destroyed.

The emigrants are to be decoyed from their stronghold. A flag of truce will be carried down to the corral. If they accept our demand to parley, we will go into their camp and arrange the terms of the surrender. If not, at least we will be able to learn what their condition is."

Bishop Philip Klingensmith wasn't pleased by what he heard. He nudged the man standing next to him, William Slade, Sr., and motioned with his head to follow him. They stepped away a short distance from the group, further up the hollow.

"This is a horrible thing we're about to enter into, Brother Slade," whispered Klingensmith.

"I agree," said Slade. "It makes my blood run cold."

"What can we do, how can we help ourselves?" asked Klingensmith.

"We can't."

Klingensmith shook his head sorrowfully and the two men moved back into the group.

"You needn't worry about shedding innocent blood," said Lee. "All children under the age of accountability will be placed in a wagon and taken out of harm's way. The wounded will be placed in a second wagon. The wagons will then start for Hamblin's Ranch. The women and older children will march on foot and follow the wagons in single file. The men will follow behind the women, also in single file. You will march down to the camp. After the wagons and the women have passed, you will march on the right side of the men up the valley to the place of ambush. Each of you will carry his gun on his left arm ready for instant use. At the right place Major Higbee will call a halt. When you hear the command, 'Do your duty', you will shoot the man next to you."

Like a sudden gust of wind a murmur of surprise rippled through the militia. A battle was one thing. But cold-blooded murder?

Lee could feel the mood of the men. He thought to head off any opposition. "Those of you too cowardly to carry out orders may fire your guns into the air and kneel down. The Indians will do your work for you. Now each of you get yourself ready. We'll be going down there soon."

The men broke up into small groups. Few of the men had anything to say, at least not loud enough to be heard by many. Some of the men were distraught, some were resigned, and some were determined to do their duty. Isaac Delaney fell into this latter group. He was full of the zeal of the recent reformation and eager to be an example of faithfulness to the orders of his superiors. Ever since the days when Brigham Young had taken him by the hand and offered comfort and solace for the passing of his first wife, it had been his experience that blessings always followed when he obeyed counsel. He was willing to die for his religion...and to kill for it. His son John did not share his feelings.

When Lee had finished speaking John Delaney stared at the ground and shook his head in disbelief. This was insane. The justifications were unacceptable. It went against every gospel principle he could think of. And the suggestion that anyone whose conscience permit him to fire was cowardly, that really stung.

He looked around at the faces of the other men. He could see nothing in their faces that betrayed their thoughts. If only he had some sign to guide him. He surveyed the scene before him. A mile away he could see the corralled wagons of the Arkansas emigrants. All around him were scrub oak and cottonwood trees. A trickle of a stream from the spring on the hillside ran past the camp down toward the wagons and into Mogatsu Creek. The grass was green and rippled in a gentle breeze. The hills and mountains to the west were brightly lit by the midmorning sun. A few wispy clouds floated in the deep blue sky. Here there should have been peace and harmony. John Delaney at last understood the saying that the mountaintops could serve as a place to perform sacred ordinances when there was no temple in which to do so. This setting could have been such a place, but the events of the past few days and the hours yet to come had desecrated it.

Young Delaney closed his eyes in silent prayer. After a few moments it came to him. He had read about it in the scriptures in his youth and had heard it preached from the pulpit many times. He felt the burning in his bosom and it grew stronger every moment. He opened his eyes and looked around. High above him, on rising currents of air, a golden eagle soared in a lazy circle, shimmering in the morning sun. Soon, another joined the first and the two birds chased one another in a playful game, free from any worldly cares.

John Delaney went and gathered up his bedroll, and then went to find his horse out on the range. John D. Lee, Higbee, and the other leading brethren had returned around the hill to Lee's camp to the north. Delaney was well away from the camp when he heard his father's voice.

"John!"

John stopped and looked back. "Yeah, Pa?"

"Where're y'goin', son? There's work to be done."

"I ain't doin' it, Pa. Don't want no part of it. I've been thinkin' it over, prayed about it, and I know the Lord doesn't want this thing to happen."

"We have our orders, John...from the Lord's anointed."

"Well, it ain't for me."

John Delaney turned and resumed walking for his horse. Isaac mind was in turmoil, old feelings of ten years past were being harrowed up. Images of his dear sweet Molly lying cold in an unmarked grave flooded his mind.

"Wait!" he cried out.

John Delaney stopped in his tracks and turned to face his father. The older man approached, tears in his eyes. He placed his hand on his boy's shoulder and said, "Son, if you won't do it for the Church, do it for me."

"I can't, Pa. You've always taught me to choose the right, to be guided by the light and knowledge made known to me. I'm sorry."

"Then think of your mother! These are the people who drove us out. She died because of them."

"No. I won't do it. Nothing in this world can make me do it."

John turned and walked away. Isaac looked around. Almost no one seemed to notice this drama unfolding. Tears were flowing.

"Oh, God help me!" he cried in anguish.

Then, in an instant, Isaac Delaney drew his Colt's revolver and fired. To Isaac Delaney it was as if time had slowed almost to a standstill. All of his senses were heightened. He felt the cold steel in his hand, saw the hammer being drawn, saw the cap explode, and saw his son slump to the ground. And then he felt purified. He had sacrificed his oldest son.

One of the southern soldiers ran to the fallen man and knelt beside him. Blood covered the entire right side of his head. The bullet had torn the scalp above his right ear before glancing off the prominence where his right eyebrow ended. He was unconscious, but very much alive.

"He's alive," the man said.

"He's dead to me," said Isaac Delaney.

Men were scurrying about. Someone fetched medical supplies and bound up the wound. Young John was soon conscious and being assisted to ride to Hamblin's ranch. The other men stood around speaking in low voices. Delaney knew they were talking about him, but he didn't care. He had shown them. None of them would have or could have demonstrated their devotion to the Church as strongly as he had done.

Samuel Knight had managed to keep away from the lower end of the Mountain Meadows since his return earlier in the week. It was just before noon when he saw John D. Lee and Philip Klingensmith approaching Hamblin's ranch on horseback with John Delaney in tow. Knight was busy doing his chores and waiting on his sick wife. Lee had been to the ranch several times in the past few days, so Knight didn't pay him much mind. Lee rode right up to where Knight was working and spoke to him.

"Got an injured man here," said Lee.

"I see that," said Knight. "I'll fix him up."

"We'll be needing your wagon, Brother Knight," said Lee.

"You're welcome to it," said Knight.

"We'll need you to drive it. There are sick and wounded that need to be transported back to Cedar."

Knight stopped what he was doing and paused to think. He knew what was going on down there and he didn't want to be drawn into it. Lee, on the other hand, wanted every available man to participate.

"I'm sorry, but my wife is sick, as you know, and I prefer helping her rather than people I don't know. Besides, you have other wagons down there."

Lee ignored the comment. Of course they had other wagons, but what Lee wanted was another gun, and Knight would fill the bill nicely.

"It's your duty," said Klingensmith.

Lee put his hand on Klingensmith's arm. "I'll handle this, Bishop," he said. Then to Knight he added, "You're a member of the militia and these are military orders."

"So that's how it is," said Knight. "All right, but my team is young horses and they ain't been broke but a few days. They're fractious and difficult to handle."

"Come right away," said Lee. He and Klingensmith turned their horses and rode south.

Jim Pearce lay in the shade watching as the militia made preparations. His digestive system had pretty well settled down, but now it was stress, instead of too much fresh beef that was tying his intestines in knots. Harrison Pearce came over to the boy and knelt down.

"How're y'feelin', Jim?"

"Better'n a couple of days ago, but..."

"You don't want to go down there, do you? Well, I don't blame you none. You just stay wrapped up in your blanket. I'll tell 'em you're too sick to come."

The younger Pearce pulled the blanket tightly around himself and turned away.

By two o'clock everything and everyone were ready. Major Higbee then gave the order for the men to advance. They marched in a very disorderly and unmilitary fashion to the California road and halted. William Bateman then took a white flag and started for the emigrant camp more than a quarter of a mile away. When he got about halfway to the corral, he was met by one of the emigrants. They sat on the ground and talked for several minutes.

The two men finally got up and shook hands. Bateman returned to the militia while the man from the emigrant company went back to the corral.

"What did they say?" asked Higbee.

"They're very anxious to receive our help," said Bateman. "They want to hear our terms before they decide."

"Very good, Brother Bateman. Major Lee, you will go down and negotiate the surrender. You have complete charge down there. You know what to do. Brother Lee, we expect you to faithfully carry out all the instructions that have been given you by our council. Most important, be sure you get all the weapons."

Samuel McMurdy and Samuel Knight were then ordered to drive their teams and follow Lee to the corral. The troops formed in two lines standing with arms at rest while Lee walked down to the corral, as the two wagons followed close behind.

Joel Deaton was dreaming that the wagons were on the move again. The oxen bellowed, the bullwhackers were cracking their whips, the wagons were creaking and rattling. Gradually, he became aware of his surroundings. He saw blue sky through the scrub oak and he heard wagons moving. He wanted to jump up and yell, 'Hey! Wait for me!'."

Joel crawled out from his hiding place and looked down at the corral. Two wagons were approaching. Off to the right some distance was a group of armed men. No Indians were in sight. He didn't know what to make of it. His first impulse was to go crashing down the hillside, but his gut reaction was to watch and see what happened next.

As Lee neared the corral, a man came out to meet him.

"Good day, sir. My name's Lee. I understand you folks are ready to negotiate an end to this fix you're in."

Lee extended his hand and the other man shook it. "My name's Hamilton. We're willing to hear what you have to say."

The emigrants loosened the chains and moved one wagon out of the way, so that Knight and McMurdy could drive into their camp.

Lee was surprised to find that the emigrants were more strongly fortified than he had supposed. Their wagons were chained to each other in a circle. In the center he saw the rifle pit that had shielded the entire company from the constant fire of the Indians. Off to one side several men were taking turns with shovels digging a large hole in the ground.

"What is this about?" asked Lee.

"Seven of our people died when the Indians attacked on Monday and seventeen were wounded," said Hamilton. "Two of the wounded died this morning. Another one died yesterday, so that makes ten."

The bodies were wrapped in quilts and laid in the grave. A few words were spoken over them and a few tears were shed. Lee stood looking on, feeling very uncomfortable.

After the impromptu service, the people gathered around Lee, very excited, several speaking at once. Though some displayed hostility and distrust, most looked upon him as the instrument of their deliverance.

Lee's soul was racked with anguish. Their simple faith in his goodness was about to be betrayed. He wanted to turn and run from the place, but his faith in his religion and in his leaders gave him strength for the onerous task ahead.

"I presume you're the head man here," said Lee to Hamilton.

"No, I am," said Alexander Fancher, stepping forward. "Mr. Hamilton volunteered to act as spokesman outside the corral. What are your terms, Mr. Lee?"

"As the Indian farmer hereabouts, I usually have considerable influence with the Indians, though in this instance I have not been too successful. I have succeeded in getting the Indians to withdraw while I negotiate in their behalf. You will notice we have called out the militia to assist, but our numbers are even less than yours. It's only because we deal with the Indians regularly that they are even willing to listen to any proposals."

"What do they want?" asked Fancher.

"They want your stock and they want your goods."

"Everything we own in the world is here," said Fancher. "That would leave us with nothing."

"You can give 'em your goods or you can give 'em your lives," said Lee. "Those are the choices."

"You won't join us in fighting them?" asked Fancher.

"Sir, when you are long gone, we'll still have to live with them. Some of our settlements are very small. We have worked for ten years to establish a relationship of trust with the Indians and that is the only thing that protects us."

Fancher looked downcast.

"Our terms are these," Lee continued. "You must give up your arms as a token of good faith to the Indians. We will carry your wounded in one wagon, and the weapons and all children under the age of eight years in the other wagon. We will conduct you back to Cedar City where you will be given shelter until we can arrange safe travel for you to California."

"It's a little late to be getting started today, isn't it?" asked Fancher.

"Hamblin's ranch is just a few miles up the valley," said Lee.

"Once we get you away from the corral, the Indians will have no further interest in you. We'll stop overnight at Hamblin's, then see you on to Cedar in the morning."

"We'll have to talk this over," said Fancher.

Fancher and the others retired to the other side of the corral for a council. Lee sat down in the back of McMurdy's wagon and waited.

Nearly two hours had passed and Major Higbee was getting restless. The sun was blistering hot. He and Nephi Johnson and Dan MacFarlane sat side-by-side on their horses, and Higbee wanted very much to dismount and sit in the shade.

"I could sure use a cool drink of water," said MacFarlane.

"We all could," said Higbee. "I wish we could hurry them up."

"Why don't we just ride down and tell 'em the Indians are coming?" suggested Nephi Johnson.

"That's an idea," said Higbee. "Yeah, we could do that."

"I'm against it," said Charlie Mitchell.

"What other choice do we have?" asked Fancher. "We're almost out of ammunition. We have little water. Some of our wounded have died. Maybe they could have been saved if help had come sooner."

"You call this help?" said one of the Missourians. "Remember Bill Aiden. It was probably one of them that done it."

"We don't know that," said Fancher.

"We've got seven thousand dollars in gold coin," said John Baker. "Are we gonna take it with us? Suppose they decide they'd like to have it? How much are our lives worth then?"

"We'll bury the gold here and come back for it later," said Fancher. "But we must think of the women and children. More people will die if we don't accept this offer."

MacKenzie Deaton listened with interest. Lying wounded on the ground, he couldn't hear all that was said. He thought back to his visit with Eli Bennett and what Bennett had said about the age of accountability and the shedding of innocent blood.

And so it went. All of the adult men had a say, and finally, they took a vote. When the council ended a majority vote had decided to accept the terms, and the wagons were being loaded. Just then Dan MacFarlane rode into the corral. "Brother Lee," he said, "Orders is to hurry up. Major Higbee is afraid the Indians will return and renew the attack."

"We're finished here," said Lee. "You may bring down the militia." MacFarlane moved to the outside of the wagon corral and waved his hat. From his position Higbee saw the signal and gave the order to march.

As MacKenzie Deaton was being placed in the wagon, he motioned for his wife to come over. "Sarah," he whispered, "Put Laura Jean in the other wagon."

"They said only children under eight and she's already nine," said Sarah.

"I know, but just do it."

"But why?"

"Something Eli Bennett said to me...something about the age of accountability and the shedding of innocent blood."

"You don't think..."

"I don't know what to think. I just believe she'll be safer there. All right, now do it before it's too late. Tell her not to tell anyone how old she is."

Now Sarah was more frightened than ever, but she took Laura Jean and did as her husband had told her.

From his hiding place Joel could see everything. He saw his sister being lifted into a wagon with the other children. From the east a rider was approaching in great haste.

As preparations for departure were underway the militia marched to within fifty yards of the wagon corral and waited. Meanwhile the weapons were loaded with the children. As Lee watched, he knew now how desperate their situation had been. Their guns were mostly Kentucky rifles, flintlocks, and their ammunition was about all gone. Probably less than twenty loads were left.

Lee stepped up to Samuel McMurdy in the lead wagon and said, "Turn left as you go out. Leave the troops to the right of us."

The opening in the corral was on the east side. McMurdy drove out and turned slightly to the east northeast in order to pass to the left of the militia. Lee followed on foot and then Samuel Knight, driving the second wagon. Dan MacFarlane came next, riding in front of the women and older children. He guided them to where the troops were standing in two ranks and passed by them. The men were following at a distance of about fifty yards.

As the men approached the militia, they waved their hats and gave a hardy cheer to their rescuers. No one seemed to notice the grim expression on most faces of the militiamen. More than a few of the militia shuddered at the thought of their hypocrisy. The women and children continued past the militia, but the men were halted when Major Higbee blocked their path with his horse. Military commands were given, forming the militia into a single file at the right side of the emigrants. The march of the men resumed, following the women and children, who were now more than two hundred yards ahead. The sun was only a few degrees above the horizon. They would have to hurry to get to Hamblin's before dark.

Joel Deaton did not want to be left behind. He began making his way down the hill. If he were lucky, he could catch one of the loose horses on the Meadows and overtake the emigrant company.

Samuel Pollock had been relieved to learn he would not go down to the emigrant wagons with the rest of the militia. Posted as a guard at the militia camp, he watched as the emigrants and militia came up near his position and turned north toward Hamblin's ranch.

William Young, being much older than the others, had been excused from duty to keep an eye on Jim Pearce. He hadn't wanted to go anyway.

The six most seriously wounded were in the wagon. Most of the rest were on foot. George Baker had been shot in the leg, not a serious wound, but it prevented him from walking. There was his wife, who had also received a minor wound, and his four children joined him. Billy was just a baby, Sallie was two, Betty five and Vina was eight. The children had been much affected by the siege and fussed a lot. Their mother held Billy in her lap, but had little to say. She just stared off in the distance. Sallie snuggled up in a red blanket next to her father. She felt warm and secure.

MacKenzie Deaton hurt really bad from being jostled around in the wagon bed. He was near the front, leaning against the side. With a little effort he could see Laura Jean in the first wagon. She looked scared. He only hoped his own fears were groundless.

The route of march was east around the south side of the small hill two hundred yards from the corral and then north paralleling the California road on the right until eventually merging with it. The emigrants had covered nearly a mile and a half in the thirty minutes since they left the corral, and even the skeptics were beginning to believe it was really true. The siege was over. They were free at last.

# 65

*Late Afternoon* The ground rose gradually as the procession approached the Rim of the Basin about a quarter of a mile away. They were in the main road now. At the front of the column first the wagons and then the women went over a slight rise and down into a declivity, out of sight of the men following. Major John Higbee was riding at the head of the column of men, regulating their pace, allowing the distance between the men and women to increase until it was more than three hundred yards. Twenty-five yards to the right were Nephi Johnson, Dan MacFarlane, Ira Allen and Bill Stewart on horseback, out of the intended line of fire. The militia marched on the right of the emigrant men at a distance of about ten feet between the two columns, paired off one-for-one, their rifles resting on their left forearms at the elbow, pointing in the direction of the emigrants.

The time had come. Major Higbee spurred his horse forward a few yards and turned it to face the column. He stood up in the stirrups, his hands resting on the pommel. "Halt!" he cried. All eyes were upon him.

Alexander Fancher was at the head of the column of emigrants. He looked into the pitiless eyes of Higbee, remembering the confrontation outside of Cedar City more than a week gone by.

"Brethren!" shouted Higbee. The rattling, clacking sound of hammers being drawn and locking into place rippled through the ranks. The emigrants turned at the sound to face their executioners. Fear struck deep into their hearts as their minds flooded with the realization of what was happening.

"Do your duty!" commanded Higbee.

In a span of about two seconds nearly fifty rifles barked pain and destruction. Most of the men fell at the first volley. Those who didn't, began to run. One man had been carrying an infant. The same bullet killed them both.

There was confusion, pandemonium. Those in the militia with revolvers drew them and continued to fire, while the others reloaded their rifles. Those men of good conscience fired into the air and dropped to their knees.

The Indians had been lying still as logs in the brush a hundred yards to the east of the gap that separated the men from the women. At the sound of gunfire they rose from their places of concealment and charged the emigrants, splitting into two groups, screaming like demons, waving their knives and tomahawks as they ran.

The women and children heard the shooting, and then the screaming Indians, and now they, too, knew that reality had become a nightmare from which they would never awake.

Back at the militia camp William Young was lying on the ground when the shooting started. He was roused by the sound of gunfire and then, in the company of Samuel Pollock, hurried around to the west side of the big hill that was on the north side of the hollow. The initial firing was many guns, but now only single shots were being fired, seemingly as fast as the ticks of a watch. The two men saw a huge cloud of smoke hanging in the air. They could see the Indians closing on the column and could hear them yelling. Pollock scrambled about seventy-five feet up the hillside for a better view.

Joel Deaton heard the shooting, but could see nothing except a cloud of smoke in the distance. The emigrants were out of sight beyond the hill on the northeast of the corral. He didn't have to see. He knew what was happening. Many emotions churned within him, anger at the betrayal, anguish for his family and friends, fear of discovery.

The wagons had stopped. The Indians were yelling. The women and children were shrieking in terror.

MacKenzie Deaton shuddered. He looked up at Laura Jean in the lead wagon. She was crying. If only he had a gun so he could die like a man!

McMurdy and Knight got out of their wagons. Each one had a rifle. McMurdy came back to the second wagon, and, raising his rifle to his shoulder, said, "O Lord, my God, receive their spirits. It is for thy Kingdom that I do this."

McMurdy fired. The bullet ripped through MacKenzie Deaton and into the man next to him. MacKenzie felt a searing pain. He gasped, unable to breathe. Silently, he slumped over dead.

Lee approached, drawing his revolver. The gun went off accidentally, cutting the thigh of McMurdy's buckskin pants. McMurdy turned and said, "Brother Lee, keep cool, you are excited. You came very near killing me. Keep cool. There is no reason for being excited."

Sallie Baker threw her arms around her father's neck. Knight fired once, hitting George Baker in the head. The same bullet ripped through Sallie's ear. "Daddy! Daddy! Daddy!" she screamed. Another shot and her mother toppled over, the bloodstain spreading on the front of her calico dress. All of the children were screaming in both wagons.

"How old are you, girl?" asked McMurdy.

"Eight," said Mary Lavina Baker.

McMurdy lifted Vina Baker from his wagon and took her away. Her brother and sisters would never see her again.

Like most of the other militia, Philip Klingensmith fired his piece and the emigrant dropped to the ground, mortally wounded. While Klingensmith reloaded he heard the Indians coming. To the west several men were running for their lives. Bill Stewart went after them on horseback. He overtook one man and shot him in the back.

Just then a very heavyset woman came running over the rise from the direction of the baggage wagons, yelling for her husband and children. Her face was red from exertion and her eyes wide with terror. A militiaman took aim and shot her in the back as she ran by. The woman dropped to the ground and did not move.

Alexander Fancher lay on the ground, stunned. The rifle ball had entered the right side of his chest just by the armpit. John Higbee had a revolver in his hand, firing at any convenient target, when he saw Fancher on the ground. He rode over to the man and dismounted. Higbee looked at the man for a moment, then put his gun away.

"Higbee..." said Fancher in a weak voice.

Major Higbee drew the Bowie knife from his belt and dropped to his knees, straddling the man.

"My god, Higbee!" said Fancher, pleading. "Don't kill me! Please! Higbee, I wouldn't do this to you!"

"You would have done the same to me or just as bad," was the reply. In one quick stroke he slashed Fancher's throat.

William Young watched the horrible panorama in a kind of detached fascination as he continued to walk toward the scene of the massacre. He was shocked by the slaughter. He saw an Indian with a knife kill a woman and the infant child in her arms. Another Indian knocked a young boy to the ground, jumped on him and smashed a large rock against his chest again and again. Another Indian dragged two girls by the hand into a group of Indians. Young couldn't see what the Indians were doing to the girls, but he thought he could hear their screams.

Other Indians swarmed in among the men, hardly pausing to kill a few emigrants, then most of them ran headlong for the wagons at the corral. They had been promised the emigrants' goods and they couldn't get there soon enough.

William Young had seen more than he could stand. He turned to go back to camp, when he saw Jim Pearce coming up the valley, carrying his blanket draped over his arms.

"Don't go up there," said Young. "It's terrible! Terrible! Come back to camp with me."

Young put his arm around the boy's shoulder and started back down the road. Jim Pearce looked back over his shoulder. The images burned into his mind and he was shocked, but also glad...glad that he had not gone down with the militia.

A boy, about fourteen years old, crying for help, came running up to the wagons where Lee, Knight, and McMurdy were conducting their bloody business. Without hesitation Knight struck him on the head with the butt end of his gun, and crushed his skull. At the same time many of the Indians reached the wagons and finished off anyone who showed even a flicker of life. One Indian from Cedar City, called Joe, ran up to the second wagon, grabbed a man by the hair, and raised his head up to look into his face. The man shut his eyes, and Joe shot him in the head.

Just then a girl, some ten or eleven years old, covered with blood, came running toward the wagons. An Indian shot her before she got within sixty yards. Another Indian ran to the front wagon and grabbed a little boy. The boy slipped from the Indian's grasp and ran to Lee, who was standing nearby.

"Help me! Don't let him kill me!"

The boy grabbed hold of Lee at the knees. Lee held up his hand toward the Indian and told him to let the boy alone as well as the other children in the wagon. The Indian looked disappointed, but paused only an instant before he rushed off to continue the slaughter.

Lee lifted the little fellow into his arms. The boy looked to be about five years old and had a bloody gash on his chin, probably from his scrape with the Indian.

"What's your name, son?" asked Lee.

"Charlie. My father is captain of the wagon train."

The boy's real name was Christopher Carson Fancher, named after the famous Indian scout, Kit Carson, but somehow he had picked up the nickname, Charlie. Lee placed him in the wagon with the other children. Scrunched down in the corner was Laura Jean Deaton. Lee gave her a curious look for a few moments, then went away.

The firing of guns had ceased except for an occasional shot to finish off an emigrant. The cloud of gun smoke was beginning to dissipate, but the smell lingered in the air. The sun had dipped below the western horizon as if to hide its face from the shame of what had just transpired.

Isaac Delaney started for the rise over which the women and children had gone. He passed John Higbee, who was giving orders to Klingensmith.

"Take charge of the little children," said Higbee. "Gather 'em up and take 'em to Hamblin's. Then we'll get things organized and get 'em back to Cedar."

Delaney stopped on the rise. He was sickened by what he saw. Bodies were everywhere and Indians were stripping them naked. Were they not already dead, they would have died of shame.

Delaney shouldered his rifle and started up the valley for Hamblin's. He didn't want to go back to camp, and he didn't want to stick around.

The killing done, Knight drove about a hundred yards from the road and dumped the bodies, then returned. Lee then ordered Knight and McMurdy to take the children and drive on to Hamblin's ranch.

Before the wagons started, Nephi Johnson came up in company with the Indians that were under his command. Lee ordered Johnson to go down to the emigrant wagons and stop the Indians from looting, then he went to the place where the dead men lay. Like most of the others, Lee was shaken by the reality of what had gone on. He had seen death, but never like this. He went over to where Higbee and Klingensmith were standing.

"The boys have acted admirably," said Higbee to Lee. "They took good aim, and all of the damned Gentiles but two or three fell at the first fire. Some three or four got away, but our boys rode 'em down and cut their throats. The Indians did their part well. Didn't take 'em more'n a minute or two to finish up once they got started. We must now examine the bodies for valuables."

Lee shook his head. "No, sir. I don't wish to do any such work."

"Well then," said Higbee. "You hold my hat and I'll examine the bodies and put what valuables I get into the hat."

Higbee, Klingensmith and Bill Stewart searched the bodies. Lee held the hat awhile, but he soon felt so disgusted that he had to give it to someone else. The search resulted in only a small amount of money and a few watches.

Joel Deaton had retreated into the scrub oak when he saw the Indians coming. They were whooping and hollering as they tore into the wagons, throwing the goods around, putting on clothing, fighting over blankets and cooking ware. A few minutes later some white men rode up and talked to the Indians. It appeared an argument was going on. Finally, the Indians, sullen, like chastised children, left with their newfound possessions. The militiamen stayed behind as if to guard the wagons.

Joel didn't want to believe what had happened, not in his heart, but his head told him his family and friends were all gone. When it was dark, he went out to try to catch a horse. There was no safety here. California was his only hope.

Samuel Knight's wife, Caroline, was lying down resting when she heard her husband coming. She didn't hear the rumble of the wagon first. It was the weeping of the children that foretold their arrival. She came out of her wagon box home to see what was the matter.

The front of Knight's clothing was covered with blood, as was the side of Sallie Baker's head. One little girl's arm had been shot clean through, shattering the bone and leaving the limb hanging by flesh alone. Knight got down from the wagon and came to his wife.

"We need to get these children something to eat and then bedded down," he said.

The woman seemed not to hear. She stared at the children for a moment. Her lips began to tremble, and then tears of anguish began to stream down her cheeks.

"Sam, Sam," she moaned. "My god, Sam, what have you done?"

Knight stood speechless, his head hung in shame, as his wife fled from the awful scene.

After the dead were searched, the militiamen were called together. The men from Cedar were ordered to camp there on the field for the night, but the men from Washington and Santa Clara were free to go. Some of the Cedar men had already left for Hamblin's. Lee went back to camp to get his horse, then he and Higbee and Klingensmith set out for Hamblin's ranch to get something to eat and stay for the night.

At the ranch Lee took his supper, then spread his saddle blanket on the ground and, using his saddle for a pillow, lay down to sleep. His exhaustion was as much emotional as it was physical. As he lay looking up at the stars, he heard an argument going on, but he didn't care anymore.

Some of the men, not satiated by the day's events, came for Laura Jean Deaton. Isaac Delaney stood blocking their way, his right hand resting on the handgrip of his revolver.

"You ain't taking her," said Delaney with resolve.

"She ain't innocent blood. She's over eight," said one of the men. "She knows too much."

"There's been enough killing for one day," said Delaney. "The girl's coming with me. I have a wife that's barren. We're going to raise this girl. I'll fight any man who tries to stop me."

Isaac Delaney took the girl and led her to the horse he had obtained of the emigrant stock. He mounted the animal, then helped Laura Jean up behind him. In a few moments he had disappeared in the darkness.

# 66

*Saturday, September 12, 1857* Scenes of blood and violence had tormented John D. Lee in his sleep. He heard the gunfire and saw the bodies falling to the ground. He heard the screaming and the loud voices of...dream was blending with reality. He heard Isaac Haight and William Dame quarreling with each other. Lee opened his eyes. It was daylight. He tried to get up, but his middleaged body just didn't want to cooperate. Lee struggled anyway, and got to his feet. He felt a little stiffness in nearly every joint.

Lee made his way over to Haight and Dame, and soon learned that they and several others had arrived at the Hamblin ranch sometime in the night. Lee and the others took breakfast at a campfire a short distance from Hamblin's house. There was little conversation about the massacre.

After they had finished eating, Lee, Haight, Dame, and several of the others saddled their horses and rode back down to the Meadows to bury the dead and take care of the property that was still there. Upon reaching the Meadows, they stopped at that part of the field where the women were lying dead and dismounted. The bodies had been stripped entirely naked, a loathsome and ghastly scene.

Lee stayed close to Dame and Haight, wondering what their reaction would be when they saw the results of their orders. Colonel Dame was silent for some time. He looked all over the field, and was quite pale, and looked uneasy and frightened. On the ground in front of him was the naked body of a woman, who in life must have been fairly attractive. She looked to be about thirty years old with long, strawberry blond hair. She had an ugly wound in the right side of her ribs and her skull had been crushed on the left side. She lay face up. The skin was already beginning to swell and discolor. Dozens of flies swarmed on her lips and the side of her head, partaking of the blood that had so recently given the woman life. It was sickening. Dame finally understood the difference between giving and executing orders for wholesale killing.

Dame spoke to Haight, and said, "I must report this matter to the authorities."

"How will you report it?" said Haight.

"I will report it just as it is."

"Yes, I suppose so, and implicate yourself with the rest?"

"No," said Dame. "I will not implicate myself, for I had nothing to do with it."

Anger flashed in Haight's eyes. "That will not do," he said, "for you know a damned sight better. You ordered it done. Nothing has been done except by your orders, and it is too late in the day for you to order things done and then go back on it and go back on the men who have carried out your orders. You cannot sow pig on me, and I will be damned if I will stand for it. You are as much to blame as anyone, and you know that we have done nothing except what you ordered done. I know that I have obeyed orders, and by God, I will not be lied on."

Colonel Dame's reaction was highly emotional. His face was scarlet, tears in his eyes, and he was overcome with the urge to just ride away and never look back.

As soon as Colonel Dame could collect himself, he said, "I didn't think there were so many of them, or I wouldn't have had anything to do with it."

Lee decided to intervene.

"Brethren," he said, "what is the trouble between you? It will not do for our chief men to disagree."

Haight came over to Lee. His face was red from anger and his dark eyes were flashing. He was unable to contain his feelings.

"The trouble is just this," said Haight. "Colonel Dame counseled and ordered me to do this thing, and now he wants to back out, and go back on me, and by God, he shall not do it. He shall not lay it all on me. He cannot do it. He must not try to do it. I will blow him to hell before he shall lay it all on me. He has got to stand up to what he did like a man. He knows he ordered it done, and I dare him to deny it."

Colonel Dame's voice was whiny and defensive, almost pleading. "Isaac, I didn't know there were so many of them."

"That makes no difference," said Haight. "You ordered me to do it, and you have got to stand up for your orders."

A crowd was beginning to gather, so Lee thought he had better put an end to the argument. "Brethren, this is no place to talk over such a matter. You will agree when you get where you can be quiet, and talk it over."

Haight said, "There is no more to say, for he knows he ordered it done, and he has got to stand by it."

Lee, Dame, and Haight began walking along the field. The militiamen still on the field were hard at work digging graves for the emigrants. Owing to the dry weather and the lack of enough tools, they were making very little progress. In the end they just piled up the bodies in heaps in the gullies and threw a little dirt over them.

Haight and Dame continued walking the Meadows as Lee gave them a detailed account of how the massacre had been carried out and each man's role in it. Eventually, they reached the emigrant corral. It had undergone a dramatic transformation. The Indians had ransacked everything. The wagon covers, the clothing and provisions, all gone. They had even emptied the feathers from the featherbeds and carried off all the ticks.

When the task of burying the dead was finished, the militia was called together at the emigrant corral. The bloody deed had been accomplished. Now it was time to put the best face on it, to cover it up.

The leading brethren, Lee, Colonel Dame, President Haight, Klingensmith, Higbee, and Hopkins gave speeches. They spoke words of thankfulness. First, that the men had been protected from harm, and second, that God had delivered their enemies into their hands. They exhorted the men to keep the matter secret and counseled them to lay the blame on the Indians.

Isaac Haight had been deeply moved by what he had seen, the results of the orders he had helped formulate. The spirit of prophecy fell upon him, and he knew what effect these events would have upon the men who had taken part. Only a few days before he had given a great speech advocating violence. Now a spirit of great humility worked upon him as he spoke.

"Brethren, this is the saddest day in the history of our Church. You are men holding the Priesthood. That Priesthood imposes a responsibility upon you to your God and to your fellow man. Pray to God for understanding and mercy. Your fellow men will condemn you. An army is approaching our gates. War is being thrust upon us by our government. The people who lie on this battleground were civilians. Their crime was against the Indians. Their threats were against the Mormons. God knows there have been many causes for conflict between Indians and whites.

"In this incident someone forgot God, or became prey to fear or revenge. This day in the presence of these dead, promise yourselves that you will not converse about what has happened here. Your silence is your safety. And judge not lest you be judged. Condemn not lest you condemn yourself. Speak not lest you be misunderstood. This is war. You were under military orders.

"These children that you have saved from the Indians must be cared for in our homes. They must be loved and protected from all harm and sorrow. They must be treated with more thoughtfulness than our own.

"You must continue to live as close neighbors and friends, attending the same church services and enjoying the same social affairs. If you must speak, speak with me of what you have seen and heard, and as your brother in the Gospel, I will do all in my power to help you. God is our salvation. We must trust in Him. May God be merciful, and help us to live as good Christian Saints, with understanding and kindness.

"The Indians are wards of the United States Government. Their part in this battle must be reported to the Governor of this territory. As your religious advisor I request that the Indian Farmer, Major Lee, report to his superior officer the causes and the results of the Indians' participation in this battle.

"We, as citizens in these scattered settlements, must be prepared for any eventuality from these aroused Indians. Be calm. Remain within the community bounds. Keep guards posted night and day. Remember, we must carry forward our Iron missions assigned to us in this part of Zion."

Col. Dame's words were not as comforting. He proposed, and it was voted unanimously, that anyone who betrayed the secret or revealed the names of those participating in the massacre would forfeit his life.

The men raised their right arms to the square and repeated the oath given by Col. Dame. They swore never to reveal what they had seen or heard or done this day as long as they should live. They were not to talk about it to anyone, their most intimate friends, or their wives, or even among themselves, and they would kill anyone who broke this covenant, the traitor to be disemboweled and his throat cut.

It was then voted to turn all the property over to Klingensmith, to be administered by him as the bishop of Cedar City. Colonel Dame then blessed the men and told them to return to their homes. Little did they know that the dark secret, like the feathers dumped by the Indians from the featherbeds, would blow on the wind, defying all efforts to keep it contained. Some would lie, others would shift the blame, and some would even reveal the secret to their enemies, but in the main most would carry the truth of the massacre locked away in their hearts, never to reveal the truth to anyone.

# 67

*Sunday, September 13, 1857* When James Haslam rode up to Isaac Haight's house, Haight had seen him coming, and came out to greet him. Haslam had made better time on the return from Salt Lake City and it showed. He was covered with a fine coating of dust and his eyes were bloodshot and glazed. There was not a part of his body that didn't ache.

"I have seen the prophet," he said, "and he sends his instructions."

Haslam dismounted and removed the letter from inside his coat and handed it to Haight. Haslam watched silently as Haight unfolded the letter and read it. A strange look appeared on Haight's face. The color drained away and he seemed to stare off in the distance, his mouth open. As he read it a second time his hands began to shake and his lips quivered. Tears welled in his eyes as he let the paper fall from his hands.

"Too late! Too late!" he cried out in anguish, then he wept bitterly. Shoulders slumped, Haight trudged slowly back to his house.

Tired and dirty, Haslam let his forehead rest against the saddle on his horse. He was heartbroken. He had failed.

# 68

The sound of gunfire and the bloodcurdling yells of the Indians mixed with the terrified screams of the women and children as they ran for their lives. Laura Jean Deaton looked down at her dress. There was blood all over it. The face of an Indian loomed before her. He raised his knife to strike. Laura Jean jumped from the wagon and ran toward her mother. Sarah Deaton was being dragged to the ground by two Indians and then bludgeoned repeatedly with clubs. Blood splattered everywhere.

"Mama! Mama! Mama!"

"There, there now, child," said Kathleen Delaney, taking the girl into her arms. "It's only a bad dream."

Isaac Delaney stood in the doorway of the bedroom as his plural wife comforted Laura Jean. Nearly a week had passed since the massacre. He was deeply troubled by the scenes of the slaughter that refused to leave his own mind. No wonder this little girl was having nightmares. Isaac shook his head. The fear and torment Laura Jean must have experienced was unimaginable. He had participated willingly, eager to display his faith and loyalty even to the point of nearly taking his own son's life. For two days now, ever since he had heard of the letter from Brigham Young, he had been too ashamed to leave his home. How could he have been so blind?

# The Long Way Home

# 69

*WANTED —Young, skinny, wiry fellows not over 18. Must be expert riders willing to risk death daily. Orphans preferred.*

*March, 1860* Nearly three years had passed since the massacre at Mountain Meadows. The newspaper Joel Deaton was reading was several months old. Joel's escape from Utah Territory had been without any further incident. He had captured a stray horse and had ridden all night. Food had been hard to come by. He stole most of what he needed along the way, a fact that he lamented, but his extraordinary circumstances had called for extraordinary measures. At the Mormon settlement at Santa Clara he left the California road and followed the riverbed through the Virgin River gorge. For ten days he hid out by day and traveled by night, across the parched desert until he reached the little town called San Bernardino.

Life had been hard for Joel in California. He had never been on his own before and he was ill-prepared for being thrust so suddenly into adulthood. Jobs were plentiful, but the pay was low. Joel needed money to get back home. He had never been keen on the idea of coming to California in the first place. He longed for the green hills of northern Arkansas.

Worst of all was the secret Joel kept locked within. There seemed to be Mormons everywhere. He knew it would be certain death to reveal that secret. But now his chance had come. The Pony Express was about to begin operation, and, though he was now a year older than the specified age, the job was just what he needed. The pay was excellent. It wouldn't take long to raise the money he needed to return home.

On the morning of March 23, 1860, Joel presented himself, at the office of Bolivar Roberts in Carson City, Nevada. Roberts was the divisional manager for the Roberts Creek to Sacramento segment of the Pony Express.

"You should've applied sooner," said Roberts. "We have a full crew for the time being."

"I came as soon as I knew about it," said Joel.

"Too bad. Service starts in about a week. Tell you what, though. Come back this afternoon. The divisional manager from Salt Lake City is coming in and he might need some people."

Joel's face lit up. "I'll be here, sir. You can count on it!"

Howard Egan was a Mormon, born in Ireland, but raised in America from the age of eight. He married at the age of 23 and settled in Salem, Massachusetts, where he was converted to the Mormon faith by Erastus Snow. After his conversion he moved to Nauvoo, Illinois, where he worked at the trade of rope maker. He was a member of the police force there and a major in the Nauvoo Legion. After the death of Joseph Smith he went west with the Saints and was in the first pioneer party that entered the Great Salt Lake Valley in 1847.

Egan was the Superintendent of the Pony Express Division from Salt Lake City to Robert's Creek. He had spent the past few weeks setting up stations along his portion of the route, and had come to Carson City to coordinate the first run with Roberts. Fate was with Joel Deaton. Had he come a day sooner or a day later, he would have missed his opportunity.

"Howard, this is Joel Deaton," said Roberts as Joel entered the room.

Egan, a heavily bearded, balding man with baleful eyes, rose from his chair and extended his hand.

"Pleased to meet you, young man," said Egan. "I have a son about your age. He's gonna ride for us, too."

"Take a seat," said Roberts.

"Thank you," said Joel.

"I hear you need a job," said Egan.

"That's right. Mr. Roberts says you're from Salt Lake City. Are you a Mormon?"

Egan looked at Roberts then at Joel. "That's right. Is that a problem for you?"

Joel's face colored slightly. His mouth went dry and he could feel his heart pounding in his throat. They would know if he was lying and he didn't dare talk about Mountain Meadows. He had been foolish to say anything. Now he probably wouldn't get the job.

"Well," said Joel slowly, "I ain't never really known a Mormon before. Oh, I met a few, but we weren't never very close, if you take my meaning."

Egan snorted. "Don't like Mormons, huh?"

"I didn't say that, sir."

"Didn't have to. But it don't matter. Most gentiles don't." Egan stroked his beard for a few moments. "I've got just the place for you...where you'll feel right at home."

Joel's heart began to race now for a different reason. This sounded like a job offer. "Where's that?"

"Camp Floyd. I need a stock tender. None of my people feel good about consorting with them soldiers. You'll do just fine."

Joel hung his head in disappointment. He would have preferred being a rider instead of feeding horses and cleaning out stalls, but it was a job and it would get him closer to going home. "Yes," he said, "I'll take the job."

"Good decision," said Egan. "Now if you would stand up, you can take the oath."

Joel rose to his feet and took the paper Egan handed to him. "Raise your right hand," said Egan, "and take the oath. Just write your name where you see the blank spot."

Joel looked it over, then raised his right hand and gave the oath. "I, Joel Deaton, do hereby swear, before the great and living God, that during my engagement, and while I am an employee of Russell, Majors & Waddell, I will, under no circumstances, use profane language. I will drink no intoxicating liquors. I will not quarrel or fight with any other employee of the firm, and that in every respect, I will conduct myself honestly, faithful to my duties, and so direct my acts as to win the confidence of my employers. So help me God."

"Good. Now sign it on the line at the bottom."

Joel signed the document at the designated spot, then handed it to Egan. Egan shook Joel's hand, then gave him a Bible. "Joel," said Egan, "welcome to the Pony Express."

With Bible in hand, Joel left the Pony Express offices in high spirits.

# 70

Camp Floyd was unlike any place Joel Deaton had ever been. It had sprung up in the summer of 1858 from the sagebrush in Cedar Valley, west of Utah Lake, beyond the mountain that hid Provo and the other settlements from view.

General Albert Sydney Johnston had marched his 2,500 troops down Emigration Canyon and through Salt Lake City on June 26, 1858. Their first camp was across the Jordan River, about four miles southwest of the temple square.

The permanent camp in the Cedar Valley had been chosen because of its ample supply of water and pasture, but more important, because of its commanding position. If called for, the force could be promptly applied either in the direction of Salt Lake City or Provo. The post covered an area of more than a thousand acres and quickly grew to more than three hundred buildings. Like most military posts there were no walls or fortifications, just a sprawling array of mostly adobe buildings that was finally ready to be officially opened on November 9, 1858.

No matter what their official purpose for being in the territory, the arrival of the troops had made an unqualified success of the Utah economy. Local labor had been paid to build the fort, using lumber purchased from the local lumber mills, and the Mormon farmers had suddenly acquired a new market for their fresh produce.

Overnight the town of Fairfield had grown from a few Mormon families to become the third largest city in the territory. The usual assortment of unsavory characters was drawn to the new post like fleas to a dog. Soon, seventeen saloons were doing business. The gamblers, thieves, and prostitutes were doing all they could to separate the soldiers from their monthly pay. Like many other such towns, this one was called Dobytown. The first one must have been built of adobes, hence the name. Some even said they were all populated with the same people. In any case, this one was no different.

John Carson, a Mormon immigrant from Pennsylvania, and one of the founders of Fairfield, built an inn to accommodate California stagecoach travelers. Now, two years later, the inn was the first major stop of the Pony Express west of Salt Lake City.

Joel Deaton arrived at Carson's Inn on the morning of April 3, 1860. It was his first trip ever on a stagecoach. Howard Egan had advanced the fare, and had made it clear that it would be repaid out of Joel's salary.

John Carson, owner of the inn, was also the stationmaster. He liked horses, and wasn't a stranger to hard work. He was waiting for Joel as he stepped down from the stagecoach.

"Are you Deaton?"

"Yes sir, I am."

"My name's John Carson. My friends call me Johnny, but you can call me Mr. Carson for the time being. You'll be working for me. I got you a place to stay in Dobytown, so get your baggage and follow me."

The streets of Dobytown were littered and dusty, and soldiers were lounging everywhere. It was not yet noon, but already business was brisk.

Joel's lodgings could not be described as comfortable or even adequate. It was a two-room shanty with a dirt floor and an outhouse in back. The worst dwelling he had seen in California was a palace by comparison. With no time for settling in, Joel put his things down and returned with Carson to begin learning his duties.

Joel soon discovered that he was near the bottom of the social scale. Shoveling horse manure was not only dirty work, but it deposited an odor that followed him everywhere, no matter how much he tried to scrub it away. Joel took notice every time a Pony Express rider came in. They slept at the inn and ate in the dining room. They were paid more and treated with deference. What did they have that he didn't? Joel knew how to ride. Maybe if he'd kept his mouth shut about Mormons the day he was interviewed by Egan, he'd be riding horses instead of cleaning up after them. In the final analysis, the job itself didn't matter as long as he was earning money to pay his way back to the States.

Spring had turned to summer when Joel met Eddie Butler, a soldier of the Second Dragoons. Their meeting wasn't exactly of the ordinary variety. Joel was partaking of the pleasures of Dobytown in one of the saloons when Eddie Butler introduced himself.

"Hey, you ignorant bastard! Get your smelly Mormon ass outta here!"

The young soldier was drunk and obviously confused about Joel's antecedents and his religious affiliation, probably because he worked for the Mormon stationmaster.

"This place is for soldiers and real men, so beat it!"

"I see," said Joel, sizing up his opponent. "Which are you, sir? A soldier...or a real man?"

In spite of his drunkenness, Pvt. Butler knew when he had been insulted. He charged forward, his fists flailing wildly, but he was no match for anyone who was sober. Joel deftly stepped aside and shoved the man headfirst into the bar, which was two planks laid across two whiskey barrels at either end.

The bartender, a greasy-looking fellow with a pock-marked face, would have none of this. He came around the bar with a bung starter in his hand, ready to do business.

"All right, you two. Get out of here before I whip the both of you."

The soldier lay face down, his head bleeding. No one seemed intent on helping him, not even the other soldiers. Joel reached down and grabbed the unconscious man by his belt and dragged him out the door. Outside, he propped the soldier up in a shady spot and took a look at his head wound. It didn't appear to be very serious. Joel was about to leave when he felt a prod in his ribs and heard the unmistakable sound of a pistol's hammer being drawn back.

"Give me one good reason why I don't blow your guts out," said Pvt. Butler.

"Well, sir," said Joel in a quiet voice, "I may be a tetch smelly, but I ain't no Mormon...just work for 'em."

"Do tell?" said Butler, with a grin. "I'm beginnin' to like you already. Help me back inside and I'll drink a toast to your good health."

"Don't believe we're welcome in there no more, leastwise not today." Joel looked up and down the street at the other saloons. "But I do believe we can be accommodated somewhere else."

Joel helped the soldier to his feet. "Don't believe we've been properly introduced. Joel Deaton from Arkansas."

"Eddie Butler. Didn't figure you for a country boy. Next time I'll be more careful."

The two young men sauntered off down the street, intent on getting both drunk and better acquainted. Joel had known a lot of people during the past three years, but Eddie Butler was to be his first real friend since Charlie Mitchell.

# 71

Eddie Butler was a backwoodsman from southern Alabama. He had enlisted in the Army because it was the only way out of a life of grinding poverty. Next to getting drunk and consorting with lewd women, he liked to hunt and fish better than anything. Joel had a liking for the outdoor activities, but he wasn't so sure about the other. The two young men got away as often as they could to the Jordan River where they spent many an hour dunking worms in the small stream.

On a hot day in early July they rode over to the Provo River to try their hand at catching trout. It was cool sitting in the shade with their bare feet dangling in the cold water that had until recently been part of a snow bank high in the Uintah Mountains. Joel was lost in his own thoughts when he was suddenly dragged back to reality.

"Hot damn!" shouted Butler. "Got me a big one!"

Indeed it was. Over a foot long, it looked like it weighed more than ten pounds. As it was already past noon, Joel and Eddie Butler decided to clean their catch and eat it. The fish were sizzling in the pan when Joel began to reminisce out loud.

"My Daddy used to take me fishin' before we came west. 'Cept it was for catfish back then."

"Didn't you say you was from Arkansas?"

"Well, not originally. Pa went bust in '49 tryin' t'get to California. We was livin' in Mississippi back then. Ended up in Arkansas."

"How'd y'get out here?"

"In a wagon."

"Very funny," said Butler. "What about your family? They livin' in California?"

Joel thought of MacKenzie and Sarah Deaton. His eyes got a little misty. He wanted to trust Butler, but he thought better of it. "Don't got no folks, 'cept some aunts and uncles in Mississippi. Thought I'd earn enough money to get me back to Arkansas. I know a few people back there."

"Y'know, we was down in the southern part of the territory last year," said Butler. "Picked up a bunch of little kids that was saved from that massacre three years back. Ever' one of 'em was from Arkansas."

Joel felt a trembling sensation up and down his legs, and a hollow feeling in the pit of his stomach. "There was survivors?"

"Yep. Not many, though. I recollect there was sixteen, seventeen. Sump'n like that. Some of 'em didn't even know what their names was, they was so little. One little gal had been shot clean through her arm. Pitiful sight that was. And the place where they was killed...hope I never see nothin' like that again. Bones scattered ever' where, skulls bashed in, pieces of clothin' hangin' on the sagebrush, flappin' in the wind. We buried 'em 'fore we left. Terrible. Terrible. I'll never forget it."

Joel got up and walked to the riverbank. He had to gulp huge amounts of air to keep himself from crying. He had seen it all, but he hadn't really thought about it for so long. And now to have the scene described in such graphic terms was more than he could handle.

"You all right, Joel? I didn't know you'd be so upset."

Joel wrestled his emotions to the ground and tucked them neatly away before he turned to face the young soldier.

"Just thinkin' of them little kids without no mamas or daddies. Kinda reminded me of my folks."

"I'm sorry," said Butler. "I won't ever talk of it again."

Could it be? Could Laura Jean still be alive? Was she back in Arkansas, just waiting for him to come home? Did she know he was alive? The possibilities seemed endless. If Laura Jean was still alive, he would find her. He said nothing aloud, but silently he swore an oath that he would not rest until he knew for certain the fate of his little sister.

# 72

Joel didn't get much time off. He was expected to put in 60 hours a week. Sundays were generally free. The only church services were either at Camp Floyd or with the Mormons. Joel had known for a long time what he must do, but it had taken him until August to get up the courage to do it. So on a Sunday, early in the month, he borrowed a horse from the Pony Express stable and headed north. He got an early start and was passing Fort Union by ten o'clock in the morning.

Church services weren't until the afternoon, so Eli Bennett was at home. When he opened his door and found Joel Deaton standing there, hat in hand, he was dumbstruck. Several moments passed as he stared at the young man.

"Eli. It's me...Joel Deaton."

"Uh...yes, but I...uh, well, sure it's you, Joel, but how...I mean...you're alive!"

"I reckon you heard about the massacre."

Bennett's eyes dropped. "Yes, Joel, I heard about it. But I heard they was all killed...'cept a few small children. How did you..."

"Escape? Pure luck, I'd say."

Joel and Eli Bennett sat on the porch for more than an hour as Joel recounted the fate of the Fancher wagon train and his subsequent escape to California. Bennett listened intently, interrupting from time to time with a pertinent question. When the tale had been told, Bennett sat hunched over, his hands clenched together, a look of deep sadness on his face.

"I can tell you're real bitter about this," said Bennett. "Probably hate the Mormons."

Joel nodded. "Only reason I come is because you were Pa's friend. I figured you deserved to know what had happened to him."

"What're you gonna do now, Joel?"

"Well, I heard the Army has found some of the little kids and sent 'em back home. I think Laura Jean was in that wagon with the others and maybe she made it back home. I dunno, but I gotta find out."

"Let it go, son. She ain't alive no more. She was too old. She wasn't innocent blood." A memory flashed into Joel's mind of the time they had visited three years before and the doctrine of accountability.

"Innocent blood!" Joel stood up abruptly, emitting a guttural sound of disgust. "You're tellin' me my sister wasn't an innocent child?" Joel's hand drifted toward the revolver strapped to his hip. "My god, Eli, I can't believe you said that! If you wasn't Pa's friend, you'd be a dead man! But seein' that you was, I'm gonna forget you said it."

Eli Bennett looked more distressed than ever. Joel stepped off the porch and headed for his horse.

"I understand your feelin's, Joel," said Bennett. Joel did not look back. "Listen to me, Joel! Please!"

Joel swung into the saddle and waited, glaring at the man as he approached.

"Don't ever tell a soul about this, Joel," said Bennett, his voice trembling. "I expect there's some people'd take your life if they knew."

"I'll find Laura Jean," said Joel, his eyes flashing with anger. "And when I know she's safe, I'm gonna track down the men that did it. I'll kill every one of 'em."

Joel turned the head of his horse and galloped off toward the west, back toward Camp Floyd. Eli Bennett watched him go and shook his head. He would have preferred to think that Joel had been killed with the others. It wasn't easy to know you were hated by the son of your best friend.

The miles ticked off ever more slowly. The horse hadn't had much time to rest and was about to give out by the time Joel reached the Pony Express station north of Point of the Mountain. He tied up outside the station and went into the tavern run by the stationmaster.

Joel ordered a dinner of steak and potatoes, accompanied by a glass of beer. The stationmaster served as host, and sometimes as cook. He had been staring at Joel ever since he had arrived. Now, as Joel was cleaning up the last few bites, the man came over to talk.

"Never forget a face," said Porter Rockwell. "We've met somewhere before."

Joel looked at the man, surprised. It was true. They *had* met. But Joel couldn't remember where either. They looked at each other for several moments, then Joel felt a sudden chill down his spine. Now he knew...and he hoped the other man didn't.

"I'm, uh, I work for the Pony Express at Camp Floyd. Maybe you've seen me there."

Rockwell pulled on his beard. "Could be," he said slowly. "Headed for town?"

"No, sir. On my way back. My horse is 'bout played out. Figured I'd rest up here for awhile."

"Your horse or Pony Express stock?"

"I don't own a horse."

"Wal, if it's got the Pony Express brand, just leave 'er here and take one o' ours. Don't make no difference, long as we come out with the right number o' horses."

Rockwell laughed, a wide grin showing through his whiskers, but his eyes gave no hint of humor. He was still sizing up the young man, trying to place where they had met.

Outside, Joel switched the saddle from one horse to the other and quickly mounted. He rode out as quickly as he dared, without seeming to be in too big of a hurry. He didn't look back and would have been glad he hadn't if he had known Porter Rockwell had watched him until he was out of sight. Joel made a mental note that he should avoid this place at all costs.

# Every Man's Sword Shall Be Against His Brother

# 73

Summer faded into fall and then winter came. Joel had settled into a routine existence, shoveling manure, feeding stock, and getting drunk with his growing number of friends among the soldiers of Camp Floyd. He had been thrifty and had saved enough to get his outfit for the trip back to the States. When spring came and the mountain passes were once again open, he planned to begin his trek homeward, at last mounted on his own horse. However, events were developing that would have a profound effect upon Joel's future.

As always, the birds heralded the coming of a new day. At the first sign of dawn they began to sing their little hearts out. The stars had lost some of their glitter and the velvet blackness of the nighttime sky was giving way to shades of gray. The sea was calm and a gentle breeze was blowing. On the eastern horizon a dark form was beginning to appear separate from the surrounding gloom. The time was 4:30 A.M. on April 12, 1861.

"You may fire when ready, Mr. Ruffin," said the artillery officer.

Edmund Ruffin of Virginia, the fiery orator and ardent separatist, pulled the lanyard on the cannon. The flash from the cannon's mouth temporarily blinded those nearby. Before the shell reached its mark, other batteries around the harbor had joined in. In the next 34 hours 4,000 shells would fall on Fort Sumter. The Civil War had begun.

Bad news traveled fast, thanks to the Pony Express. Almost immediately, many of the southern soldiers at Camp Floyd began making plans to return home. Joel Deaton didn't care either way. Regardless of the impending conflict, he was going home to find his sister. There was other bad news, though, and it, too, was brought to Joel by a man on horseback...Eli Bennett.

Joel was busy feeding the horses when Bennett entered the Pony Express stable.

"What brings you out here, Eli?" said Joel.

Bennett took off his hat and slowly turned it around the index finger of his right hand. Considering the attitude Joel had displayed when they last met, he wasn't exactly sure how to begin this conversation.

"Come to give you a warning, Joel."

Joel continued to feed the horses as if nothing had been said. Bennett had expected some response and looked a little perturbed that he hadn't gotten one. "I've heard talk, Joel."

"What about?"

"About you."

"Nothin' good, I reckon."

"No," said Bennett slowly.

"Then what is it?"

"There's talk that the leading brethren want you put out of the way."

"Is that so?"

"You don't seem much bothered by it."

"Should I be?"

"Don't you know what this means?" asked Bennett.

"Sure. Porter Rockwell's finally figured out where he's seen me. Well, it don't matter much. Long as I mind my own business here, nobody's gonna bother me. Too public."

"Joel, I'm real sorry you don't have the sense your father did. If Porter Rockwell's on your trail, you're a dead man just waiting to be planted."

"I've heard about 'im," said Joel, "but he don't scare me none. I ain't long for the Territory anyway. 'Spect I'll be leavin' for Arkansas any day now."

"I'm glad to hear that, Joel. You're the only grownup witness to the massacre. Knowin' that makes a lotta people nervous."

"They ought t'be. 'Specially the ones that done it. You put the word out. Judge Cradlebaugh couldn't arrest the guilty parties. Couldn't even get 'em charged by the grand jury. But I'll be back...and I'll see that justice gets done. You tell 'em that."

Bennett shook his head slowly. "I can't even let on that I know you, Joel. I think you'd better be movin' on...just as soon as you can."

Joel pitched some more hay for the horses and then turned around to say something. Eli Bennett was gone. In spite of his bluster, Joel really was scared. He had indeed heard about Porter Rockwell. He was the toughest, most dangerous man in the Territory...maybe even in the West. Joel reasoned that if he went public and told the story they just might be afraid to bother him. If he did, though, there would be so much publicity that he would find it impossible to carry out his plans. Eli Bennett was right. It was time to be moving on.

# 74

Joel and his southern compatriots sat huddled around the campfire. The nights on the trail were colder than he had remembered. They had left Camp Floyd before the end of April and were making good time. They had avoided going through the Mormon capital by taking the military road up Provo Canyon. Nevertheless, Joel couldn't shake the feeling that he was being stared at every time they came in contact with Mormons. Somewhere, a short distance east of Fort Bridger, they had noticed a party of a few men following less than a mile to the rear. Now, as they warmed themselves by the fire, it seemed like a natural topic of conversation.

"What do you make of it?" Joel asked Eddie Butler.

"Dunno. They move when we move. Camp when we camp. Never get no closer. Never get no farther away."

The time had come. Joel would have to trust someone. Besides, now that the Mormons knew about him and that he was an eyewitness, it was pointless to keep it a secret.

"Remember when you told me about the Mountain Meadows massacre?"

Butler was surprised. He had been impressed that Joel found the massacre a subject too distasteful to discuss. In the pale flickering light of the fire his eyes were shaded from view by the brim of his hat. He took a few moments to size up his young friend.

"Reckon I do. Why do you ask?"

"I was there, Eddie."

"Where?"

"At Mountain Meadows."

"When?"

Joel leaned forward and looked directly into Butler's eyes. He spoke the words slowly and with great intensity. "When they murdered my parents and all the rest. I was there. I saw it all."

Butler's face went blank at first, then his eyebrows took on a look of great thoughtfulness. "Now I see why you was so riled up that day when we was fishin'. How did you get mixed up in all that?"

Joel proceeded to tell Butler and the others everything: coming west, the humiliation by the Indians, Cordelia Huff, Charlie Mitchell, the arrogance of the Missourians, and the run in with the law at Cedar City. The telling of the massacre was more painful than the wound he had received to his leg from the Indians. Eddie Butler listened until Joel was through, not asking a single question. Then followed a long silence.

"Anyone else know about this?" asked Butler finally.

"Could be," said Joel. "I've heard they're out to kill me. I can't help wonderin' if them ol' boys camped over 'cross the way might not be some of them destroyin' angels I've heard about."

Every head turned in the direction of the other campsite.

"That would explain a lot," said Butler. "Question is, what're y'gonna do about it?"

"I figured I'd just go over and ask 'em."

"Go on!" said Butler incredulously. "You wouldn't!"

"Don't see why not. Can't think of a better way."

Joel stood up and strapped on his revolver. He wanted some answers, but he didn't want to take any unnecessary chances. If Eli Bennett had been present, he would have just shaken his head in disbelief at that idea.

At the other campsite five grim-faced men huddled around the fire. Joel scouted the vicinity and found no sentry posted. He took a deep breath and strode into the camp.

The men were obviously startled to see someone suddenly appear out of the darkness. There was a brief flurry of movement, then all was still.

"Who might you be?" asked one of the men.

"I'm from the other camp. You men have been shadowin' us for a few days, now, almost as if you was followin' us. Any reason for that?"

"None in particular. We prefer to keep to ourselves, but don't mind havin' someone nearby in case there's Injun trouble."

None of the men appeared to be wearing sidearms. Joel relaxed, but only a little.

"The name's Joel Deaton, if that means anything to you."

It apparently did to one man. He jumped up and sprinted toward a shotgun that was propped against a rock.

"Don't do it!" yelled Joel, drawing his revolver.

The man picked up the gun and whirled around. Joel fired three times and the man fell in a heap. Then things began to happen too quickly. The other four men were all moving. Joel couldn't tell if they were going for guns or scrambling for cover. In an instant Joel was surrounded by the men from his own camp. Each man was well-armed and ready to shoot. Their opponents stopped moving and raised their hands.

"Looks like you had more'n you could handle," said Eddie Butler.

"I didn't think this would happen," said Joel. "What do we do now?"

"Well, looks like we're gonna have to kill 'em," said Butler.

"No!" said one of the men. "We've got families."

Joel thought of his vow to avenge his own family. He felt no anger toward these men. The fire didn't burn in his belly. He wasn't really sure what all this meant, whether they had meant to harm him or not. Oh, he didn't feel any guilt for shooting the man who had gone for the shotgun, but killing these other men didn't seem right.

"I don't think we ought t'do it," said Joel. "As far as that other fellow is concerned, I think everybody'd agree it was self defense."

"Oh, yes. Absolutely," said one of the men with his hands in the air. A general chorus of support for that idea was voiced by his companions.

"They'll hang you, Joel," said Butler. "It'll be their word against yours. We can't just let 'em ride outta here."

"Damn!" said Joel. "I don't know what to do."

"Leave it to us," said one of the southern soldiers. "We c'n take care of 'em without killin' 'em."

Joel thought it over for a few moments, then holstered his revolver and started back for camp. He didn't look back.

The next morning Joel awoke to find no sign of the other camp. He didn't ask and no one offered to tell. He did notice they had acquired a few extra horses. When the soldiers left the main trail and struck out cross-country toward the southeast, Joel didn't have to ask if they were trying to avoid pursuit.

The weather continued to improve and they made good time. They picked up the same trail the Fancher wagon train had traveled four years before. A small settlement called Denver was now where Cherry Creek met the South Platte.

Before three more weeks had passed, they had crossed the imaginary line between the Indian Nations and Arkansas. It was only an illusion, but for the first time in years Joel Deaton felt at peace with the world. He was home.

# 75

Joel Deaton paid no attention to the crowd gathering near the Carroll County courthouse. It was a bright sunny day and he had business to take care of. Eddie Butler was anxious to be moving on. He had stayed on while Joel was making inquiries about the surviving children, but, like every other southerner, Eddie Butler expected little trouble whipping the Yanks and he certainly didn't want the adventure of a lifetime to pass him by.

Joel found several of the children, and those old enough to talk were too young to remember much of their experience in Utah Territory. Meanwhile, Joel and Eddie Butler were staying at the Samuel Benton farm, and they had to spend a few hours each day earning their keep.

This day Joel was fetching the supplies from town. He continued on down the street and stopped the wagon in front of the feed store.

While his order was being filled, Joel strolled down to the courthouse to see what all the excitement was. A well-dressed man was haranguing the crowd about the damned Yankees and southern pride and patriotism. Joel had heard it all before from the southern soldiers during his last days at Camp Floyd.

While other southern states had seceded from the Union, Arkansas had taken a wait-and-see attitude. When called upon to send troops to support the Union, Arkansas Governor Rector had refused. An election was scheduled for the summer to let the people decide whether or not to join the Confederacy. Joel didn't care one way or the other. His only thoughts were to learn the fate of Laura Jean, perhaps even find her.

"...and the legislature has voted today, sixty-nine to one, to secede from the Union," said the well-dressed man. "We'll hang the Union sympathizer who voted against it as soon as we find out who he is." A ripple of laughter went through the crowd. "I'm here to organize a company of volunteers to join me in driving the damned Yankees from our fair state and to preserve our southern way of life..."

When he set out for home, Joel hadn't thought of the possibility of being asked to fight for the Confederacy. Fighting in a war didn't fit into his plans. States rights, slavery...those things didn't mean anything to him. His only desire was to find his sister, dead or alive, then take his revenge upon those who had destroyed his family. He would be pressured to volunteer if he stayed in Arkansas. Neither going north nor going back to Utah was a viable option. His father had kin in Mississippi. Perhaps there he could be sheltered from the forces that would delay or thwart the mission he had pledged himself to fulfill.

Back at the farm Joel found Eddie Butler packing.

"Leavin' already?" asked Joel.

"Sure 'nuff. When the shootin' starts for real, I wanna be in the right place. Why, with my military experience I might even get to be an officer. Yeah, maybe even a general. What d'you think?"

"A general layabout, I'd say, judging from what I saw at Camp

Floyd. Course, if they need someone that's good at fishin', I reckon you'll do."

The conversation then turned from lighthearted to serious. Joel told of his frustrations and his thoughts of going to Mississippi.

"That'd work out just right," said Butler. "Mississippi is on the way to Alabama. We could ride together at least that far."

The next morning Joel and Eddie Butler said goodbye to Mr. Benton and his family and headed east.


# 76


In spite of his best intentions, Joel Deaton found himself unable to resist the popular attitudes toward voluntary service in the Confederate Army. Most all of his uncles and cousins had signed up to whip the Yankees, and Joel found himself being swept along by the tide of history.

It was an exciting time. The people were euphoric over the prospect of getting the hated Yankees out of their lives forever. States rights, guaranteed by the Constitution, would at last be respected after having been trodden under foot for so many decades.

Joel enlisted in a new company calling themselves the Adams Rifles, because the company had been recruited by Captain Fleming W. Adams of Harrison County. Other than Adams, the men were to elect their own officers, and a lot of electioneering went on as the various candidates put themselves forth. Joel was quite flattered by the attention showered upon him by those seeking his vote. He had never realized how handsome, talented, and intelligent he was. Captain Adams was a tolerable enough leader by Joel's way of thinking. He seemed to be fit for the job. The real problem, though, was how fit the soldiers were for their job.

The Adams Rifles were marched to Corinth, Mississippi to begin their training under the tutelage of Brigadier General Charles Clark. One company did not a regiment make, so they went about the onerous duty of being transformed from country boys into soldiers.

"This here's a cartridge," said the sergeant, holding up a minie ball with a paper envelope attached containing a measured charge of gunpowder. "Now I know you country boys are used to pourin' powder down the barrel, but them days is over. To load your piece, stick this end of the cartridge in your teeth and tear the end off. Pour the powder down the barrel. Stuff the cartridge into the barrel and ram it home."

The sergeant demonstrated each step as he described it.

"Now be sure you never...I repeat, NEVER...never put a cap on the nipple before loading the cartridge. I don't know a better way to blow your own head off than that. We're s'posed t'kill Yankees, not ourselves."

The sergeant drew back the hammer half way and placed a percussion cap on the gun's nipple.

"This is the safety position," he said. "You can't fire your weapon when the rifle is halfcocked."

He cocked and pointed the musket at the target 30 yards away and fired. Joel Deaton noted that the sergeant was good at loading a gun, but not very good at shooting it. The shot was well off the mark.

"Now I'm gonna do it again to show you just how fast y'gotta be."

The sergeant loaded and fired three times in quick succession. The recruits were suitably impressed with the demonstration. Joel Deaton, like almost all the others, had done his share of shooting over the years, but this was a new approach. He sensed that survival in battle would largely depend on how well he learned the skills of the infantryman. He paid strict attention to the instructions and resolved to try his best to carry them out with precision.

The sergeant was one of the few men in the company with military experience. He had served in the army during the Mexican war in 1847, and so he was a natural to be training the recruits, though most of them viewed military training as more of a nuisance than a benefit. After all, how much training was necessary to kill "damn Yankees."

Next to close order drill, sentry duty was viewed as the most onerous aspect of military life. Nobody particularly liked it, but everybody had to take a turn at it. And so it was that Joel Deaton found himself walking his post along a stretch of country road in northern Mississippi just outside of Iuka. Joel didn't view it with the same disdain as the other soldiers. He already had plenty of experience from his trek across the plains with the Fancher train. As he marched back and forth in the darkness his emotions were stirred by memories of those days that now seemed so long ago, of his parents, Charlie Mitchell, and the beautiful Delia Huff, all of whose bones now lay above and below the ground in that beautiful valley, Mountain Meadows.

"Lucky for you I ain't no Yankee," said a voice in the darkness.

Startled, Joel snapped out of his reverie. "Who's there?"

A cackling voice called back, "Don't fret yourself none. I ain't gonna shoot you." The vague form of a man with a scruffy beard appeared out of the darkness. "Hutchins's the name. John Richard Hutchins. You c'n call me Johnny or you c'n call me Dick. Just don't call me Johnny Dick. M'folks call me that, an' I ain't never pertickerly liked it."

Joel could see the man was a soldier, but he didn't look like any of the men he had been training with. On closer examination, the beard was more fuzz than hair. The man couldn't be more than nineteen.

"Don't recollect seein' you 'round during training," said Joel.

"Don't reckon y'did. I'm with the Barksdale Grays. We're trainin' just down the road a piece."

"Where y'from?"

"Webster."

"I'm Joel Deaton," said Joel, extending his hand, "from over by Greenwood...well, not really. I growed up mostly in Arkansas, though I was born in these parts. We went west, and now I'm back, so I guess Greenwood's the closest thing I c'n call home."

"How'd y'get into the Adams Rifles?" asked Hutchins. "Ain't they from down on the gulf?"

"I been out west the past few years," said Joel. When I got home, all the folks had mustered up and gone. The Adams Rifles were passing through, so I signed up with them."

Hutchins took a good look at Joel while accepting the handshake. The conversation turned to idle chitchat as each man relished the break in the routine of sentry duty. They both quickly forgot they were supposed to be pacing back and forth on adjacent sections of road. It was great to have someone to talk to as they listened to the sound of June bugs, watched the fireflies flashing their secret code, and breathed deeply of the fragrant summer air in the deep south. Joel was a country boy at heart and always would be. He felt a closeness with the earth, with all the good things in it and on it. For now, the terrible memories of blood and tragedy were lost in the far recesses of his mind.

"What're you men doing out here?"

Joel and Johnny turned at the sound of the voice, curious, but unafraid.

"Reckon we ought t'be askin' you the same thing," said Hutchins.

"Do you know who I am?" demanded the stranger.

"Don't reckon we do," said Hutchins.

"I'm Lieutenant Sharp. Now I'm asking you again, what're you men doing out here."

Joel and Johnny looked at each other, each of them trying to stifle a grin.

"We're kinda like sentries," said Hutchins.

"I see. You're kinda like soldiers, but not really. Neither one of you knows the first thing about soldiering."

"Hey, now that ain't fair," whined Hutchins. "We've been trainin' for several weeks."

"Is that so? Then you should know that it's customary for soldiers to salute a superior officer."

"Sorry, sir," said Joel. "We couldn't tell you was an officer, what with it bein' so dark an' all."

"That's right, Lieutenant. It's just too dark out here."

"I see." The Lieutenant looked thoughtful for a few seconds, then turned to walk away. He took two steps, then quickly turned around, glaring at the two sentries. "Well!" he thundered.

Joel and Johnny looked at each other furtively, then each man gave a perfunctory salute.

"Not very good," said the Lieutenant. He turned away and quickly disappeared in the darkness.

In the morning Joel wondered what had happened to his newfound friend. As for himself, he was sitting astride a wooden rail for eight hours as regimental punishment. It was extremely uncomfortable and becoming more so by the minute.


# 77


The summer heat was oppressive, and the constant drilling was even worse. Inevitably, the troops became restless. Passes were granted and the soldiers went into town to partake of strong drink, the favors of the young ladies, and whatever other delights the town might offer. Joel was jaded by his experience back at Dobytown outside Camp Floyd, and saw little reason to join the others on their excursion to Iuka. Even the entreaties of Johnny Hutchins were of no avail. Instead, Joel spent the time updating his journal and reading a book he had borrowed.

Joel had been sleeping soundly when he was shaken awake by someone obviously under the influence and almost incoherent.

"Joel... Joel... y'gotta wake up... c'mon, Joel... I'm in big trouble... y'gotta help me... c'mon... wake up."

For a moment Joel was confused, but he soon came to his senses. The stench of alcohol emanating from the shadowy form looming above his cot was overpowering.

"Who is it?" he asked.

"It's me... Johnny Hutchins."

"Go to bed and leave me be. You're drunk." Joel rolled over and tried to go back to sleep.

"Joel," said Hutchins, pleading, "Y'gotta help me."

Joel raised up on his elbows.

"All right. What is it?"

Before Johnny could answer, the sound of angry voices rose like a sudden storm and a small group of men burst into the tent. A brief struggle ensued, almost collapsing the tent, and a screaming Johnny Hutchins was dragged outside. Joel rolled off his cot and rushed outside.

"What's happening? What's going on?"

A burley, heavyset man stepped away from the group of men that had wrestled Johnny Hutchins to the ground. He was obviously not a soldier.

"This ol' boy raped one of our girls and damn near strangled her. But it's all the same. We're gonna hang 'im either way."

Several of the soldiers in camp rushed up to the group, rifles cocked and ready. The tension instantly escalated to a greater level as both groups were armed. Captain Adams appeared a few moments later, demanding to know what the trouble was. The heavyset man gave a hurried explanation.

"Gentlemen," said Captain Adams. "This man is a soldier of the Confederacy and we will deal with him according to military law."

"See here," said the heavyset man, "we know you and your soldiers are going to be leaving any day. We aim to see that justice is done. You'll just take him outta here and forget about it. We can't have that."

Captain Adams knew he was in a difficult situation. The army needed the support of the people, but he didn't feel he could just turn one of his men over to a lynch mob, nor could he leave him behind for trial. If he did, there would probably be a lynching anyway.

"We will hold a court-martial in the morning," said the Captain. "Bring your witnesses. Until then, this man will remain in our custody."

After a moment of hesitation the civilians silently released the frightened young soldier.

"We'll be back in the morning to see that justice is done," said the big man. "See that it is."

Joel slept fitfully. At first light he was up and getting ready for the day's activities. The local citizens were also early risers. They were on the scene before most of the soldiers had gathered for breakfast. The heavyset man ate breakfast with Captain Adams and laid out his complaint.

The court-martial convened at 10:00 A.M. beneath an open canopy. Four officers, two each from the Adams Rifles and the Barksdale Grays, comprised the court: a president, a judge advocate, and two others. The president read the order to establish the jurisdiction of the court. Next, the judge advocate swore in the other members of the court, and he in turn was sworn in by the president. The judge advocate then read the charges against Johnny Hutchins.

*"Charges: assault, rape, and attempted murder. Specification: on or about the 2nd of July, 1861, during the evening hours, Pvt. John Richard Hutchins did willfully assault, violate, and attempt to take the life of Becky Stubbs, age 16, of Iuka, Mississippi. The said Pvt. Hutchins was in a state of intoxication from strong drink. He attempted to force his attention on the said Miss Stubbs, and upon being rejected he did force her to the ground, tear her clothing, and proceeded to violate her person. When the said Miss Stubbs resisted the assault, Pvt. Hutchins clasped his hands about her throat and strangled her almost to the point of death. All this near the town of Iuka, Miss. On or about the 2nd of July.*

*"F.W. Adams, Capt. C.S.A. Comdg Adams Rifles*
*"Witnesses: Lieut. R. Wilson Paine*
           *Sergeant John Quincy Reed"*

The judge advocate faced the prisoner and said, "Private Hutchins, you have heard the charges preferred against you. How say you...guilty or not guilty?"

Hutchins rose to his feet, glancing around nervously. "Not guilty, sir."

The trial was short and to the point. Mr. Stubbs, the heavyset man Joel had seen in his tent during the night and who was also the father of the girl, was the main witness for the prosecution. The young lady's torn dress was introduced as evidence. The girl testified, but appeared to be a reluctant witness. Johnny Hutchins then told his story, that the girl had been a willing participant, and that their tryst had been interrupted by the irate father before Johnny had finished his business. As to the bruises on the person of the young girl, he could only speculate that the injuries had been inflicted by her angry father or some other unknown person.

By 11:30 A.M. the officers of the court retired to consider the evidence. They returned before noon to deliver their verdict: guilty as charged. A shaken, hung over Johnny Hutchins stood before the court, his face pale and his eyes downcast.

"Private Hutchins," said the presiding officer, "do you have anything to say before sentence is passed?"

"No, sir. 'Cept I didn't do no such thing like they said I did. I'm an only child and my Ma is a widow woman. I expect that don't mean much to you gentleman, but she needs me to come home this winter when my enlistment is up to take care of her and the farm...I guess that's all I got to say."

"Gentlemen," said the presiding officer. The members of the court leaned their heads together and spoke in whispers for several seconds. The president nodded his head finally and each officer resumed his place at the table.

"Private Hutchins, it is the sentence of this court that you be taken from this court to a place to be designated and put to death by musketry at sundown today."

Johnny Hutchins staggered backwards, his eyes rolling wildly. Two soldiers took him and bound his arms, then led him away. As for Joel, he had witnessed the entire trial, and he was firmly convinced that Johnny was telling the truth. But there was nothing he could do.

After the evening meal the soldiers were formed into ranks. They were made to count off and every tenth man stepped forward. From this group lots were drawn to form two firing squads of twelve men each. The second firing squad was to be held in reserve in case the first one didn't get the job done. Each man surrendered his rifle to be loaded by one of the officers. Six rifles had bullets and six didn't, so that no man would know if he had fired a fatal shot.

Joel Deaton was horrified that he had been one of those chosen for the first firing squad. He hurriedly presented himself to Captain Adams.

"Captain Adams, sir. Johnny and me are real good friends. I would take it kindly if I might be excused from this thing. I can't do it, sir, I just can't do it."

Adams placed a hand on Joel's shoulder. "I'm sure there's a lot of these men who are friends with Private Hutchins. We're in the army. Each man must learn his duty and then do it. I'm sure I hate this thing as much as you do, but raping our young women...we can't allow those things to happen."

The soldiers were formed into a three-sided square near a grove of trees. The two firing squads were formed in two ranks within the square facing the trees. Then came the chilling sound of the drum roll. Johnny Hutchins was being marched at slow step toward the trees. The formation parted to let him and his escort pass.

Johnny was almost to the trees when a commotion arose in the rear. Colonel Russell, who had been away from camp the past two days, had just ridden in.

"What's going on here?" said the Colonel to Captain Adams. "This looks like an execution."

"It is, sir," said Adams, who hurriedly explained what had happened that day.

"I'm afraid you'll have to call it off," said the Colonel. "A death sentence must be reviewed by the commanding general. No exceptions."

Johnny Hutchins was being tied to a tree when a sergeant rushed forward with the order to halt the execution. Johnny fainted.

The news of the Confederate victory at Bull Run came by the time Joel and his comrades had completed their training and were awaiting orders. The biggest concern of the troops now was that the war might end before they had the chance to fight. They would soon learn their fears were unfounded.

Johnny Hutchins was in a constant state of anxiety as he awaited news of his fate. By mid-July enough companies had joined the Adams Rifles to form a regiment. The Adams Rifles became Company E of the Twentieth Mississippi. Orders came through for the regiment to deploy to Lynchburg, Virginia, as soon as transport could be arranged. Days passed and several trains came and went, but not the one for them. Everyone was anxious to leave, and no one more so than Johnny Hutchins.

# 78

The lynch mob from Iuka had been right. The train came and Johnny Hutchins left with the other soldiers for Virginia. Though technically under arrest, Johnny enjoyed the same freedom of movement as the other soldiers. No one spoke of the review of his death sentence, and Johnny Hutchins wasn't going to bring it up. Certainly, no news was good news.

As the regiment moved east, an almost carnival-like atmosphere existed at every town and settlement as they passed. These young soldiers were showered with praise, love, and affection as they went forth to defend the rights of the southern states.

The war in the East got all the headlines, perhaps because the two capitals of North and South were less than 100 miles apart. The primary goal of each side seemed to be to capture the capital city of the other. "Cautious" was the politest term applied to General

McClellan's leadership of the Army of the Potomac. From Bull Run to Ball's Bluff, the Union troops were driven and defeated at every turn, while "Little Mac" planned and planned, but did little. Congress was outraged by the lack of results and the Joint Committee on the Conduct of the War was set up to look into what the generals were doing. Bigger things were shaping up in the West.

The regiment encamped at Camp Davis, near Lynchburg, from July 27 until August 31. In September 1861, Kentucky finally got off the fence and cast its lot with the Union. A heavy concentration of Federal troops occupied Cairo, Illinois, and it was only a matter of time before they invaded the south. Meanwhile, General Albert Sydney Johnston received command of all Confederate forces in the West on September 10, 1861.

On the seventeenth of September Colonel Russell received orders from Richmond to report to Brigadier General John B. Floyd at Lewisburg. The regiment arrived at Sewell Mountain in the Kenawha Valley on the twenty-sixth, where General Floyd had been driven back before their arrival and General Robert E. Lee had been assigned to command in the field on the twenty-first. Upon arrival the Twentieth Mississippi Volunteer Infantry regiment had the distinction of being the first Mississippi unit to serve under the command of that greatest of Confederate generals.

Throughout the campaign in the western Virginia mountains the men were exposed to inclement weather, were without adequate food or shelter, suffered much, and lost many from sickness and death. A regiment of troops accustomed to the rigors of the winter climate in western Virginia was deemed ideal to be stationed at or near Lewisburg, South Carolina.

On the seventeenth of December the War Department detached the regiment and two other units from General Floyd's command and transferred it to South Carolina, where General Lee had been transferred after the retreat of General Rosecrans in late September.

The Mississippians took the train and traveled one entire day to their destination, and, upon arrival, were notified that the order had been countermanded and that they were to rejoin General Floyd whose brigade had been sent to Kentucky to reinforce General Albert Sydney Johnston. The regiment arrived at Chattanooga, Tennessee, on the first day of eighteen sixty-two and was hurried along to Bowling Green, Kentucky, where a great battle was expected.

The Union army had occupied Paducah, Kentucky, a few days before and General Albert Sydney Johnston responded by establishing a passive defense from Columbus, Kentucky, through

Forts Henry and Donelson to Bowling Green, which came to be known as "the long Kentucky line."

General John C. Fremont, judged by many to be incompetent as commander in the West, nevertheless did make one brilliant decision: he appointed a little known Brigadier General, Ulysses S. Grant, to command the troops at Cairo.

Grant had two options: invade via the Mississippi or up the channels of the Tennessee and Cumberland Rivers, the one guarded by Fort Henry and the other by Fort Donelson. Meanwhile, the Confederacy was content to sit and wait. As for Joel Deaton and Johnny Hutchins, they were now part of the Twentieth Mississippi assigned to General Johnston's main army at Bowling Green. What had been promised to be a short and decisive war now began to wind down for the winter. They now knew they were in for the long haul and the routine, boring life of the garrison soldier.

General Johnston knew the loss of the Mississippi and Tennessee River valleys would lay open the very heartland of the South and make ultimate victory extremely difficult if not impossible. The ability to move men and materials was the key to success, and the most efficient modes of transportation were by riverboat and by railroad. The rivers and rail lines must be protected at all costs. So, Johnston spent the winter preparing for the inevitable Union offensive, but time was not on his side.

Grant struck southward, up the Tennessee River. On February 6, 1862, Fort Henry fell so easily to the attack of Union gunboats, that it was in Federal hands before General Grant could even get there. News of the defeat reached the Confederate garrison at Bowling Green the following day.

The Confederate forces were spread too thin. Johnston then made the worst possible decision: he detached 12,000 men, including the Twentieth Mississippi, from his main army at Bowling Green and sent them to Brigadier General Gideon J. Pillow at Fort Donelson. It was not enough to make a difference and it unnecessarily weakened his forces in eastern Kentucky. Instead the troops were called upon to meet Grant's advance up the Cumberland River, which had made it necessary for the Confederate forces to abandon their position at Bowling Green. Gen. Floyd's troops were sent to Russellville and then to Clarksville, and as soon as Fort Henry fell, they were hurried to Fort Donelson.

The soldiers of the Mississippi Twentieth Infantry arrived at daybreak on the 13th of February. Brigade Commander was Colonel William E. Baldwin. Major William N. Brown commanded the Twentieth Mississippi. During the day the

Twentieth were held in reserve as the Federal attack on Fort Donelson began and grew in intensity throughout that day and into the next. While being held in reserve, Union artillery reached their position and one man died, and a handful were wounded. As darkness fell the dead and wounded were left on the battlefield to take a terrible snow storm, several inches deep.

At midnight the men of the Twentieth relieved the Seventh Texas Infantry in the trenches before Fort Donelson. The first job was to clear the trenches of snow and water. It was miserable work, and the men cursed the Seventh Texas for leaving the work to them, and all this while a brisk firing was going on due to Union sharpshooters. The rest of the night was spent strengthening the trenches. By morning the men were beginning to falter from lack of sleep.

During the early afternoon the Twentieth, with the rest of the Fourteenth Brigade, began to advance on the Federal lines. They soon found themselves in an exposed position, taking heavy Union fire throughout the rest of the day. Late in the afternoon Joel Deaton and Johnny Hutchins huddled together behind an embankment.

On the next day, the 15th, they were the last regiment to be recalled after suffering heavy casualties. It had been their first experience in combat, and they were bedraggled and dirty. Their looks of fatigue slowly transformed into half smiles. Each man quietly celebrated their survival.

Johnny's enlistment had been up in December, leaving him with two choices: return home, where he would be uncomfortably close to Iuka, or reenlist. He chose the latter, especially when he was assured by Captain Adams that charges against him could no longer be pursued once he had spent one day as a civilian between enlistments. Now, with an important battle imminent against a large Union force, he was no longer sure his decision had been the right one.

"It don't look good," said Hutchins.

"I know," said Joel. "Sorry you reenlisted?"

"Right now I am. I should've gone home. Ma needs me. Besides, them folks from Iuka don't know where I'm from."

WHOOSH! Instinctively, Joel and Johnny hugged the ground as the canister round came in and exploded about fifty yards away. They looked in the direction of the explosion. Bodies were scattered on the ground and men were screaming. Some were running around in a desperate attempt to get away from the pain.

"Damn!" said Joel, rising to his feet.

"Get down, you fool!" yelled Johnny as he pulled Joel to the ground by his belt.

The two young soldiers sat there staring, numbed by the sight. Canister was just that: a can full of grape shot, nails, pieces of scrap metal, and black powder, designed not only to kill, but also to maim. A fuse was ignited by the primary charge as the canister left the mouth of the cannon. Ideally, the fuse would set off the canister charge in the air just as it reached the enemy position, thus doing the greatest amount of damage. Cruel, but effective, the infantryman feared it more than anything else.

The Union forces had been content at first to surround the fort and shell the fortifications. Rifle fire was sporadic. The Confederates returned the fire to little effect. It didn't take a military genius to figure out they were outnumbered and outgunned. The Union gunboats shelled them from the Cumberland River on the east and the infantry laid down fire from the west.

Loaded with knapsacks, blankets and three days' rations, Colonel Baldwin's brigade was ready to march by four o'clock Saturday morning, the 15th, and at six o'clock was ordered forward to the attack. Skirmishers of the Twenty-sixth were soon under fire and driven back, and the regiment deployed into line on the right under heavy fire, taking the pivotal position for the ensuing battle. Other regiments were then brought up.

The Twentieth went into action by direct order of General Pillow, taking up an exposed position, but unable to return fire with effect. They were soon recalled, but not before suffering heavy losses. The men were in disarray. Huddled together in a defensive position, their faces blackened by gun smoke, some men crying, others praying, they waited for further orders. Joel and Johnny were unscathed. They looked at each other and began to laugh hysterically.

"Just look at you!" said Johnny.

Minie balls had ripped Joel's shirt, pants and hat. He believed it almost miraculous that he hadn't been hit. He thought of his family and the mission he had set for himself to find his sister. Perhaps his fate had been ordained by God. Maybe the Yankee bullet hadn't been cast that could kill him.

Baldwin's brigade advanced some fifty yards up a slope toward the enemy positions, but were stalled there for nearly an hour by the fierce resistance. The men of the Twentieth watched and waited.

The roar and fury of the battle continued unabated. Major Brown, the regimental commander, rode up to Joel's company with new orders.

"Where's Capt. Adams?" he demanded.

"He's wounded, sir," said one of the soldiers.

"Lt. Paine?"

"He's killed."

The major looked around at the men, exasperated. His gaze fell upon Joel. "You there! What's your name soldier?"

"Private Deaton, sir."

"Well, it's Lt. Deaton now, soldier. Rally the men from your company and advance to the left of Colonel Baldwin's brigade."

"Yes, sir!" said Joel, as the major rode away. "You heard 'im, men. Gather 'round!"

The Twentieth Mississippi came up across the field and took a position slightly covered by an irregularity of the ground. The Federals were forced to bring troops into position opposite the Twentieth, giving Colonel Baldwin the opportunity to attack on the right flank with a fresh regiment. The enemy was almost immediately dislodged from their position and began to fall back.

Screaming and yelling, the rebels rose from their positions and charged, reloading and firing so fast they ran out of ammunition and had to scavenge the cartridge boxes of the dead and wounded. After six hours of fighting the Confederates had completely routed the Federals, but the fighting was not yet over. The day had not been won.

The Federals regrouped and pressed the attack for the remainder of the day. The Confederates ended the day by holding a corridor from the fort to the landing on the river. At one o'clock Sunday morning Major Brown of the Twentieth Mississippi was summoned by General Floyd.

"I have bad news, Major," said the General. "We have decided our situation is hopeless. General Pillow has given the order to surrender. As for me, I intend to cut my way out with as many men as I can. You are ordered to post your regiment at the landing to protect our retreat."

Major Brown stood dumfounded. "What of us, General?"

"That's entirely up to you, Major Brown. Surrender if you must, or get away as best you can. This is a sacrifice I hesitate to ask, but we must get as many men away as possible."

"I see. The Twentieth is a good regiment, General. We'll do our duty."

Word of the surrender spread quickly through the camp, causing many to flock to the river, almost panic-stricken and frantic to get aboard the boats. Major Brown gathered the soldiers of the Twentieth and spoke to them.

"We are surrendered, boys. We have fought a gallant fight, but further resistance is useless. We are ordered to guard the landing to allow some of our boys to get away. The generals have agreed to terms with General Grant to turn over everything under their command at daylight. We are honor bound to comply. But that doesn't say we can't get some of our boys away to fight again another day. I know this is hard, but it is our duty and I know you men will do your best."

In the midst of chaos the Twentieth Mississippi represented order. Stoically, they stood their posts at the river landing as hundreds of their comrades boarded the boats. At daylight, the last boat underway upriver, the soldiers of the Twentieth stacked arms and awaited the arrival of the Federals to take them prisoner.

# 79

"Keep it moving! Keep it moving!"

Joel wondered how so few guards could control so many prisoners of war. He didn't think of it for very long, though. He and thousands more shuffled along, boarding riverboats for the journey north. Joel had been south and west, but never dreamed he would ever see the northern states.

The journey into captivity was only a taste of the rigors that lay before the men of the Twentieth Mississippi. A freezing rain started to fall shortly after they were underway and the temperature fell rapidly. Some men sought shelter in the dark hold of the vessel, but were soon driven out by the terrific stench, which came from the decaying remains of dead Federal officers and soldiers being transported to their homes for burial. At Cairo, Illinois, Joel's group was held for several days, then loaded onto a train. With no prison large enough to accommodate all of the prisoners, some were sent to Camp Chase at Columbus, Ohio, and others to Camp Douglas, near Chicago. The destination for Joel's group was Camp Morton at Indianapolis  The slow-moving train stopped twice each day and a field kitchen set up to feed the prisoners from their own captured supplies. Often, when the train stopped in a town, the people came down to look at the "rebs." Some just stared, but most did little to conceal their hostility.

From the moment of capture escape was on the mind of nearly every confederate soldier. The farther north the prison train went, the more relaxed and careless the guards became, and the greater the opportunity for the prisoners to take leave of their captors.

On the evening of the second day out of Cairo, Joel, Johnny, and some fellow prisoners were engaged in earnest conversation about army life, the possibilities of escape and sundry other topics.

"I saw a man shot through the head...and he lived!"

"That's nothin', I seen one ol' boy whose arms and legs had been carried away, and he lived!"

"Is that so? Just how d'you reckon he fed hisself?"

"Cain't say for sure, but it's a true story."

"Wal," said one of the men who had been sitting quietly, smoking his pipe, "I once saw a man shot in the side and in the head. He lived."

"Incredible!"

Joel decided he ought to get in on this, too. "I saw a man shot clean through the body by a ten-pound cannon ball."

"And he lived?" Exclaimed all the others, almost in unison.

"No, he died."

As the laughter died down they were joined by a man named Chauncey Maxwell. "Boys, I'm gonna make my escape," he said.

"How're y'gonna do it," someone asked.

"Been down twice t'get a drink at the water tank, an' the guard by the door seems to be half asleep. Next time I'm gonna knock 'im with my fist and jump out the door."

"You're crazy," said one of the prisoners.

"You'll be a dead man for sure," said another. "It's dark. You won't know if you'll hit a bridge, a tree, or a pile of rocks."

"That's the best reason. They cain't find me in the dark. Anyway, my mind's made up, boys. Y'all are welcome to come along if y'have a mind to."

The conversation drifted into other areas, and after a good interval Maxwell made his way once again to the water tank. As planned, he struck the guard with a crushing blow and threw open the door. As he jumped, another prisoner saw his opportunity and ran for the door. Just as he reached it, the guard had recovered sufficiently and shot the man dead. The remaining prisoners dropped to the floor.

The train was stopped and the guards fired several shots into the darkness. Apparently, Maxwell had made good his escape. Joel considered escape a two-sided coin. A soldier's duty was to escape, but it carried the potential of freedom or death. In any case, opportunities would be fewer in the near future as the guards were now more alert.

On February 22, 1862, barely a week after their surrender, the trainload of Confederate prisoners arrived in Indianapolis and were marched to Camp Morton, situated on 36 acres on the north side of the city. As if it were a festive occasion, the entire city turned out to see the captured rebel soldiers.

Camp Morton, named for the governor of Indiana, had not begun life as a prison camp, or even as a military post for that matter. People entering the facility before the war had been required to pay for the privilege. Entrance was through an ornate gateway, and, though crowds had been so eager to enter before the war, the present occupants were more eager to get out. The camp was the former site of the Indiana State fairgrounds. It had opened for business as a military training center on April 17, 1861, and during the fall and winter of 1861-62 had served as barracks for Indiana troops. The sheds where horses and cattle had been shown and the halls where agricultural products had been exhibited were turned into barracks for prisoners. Oak and walnut trees dotted the area and a creek that came to be known as the "Potomac" by the prisoners flowed through the property.

The camp was surrounded by a high board fence with armed guards. The cheap construction of the buildings allowed easy penetration by snow, wind, and rain. Sanitary conditions were abominable. Sewage flowed through an open drainage ditch that ran through the camp. Within days of their arrival, several prisoners had died of disease. In such a miserable situation Joel was not alone among the prisoners in his desires for freedom.

From the Federal point of view it was a good facility to use as a prison. It was already fenced and buildings were in place. The prisoners were put immediately to work constructing additional barracks for the expected influx of more prisoners. A low rail fence inside the perimeter served as the "dead line." The first rule the prisoners learned was that any man who crossed the line would be fired upon without warning. And many were while in the act of relieving themselves. Joel Deaton vowed to cross that line as soon as possible. He did not intend to spend the war sitting in a prisoner of war camp.

Joel decided there were only three ways out of the camp: through the front gate, under the fence, or over it. Getting over the fence appeared to be so incredibly easy, Joel eliminated the other two options without any real thought. The wooden fence looked to be only ten feet high. The materials needed to build a ladder were everywhere.

The inside of the barracks was open with square posts every twenty feet to support the rafters. On each side of the barracks there were four tiers of bunks, one above another, with a narrow space down the middle, and a heater in the center. The walls were made of studs with 1 x 6 boards nailed to the outside. A lack of insulation allowed light to be seen between the boards. Obtaining an eight-foot board was easy, and nails could be removed here and there, and not be missed. Joel nailed smaller pieces of wood to the larger board about a foot apart. Once the makeshift ladder had been put together, Joel concealed it under the dirt and straw that was the barracks floor. The ladder was an open secret among the prisoners. Most everyone thought Joel was crazy, but he remained undeterred. He was going out, and that was that. He needed only wait for the right opportunity.

Joel studied the situation for several days. The guards walked their posts along the scaffold. Fires were built at the end of each guard's beat. They stopped to warm their hands for a few moments, then pulled their capes over their heads and walked to the other end of the beat to the next fire and then back again. At night, the guards seemed to disappear into the darkness between the two fires.

During the second week of March 1862, Joel decided he couldn't wait for ideal conditions. While the weather was still cold and wintry the guards would probably follow the same routine. With warmer weather the opportunity to leave might be less and perhaps even disappear. The moon was just past full, so Joel would have to wait until it had set before making his attempt.

"I've decided to take my leave of this godforsaken place," Joel said to Johnny as they ate their evening meal.

"How soon are y'leavin'?"

"Tonight," said Joel.

"If I thought you was serious, I'd try to talk you out of it."

"I am serious, Johnny. There ain't never gonna be a better time."

"You gone daft on me, boy? It's freezin' out there."

"That's why it's the best time," said Joel. "They ain't gonna be looking for anyone to escape when it's like this. The only reason I'm tellin' you is 'cause I want you to come with me."

Johnny Hutchins ate in silence, thinking over the proposal. Finally, he said, "Y'got a plan?"

"Sure do."

Joel spent several minutes describing his preparations and what he intended to do once he was over the fence. In the end, Johnny Hutchins decided not to go. Prison life wasn't particularly to his liking, but he didn't have the fortitude to risk his life trying to get out.

The lights had been out for more than two hours when the moon finally set. Everyone was asleep in the barracks except Joel and Johnny. Joel had retrieved his makeshift ladder and was ready to go.

"Y'sure you don't wanna come along?" asked Joel.

"Sure would, but I don't think it's worth the risk. I already dodged the bullet once down in Iuka. Don't figure a man's got too many chances in life and I don't wanna use up the ones I got left."

"I reckon I'd feel the same way, too, if I was in your shoes," said Joel. "Y'all take care now, y'hear. Maybe we'll meet again when the war's over."

The two men shook hands and then Joel slipped out the door. He crawled toward the midway point of the sentry's beat dragging the ladder behind him. The ground was cold and muddy, but there was no other way. After much exertion he lay hugging the ground not ten feet away from the dead line as the sentry passed by. When the sentry was out of earshot, Joel crawled to the fence and was about to set up his ladder when he saw the man hadn't stopped at the fire, but had turned and was on his way back. Joel was filled with panic. If the guard saw him, he would be shot dead on the spot. The guard was looking in his direction, so he dare not move either. Joel pressed himself facedown against the bottom of the fence and prayed. He heard the approaching footsteps. He could hear the pounding of his pulse in his ears. Desperately, he tried to slow his breathing. The footsteps came, and then slowly faded away.

Silently, Joel raised the ladder into position. He was halfway up when he saw the sentry stop at the fire and warm himself as he spoke to the sentry walking the adjacent beat. Joel scrambled up and straddled the fence. He looked again at the sentries. They had neither seen nor heard anything. He pulled the ladder up and heaved it over the fence, then dropped to the ground and quickly started walking in the direction he took to be south, based on his orientation to the camp. Joel figured there would be at least six hours to daylight. If his absence was not discovered before then, he could make at least fifteen miles before the alarm went out.

When morning came Joel had done much better than he had expected. Less than a mile from the camp he had come upon a farm with a horse in the barn. He made good use of the animal, covering nearly forty miles by daybreak. He abandoned the horse in some woods and began walking west. Joel reasoned that the theft of the horse would be discovered and they would come south looking for him. No one would expect him to go west.

Six days after his escape from Camp Morton, Joel finally reached the Ohio River near Evansville, Indiana. With no bridges and no boats, his only option was to swim. There was a hint of spring in the air, temperatures in the sixties, but the water was very cold. Joel found a small log for flotation, tied his clothes into a bundle, and entered the water at twilight. Halfway across the bundle of clothes slipped from his grasp and sank out of sight.

After reaching the southern riverbank, Joel was forced to walk all night just to keep warm. His body covered with welts and scratches, and nearing exhaustion, he came upon a plantation at dawn and slipped into the barn. He found an old horse blanket and curled up to sleep. If he were discovered and sent back to prison, he didn't really care.

Kentucky was a border state. Slavery was legal, but the state had chosen to remain in the Union. The citizens were deeply divided on the issue. Most did not own slaves, but those who did faced economic disaster if slavery should be abolished. Those sympathetic to the southern cause had gone south to join the Confederate army. Meanwhile, Kentucky was a hot bed of Union activity. Joel was far from safe.

# 80

It was a dreamless sleep from which Joel was awakened. He saw a large black man standing above him holding a pitchfork in his hand.

"Whut y'doin' heah in Massa Randall's barn? Y'heah me talkin', boy? Whut y'doin' heah?"

"Where am I?" asked Joel.

"Wheah iz you? You in Massa Randall's barn, dat's wheah!"

Joel decided to take a chance. "I'm a Confederate soldier. I've escaped from prison in the North, and I ain't had nothin' t'eat in nearly a week."

"Well, now, dat's a mahty diffrunt story. Massa Randall iz off fightin' in dat war. I belieb de missus, she be mahty proud t'hep a po suthin boy."

The black man escorted Joel to the big house, his pitchfork ready in case Joel turned out to be more dangerous than he looked. Mrs. Randall was sitting in the parlor, tying a quilt when Joel was ushered into her presence.

"Samuel! Who is this man? What is he doing here?" asked Mrs. Randall.

"Found 'im in de barn, Missus Randall. Sez he iz a soldier, dat he iz got away from dem Yankee men. Sez he needs yore hep t'get home."

"Is this true?" asked Mrs. Randall.

"Yes, ma'am," said Joel, drawing the blanket closer around himself. "I was taken prisoner at Fort Donelson. Got away about a week ago. Lost my clothes when I swam the Ohio River."

"You look a sight, young man. When did you eat last?"

"Been scroungin' anything I could," said Joel. "Last regular meal I had was before I left the prison camp. Could sure use a bite to eat."

"First things first, young man. First, tell me your name."

"Joel Deaton, ma'am."

"Joel, my husband is away, serving our southern cause."

"I know that, ma'am."

Mrs. Randall gave Samuel a sharp look. The black man hung his head, looking nervous.

"I hope my personal affairs are not being told to every stranger who comes around," said Mrs. Randall. Turning back to Joel, she added, "Major Randall was in Nashville the last I heard. Don't expect I'll be seeing him very soon."

Joel was puzzled by all this talk. He didn't particularly care where this woman's husband was or when he would be coming back. All Joel wanted was to get back home.

"Samuel, tell Nancy to prepare a meal for this man."

"Yes'm. I'll get raht to it."

Joel watched the black man leave, then turned his attention back toward Mrs. Randall. "I appreciate your help, ma'am. I'll try not to trouble you too much."

"No trouble. It's good to have a man around the house again. Now, let's get you a bath and some clothes. My husband's a little bigger than you, but I think we can find something that'll fit."

After a bath and a new suit of clothes that belonged to the absent mister Randall, Joel was sitting down to the first decent hot meal he had eaten since leaving Mississippi. Mrs. Randall was an attractive woman in her early thirties with two pre-adolescent daughters at home. They peered at him from the doorway to the parlor and whispered all the while Joel ate.

Mrs. Randall trimmed Joel's hair, and, after a close shave, he looked like a respectable citizen instead of an escaped Confederate soldier. It was late afternoon and Joel was beginning to feel he should be on his way.

"You've been mighty helpful, Mrs. Randall. I'd best be going. Gotta put some miles behind me before dark. I don't even know where I am"

Mrs. Randall looked thoughtful. "You're in Henderson county... Kentucky. You could stay here tonight, get an early start in the morning. You'll be rested."

Joel didn't need to be persuaded. He was dead tired. The house had only two bedrooms, the master bedroom and another shared by the Randall girls. Mrs. Randall had Samuel set up a cot for Joel in the kitchen. The girls were in bed, Samuel and Nancy had retired to their quarters, and Joel was sitting on the cot pulling off his new shoes when Mrs. Randall appeared in the kitchen doorway. She was in her night clothes. The back light from a lamp in the parlor revealed her feminine form. Joel looked at her, but could not see her face in the dim light. She stood there for several moments, saying nothing.

"Ma'am?" said Joel.

"I wanted to say good night," said Mrs. Randall. "If you need anything...anything at all...come knock on my door. It's the one at the end of the hall."

"Thank you, ma'am," said Joel. "Good night."

After Mrs. Randall left, Joel undressed and slipped under the covers. He lay staring at the ceiling for a long time. Even a country boy like Joel could figure out what Mrs. Randall wanted. He was only twenty-one and she was at least thirty. Was she unhappy in her marriage? Or just lonely? Should he follow his carnal instincts? Or should he exemplify the best of southern chivalry? While mentally reviewing the situation, Joel drifted off to sleep.

Suddenly, Joel was awake. He felt a hand on his shoulder and his name being whispered. He raised himself on one elbow. Even in the dark, he knew who was sitting beside him on the cot.

"I declare, Joel! You are a stubborn young man!"

"Mrs. Randall?"

"Well, it ain't Nancy!"

Joel thought of the black woman who cooked and cleaned house for the Randall family. He almost laughed. Of course it wasn't her.

The woman took Joel's right hand and held it in hers for a few moments, then kissed it on the knuckles. She stroked the back of his hand against her cheek, then placed it in her clothing against the skin just below her navel. A few awkward moments later Mrs. Randall spoke again, "Joel? Ain't you never been with a woman before?"

"None I'd be proud t'tell about."

Mrs. Randall laughed merrily. She stood up and pulled Joel by the hand. "Come with me," she said.

As Joel stood up, Mrs. Randall started for the door. Joel spun her around and took her into his arms. They kissed passionately. Suddenly, Joel seemed out of breath, and not from exertion. He lifted the woman into his arms and carried her back to her room.

# 81

Six days later, the 30th of March, Joel was strolling down the streets of Corinth, Mississippi. It had been an exhausting trip. He walked most of the way, but hitched an occasional ride in a farmer's wagon. Dodging Union patrols had been his biggest problem.

With his entire regiment in captivity, Joel didn't know exactly what, if anything, would be required of him in the way of military service. Should he just go home or what? In any case, he couldn't help noticing an unusually large number of Confederate troops bivouacked in and around Corinth. With no other pressing business, and after making inquiries, Joel presented himself at military headquarters. Within the hour he was being interviewed by more high-ranking officers than he had ever seen before.

The man who asked most of the questions, General Pierre Gustave Toutant-Beauregard, was a rather unimposing figure, middleaged and of Creole descent. His eyes had a sad look. Some said they resembled those of a bloodhound. Beauregard was the hero of Fort Sumter and had been the tactical commander of the Confederate victory at Bull Run. After the reverses of Fort Henry and Fort Donelson many southerners looked to him as the best hope for victory in the West.

Joel gave his best estimate of enemy forces along the west bank of the Tennessee River, especially in the vicinity of Pittsburgh Landing. He recounted his experiences at Fort Donelson, his imprisonment and escape, and his subsequent journey south.

"I'm curious," said Beauregard, who spoke in a wheezy voice because of a chronic case of bronchitis, "how did you pass so easily through the Federal lines?"

" 'Tweren't easy. No, sir. I had to answer more questions than was posed by you gentlemen. But they believed me when I told 'em I was against secession, but I wasn't gonna take up arms against my friends and neighbors neither."

"Fortunately for you," said Beauregard, "you weren't shot as a spy."

Sitting quietly to one side during the interrogation, a man with penetrating blue eyes finally spoke when the questioning was over.

"Young man? General Johnston. I would have a few words with you. Come to my quarters in an hour."

General Albert Sidney Johnston was one of the handsomest Southern generals. Tall, erect, and muscular, his six-foot two-inch frame had a unique combination of dignity and grace. Though he wore a well-groomed moustache, the rest of his strong, even features were unobscured by whiskers, and his thick hair was sprinkled with just enough gray to give the impression of mature wisdom. Despite his fine reputation in the military establishment, he was not filled with self-importance and bombast. He was soft-spoken and pleasant, and his blue-gray eyes twinkled with gentle humor.

Originally from Kentucky, Johnston later called Texas home. A West Point graduate, he had resigned his commission to be with his first wife in her final illness. For a time he worked a farm in Missouri, but moved to Texas where he was Secretary of War and General of the Texas Army. In the 1850's he received an appointment as colonel of the 2nd Cavalry by his old West Point friend, Jefferson Davis, the Secretary of War. He led the army to Utah in 1857 to subjugate the Mormons and then went on to California, where his pro-Southern attitude made him a virtual prisoner. When Texas seceded, Johnston resigned for the second time and headed for Richmond, dodging Federal authorities who had ordered his arrest. He was looked upon as a brilliant commander, though his successes had been few.

"So they made you a lieutenant at Fort Donelson," said Johnston to a wide-eyed Joel Deaton.

"Yes, sir, they did, but I ain't had no real experience at bein' an officer."

"I would certainly agree with that," said the general. "The problem we have is that the army has recently been reorganized. Your regiment is either captured or dead, so there's really no place for another lieutenant. I'm sure you'd feel right at home returning to the rank of private, wouldn't you?"

Joel's face fell. "Well, I s'pose so, general, if that's the way it's gotta be."

"Well, someone must have recognized leadership qualities, and I wouldn't like to see them go to waste. I'll have my aide announce that you're now a member of my staff. Does that suit you...Lt. Deaton?"

"Yes, sir!" said Joel with as much enthusiasm as he could muster.

"Report to the quartermaster and get fitted with a proper uniform. That'll be all."

"Thank you, sir," said Joel, extending his hand. The general looked at the hand, then gave Joel an icy look. Joel snapped to attention and gave the general a smart salute. Johnston smiled slightly as he returned it. At the door Joel turned and said, "General Johnston, were you the commander at Camp Floyd?"

"Yes, I was."

"I worked there for awhile. Pony Express station." Johnston seemed unimpressed. "Did they find all the children?"

"What?" said the general, momentarily confused. "Do you mean the survivors of the Mountain Meadows massacre?"

"Yes, sir, I do."

"What do you know about that?"

"I was there."

"You what?" said the general, rising from his chair, his face turning red with anger.

"You don't understand, general. My family was killed at Mountain Meadows."

"Oh," said the general, softly. After a long moment of silence he added, "Please forgive me, but I have never before heard of any survivors besides the children. How did you get away?"

"Me and three other men lit out for California. One horse came up lame and I was left behind, so I hiked back to camp, but I wasn't able to get in. I hid in the bushes. Never did know what happened to them other three."

"They were hunted down and killed, I'm told."

"Anyhow, I saw them take a wagonload of kids out of the corral and it wasn't till four years later that I heard they was spared. My sister was in that wagon. I've looked for her since I heard, but I ain't been able to find 'er."

"Amazing," said Johnston. "You and I shall have some interesting conversations after we've whipped General Grant and driven the Federals out of the south. How old was your sister?"

"Nine."

"Nine? That *is* interesting," said the general. "We did hear rumors of an older child, a girl, that was saved, but hidden from us because she was too old...old enough to tell the tale. We looked for her, but could never find her." There was a look of growing excitement on Joel's face. "Of course I couldn't say whether or not she was your sister. When we have more time, I'll tell you what we learned. Maybe it will help you find her some day. For now we have another job to do. Report to Captain O'Hara in the morning."

Joel left the general's quarters in better spirits than he had felt in a very long time. War or no war, when his enlistment was up he was heading west.

# 82

Only 23 miles separated Corinth from Pittsburgh Landing. Because of the humiliating defeats in recent weeks, a Confederate victory was both a tactical and a political necessity. Federal gunboats had made the Tennessee River their own, traveling its navigable length at will. Meanwhile, Grant had moved his headquarters to Savannah, Tennessee, and was massing his troops at Pittsburgh Landing. As soon as the Army of the Ohio arrived, commanded by Major General Don Carlos Buell, the push into the heart of the South would begin.

The military intelligence gathered over the recent weeks convinced General Johnston that he should give up the advantage of the defensive position and attack the Federal forces before they became too strong. General Beauregard drew up the battle plans and they were approved by Johnston with neither comment nor change.

Amidst mass confusion, the Confederate forces moved out for Pittsburgh Landing on the morning of April 3, 1862, for an assault planned for the early morning hours of April 5. On the morning of the 4th Johnston prepared to leave for the front, fully expecting to lead the attack the following morning.

"General Johnston, you haven't eaten this morning," said Mrs. Inge, the lady whose house he had been using as his headquarters. "Let me fix you some sandwiches and some cake."

"No, thank you, Mrs. Inge, we soldiers travel light."

Mrs. Inge frowned and left the room. The general was old enough to be her father, but she acted more as if she were his mother. She retired to the kitchen and started fixing sandwiches anyway. When the general wasn't looking, she slipped the food into his coat pocket.

The general spent a few more minutes making final preparations and then he was ready.

"Lieutenant Deaton, you'll ride with me this morning," said the general.

"Yes, sir."

Joel followed him out the door. Johnston stopped on the front steps, looking as if he had forgotten something. After a few moments he said, "Yes, I believe I have overlooked nothing", then mounted his horse and, with his staff, set out for Monterey, Tennessee, some twelve miles away.

At Monterey Johnston expected to find the army corps under generals Hardee, Polk, and Bragg in position for the attack the following morning. Instead he learned that his army was scattered all over the countryside, unprepared for battle and in constant danger of being discovered by the enemy. Stormy weather, muddy roads, and poor communication had worked against the plans.

Johnston was resolute. He conferred with Beauregard and Bragg throughout the afternoon and into the evening. Joining them was Breckinridge, commander of the reserve corps. In the end Johnston decided to forge ahead, issuing orders to launch a full-scale attack in the morning. At 2:00 A.M. a storm front moved in. The rain fell in torrents the rest of the night.

The cold temperature and flooded roads made it impossible to start the battle at 8:00 A.M. as planned. The troops that hadn't yet reached the front continued to move. Johnston and Beauregard left Monterey at first light. By noon Johnston knew there would be little chance of engaging the enemy this day. Disgusted and frustrated, he rode off with three of his staff officers in search of the missing troops. By the end of the day the army was present in sufficient numbers for Johnston to give the final orders to attack in the morning, April 6.

The Sixth Division of the Union Army of the Tennessee was camped along the Eastern Corinth Road. The commanding officer, Brigadier General Benjamin M. Prentiss, had retired for the night secure in the belief that the sporadic sightings of Confederate infantry and cavalry in the vicinity was nothing to be concerned about, an opinion not shared by some of his subordinates. After midnight, brigade commander Colonel Everett Peabody met with a handful of his subordinate officers who took the Confederate threat more seriously. The situation was discussed at length before Col. Peabody decided to take the initiative. He ordered Maj. James Powell to take three companies of the 25th Missouri and two companies of the 12th Michigan out at 3:00 A.M. to reconnoiter.

Private Franklin Bailey of the 12th Michigan Infantry was a youthful seventeen years old, but itching for a fight. Like most other youth, to him death was something distant and remote. It didn't matter that he had been sick for several days with the flu, nor did he care that his captain had refused to issue him ammunition or allow him to go on the night patrol. Pvt. Bailey persuaded a sergeant to get him a supply of cartridges, and under cover of darkness mustered up with the others of his company and marched off into the woods.

Beyond the picket lines Maj. Powell divided the patrol into three columns, each moving off in a different direction. The moon, in its first quarter, had set several hours before. The air was full of night sounds as they stumbled along.

"What the hell are we doin' out here?" asked the soldier behind Bailey. "If we run into anyone, how're we gonna tell if they's Rebs anyhow?"

"Dunno," said Bailey. "But they're out here. I c'n smell 'em. Gonna bag me a couple if I can."

"Quit talking!" said someone up front.

The column pushed on southward. Half an hour later they broke into a small clearing. Not twenty yards away another group of men emerged from the trees. "There they are!" Someone shouted. Guns were unslung, hammers were cocked. The bustle of activity bordered on panic.

"It's the Rebs!" yelled someone in the other group.

"Hey! We ain't Rebs!"

"Then who are you?"

"12th Michigan!"

"The hell you say. So are we."

A potential disaster averted, the two groups moved on together. About the same time, the other column of Powell's patrol entered a clearing of some forty acres, called Fraley field, shortly before 5:00 A.M. In the dim, half-light of the approaching dawn they saw a mounted Rebel in the distance. They immediately turned to withdraw when three shots rang out. The Federal troops promptly retreated and rejoined the rest of Major Powell's command in Seay field on the other side of the Pittsburgh and Corinth road.

"Who's doing the shooting?" asked Powell.

"There's some Johnnies in the field across the road."

"How many?" asked Powell.

"Can't rightly say, sir. Only saw one man."

Powell formed his men into a skirmish line and crossed the Pittsburgh and Corinth road into Fraley field. Slowly, they advanced in a southerly direction. Apparently only a few enemy pickets were in their front. When Powell's men reached the middle of the field, the Confederate pickets opened fire and fled. Powell looked around. None of his men had been hit. The advance continued until they reached a small, brushy knoll where Fraley field joined with another. There, two hundred yards distant in the gloom, some three hundred soldiers of the 3rd Mississippi were kneeling, waiting. A heavy white mist hung in the air, shrouding the trees in an eerie fog. Was it a dream? Or was it real? Powell's men didn't wait for orders. They unslung their muskets and opened fire.

Like some gigantic engine of immense power, the military engagement that began with a cough and a sputter would grow in a furious crescendo over the next few hours. The terrible, bloody Battle of Shiloh had begun.

# 83

General Johnston and his staff were too excited to sleep much. Twenty-four hours ago they had been drenched in rain, but now it was clear and cold. Sydney Johnston and his staff were sitting by a blazing campfire having a breakfast of coffee and biscuits while listening to the serenade of birds in the trees that foretold the coming dawn. There was little conversation. Lt. Joel Deaton was the last to arise from his bed. In spite of his farmer upbringing he had never been an early morning person.

Joel was pouring himself a cup of coffee when the birds fell silent. Sydney Johnston rose, cup in hand, and stepped to the north side of the fire and stared into the gloom. The faint, but unmistakable, sound of gunfire could be heard in the distance. He lifted the cup to his lips and sipped his coffee. Turning, he said, "Gentlemen, please note the time in your notebooks. It appears we may have been discovered and the battle has been joined ahead of schedule."

Johnston tossed the remainder of his cup of coffee into the fire, mounted his horse, and, with his staff, rode off in search of the battle.

The skirmish in Fraley field grew in intensity. At first the Rebs fell back one company at a time, only to be replaced by fresh troops more numerous than before. Pvt. Franklin Bailey was reloading his musket when he noticed a unit of Confederate cavalry working their way around the Union left. "Major Powell! Major Powell! Look sir! The Rebs are tryin' to flank us on the left!"

Powell moved a short distance to the left behind a tree to study the situation. After a few moments consideration he ordered the bugler to sound retreat. The Federal forces did not panic, but moved to the rear in good order, pausing to fire from time to time as they moved into the woods. Behind them they saw a sight they would never forget. What had started out as a trickle of Confederate skirmishers had turned into a flood of more than nine thousand soldiers in twenty-two regiments. The retreat quickly became a rout.

Sydney Johnston and his staff rode north on the Pittsburgh and Corinth road to the junction with Bark Road, where Johnston dismounted to set up his headquarters only a mile southwest of Fraley field. Beauregard was the first of the generals to arrive. It wasn't a formal meeting at first, just casual reference to the gunfire that had begun to lessen in the distance. One of the generals remarked that the shooting had started when an enemy patrol had fired on advance elements of Hardee's Third Army Corps.

"We have obviously lost the advantage of surprise," said Beauregard. "By now Grant's entire army must be fully alerted to our presence. We weren't ready for the battle yet, and I dare say we are in a most dangerous position. There's no telling what the Federals may be up to. I am hearing reports that there is mass confusion among the troops. If you would heed my advice, General, I would recommend a retreat to Corinth where we can fortify and better prepare for the inevitable confrontation."

As Sydney Johnston pondered the words of his second-in-command, gunfire rang out in the nearby woods and rose quickly in intensity and was then joined by the sound of artillery.

"The battle has opened, gentlemen," said Johnston. "It is too late to change our dispositions. Many good men shall die from want of leadership if we tarry longer. I have decided to leave General Beauregard in command here to follow the course of the battle and commit the reserve forces when and where needed. As for me, I shall ride to the front and lead the attack myself."

The meeting broke up and the generals left for their respective commands. Johnston summoned his staff and sent for his horse. Mounting the animal, he exclaimed to his subordinates, "Tonight we will water our horses in the Tennessee River!"

The surprised Federals reeled under the enemy onslaught. The Confederates overrunning the Federal camps found breakfast still on the table and no evidence that anyone had foreseen their coming. Though some of the Union soldiers contested every step of ground, others, even entire companies, fled in terror. Reinforcements moving to the front encountered ever-increasing numbers of panicky soldiers from the Sixth Division streaming toward the rear. The arrival of two brigades under Stephen Hurlbut stemmed the flow of terrified soldiers and allowed General Prentiss to rally his troops, what was left of them, by midmorning.

Hurlbut established a defensive line about a half mile behind the Sixth Division camps, but, thinking his left flank was being turned, retreated a hundred yards and took up position in a peach orchard and along a heavy split rail fence at the edge of the woods. Hurlbut's troops had good cover as they faced a trampled cotton field in their front. To the west, elements of the Federal Second Division under General William H. L. Wallace moved into position on Hurlbut's right along a sunken road that ran through open woods. The remnant of the Sixth Division filled the gap between Hurlbut and Wallace. Spread out over half a mile, the Federal defenders, more than eleven thousand strong, watched and waited.

Opposite the Federal position, the Confederate forces were in disarray. They had advanced more quickly than expected, causing a breakdown in communications and command structure. After a long delay and much confusion, sufficient troops were finally organized to mount an assault against Hurlbut's line.

The Rebel attack was terrible. For an hour the two sides exchanged artillery fire, the din seeming to be one continuous roar, the air heavy with the smell of burned gunpowder. About 11:00 A.M. the Confederates sent three regiments across three hundred yards of open ground against the Federal stronghold. When only a hundred yards separated the two sides, the Yanks opened fire. The slaughter was sickening, but it was only the beginning. A second and a third time the Rebs came. The Northern batteries tore them to pieces with canister and shells while the infantry laid down a withering fire at point blank range. The fire was so intense that for hundreds of yards the vegetation had been ripped to shreds. Barely a single leaf was left on the budding trees. Before the day was done the Rebs would be calling the enemy redoubt, "The Hornet's Nest."

# 84

Joel Deaton had been at Johnston's side most of the morning as the general rode back and forth surveying the scene and giving encouragement to the troops. Around eleven o'clock Johnston sent Joel to the left flank of the attack to assess the situation there.

Joel took the Hamburg-Purdy road west. To his right was the incessant rattle of musketry. All around him was what sounded like rain falling on the trees. It didn't take him long to figure out that the sound was from the firestorm of bullets striking the leaves and branches overhead. Joel arrived at the rear of Gibson's brigade just as they were making their second assault on the Hornet's Nest.

The fire from the Federal positions was overwhelming. Gibson's men had no choice but to fall back. As Joel rode up he saw Major General Braxton Bragg himself arguing with Colonel Gibson. Bragg was attributing Gibson's lack of success to the cowardice of his men. He demanded they reform and mount another attack.

The sound of musket fire died out as the Federals waited for the next assault. A battery of Union artillery had been abandoned in the field. Bodies were everywhere. Satisfied that he had a good understanding of the situation, Joel turned his horse and started back the way he had come.

"Where're you going, lieutenant?"

Joel stopped and looked back. It was General Bragg.

"Sir?"

"Take your place in line with the others. I'll have no cowards in my command."

"But, general..."

"Get in line or I'll shoot you myself!"

Armed with only a revolver, Joel joined Gibson's men and moved out when the order was given. Forward they went in three ranks, muskets ready. The field in front of them seemed to be alive, quivering and shaking. Then Joel knew why. Among the dead lay hundreds of wounded soldiers, writhing in pain, their pitiful cries rending the air.

Being on horseback, Joel was in the front. He passed a man whose abdomen had been ripped open by a shell fragment, trying to push his intestines back in as he whimpered over and over, "Help me, please help me."

Joel looked back. The men, their faces dirtied by the clouds of gun smoke, were grimly determined. Some had an excited look about them. Then it happened. Joel felt it, too. He was caught up in the spectacle. His heart raced. He wanted this. He couldn't wait to look the Yanks in the eye and fire his revolver. He had to restrain himself from spurring his horse forward ahead of the others.

When Gibson's brigade had crossed the field to within one hundred yards of the Federal position, Joel saw the flash of the guns and the clouds of smoke as the Yanks opened fire. The Rebels didn't return the fire yet, they only quickened their pace. Here and there a Confederate soldier cried out and fell to the ground. The men began to run toward the enemy line and Joel felt an uncontrollable shiver pass through his body as the Confederates raised their voices in the "rebel yell."

The firing from the Federal ranks ceased for a few moments until the Rebs were almost upon them, then a sheet of flame and a dense cloud of smoke erupted from their ranks. Dozens of Rebels dropped to the ground, dead or wounded. Joel's horse jumped suddenly and he felt a stinging on the inside of his left thigh. A bullet had passed between him and the horse, tearing up the stirrup and striking both Joel and the horse. The animal began to rear up and swing around. Suddenly, the horse dropped to the ground, sending Joel tumbling. He looked and saw a bloody hole in the horse's forehead. Using the horse's body as cover, Joel drew his revolver and began firing. When the gun was empty, he grabbed a musket and cartridge box from a dead soldier. He bit off the end of the paper cartridge with his teeth and rammed the charge down the barrel. He continued to load and fire as fast as he could. He didn't aim at anyone in particular, just fired in the general direction of the Federal line.

It seemed like an eternity, but only fifteen minutes later the men began to withdraw. The Federal batteries were pouring in a deadly fire of canister. If the Rebels didn't retreat, the only ones left on the field would be dead men. Most of the men turned and ran, but the more stouthearted stopped every few yards, reloaded and fired. Joel was not one of them.

Back at the starting point Joel found Col. Gibson and reported. "Colonel Gibson, I need a horse. Mine was shot from under me."

"Take any one you can find," said the colonel, "but just who are you?"

"Lt. Deaton, sir. I'm with General Johnston's staff. He sent me over to learn what was afoot in this area. I need to return and report."

"Looks like you've had rather warm work, lieutenant. We'll find you a horse."

While a horse was being found, Joel took a few moments for self-assessment. Beside the slight wound in his left thigh, he found several tears in his uniform where Yankee bullets had struck harmlessly, and for the first time he noticed the right side of his neck felt wet. He touched it and then looked at his bloody fingers. A projectile had apparently clipped the edge of his right ear, though he had felt no pain.

When a horse was found, Joel started back. It was after two o'clock.

General Johnston and his staff were not where Joel had left them near the peach orchard. Joel sat pondering his next move when two staff officers galloped by in a great hurry. Joel decided to follow them. A few moments later he came upon a soldier running around, obviously in a great state of agitation.

"Have you seen the General?" Joel yelled.

"Yes, sir! He's been shot!"

"Shot! Where is he?"

"They took him into that ravine yonder."

Joel galloped up to where several officers were gathered around Sydney Johnston lying on the ground, his head in the lap of Governor Harris of Tennessee.

"Johnston, do you know me?" said Col. William Preston, his voice trembling with anguish. The general did not respond. Joel slid from his horse and joined the others. Dudley Hayden tried pouring whiskey down the general's throat. It just ran out of his mouth.

Joel looked around. If it were not for the sound of gunfire in the distance, this could be considered a place of peace and tranquility. He surveyed the faces of the others. Never before had he seen such emotional pain. He looked at Sydney Johnston. The general's coat and shirt had been torn open, but no wound could be seen. The front half of the sole of his left boot had been torn away, probably from a stray bullet. The general's breathing became intermittent and labored. He shuddered, then was still. Tears streaming down his cheeks, Gov. Harris looked up at the others and said, "It's all over."

Hayden felt Johnston's chest for a few moments. "There is no heartbeat," he said.

"My God, Hayden, is it so?" asked Preston.

Hayden looked up and nodded. Joel felt a numbness begin to set in. Tears came. It was not that he cared so much for this man, but with Albert Sydney Johnston died the best chance for Confederate victory and Joel's best chance to find his sister. Joel wept.

# 85

The battle at the Hornets Nest raged for hours. Grant had ordered General Prentiss to hold the position at all costs. The Rebs charged a dozen times to no avail. The Union line bent, but did not break.

"Get me every gun you can find," ordered Confederate General Daniel Ruggles.

The Confederate gunners rolled 62 cannons into position along the southwest edge of Duncan field opposite the Hornets Nest. The roar of 12-pounders and the screech of 3-inch Parrott rifles created a continuous din and the billows of smoke blotted out the sky as the Rebs pounded the Union position with more than 11,000 rounds. The Federal troops were pinned to the ground, unable to rise and return fire.

By 5 o'clock the Union forces retreated once again, and at 5:30 General Prentiss surrendered the 2200 remaining defenders of the Hornets Nest. He had bought hours of precious time for Grant with the lives of hundreds of the best of American young manhood.

The Confederate army rolled up the Union forces like an old rug. By nightfall the Union Army of the Tennessee was nearly encircled, their backs to the Tennessee River at Pittsburgh Landing.

Thousands of dead and wounded from both sides lay scattered over the several square miles of battlefield. The Confederate wounded who could walk, straggled to the rear. The army surgeons were overwhelmed with serious wounds and had no time for men like Joel. His wound was only superficial. It looked worse than it was. He was given some bandages and left to dress the wound himself.

Thousands of stragglers were wandering everywhere, most of them ransacking the Federal camps for food and souvenirs. Joel's heart was heavy and there was no more fight left in him. He began to think of his own hunger. He hadn't eaten in more than twelve hours. He only had a vague idea of where he might report for rations, so he joined the others in scavenging what he could. By dark he was filled and feeling quite comfortable. A storm was brewing, so he sought shelter in one of the abandoned Federal tents.

The thunder and lightning of the storm seemed quite docile when compared to the manmade thunder earlier in the day. Joel drifted off to sleep, but was soon awakened by a tremendous, ground-shaking concussion. The Union gunboats were lobbing shells into the Confederate positions and continued at fifteen minute intervals throughout the night. Joel slept in snatches, but got little rest. At daybreak the shelling stopped and he plunged into a deep, dreamless sleep.

Joel had no idea what time it was, but the sound of rain on the tent and the rumble of thunder told him the storm of the night before had resumed its onslaught. He opened his eyes, stretched, and yawned. He looked around. Something wasn't right. There was no silence between the claps of thunder, only a lessening of the rumble. Joel sat up and looked out the tent flap. No rain. No thunder. Minie balls were ripping through the tent fabric. Artillery batteries were dueling with each other. The Yanks were back, reinforced during the night. General Lew Wallace's Division from Crump's Landing had arrived just after dark, and General Don Carlos Buell's Army of the Ohio had marched from Savannah along the eastern shore of the Tennessee River and had been ferried across on Union gunboats.

Joel studied the situation and considered his choices. He was in a "no mans land." He could try for the Rebel lines, but he would be the focus of Union fire. If the Federals overran the camp, he would be taken prisoner. Joel checked his revolver. It had two loads, and his cartridge box was empty. He decided to just wait it out.

The fighting raged for hours. At some point Joel was overcome with boredom and fell asleep. Some time later he awoke again. All was quiet. Then he heard voices. He was afraid to look out to see which side it was. He didn't have to wait long. A redheaded, freckle-faced kid stuck his head in the tent.

"Well, I'll be jiggered!" said the kid. "How'd you get here? Well, it don't matter none. Get your hands up! You're my prisoner."

Joel stuck his revolver in the kid's face. "You're wrong, kid. You're my prisoner."

The kid had a big grin on his face. "Now, if this don't beat all. How in the hell do you expect to take me prisoner? Good lord, Johnny, there's hundreds of us out here and only one of you in there."

Joel wondered if he looked as silly as he felt. He turned the revolver butt-first and handed it to the kid. An hour later he was sitting with the other prisoners on the river's edge at Pittsburgh Landing.

Shiloh was the high-water mark of the Confederate campaign in the West. It had been a "must win." For the first time soldiers of both sides had seen the ugly, brutal face of war. Politicians would paint glorious pictures in their speeches, the generals would write self-serving reports, each claiming the credit for himself or pointing the accusing finger at someone else. But for the most part the common soldiers were glad they had survived and prayed they would never again witness, let alone take part in, such a fight.

The carnage was everywhere apparent. Trees topped by artillery shells, stripped of their foliage by the unrelenting storm of bullets, the bodies of hundreds of horses and thousands of men scattered everywhere in every grotesque position imaginable. Of some 111,000 combatants, more than 23,000 had become casualties...one in every five.

For the South, what was almost a glorious victory had become a crushing defeat. Their best general lay dead and the heart of the Mississippi Valley lay open for invasion by Union forces. It was said that after Shiloh, the South never smiled again.

Like every other man who had taken part in the battle of Shiloh, Joel Deaton would never be the same. He went into captivity resolved to never again swerve from his goal of finding Laura Jean.

Most of the Confederate soldiers captured at Shiloh were transported to Camp Douglas. It had received its first prisoners in February 1862. Located on the south side of Chicago, the camp was not suited for its role as a prison camp. It was situated on low ground and flooded after every rain. During one month, February 1863, one tenth of all the prisoners had died of disease. Security was lax and it would have given Joel another chance to escape to the South.

Joel was not so fortunate. Alton Prison, in southern Illinois was Joel's destination. Unlike Camp Morton this was a real prison. Built like a fortress instead of a camp, its walls were made of stone 30 feet high. Each cell was a mere four by seven feet. Overcrowding, starvation, scurvy and a complete lack of medical attention made the place into a living hell.

Hear That Lonesome Whistle Blow

# 86

On a sunny day in July 1865, the gates of Alton Prison swung open and a host of Confederate prisoners emerged to face an uncertain future. Joel Deaton had endured more than three years in the place. Joel had survived because he had a purpose in his life, a goal to fulfill. He took the loyalty oath along with the others and was set free, penniless, dressed in rags, and no place to go.

Joel had no desire to return to the South. Stories of carpetbaggers and oppression under the military occupation were widespread. Joel wanted none of that. He kicked around doing odd jobs for several months until he heard of recruitment for the Union Pacific. Unlike his experience with the Pony Express, Joel didn't arrive too late for this opportunity.

The Union Pacific Railroad was created by an act of Congress in June 1862, but by the end of the Civil War the first rails west of Omaha were yet to be laid. Work was finally started in July 1865, but by the end of the year little progress had been made.

In February 1866, a track-laying contract was let to Jack and Dan Casement. Jack had been a brigadier general in the Union Army. The Casement brothers spent little time in getting organized, and by April they were laying track westward, completing 250 miles in their first 182 days.

The railroad workers were a wonderful mix of mostly Irish extraction with an infusion of former soldiers from both sides of the recent conflict, mule skinners, Mexicans, ex-convicts, and even former slaves. Each man was trained to do a specific task, and because of this specialization the work was able to proceed like an assembly line. Joel's job was placing rails. It was hard work, requiring little thought, but the pay was good. Thirty-five dollars monthly, plus board. Most important, from Joel's point of view, was that he was headed west again. He wasn't sure what the future might bring, but he knew that the only way he would learn of his sister's fate was by returning to Utah, and maybe even to Mountain Meadows.

Except for the blacks and Mexicans, little social distinction existed among the railroaders. The Civil War veterans, both North and South, mingled freely, but they had little regard for the "niggers and greasers."

None of this had any effect upon Joel. Basically a loner, he didn't mingle with anybody. Though only twenty-five, his experiences had hardened him, adding years to his appearance. The carefree personality he exhibited on the westward trek of 1857 had completely disappeared. He turned to drink in spite of his bad experience with it nine years before. Most of the men used tobacco freely, but Joel had never been particularly attracted to the filthy practice.

As the rails pushed ever westward, a new influx of emigrants followed. This time, instead of crossing the plains, they came to settle it. Towns like Elkhorn, Grand Island, and North Platte sprung up along the tracks.

Another kind of town grew up around the track laying camp, just like the "Dobytown" Joel had found outside of Camp Floyd, except these "Hell on Wheels", as they were called, were portable. They moved when the railroaders moved. Sometimes the towns survived after the railroad left, but usually they didn't.

Joel took a few turns with the girls at the camp brothel, but he soon lost interest. He always felt guilty afterwards. The girls doused themselves with cheap perfume, but they were dirty and it was not at all like the tender relationship he had experienced with Delia Huff so many years before. As he lay grunting in their carnal embrace he couldn't help but compare it with the sweet kisses he had exchanged with Delia that night while guarding the wagon train. He was a man, and had the appetites of a man, but he had had enough of whores and resolved to keep himself for the girl he would someday marry. After he had found Laura Jean.

The miles continued to mount and little happened to break the tedium of the daily regimen. Indians were a constant threat, but they were partially held in check by the army of Pawnee that had been hired to protect the workers. This time Joel was able to take a better look at the Great Plains. Travel distances were only a mile and a half per day instead of fifteen to twenty. Prairie thunderstorms alternated with the heat and the dust, and even an occasional herd of buffalo rumbled by. Everything looked the same, but it was different. In their passing, the forerunners of civilization had left an indelible mark on the landscape, not yet civilized, but no longer wild and untouched.

By May 1867, end of track had left North Platte, Nebraska, in its wake. The town consisted of only fifteen buildings, of which nine were saloons and one a billiard parlor. The population quickly grew to more than five thousand: Union Pacific workers, bunco artists, gamblers, and whores. The only law was a vigilance committee that took care of business with warnings to leave town to those miscreants who would and "neck tie parties" for those who wouldn't. Nevertheless, hardly a day went by without at least one killing, and the amount of loot separated from the railroad workers was beyond anybody's reckoning.

Out of boredom, more than anything else, Joel found himself a more frequent visitor at the saloons. After a particularly hard day of work he found himself in a large tent with a square wooden false front, two windows, one on either side of the swinging doors, and the word "Saloon" painted near the top were all that identified it from other establishments.

Joel was enjoying a shot glass of Taos Lightning, a potent drink made in New Mexico and freighted up to the saloons along the Union Pacific line by way of Denver. That city was not yet ten years old, but unlike many other towns that sprung up where gold was found, Denver had managed to flourish, even after most of the miners had left. The people of Denver had lobbied hard for the main line of the transcontinental railroad, but money and a deadline dictated that the tracks follow the more direct route through southern Wyoming.

Joel's thoughts had turned inward. He was thinking of his family when he noticed three men at the other end of the bar, one of them hunched over and the other two on either side snickering and guffawing. Suddenly, the man in the middle spun around.

"It ain't none of your goddamned business!" he shouted. There was a momentary lull in the noise of the crowded saloon, but since fights and other ruckuses were more or less common place, most people paid no mind to the goings on, at least as long as no guns were drawn.

"Now don't get your hackles up, Zack. We's just curious, that's all."

"Don't call me that, neither!"

Without warning one of his tormentors punched the man in the gut, sending him crumpling to the floor.

"Hey, there!" said Joel. "Two on one, that ain't right."

"You want some of this?" said one of the men. "Come'n get it."

"You a Mormon lover or sump'n?" said the other. "We was just askin' 'im how many of them Mormon whores he had for wives."

The two men both laughed. The man on the floor saw his opening and he gave it his best, got in a few good licks, but he was no match for the other two. When the two rowdies were finished, they threw a few coins on the bar, took their bottle of whiskey and left the saloon. Joel looked at the man on the floor, bruised and bloody. He felt no pity. In fact, he felt an urge to get in a few licks of his own.

The man got to his feet and shook the barroom floor sawdust from his clothes. A few people looked his way, but no one really cared. The man had a sad, forlorn look on his face, a look of total resignation. He looked at Joel and there was a flicker of fire in his eyes.

"I'll be remembering you," he said.

"Do tell. Well, I ain't partial to Mormons in the first place, so don't give me none of your sass."

"I'm not a Mormon...at least not anymore."

"Seen the light, huh?" said Joel.

"It ain't none of your business, neither."

"Well, I'm always happy to see a man who's mended his ways. What's your name? I heard 'em call you Zack."

"The name's Isaac. Isaac Delaney."

"Pleased to make your acquaintance," said Joel, extending his hand.

Isaac Delaney brushed past Joel and shuffled out the door.

"Ain't no pleasin' some people," said Joel to no one in particular.

The seemingly endless, rolling sea of grass stretched to the horizon and beyond. There were no trees except along streams and the only signs of civilization were provided by the railroad workers themselves and the camp followers. The great slaughter of buffalo was already underway, and sightings of buffalo herds were much less frequent than ten years before.

Indians were becoming more of a problem. They didn't need to be told that the twin ribbons of steel meant the intrusion of the white man would continue to grow and threaten their traditional way of life. Rails were being torn up and survey crews were coming under attack. The U. S. Cavalry was of little help and the Pawnee hired to protect the railroad workers wouldn't come this far west. The Union Pacific was forced to divert men from laying track to acting as armed escorts. The pay was the same, but the work was much less strenuous. There was no lack of volunteers.

Along with Isaac Delaney, Joel Deaton found himself among the lucky few selected. It didn't take long, though, for him to realize that he wasn't as lucky as he first thought. After only three days out on the prairie a party of Cheyenne "dog soldiers", numbering more than forty, swept over a rise at full gallop whooping and firing rifles and shooting arrows. Two men fell immediately and three more were hit before the fight was over.

Joel had dropped to the ground and would've crawled under it if possible. The sound of gunfire and the whizzing of bullets overhead transported him mentally back to the Shiloh battlefield. Images of scattered bodies, including his own, filled his mind with terror. He looked up and saw next to him Isaac Delaney resting on one knee, firing his Henry rifle at the oncoming Indians. Delaney seemed not to care that his life was in danger. Coolly, he picked off five Indians by Joel's count. Inspired by the example, Joel got to his feet and opened fire. After only a couple of minutes the Indians turned tail and rode out in the direction they had come.

The men of the survey crew all stood up and looked around, most of them grinning at each other, not humorously, but from the relief of knowing that they were still alive. A quick nose count was done. Only one of the railroad men was dead. Seven Indians had fallen, four of them still alive.

"What're we gonna do about them, Mr. Sullivan?" said Joel to the survey boss.

"We ain't got time to fool with 'em," said Sullivan. "Finish 'em off."

"Kill 'em?" asked Joel.

"Yeah, kill every one of them red niggers," said Sullivan, "and maybe the rest will get the message."

Joel and Delaney and the rest of the armed guard quickly dispatched the wounded Cheyenne. Joel felt no remorse. He fortified himself by thinking of the Paiute Indians killing the women and children of the Fancher wagon train. He did feel a sense of revulsion as one of the men lifted the scalps of the dead Indians.

"You're pretty handy with that rifle," Joel said to Delaney. "Did you fight in the war?"

Delaney looked at the younger man and slowly shook his head. "Don't believe much in war. Seems it's always the wrong ones that get killed."

"Well, I shudder to think the fix we'd be in if you hadn't taken charge."

"Just doing my job."

"I was in the war," said Joel. "Saw a lotta brave men die. Weren't none of 'em showed more courage'n you did."

"Listen, son. All men die...someday. None of us know when that's gonna be. Until then, I'm gonna live like a man, and when it's time, die like a man. A man's life don't count for much if he has to live with his head hanging down."

"That sounds good," said Joel, "but what about that run in you had with them bullies back at North Platte?"

"I fought back, didn't I?" said Delaney.

"Yes, but..."

"But what? I may keep to myself, that's my business, but I don't step aside for no man...and that includes you."

Delaney took some shells from his pocket and reloaded his rifle.
Joel was beginning to feel a grudging admiration for this strange
man in spite of his first impression. He wanted to ask Delaney about
his Mormon background, but thought better of it. Before Joel could
think of anything else to say, Delaney hoisted his rifle onto his
shoulder and walked away. There would be no more work this day.
The dead man needed burying and the wounded had to be taken
back to North Platte.

Within six weeks North Platte had lapsed into its former
obscurity, most of the rowdies having packed up and followed the
tracks west. The "Hell on Wheels" had not been abandoned, but
had simply moved to a new location, Julesburg, Colorado.

# 87

By the end of July the population of Julesburg had grown to four
thousand, and provided abundant opportunities for the men of the
Union Pacific to indulge their appetites for alcohol and gambling,
and plenty of "soiled doves" were available to take care of the need
for female companionship. Of all the "Hell on Wheels" towns,
Julesburg was the worst. A wide open town, the Sabbath came and
went with little notice by anyone.

Joel and Isaac weren't exactly friends, but circumstances had
thrown them together and an uneasy relationship was beginning to
develop. It was early evening as they rode into Julesburg after several
days on the prairie guarding the survey crews. The main street was
filled with people, many engaged in animated conversations and
most others either milling about or seemingly on their way
somewhere. It had the appearance of a crowd just leaving the theater
and coming in conflict with people on their way to a fire. Joel and
Delaney had to be careful they didn't run someone down with their
horses.

"Well, Isaac, what'll we do first?" asked Joel. "I'd say there's a
whole bunch of possibilities. This town don't lack for saloons. We
can get drunk or find us a game, or a woman or two."

"Thought you didn't mess with whores," said Delaney.

"I don't," said Joel. "I was only thinking of you."

"I'm hungry and tired," said Delaney. "Let's eat first and then
we'll see."

Had Joel known much about the Mormon religion he would've been surprised that Delaney would even consider getting drunk or gambling or paying for the sexual favors of a woman. But then neither did he know that he and Delaney shared the same dark secret...that they were two sides of the same coin.

Much had changed for Delaney since the day of the massacre. He had done his duty as a soldier and as a loyal Latter-day Saint. He had done only what he thought was the bidding of his friend and prophet, Brigham Young. Like some of the others, he felt betrayed by his leaders, shattered by the realization of the grievous wrong he had been a party to, devastated by the knowledge that he had almost taken the life of his own son, all this in the name of religion.

Like the other participants in the massacre he was shunned by the citizens of the community and became the subject of vicious gossip. His services as a carpenter were less and less in demand. Finally, he had been forced to move his family and, with Bishop Philip Klingensmith, had helped homestead a new settlement called Adventure. As if by the wrath of God, the new community was wiped out soon after in a flood. Klingensmith soon left the church and the territory. Feeling his wives had also turned against him, Isaac Delaney soon followed suit. He had drifted around from town to town looking for work, looking for absolution for his sins, and perhaps, like the Ancient Mariner, hoping that someone would end his misery upon this earth.

Though he longed for human comfort and companionship, Delaney avoided relationships. In the ten years since the tragedy at Mountain Meadows, Joel Deaton, young enough to be his son, had been his only friend. And Delaney was careful to not be too friendly.

Joel Deaton and Isaac Delaney tied up in front of a restaurant where customers were lined up, waiting to get in. Although Joel had learned to hate standing in lines because of his military experience, he figured that a long line was a good recommendation for the quality of the cuisine, at least in comparison to the other establishments in town.

"How's your dinner?" asked Joel.

"Ain't exactly home cooking," said Delaney, "but I can't complain. It's a damn sight better than what they feed us back in camp."

"Wish I could say the same for the surroundings," said Joel.

If cleanliness was next to godliness, this restaurant would be closer to the lower region. It was one large room about the size of the inside of a barn. The studs and rafters were exposed, as were the

4 x 4 posts that held up the roof. The tables were made of rough planks, and seating was benches made of more planks. Only one item was on the menu: steaks cooked outside on a large grill and served with a side order of beans and half a loaf of bread. The only beverages were coffee and beer.

Afterwards, their hunger sated, Joel and Delaney strolled down the street leading their horses. It was a warm and pleasant evening under a clear, starry sky. The sound of music mingled with hundreds of voices, giving the two men an exciting feeling of anticipation.

"What d'you say we find us a game?" said Joel. "I feel lucky."

"You go ahead," said Delaney. "I ain't much for gambling. You play and I'll watch."

"Don't believe in it, huh?"

"I didn't say that," said Delaney.

"That's okay. No need to feel ashamed of it."

"I ain't ashamed of it. Hell, you're just trying to goad me into playing, ain't you."

Joel laughed. Delaney didn't miss a thing. Ever since they first met, Joel had been trying to get him to open up and talk about himself. Something about this man intrigued Joel, and he wanted to know what it was.

"Funny thing about gambling," said Delaney. "All of God's creatures have the need for food and shelter, but only men drink and gamble."

"You left out sex," said Joel.

"That, too," allowed Delaney. "I've seen animals fight for food and shelter and mates, but I ain't never seen one wager his property to take the valuables of another. No, sir, gambling ain't natural."

"Well, you're right, Isaac. Only men know how to have fun."

Delaney just shook his head.

Their choices were many, so Joel and Delaney stopped at the first gambling hall they came to. This place was about twenty feet wide by forty feet deep and built of sturdy lumber imported from the Midwest. The bar down one side was doing a booming business, and three faro tables, each in a corner, were separating the customers from their money. Along the wall opposite the bar were several tables with lively games of stud poker. There must have been nearly two hundred men and women jammed into the place. The women weren't there to drink or gamble, but to accommodate the carnal desires of the men. The saloon was filled with smoke and so much profanity it seemed to flow like a heavy spring runoff. Joel and Delaney each bought a glass of beer and began mingling with the crowd, looking for a game.

"What d'you say, Isaac?" said Joel over the noise of the crowd. "Shall we play faro or poker?"

"I told you I was only gonna watch."

"Yeah? Well, if I was to find me a whore you'd probably just want to watch, wouldn't you?"

"I ain't no pervert," said Delaney.

"Then let's play cards," said Joel.

The action was fast, and when a man vacated his seat it was usually because he was busted. No seat stayed empty for very long.

"My daddy liked poker," said Joel, "but I'm partial to faro. Y'got a better chance to win."

Finally, a seat opened at one of the faro tables. Joel slipped into the chair just ahead of another man. The two exchanged hostile looks, then Joel ignored the man and turned to the dealer and asked, "What're the stakes?"

"Cost you a dime to play and six bits is the limit."

Joel put a dime on the seven. When the bets were down the dealer drew two cards from the box. The first was an eight and the second was a king. The dealer collected the money from the eight and paid the wagers on the king.

"Wagers, gentlemen," said the dealer.

Joel decided to let it ride. The next two cards were two sevens. A push. Joel moved his bet to the deuce. This time the cards were a jack and a deuce. He had won. The game continued. Joel won some and lost some. After half an hour he was a few dollars ahead.

As he said he would, Delaney had stood at Joel's shoulder watching the game. When he had seen enough, he leaned over and whispered into Joel's ear.

"Don't put your money on the same card as the majority do."

Joel looked up at the older man. He did not speak, but his expression asked the question.

"Just watch," whispered Delaney.

Joel did watch, and it didn't take long to see what Delaney had seen. The cards with the most money wagered lost more often than not. Joel watched the dealer, but couldn't see how he was doing it. Joel counted his stack and, seeing he was still a few dollars ahead, decided to get out of the game. But then he did a foolish thing.

"That's it for me," said Joel. "I ain't throwin' my money away on a crooked game."

"What'd you say?" said the dealer, rising part way from his chair, looking Joel over from head to foot.

"I said..."

Without warning the dealer lunged across the table and punched Joel in the jaw, sending him sprawling. Joel was shaken, but unhurt. The dealer's placid demeanor had changed. His eyes glistened with fire and ice.

"Nobody calls me a cheat and gets away with it. If you were

armed, you'd be dead on the floor, mister! Now get your ass out of here before I do it anyway."

Joel rose from the floor and it was plain to see what his intentions were. He took one step toward the faro dealer when suddenly the lights went out... his lights. Delaney stood over his young friend, a bottle in his hand.

"Sorry I had to do that, Joel, but you were fixing to get yourself killed."

When Joel woke up he was sitting on the ground against the outside wall of the saloon. He had a salty taste in his mouth from the blood trickling down from the cut on his head. Most people on the street paid him no mind, but some stared at him...particularly the two standing in front of him.

"I heard what y'said in there," said the older of the two. "You were right, but you were stupid. Mister, you don't tell a dealer he's crooked 'less y'intend to back it up. You're lucky you ain't dead."

"Who hit me?"

"I did," said Delaney. "It was the only thing I could do to save your life."

"I expect I should be sayin' my thank you's, but my head tells me to get up and beat the hell out of you."

Joel felt the bump on his head. It was about the size of a hen's egg and very tender. He looked up at the stranger, a man in his mid-twenties, stocky and well-dressed. With him was a younger man around twenty, with a moustache and piercing eyes. The younger man had long, slender fingers and soft hands. He didn't appear well acquainted with manual labor. Joel addressed himself to the older of the two. "Who're you?"

"Earp's the name, Virgil Earp. This here's my brother, Wyatt. We work for the U.P., same as you. We saw what y'done in there. Most of them games are crooked. 'Bout the only way you c'n keep from gettin' skinned is to not play, but I don't reckon that'd keep you from it."

"No, sir, it wouldn't."

"Well, that's your business," said Virgil Earp. "Just wanted to give you some friendly advice. If you're gonna play, keep your mouth shut around them dealers or you'll be eatin' lead, if you take my meaning."

"Give me a hand up, Isaac," said Joel.

Delaney helped his young friend to his feet. Joel dusted himself off and tried to shake the cobwebs from his mind.

"Be seein' you," said Virgil Earp as he and his younger brother shuffled off down the street.

Joel felt his head one more time, then turned to Delaney. "Next time don't try so hard."

"Do you want to go back to camp?" asked Delaney.

"Nah. The night's young and so are we...well, at least I am."

The two looked at each other and Delaney managed a smile. Joel was pleased. In the past few weeks Delaney had displayed only one expression. Maybe he was finally going to open up.

When Joel awoke in the morning, he found himself in the bed of a half-naked, overweight woman old enough to be his mother. He shook his head and almost laughed as he recalled the story his father had told him of the mountain man and the "coyote ugly" Indian squaw. Joel hadn't remembered much after the first few drinks. He wondered if Delaney had had any fun. Hell, he couldn't remember if he'd had any fun himself.

# 88

General Grenville Dodge, superintendent of the railroad, read the telegram from the land agent in Julesburg and his hands trembled from anger.

"Who the hell do they think they are?" he roared. "The U.P. owns that land, and if they want it they're gonna have to pay for it!"

Before the coming of the railroad Julesburg had a population of only forty men and one woman, and was little more than a stop for the overland stagecoach. The Union Pacific owned the land and Dodge had laid out the town and left an agent behind to sell the lots. The "entrepreneurs" who came to town with the railroad had simply ignored the question of ownership and set up business. When the agent demanded payment of rent or outright purchase, they laughed in his face. Dodge sent a telegram of his own to Dan Casement; make 'em pay or clean 'em out.

Casement responded to the assignment with a great deal of enthusiasm. He gathered a force of two hundred men, Joel and Delaney among them, and headed for Julesburg.

It was only a short train ride to Julesburg. Isaac Delaney pulled his hat down over his eyes as if going to sleep, extended his legs in front of him and folded his arms. His Henry rifle was beside him, the butt on the floor and the barrel leaning against his hip. He wasn't sleepy, though. He just wanted to be left alone. He wanted to think.

Through the medium of his imagination Delaney was able to transport himself to happier times, away from the miserable life he now led. Somewhere out here in an unmarked grave on the prairie lay his beloved Molly. How long had it been? Nearly twenty years. So much had changed. In those days it truly was a wilderness. The only real town between the States and California had been Salt Lake City. Now towns were springing up all over the plains. People traveled by stagecoach and soon they would be traveling all the way to the Pacific Ocean on trains.

Delaney thought of those days of privation with the Mormon Battalion and the heady feeling of chipping gold flakes from the rocks in California. And his disappointment with the Salt Lake Valley and the agony of learning of Molly's death on the trail. The joy of his newfound love of Harriet after that night he had been lost in the blizzard in Millcreek Canyon did much to balance the pain of losing his first wife. The early days in southern Utah were hard, but he had many happy memories of watching his children grow and flourish.

Curse the day that he had given over his conscience to the control of others! Damn them for what they had led him to do! Damn them for turning their backs on him when it was all over! There had been no more loyal follower than himself. How low he had fallen! A partaker of liquor and lewd women. He had contemplated taking his own life on many occasions, but he did not want to add murder to his other sins. He did not consider the slaughter at Mountain Meadows to be upon his own head, but upon the heads of those who had ordered it done. Nevertheless, he counted himself as being unworthy of the company of decent men and lived apart from them, though he could not account for the growing friendship with Joel Deaton. Something about this young man drew them together, but for the life of him, Delaney could not put his finger on what it was.

"Wake up, Isaac. We're there."

Delaney pushed the brim of his hat up and looked at young Joel. A glisten of tears was in Delaney's eyes.

"You okay?" asked Joel.

"Just remembering," said Delaney, "happier days."

"Yes," said Joel wistfully, "happier days."

Casement had wired ahead to the land agent. A crowd of Julesburg's "leading" citizens were awaiting the arrival of the railroaders, though they had not expected a small army. Casement was short and to the point; rent it, buy it, or get out. One of the squatters stepped forward.

"This is a free country...or at least it used to be. What gives you the right to demand payment for this land. You sons-of-bitches didn't buy it from nobody..." The crowd shouted their agreement.

"...We got as much right to this land as anybody. Hell, the Injuns got more right to it then you do!"

"Gentlemen," Casement practically choked on the word, "the United States Congress has given us a patent on this land. We're building a railroad, or hadn't you noticed? There ain't a decent man or woman among you. You rob, lie, cheat...this ain't a town...if there's a heaven, this is hell...and we aim to clean it up."

Delaney stood staring at the ground. He had a queasy feeling in his stomach. Joel was scanning the crowd, looking for one particular man. Then he saw him, the faro dealer who had knocked him to the floor. The man was standing there, seemingly bored by all the rhetoric.

"You're makin' a livin', ain't you?" said one of the gamblers angrily. "We gotta right to make a living, too?"

"That's right," said another. "There's farmers squattin' all over this territory. What gives them more right to the land than us?"

"We're stayin' and we ain't payin'!" said still another.

Casement looked the crowd over. He was disgusted. He thought of the men cheated, beaten and killed by these lowlifes. He was through talking. He turned to his posse.

"Talking's over men. Fire into the crowd!"

Joel was electrified. He felt the same thrill as he did when charging the Yanks at Shiloh. He raised his rifle and took dead aim on the faro dealer. He dropped him with one shot. The gamblers had a few handguns among them, but no long guns. People screamed and scattered in panic as the railroaders raked them with a murderous fire.

Delaney stood there transfixed, a sound of sheer horror escaped his lips two, three times. "Oh, God! No! Not again!" He looked around at the men firing into the crowd. Some were laughing. He looked shocked and bewildered. Then as quickly as it began it was over.

Joel had only aimed the first shot and fired three more times at random. He didn't know if he had hit anyone else but the faro dealer, but he didn't care. There were obviously several fatalities, but Joel felt no remorse. Most of these people were only taking up space on the planet, serving no useful purpose whatsoever. It was likely that mischief in Julesburg would continue, but at a much lower level.

While the railroaders planted thirty-three new bodies in the cemetery outside of town, a substantial portion of the citizens were seen to be heading back east. Before the day was over, Joel, Delaney, and the other railroaders were on the train heading for end-of-track. Since the shooting Delaney hadn't said a single word in spite of all of Joel's attempts at conversation.

In the morning Delaney was back to normal...almost. He spoke, but only when spoken to. His thoughts had turned inside himself and Joel found him a harder nut to crack than ever.

# 89

The next Hell on Wheels town was Cheyenne, Wyoming. It had sprung into existence in July 1867, long before the tracks arrived and before Julesburg had even built up a good head of steam. The Union Pacific intended it as a railroad center with maintenance shops and storage facilities. It wasn't as boisterous as Julesburg had been, but then neither was Julesburg. That locality had gone back to being a sleepy frontier town as soon as Cheyenne was open for business in the fall. In this town of more than a hundred saloons, killings and robberies were commonplace, the same as they had been at Julesburg. Even a lynching from a telegraph pole down by the station of one badman, ordered out of town and stupid enough to come back, did not dampen the enthusiasm of the criminal element. For the most part, though, this town was much quieter than the last one in spite of the daily newspaper column titled, "Last Night's Shootings."

Track reached Cheyenne in November and work on the railroad stopped for the winter only twenty-two miles farther west. Joel and Delaney didn't care. The railroad workers were paid regardless of the weather.

For the time being, Cheyenne was the western terminus for the Union Pacific, and passengers and freight arrived everyday. The wagon freighting business was doomed to extinction, but plenty of entrepreneurs were trying to milk the last bit of money out of the business before the railroads took it over. It was at Cheyenne, after the spring thaw, that Joel got the idea to go into the freighting business. All he needed, he figured, was a freight wagon and a good team of mules.

"It ain't no good," said Delaney when Joel presented the idea.

"And why not?" said Joel. "I see wagons loading up everyday. Some of 'em are even carrying passengers. I hear that a man with a wagon can hire out at twenty-five dollars a day. Y'figure what our room and board is worth, we c'n make a month's wages in only two days."

"Have you ever run a business, lad? Have you?"

"No."

"Well, then, I have."

At last! Joel was finally going to hear Delaney talk about himself. What Joel didn't grasp was that Delaney wasn't merely opposed to Joel starting up a business, but that in doing so they would inevitably part company, probably permanently, and Delaney would be minus the only friend he had. Delaney wouldn't say that. Perhaps the thought had not even occurred to him, at least not consciously. Nevertheless, it was true.

"You hauled freight, I suppose," said Joel.

"No, I didn't," said Delaney, "but during the gold rush there was a fortune to be had picking up the discards of the forty-niners. You see, most of 'em were greenhorns. Hadn't the foggiest notion what to bring with 'em on the trail. There was hardly a wagon that didn't lose an ox or two."

"Why was that?"

"They worked 'em to death," said Delaney. "Why, they were carrying mining tools, four-poster beds, cast iron cook stoves, trunks of useless things, and more food then they could eat on two trips. So they dumped it along the trail."

"That was stupid," said Joel.

"Of course it was. And the people coming along the trail, they couldn't pick it up, 'cause they were overloaded, too. Even wagons were discarded when they broke down. I used to be a carpenter, so I fixed 'em and brought 'em back to Salt Lake...fully loaded mind you...and sold the whole outfit. I would've been a rich man, too, if they hadn't called me on a mission."

"A mission?"

"Not to preach, mind you, but to colonize."

"Where'd they send you?" asked Joel.

"To Parowan," said Delaney.

Joel turned away. Parowan. They had closed the gates of the town, forcing the Fancher company to blaze a new road around the settlement.

"How long were you there?" asked Joel.

Delaney looked at Joel, surprised that he had told so much about himself.

"It was a long time ago," he said. "Anyway, you ain't ready to start a business."

"Why not?"

"You've got to have money," said Delaney, slapping the back of his right hand into the palm of his left.

Delaney went on, but Joel wasn't listening any more. Just when had Delaney been in Parowan? Did he know anything about the massacre? Had he ever heard anything about the children? He wanted so badly to ask those questions, but he knew he wouldn't get an answer.

Days passed, and then weeks. One day Joel and Isaac Delaney were in Cheyenne again acting as armed guards, this time for the company payroll. They were standing outside the train station when Joel heard someone call his name. He looked up at a man sitting astride a horse. It was Eli Bennett.

"Joel Deaton? That is you, isn't it?"

"I do declare," said Joel, smiling. "Thought I'd never see you again. How've you been?"

"Just fine," said Bennett. "My, how you've changed. You look so much like your dad, rest his soul."

The smile fled from Joel's face. Bennett realized instantly that he'd said the wrong thing.

"Y'married?" he asked. "Got any kids?"

"No," said Joel, "ain't never had the time. What brings you here?"

Bennett explained that he was in Cheyenne to pick up a party of Mormon emigrants from Europe and escort them the rest of the way to Utah. Bennett dismounted and the two men talked over old times and when it was time to go, on impulse Eli Bennett gave Joel a warm embrace. Standing to one side, Delaney had been watching all this and listening to the conversation. For someone who "wasn't partial to Mormons", Joel was doing a right smart imitation of being quite fond of this one. Delaney realized there was a lot he didn't know about his young friend. He wanted to know more.

Summer came and the tracks pushed farther into Wyoming. The business of building a transcontinental railroad had turned into a contest between the Union Pacific and the Central Pacific. Indians were more scarce than on the plains, making the need for armed guards unnecessary, so Joel and Delaney went back to laying track. They didn't see as much of each other as before, and Delaney was glad. He wanted to be alone. But Joel felt empty. Having a friend had soothed some of the hurt and made the days go faster. It wouldn't be long before they got to Utah.

The race between the Central Pacific and the Union Pacific was rapidly changing from a marathon to a sprint. During the summer and fall of 1868 the pace of track laying was as high as six miles per day. By September, end-of-track and the newest Hell on Wheels town was at Bear River City, Wyoming. Grading, tunneling, and bridging to the mouth of Weber Canyon in Utah were nearly complete and everyone felt the transcontinental railroad would be finished before the following summer. The only question was where.

The Hell on Wheels towns were progressively nastier as the tracks moved west. Julesburg had received more attention because it had endured so long, but Bear River City was beginning to rival it as a place to lose your money, your virtue, and your life.

A pair of brothers, Leigh and Richmond Freeman, arrived in Bear Town, as the place was more commonly called by the locals, with a printing press and began publishing the Frontier Index. The Freeman boys were from Georgia, Civil War veterans, and totally unrepentant of the sins of the South. Their publication was not a newspaper in the traditional sense, but seemed dedicated to tweaking the noses of almost everyone. The local citizenry organized a "vigilance committee" to effect law and order, but it was little more than a lynch mob, and it was said that they were bent on hanging half the town and shooting the rest. When three of the Union Pacific men were lynched, an armed mob of 200 of their fellow railroaders descended on the newspaper office, a tent with a false wooden front, and destroyed the press. The brothers Freeman barely escaped with their lives when they were forewarned by a man named Alex Topance, who cut a slit in the back of their tent.

The vigilantes, who had little use for the newspaper either, but who thought even less of the railroaders, attacked in force and when the smoke cleared, fifty-three new graves were in the cemetery. Remembering the experience in Julesburg, Delaney had refused to take part, but not so Joel Deaton. He had waded in with great enthusiasm, and had been fortunate to escape death or injury. Winter was coming and the railroaders moved on to Wasatch in Utah Territory to lick their wounds and get ready for the final push in the coming year.

# 90

Echo Canyon, twenty-three miles long and a few hundred yards wide with sheer rock walls on both sides, had received its name from the Mormon pioneers of 1847. The pioneers had been impressed by the echo, which to them made the rattle of the wagons sound like carpenters driving nails, and made a gunshot reverberate like a clap of thunder.

Progress on the railroad down the canyon from Wasatch had slowed to a crawl because of the harsh winter weather. Previously, work was measured in miles per day. Now it was measured in days per mile. Echo was the first town with decent citizens that most of the men had seen in a very long time. But before the railroad came to Echo, Echo came to the railroad.

Mormons generally were not given to mingling with the railroaders, except in one regard. Their leaders had taught them well to seize upon any business opportunity that came along. Thus, many of the women were earning extra money selling home-cooked lunches to the railroad men, much to their delight.

"It's fried chicken, boys!" someone shouted. "Fried chicken!"

The men scrambled to get in line. Pushing and shoving soon led to a scuffle or two, but the men quickly realized that even a home-cooked meal was not worth a broken nose or a split lip.

When Joel finally got his chance at one of the lunches, he couldn't help noticing a girl handing out meals. The look on her face betrayed the disdain she felt for these rough and ready railroaders. She seemed barely able to even look at them. But when Joel got to the head of the line, the girl looked directly into his eyes and smiled. She had a simple beauty that took his breath away. Her soft brown tresses were gathered in a bun on top of her head and her complexion was without blemish. Most striking was the pale blue of her eyes. Joel wanted to ask her name, but couldn't find the courage. He gave her twenty-five cents for the lunch and walked away.

Joel's mind was not on the food. Delaney sat next to him and said something that Joel didn't hear. It didn't take much to notice that Joel was more interested in the girl than in conversation. When the girl and the other women gathered to leave, she looked in Joel's direction. She saw that Joel was watching her and she looked away, then stole another glance.

After the women were gone, Joel had a painful thought: suppose she didn't return? One way or another, he was determined to learn her name and anything else he could.

At the end of the day Joel and Delaney adjourned to one of the saloons at Wasatch, this one little more than a tent.

"Don't get no ideas about Mormon women," said Delaney.

"I don't know what you mean," said Joel.

Delaney laughed. "You don't need to hide it from me, Joel. I've seen that look before. You're interested and so is she, but there ain't no profit in it for either one of you."

"Why do you say that?"

"She's a Mormon, and you ain't. That's all you need to know. Besides, I thought you weren't partial to Mormons."

"I'm partial to you," said Joel, grinning.

"That's a horse of a different color," said Delaney. "Things ain't what they used to be...I ain't what I used to be."

"How's that?" asked Joel.

Delaney glanced at Joel, then seemed to look off toward infinity. He was quiet for a while. Then he spoke, in a more serious tone than Joel had ever heard him use before.

"I was a good Mormon, Joel. I lost a wife...I gave up a business to go on a mission...I did all that was required of me and I never complained...well, I wasn't too happy when my wife died. But I just can't do it anymore."

"I reckon losin' one's faith is a hard thing," Joel offered.

"It's not that. No, sir. I still believe. The Gospel is true. I know it as surely as I'm sitting here. I believe in it...I just don't believe in people anymore. There's a lotta things done in the name of religion that I'm not so sure the Lord approves of."

"I'll drink to that," said Joel.

"What about you? What's your religion, Joel?"

"Don't have one. I used to go to church when I was a kid, but I don't believe in it anymore."

"Joel, every man should believe in something."

"Is that so? Well...I believe I'll have another drink."

It was very late when Joel and Delaney retired to their tent, and their condition would have kept less hardy men from their duties in the morning. Joel had a fitful sleep. He dreamed of the girl he had seen selling lunches. She was with people, always hurrying, and no matter how much he tried, he could never catch up to her.

In the morning Joel was up early. The effects of the alcohol had taken less of a toll on his body than on Delaney's, but he had difficulty eating breakfast because of a nervous stomach. Thoughts of the girl filled his mind even though he kept telling himself it was stupid to be thinking of a Mormon girl, seeing as how he hated Mormons so much. In a perverse sort of way he rationalized that it would be poetic justice to romance one of their women, compromise her virtue, and then leave her in the dust. Love 'em and leave 'em, that was his motto.

By lunchtime the crew had laid only a quarter mile of track. Joel kept pulling out his pocket watch to check the time. After the fifth or sixth time, Delaney knew he had to say something. "You're gonna wear the numbers off that watch if you ain't careful. They'll call us when it's time to eat, just like they do everyday."

Joel was a little embarrassed. He put his watch away and said nothing. In a little while he felt the urge to take it out again. How long had it been? Ten minutes? Half an hour? Finally, he saw a wagon coming up the road, carrying the Mormon women with their lunches. They were too far away to be identified individually. Joel wasn't the only one looking. Everyone had stopped work, including Delaney.

"Guess they won't have to tell us today," said Joel to Delaney with a grin.

The men who wanted to buy lunch from the ladies began forming a line. Joel wanted to get at the end of the line so he could take his time talking to the girl without a lot of "hoorahing" from the other men. But he was afraid if he did, there might not be any lunches left when he got there, and he wouldn't have a chance to talk to her. So, he got somewhere in the middle of the second half of the line.

The girl had come and, no mistaking it, she was looking at him every chance she got. By the time Joel got to the head of the line he knew exactly what to say.

"I enjoyed the lunch yesterday," he said.

"Thank you," said the girl in a voice barely above a whisper. Joel heard a "hmpf" from somewhere, and he looked around. One of the older ladies was giving him a look that would peel the paint off the walls. "That'll be twenty-five cents, please."

Joel dug for the money in his pocket. "Will you be coming tomorrow?" he asked.

The girl looked at the ground, trying to hide her grin. "Maybe," she said in a teasing voice.

"Lavina!" said the older woman. "There's more men to feed!"

Joel gave the money to the girl and thanked her. He was quite pleased with his good luck. He had learned her name and hadn't even had to ask. He sat down on the ground a short distance away and began to eat. Watching Lavina was becoming a downright pleasure, and he would've told her so if he'd had the chance.

Joel watched her work, but today she seemed to hardly notice him. The one time she did look in his direction, the older woman tugged on her sleeve and gave her a sharp look.

The next day the lunches came, but Lavina did not. Nor did she come on the following day. Joel figured the older woman must have been her mother or some other close relative and they were keeping her away because of him.

"Don't flatter yourself," said Delaney. "You wouldn't have a chance with her and her mother knows it. She probably doesn't want her gal teasing you like she's been doing."

"Teasing?"

"Of course. No decent Mormon girl would be interested in an outsider, especially one as dirty and ugly as you."

Dirty? Yes. But ugly? Delaney must have been thinking of himself instead of Joel.

The tracks pushed on toward Echo and Joel was beginning to

wonder if he would ever see the girl again. But he had a plan, a desperate plan, requiring him to do something he hadn't done in years. Joel cleaned himself up, got his hair cut, put on his best clothes...and went to church. That's right. He went to church.

Joel had never felt more uncomfortable. Some of the people came up and shook his hand, even called him "Brother", but most of the congregation regarded him as a curiosity. Those who did speak to him quickly discerned that he was not a fellow Mormon. He didn't act like one and he didn't talk like one. The missionary spirit prevailed, though, and Joel found himself the recipient of a few invitations to Sunday dinner, all of which he politely declined. It was hard disguising the real feelings he had for Mormons, but he was careful not to say or do anything that might hurt his chances with the girl.

Lavina had seen Joel come into the church and showed her approval of his presence the first chance she had by giving him one of her most friendly smiles. Joel paid little attention to what was going on, and when the meeting was over he hurried outside. Lavina was standing next to a tree waiting for her family to finish visiting with the other church members. Joel puffed up his courage as much as he could, then made his move.

"Hello, Miss Lavina," he said.

The girl looked into his eyes, then, leaning to the side, looked around him in the direction of her family. She looked at Joel again and smiled.

"Hello. How did you know my name?"

"Heard one of the ladies call you that. Didn't hear your last name, though."

"It's Curtis."

"Well, I'm pleased to make your acquaintance, Miss Curtis," said Joel. "I was afraid I wouldn't be seeing you again."

"Does it matter?" said Lavina, teasing again.

Joel twisted his hat in his hand, and gave his best "Aw shucks" routine.

"Well, hell's bells, girl, but you are about the prettiest gal I've seen in a long time."

Lavina looked away, her head down. Joel suddenly realized his language may have offended her feminine sensibilities.

"Damn," he said half aloud, then uttered a sound of exasperation at his inability to speak like a gentleman. There was a moment of silence and Joel stood shuffling his feet trying to think of what to say next.

"So, you came to church just to see me?" said Lavina, finally.

"I reckon so," Joel allowed. "My, you sure do speak your mind, don't you?"

"When you're the only girl in the family, you have to either speak up or shut up."

"Y'know, it won't be long before the tracks get here, and then we'll be gettin' farther away from here every day," said Joel, "and it looks like you ain't coming out to sell lunches no more..."

"Lavina!" It was the older woman again. She must be Lavina's mother.

"I have to go," said Lavina.

"May I call on you?" asked Joel.

"We live on the other side of the river," said Lavina. "The house up against the mountain."

Lavina hurried away to join her family. As they drove away in their wagon, Lavina didn't look back, but her mother did. Joel wasn't sure he liked what he saw in her eyes.


Joel waited about an hour before he started for the Curtis house. He figured it would give the family time to eat dinner, get settled for the evening, or whatever they did after church.

Mrs. Curtis answered Joel's knock. "Yes?"

"I'm here to call on Miss Lavina."

Mrs. Curtis looked him up and down, and, apparently finding no obvious shortcomings, invited him to wait. In a few moments Lavina appeared in the doorway.

"Evenin', Miss Lavina."

"Good evening," said the girl. "This is an unexpected pleasure."

"Ma'am?"

"Your visit."

"But I thought..."

Lavina gave him a knowing smile. She apparently didn't want her mother to know she had encouraged Joel's visit.

"I'd like to introduce you to my mother," said Lavina, "but I don't believe I know your name."

"Deaton, ma'am. Joel Deaton."

"Mother!" The woman appeared once again in the doorway. "Mother, this is Joel Deaton. He bought a lunch from me the other day."

"Pleased to make your acquaintance, ma'am."

Mrs. Curtis gave him a withering look and only nodded. "Don't you go nowhere, Lavina," she said.

Joel and Lavina sat on a bench on the porch and talked for what seemed hours, but was only about forty-five minutes. It was mostly "get acquainted" talk, but Joel found himself thinking of this girl in different terms than he had at first. She had such a freshness about her and an enthusiasm for life that was different from what he was used to.

Lavina was eighteen and Mormon from the top of her head to the tips of her toes. She displayed a level of cultural refinement that was not to be found in the women Joel had previously known. She was educated and could play the piano.

All too soon, Lavina excused herself and went inside, but not before Joel had obtained permission to call on her again. He only rode his horse back to camp because he couldn't leave it at the Curtis place. He felt as if he could fly.

The tracks finally reached Echo on January 15, 1869, and halted for three weeks because of the worst snowstorm anyone in the vicinity could remember. Joel was not at all disturbed by this, delighted that he would have greater opportunities to see Lavina. He saw her almost every day, usually under the watchful eye of her mother. They sat and talked, went for walks, and attended church together on Sundays. When the weather finally broke, followed by the late January thaw that was typical in Utah, the track-laying moved on to the mouth of Echo Canyon and down Weber Canyon toward Ogden. Joel's visits were now restricted to Sundays, and when the weather turned warm the young couple spent one Sunday afternoon enjoying a picnic beneath a clump of trees on Echo Creek.

The mixture of sound from the gentle breeze in the trees and the rush of water in the creek was a symphony to the ears of the young couple. Joel lay on his back, hands behind his head, looking at the different shapes of cumulus clouds being pushed along by the wind. Lavina was spreading out food on the blanket.

"It hardly seems like only two months since we met," said Joel. "But I have enough memories to keep me goin' for a good while. How about you?"

"It's been fun."

"Fun?"

"Well, I'm sure you know Ma and Pa don't think much of my spending so much time with a gentile. I'm a little surprised myself."

*Not as surprised as I am,* thought Joel. This young Mormon girl had touched his heart in a way he never thought possible. He hadn't thought of the massacre or his sister in several days. It was easier to think of the pleasant times with Lavina.

The afternoon passed more quickly than either of them wanted. Toward dark they started back, and by sunset they were standing on the front porch of Lavina's home. Joel leaned toward the girl to kiss her gently on the cheek, but when his lips arrived, the cheek was no longer there. He tried again. Once more Lavina avoided him. Joel felt embarrassed by all this maneuvering.

"What's wrong?" he asked.

"Nothing. I'm just saddened that you have such low regard for me."

"Low regard?"

"I'm not one of those girls I hear about who follow the railroad, and I won't be treated like one."

Joel turned away and stood there thinking, twirling his hat in his hands. He felt defeated.

"I've not had an easy life," he said. "Besides my mother and my sister, I've loved but one woman until now. There's a lotta ugliness and misery in this world. A gal like you...I don't know how to say this, Lavina, but my life's a bit easier, havin' known you. I ain't likely to forget you." There was a long silence, Joel feeling more uncomfortable with each passing second. "So I'll be goin' now."

"When will I see you again?" asked Lavina.

"You won't."

"But why?" asked Lavina, sounding almost desperate. "Just 'cause I wouldn't let you kiss me?"

"I don't believe you think much of me," said Joel. "I reckon you won't know how much I care for you, 'less I walk away. I'd rather have you remember me as a fella who'd walk away to prove how much he cared for you, than to go on thinkin' I was only wantin' t'have my way with you...and that's more'n I've said to any woman in more'n ten years. So, I'll be seein' you."

Joel stepped off the porch and had taken two or three strides toward his horse when he heard Lavina call his name. He stopped and turned around. Lavina had come to the edge of the porch and was standing with her arms folded, looking like a spoiled child who wasn't going to have her own way.

"Don't go," she said, in a pleading tone.

Joel stepped up to the porch. Now he had to look up at her instead of down. The pale blue of her eyes was striking in the fading light. "I don't know how to put this in words, Lavina. I ain't very good at sayin' what I'm feelin'. I knew when I first saw you that you were special. I got a special feelin' for you that I don't reckon happens to a man too many times. So, I reckon it's come time t'cut to the chase."

"Then cut to the chase," said Lavina.

"All right. We're layin' track two, three miles a day. I ain't got time for a proper courtship, and when we're gone I may never come this way again."

"Is this a proposal of marriage?"

"I don't rightly know," he said. "Ain't got no place to keep a wife if I had one. But I'd sure like to know I had something to come back to."

Lavina reached out her left hand and touched Joel's cheek. She looked into his eyes, and Joel felt as if she were peering into his soul. A shiver shook his body.

"Joel," she said softly, "My heart says yes, but my spirit says no. For us marriage is forever, when a man and woman are joined by one who has the power to seal us together for eternity."

"So we just need the right preacher, is that it?"

"It's not that simple," said Lavina.

Joel moved slightly toward Lavina, then he felt a gentle tug from her hand on his cheek. Their lips met and she slipped easily into his arms. In between Delia Huff and Lavina Curtis, Joel had kissed, fondled, and otherwise explored the charms of a goodly number of women. Even so, he had never before felt the thrill like he was feeling now.

"Will you go for a walk with me," asked Joel, his mouth dry and his voice almost cracking. Lavina pulled away from Joel and looked into his eyes. He kissed her on the forehead, the nose, and gently on her lips. "I love you, Lavina...more than life itself."

Lavina did not speak, but let out a sigh as she hugged him as hard as she could. Beneath a brilliant starry sky, Lavina walked and talked with the handsome young man from Arkansas.

When they returned to the house, Mrs. Curtis was waiting. "Lavina, go inside," she said.

"But, Mother..."

"Now!"

The girl did as she was told.

"And now you, young man. I haven't thought much of you comin' 'round here, but I've held my tongue. Girls her age have enough to be rebellious about without me giving her something else to make her fret. We don't hold with our girls marrying outside the church. Besides, she's a mite young for the likes of you."

Joel couldn't help but wonder if this was Mrs. Huff come back from the dead. Were all mothers like this?

"I'm sorry you feel that way, Mrs. Curtis," he said. "I've done the best I know how to be sociable. I don't think I've given cause for anyone to take offense."

Mrs. Curtis seemed to soften a bit. "Well, that's true, and I don't want you to think that's how I feel. She's my only daughter..."

"And you want her to marry a Mormon."

"Yes, I suppose that's it."

"Not much chance of that happening to me," said Joel. "But Lavina's almost full growed. I think it's wrong for you to stand in her way."

"You don't understand, do you?" said Mrs. Curtis. "No, I guess not. You have to have had children of your own before you'd be able to think and feel as I do."

"I reckon there's a lotta truth in that ma'am, but you've gotta remember that you was young once, and you knew what you wanted to do. How would you feel if someone said you couldn't?"

"As a girl I always obeyed my parents, and I expect my daughter to do the same. As for you...well, I think it'd be best if you didn't come around anymore."

"I think I'll let Lavina decide that, Mrs. Curtis."

"I guess that's all we have to say," said Mrs. Curtis. "Good night."

Mrs. Curtis went into the house, leaving Joel standing on the porch. He could hear conversation inside, then some angry words, and then a door slamming. Joel lingered a few moments, and then headed back to camp. He couldn't help comparing Mrs. Curtis to Delia Huff's mother. He resolved that this time things would be different.

# 91

The sermon seemed to drone on for hours, though it had only been twenty minutes. Lavina looked out the window of the little church and wondered if Joel was at her home already or somewhere along the way. She couldn't understand the emotions that churned within her. She was anxious to see Joel again, yet the prospect filled her with dread. Why couldn't her parents and Joel get along? She knew what her duty was and she was mindful of the covenants she had made. Nevertheless, she was in love with Joel. What could she do? Why did her choices have to be so black and white?

"Lavina!"

The girl turned her gaze from the window to see why her mother had poked her in the ribs and spoken to her sharply. Then she noticed that all heads were bowed except for hers and that of Brother Stevens, who was glaring at her from the pulpit. Lavina bowed her head and Brother Stevens then offered a fervent prayer to bring the services to a close.

Sunday meeting was more than a religious activity. The Mormon ward house was also the social and political center for the community. Though the meeting was over, most of the people lingered to visit with their friends. It was often the only opportunity for many of the people to mingle with one another. Lavina and her family were no exception, but this day she was anxious to get on home in case Joel was there. Several of her friends stopped to pass the time of day, but she was short with them, almost to the point of being rude.

When at last the Curtis family drove up to their house, Lavina was not disappointed to see Joel sitting on the front steps.

"What's he doing here?" asked her father.

"Daddy, I have to speak with him," said Lavina.

"Well, keep it short."

The greetings were restrained as the Curtis's passed Joel on their way into the house. Mrs. Curtis wouldn't even look in his direction. She knew why he had come and she wanted no misunderstanding about how she felt.

Lavina waited until the others had gone inside before she came near Joel.

"How have you been?" she asked.

"Tolerable."

Joel stood looking away from her. The ugliness that had been the railroad town, had been replaced by the beauty of Echo that had been before the coming of the Union Pacific. Only the iron rails indicated that Joel and his fellow railroaders had ever passed that way. Lavina's heart was breaking as she saw the sorrow reflected in Joel's eyes.

"Why so sad?" she asked.

"I don't know. I'm just having a hard time with my feelings. I haven't felt this way since I was a teenager. I didn't know it was still possible."

"Of course it is. You're not as hardhearted as you think you are. You're such a tender and caring person."

Joel laughed inside. No one who knew him in the years after the massacre would have found that assessment even remotely accurate. But she had changed him, softened his outlook on the world.

"Really think so, huh?"

"Yes, I do," said Lavina. "I know that you're sensitive and that you're hurting inside and it's my fault."

"No, it's not that," said Joel. "It's just hard to have these feelings and know that you don't feel the same way about me, 'cause if you did you'd set your ma straight about us."

"You're wrong. I do have those same feelings. But there are limits we cannot go beyond. We're both prisoners of circumstances. I have a very deep sense of who I am and I cannot violate that."

"I don't understand," said Joel.

"I am who I am because of everything I have done and everyone I have known. The person I want to be and the things I want to do would simply disappear. You could never be happy with me because I would not be happy with myself."

Joel turned to Lavina and looked into her eyes. He saw peace and happiness. All the hurts he had suffered could be made well. As a man he could be made whole.

"There's not an hour goes by that I don't think of you," he said.

Tears welled up in Lavina's eyes. She stepped forward and gently took Joel's hands into hers.

"I'm sorry I've done this to you," she said barely above a whisper.

"Don't be. I did it to myself. I had no right to think anyone would ever care for me."

"But I do. I really do."

"Then come with me," said Joel.

"I can't."

"That's your mother talking, not you."

"No, Joel, I was angry at first, but now I know she was right."

"But if you really love me, Lavina, you'll come with me."

Lavina lowered her head as she fought back the tears. She couldn't raise her eyes to look at Joel. She didn't want him to see her cry.

"I'm sorry, Joel, but I can't turn my back on my entire life."

"I'm not asking you to do that."

Lavina looked at Joel. He saw the tears streaming down her cheeks, but she didn't care.

"I love you," she said, "but we're different people. There is such a distance between us and only you can bridge that distance."

"You mean, become a Mormon."

"Yes," said Lavina in a small voice.

Joel put his hands on his hips and looked away in disgust. That's what she had meant when she had talked about being married for eternity. Several moments passed as he tried to frame a reply. He turned his back on Lavina and took a couple of steps, his eyes sweeping the surrounding mountains. When he turned around, he looked up at Pulpit Rock for a moment, then finally at Lavina. It was no use. No other way could convey how he felt.

"Darlin' " he said, "There ain't no way in hell I could ever be a Mormon."

"Then there is no hope for us."

Lavina turned to go inside. Joel stepped up on the porch, caught her by the elbow and turned her around.

"That ain't good enough, Lavina! Give me a reason. Don't tell me that you love me and just walk away. There ain't no religion in the world that important."

Suddenly the door burst open. Lavina's father stood there with a shotgun in his hands. His voice was firm and threatening as he said, "I guess you're deaf, boy, but I know you ain't blind. I got two good reasons right here and they're all you need."

Joel saw the two barrels and reacted instinctively. He swung, hitting the shotgun with his left forearm. The gun discharged and

Joel screamed in pain. He staggered back, staring at the powder burns and buckshot wounds. They were only superficial, but they hurt like hell. Joel sprang at Curtis, pummeling him with his fists. The older man was driven back as he tried to fend off the blows.

"Stop! Stop!" screamed Lavina, but the two combatants paid her no mind. Her father threw his shoulder into Joel, driving him back. Joel charged again. A huge right hand crashed into the young man's jaw, driving him backward over the porch railing. Joel hit the ground rolling, and came to a halt on his back. As Curtis made a move to step off the porch, Joel drew his Colt's revolver and pointed it at the man.

"Joel!" screamed Lavina.

Joel glanced at the girl, then back at her father. He cocked the gun. Lavina came to the porch railing and looked down at Joel. In a tiny voice, quivering with emotion, she pleaded, "Please don't kill my Daddy."

Instantly, Joel's mind was transported back to his hiding place on the hill overlooking Mountain Meadows. He relived that terrible moment, once again seeing his family and friends brutally murdered. Joel looked at Lavina and the fire went out. No, he couldn't do it. He couldn't do to her what had been done to him. The young man uncocked his gun. Rising to his feet, Joel holstered the Colt, then picked up his hat and started dusting himself off.

"Thank you, Lord," said Curtis, lowering his eyes.

"You'd best be thanking your daughter," said Joel. "It's only because of her that you ain't dead."

Joel turned and started for his horse. Blood was running down his left arm and dripping on the ground. Lavina stepped from the porch and ran after him.

"Joel! Your arm is hurt. Let me tend it for you."

"Come back here, girl," said Curtis.

Lavina ignored her father. When she caught up to Joel, she put her arms around him from behind.

"I'm so sorry," she said.

Joel twisted out of her embrace and turned around. He looked into her eyes. A tremor went through Lavina. She saw a hardness in Joel's eyes that she had never seen before. Joel spoke to her, his voice quiet and restrained.

"You said you couldn't turn your back on your whole life. Well, that's what I did...for you. You blinded me to my duty, but your father has helped me see again. Some things are meant to be and some things can never be. We just gotta be able to tell the difference. It *is* over for us and I'm sorry for it."

"Joel, it doesn't have to be."

Joel looked at his bloody left arm and snickered. "A fine

relationship I'd have with my father-in-law. No, Lavina, it would never work and I should've known it." Joel mounted his horse. "Goodbye, Lavina."

Joel spurred the horse to a gallop. He wanted to put as much distance as possible between himself and Echo. His heart was aching, but he didn't know if it was for his lost love or because old wounds had been torn open. He only knew that the time was at hand to get serious about finding Laura Jean.

Isaac Delaney was lying on his cot when Joel rode up to their tent. He sat bolt upright when the younger man entered.

"Good Lord, boy! What happened to your arm?"

"Her daddy has a hot temper."

"Come over here, Joel. We have to clean that wound so you don't get gangrene."

Delaney cleaned the wound with soap and water. It hurt some, but Joel took it like a man. Delaney handed Joel the liquor jug and said, "Drink some of this."

"Will it make my arm feel better?"

"Yes and no. Drink enough of it and you won't feel any pain at all."

Joel drank deeply of the fiery liquid. He remembered that day when the Indians had wounded him in the thigh back in '57. The liquor didn't taste any better now than it did then.

"Give me a chug of that," said Delaney, taking the jug. He took a big drink, then poured some on Joel's arm. Joel screamed in agony.

"Here," said Delaney. "You better have some more."

Several more drinks and Joel was developing a better attitude toward the world. Together the two men staggered to the place in camp where the "soiled doves" were plying their trade.

Delaney approached one of the young ladies. She wasn't particularly good looking. In fact, she was ugly, but in Joel's condition he wasn't likely to care.

"I give you my young friend," said Delaney with a bow. "Cupid has shot him through the heart. You, my dear, shall be the instrument of healing. I shall call for him in one hour."

Delaney flipped the tart a five-dollar gold piece and retired to his tent. After an hour he returned.

"Your money was wasted, mister," said the whore. "He weren't in no condition to do nothin'."

Looking at Joel, passed out on the floor, Delaney said, "Not to worry, my dear. I won't tell him if you don't."

It was difficult, but Delaney managed to get Joel back to the tent and onto his cot. The young man was semi-conscious and talking. At first Delaney paid no mind to what Joel was saying, but a word, a phrase caught his attention, and then he began to listen carefully as Joel told of the massacre at Mountain Meadows.

Far into the night Delaney sat on his cot, head in hands, and listened to the drunken babblings of the young man from Arkansas. He wept bitter tears as those dark days were brought back into his mind, and he wondered: would it never end?

# Redemption

# 92

The rails reached the mouth of Weber Canyon on March 7, 1869, and the men hardly had a chance to catch their breath in the Mormon town of Ogden before continuing the race with the Central Pacific. Grading had already been done north from Ogden and then west around the north shore of the Great Salt Lake. In fact, the grading crews of both railroads had passed each other going in opposite directions. By April 7 the rails had arrived at the site of Corinne, the last Hell on Wheels town and the first non-Mormon settlement in Utah.

On April 10 the men were called together and heard the announcement that the rails of the two competing railroads would be joined at Promontory, Utah. Now that the race was over, a certain number of men, now deemed unnecessary, were paid off and released. Joel and Delaney were among those who managed to stay on. Four more weeks passed as the final twenty-eight miles of track were laid. On the night of May 8, their termination pay in hand, Joel and Delaney joined the celebration that was in full swing at Corinne.

Alcohol has a wide variety of effects, depending on the drinker. Some men become violent, others sullen and morose, while others become gregarious in the extreme. Delaney had never been a violent or a silly drunk. Usually he became quieter than usual, as if taking a silent inventory of his internal working parts. In contrast, Joel usually loosened up a bit from his customary reserve. On this particular evening both men had a lot to drink, but neither was enjoying himself. Toward midnight the pair retired to their tent for the last time. On the morrow they would each be going their separate ways.

Joel flopped down on his cot, one arm flung over his eyes. He was drifting toward sleep when he heard a sobbing sound. Delaney had gotten out a leather case that Joel had noticed on many occasions before in their tent. The older man was holding a tintype of his family and a leather-bound book lay open before him. Tears were streaming down his cheeks and his body shook gently as he cried.

"Isaac?" said Joel. "What's wrong?"

Delaney didn't answer. Joel got up from the cot and stood behind his friend, putting his hand on his shoulder. He had never seen Delaney like this before.

"Is that your family?" asked Joel.

Delaney said nothing. Joel leaned closer and looked at the picture. He recognized Delaney, and there were two women, a young man, and three young girls.

"I reckon you're missin' 'em now, ain't you?" said Joel.

Delaney seemed to nod.

"Well, as long as you're here, y'ought t'go see 'em, Isaac. I'd wager they're missin' you too."

Delaney didn't answer. His chin rested on his chest and his hands hung at his side as if unconscious. Joel looked at the picture again, and a shiver went through his body. He leaned closer for a better look. Then he snatched up the tintype and held it closer to the light. He looked back at Delaney, who appeared semiconscious, his eyes red and his nose runny.

"Isaac, what's my sister doing in this picture?"

"Your...oh, God, no..." Delaney's lay his head in his left arm on top of the table and appeared to go to sleep.

Joel stared at the picture for a long time, then at Delaney, who was snoring softly. All this time the key to his lost sister had been so near. How was it possible? Then he saw the book on the table and opened it. It was a diary that went back nearly twenty years. Normally, Joel wouldn't intrude on another's privacy like this, but he felt if anyone had a right, he did.

Dawn was near when Joel finally put the book down. Delaney was a man he should hate for what he had done at Mountain Meadows, but he couldn't. Too many things had passed between them in the past few years. He reached down and shook Delaney awake. Delaney sat up, looking confused. Joel showed him the picture.

"This is my sister, Isaac. What do you know about her?"

Joel sat down next to Delaney and waited for an answer. Delaney wiped his eyes, and blew his nose. In spite of his knowledge of Joel's involvement, Delaney had no idea that the girl he had raised was Joel's sister. The good memories, the bad memories, the cries of the emigrants as they were slaughtered, the tears of the children being led away, the feelings of guilt he had never been able to shake, all came flooding into his mind, overwhelming him. Delaney muttered something.

"I didn't hear you," said Joel.

"I was there," said Delaney. "I helped 'em do it."

"I know."

"I was there," said Delaney. "I killed at least one man that I know of. I knew you were there. You told me that night when you were drunk, when you came back from Echo."

"How could you do it, Isaac? A good man like you?"

"A good man? Yes, I was a good man, a good husband, a good father." Delaney's head hung low, but his eyes lifted as he spoke to Joel. "Don't you believe that good men can do evil things...for the greater good?"

Joel stood up and paced the floor, his fists clenched, then sat down again. He placed his hand on Delaney's shoulder and looked him directly in the eye. "Where is she, Isaac? Where's my sister?"

"I'm sorry," said Delaney. "I should've known better."

"Please," said Joel. "Where is she?"

"When it was over, I took her. They were going to kill her, said she was too old. But I wouldn't let 'em have her. They said I was a traitor, threatened my life if I didn't give her up. Then, when word came from the prophet in Salt Lake, they didn't dare harm her. I gave her to my other wife. She was barren and needed a child of her own. When the army came, we hid her."

"Where is she now?" asked Joel.

"I don't know. Last I heard, she was in Ephraim."

Gold. Twenty years before, it had set a nation in motion and opened the settling of the West. Men from all walks of life had abandoned their former situations to seek their fortunes in the gold fields of California. Gold. Few had it. Everybody wanted it.

Information. More precious than gold. If General Beauregard had known how desperate was the plight of the Federals when he had driven them to the banks of the Tennessee at Shiloh, the Confederates would have destroyed Grant's army and perhaps could have driven a wedge so deep into the Union that the South may have won the war.

Information. Joel had been seeking information about his sister Laura Jean for years, and would have given anything to get it. Now he had it, and he was going to make good use of it. Delaney had given him names, dates, and places. Joel intended to find Laura Jean and save her from her miserable existence.

When morning came Joel packed his few personal belongings and rode out of Corinne. Delaney had still been asleep and Joel didn't wake him. What could they have said to each other? In spite of their longtime friendship, the revelations of the previous night had created a gap between them that could never be bridged. What happened to Delaney now was of no further interest to Joel. His mind was right and focused upon his sister, as it should have been all along.

# 93

The trail was long since cold, but the information Joel had managed to glean from Isaac Delaney's journal led him south. He found no one willing to talk about those days and events related to the massacre. Days became weeks and then months. Joel soon learned that he was better received if he said "Brother" instead of "Mister." He had been around Isaac Delaney long enough that he knew how to sound like a Mormon. He regretted the deceit, but justified it because of his purpose.

At last, Joel found himself astride his horse on a ridge overlooking a small Mormon village. He had followed many leads with no success. He wondered if this would only be another dead end. He felt a knot in his stomach as he spurred his horse forward.

It was a terrible moment for Joel Deaton as he knocked on the door of the farmhouse. After so many years he was not sure how to act. He could not bear the thought of failure. His pulse and breathing quickened. In his heart he knew his search was over, but the queasiness in his stomach told him otherwise.

The door opened. Light from a solitary kerosene lamp spilled onto the porch, a delicate counterbalance to the fading hues of the recent sunset. A young woman stood silhouetted in the doorway.

"Yes?" she said.

In the dim light Joel was unable to make out the young woman's features. He moved closer for a better look. Instinctively, Rebecca Delaney stepped back. Sensing something was wrong, her husband John rose from his chair in another room and called to her, "Who is it, Rebecca?"

Rebecca did not answer. There was something vaguely familiar about the scruffy-looking man on her porch. Her feeling of fear subsided.

As for Joel, he fought the tight, strangled feeling in his throat. The woman standing before him was the image of his mother, only younger. She was beautiful...not the painted-face beauty of the "Hell-on-wheels" girls nor the haughty beauty of the society ladies. She radiated a warmth and vitality unusual for the frontier. The harshness of pioneer life had not yet taken its inevitable toll. She was a head shorter than Joel's six feet and of slender build. Her hair, golden brown, was parted in the middle and spilled playfully about her shoulders. The eyes were soft blue and sparkled with life. Her face had a pleasant look and her lips appeared ready to smile at any moment.

Joel had no doubts. He was almost overcome with emotion. Finally, he forced the words from his lips in a low, hoarse voice barely above a whisper.

"Hello, Laura Jean."

Rebecca's body stiffened, her right hand involuntarily rising toward her mouth.

"Laura Jean?" she said, repeating the name in a voice that trailed off.

Since her adoption she had always been Rebecca. Since that horrible day at Mountain Meadows no one had called her Laura Jean. Tears welled in her eyes and her chin quivered uncontrollably.

"My god," she said weakly. Then, in a rising voice, "Joel? Joel, is it you?"

It was impossible to tell who took the first step. Rebecca Delaney and her brother Joel Deaton embraced for the first time in nearly twelve years. They spoke each others name over and over as their eyes filled with tears.

John Delaney stood in the doorway to the parlor. His initial look of puzzlement was turning to something darker, more ominous.

"What's going on, Rebecca?" he asked.

But he knew the answer already. He had heard the stranger calling his wife Laura Jean. There could be only one reason for that.

Rebecca turned toward her husband. Her eyes were bright and shining, and her smile was framed by the tear streaks on her cheeks.

"John, this is my brother Joel. I haven't seen him since..." Rebecca stopped in mid-sentence. She couldn't make the words come.

John stepped toward them and self-consciously extended his hand. It was an awkward moment. Hesitantly, Joel accepted the handshake, but it was impossible to mask his real feelings. John took his hat and coat from the peg by the door and brushed past them.

"I'll be feedin' the animals," he said.

"John! Wait! Please!"

Rebecca's husband stopped, but did not turn around. She stepped toward him and grasped his left arm just above the elbow. She rested her head against his shoulder and said in a quiet voice, "John, I know this is hard for you, but please... please don't make it hard for us. Try to understand."

"I guess you'll be wantin' to talk," said John.

"Yes."

"I can be in or out."

Rebecca thought for a moment before she spoke. "All right. I think I'll take Joel for a little walk."

Delaney returned his hat and coat to their peg and turned toward Joel.

"You be careful with her. Y'hear?" he said, then strode past him into the parlor.

Joel's jaw clenched and his fists tightened. His anger flickered briefly, then faded away. He wasn't one to be told how to treat his own sister...and especially not by a Mormon!

Joel felt a gentle tug on his sleeve. Rebecca had wrapped a knitted shawl around her shoulders and was holding the door. Joel took his sister by the hand. They walked in silence for several moments. It was a cool evening and the moon, approaching its first quarter, illuminated the landscape with its soft light. The sky was sprinkled with a growing number of stars. The faint orange streak along the western horizon bore witness to the recent setting of the sun. Their footsteps made crunching sounds in the unpaved road. Somewhere in the distance a dog barked. Nearby was the sound of rushing water...perhaps a creek or an irrigation canal. For the first time in years Joel felt at ease.

"Why do they call you Rebecca?" he said.

"It's my adopted name."

"I don't like it. A person should be called by the name they was born with."

"Oh, I don't mind," said Rebecca. "Ma and Pa Delaney named me that when they took me in. It was the name of their little girl that died at birth in '53."

"Well, it just ain't natural," said Joel.

"You can call me Laura Jean if you want."

"Thanks. I will."

Rebecca stopped and turned toward Joel, taking both of his hands in hers.

"Will you be staying long?" she asked. "There's so much I want to tell you, and so much I want to find out about you, what you've been doing all these years, and how you got away at the Meadows. I mean, we all thought you were dead. They said them that got away were all hunted down and killed."

"Stayin'? Laura Jean, I ain't stayin' at all. I've come to take you home with me."

Rebecca released her brother's hands and turned away from him.

"Home?" she said, her voice agitated. Looking fiercely determined, she turned back to face him. "I am home, Joel. This is my home."

"But you don't belong here...not with these people."

"Yes, I do! I have a husband and a child. I'm happy."

Joel felt helpless, the same as he had that day at Mountain

Meadows, seeing the women and children running, screaming, being dragged down by the Indians with upraised weapons in their hands, knowing his family was dying horrible deaths, and that he was helpless to do anything about it.

"Laura Jean," he said, pleading. "They killed Ma and Pa. They took everything we had."

"My husband didn't kill anyone. My daughter is innocent."

"We'll take her with us."

"Where, Joel? Home? To Arkansas? There's nothing in Arkansas for me. Joel, there comes a time when you have to let go of the past or it will consume you, steal your soul. The past is only a memory. Like a dream it just fades away. I'm alive...here and now. I have a future and I want to live in it."

"I was only sixteen, Sis. They stole what was left of my youth. And then I think of Ma and Pa lying there dead on the ground, and who done it."

"I ain't forgot it, Joel. But when I think of them, I remember Mama singing as she worked. I remember Daddy holding me in his arms when I was so sick with measles they thought I was going to die. I remember the good times, the love and the caring. I wish to God they were still here, Joel, but they're not, and I can't change that. And neither can you."

Joel stood staring at the ground, shoulders slumped. His sister felt his disappointment.

"I'm sorry I don't live up to your expectations," she said.

Joel did not reply.

"Come, let's sit a spell," said Rebecca, pointing toward a bathtub-sized chunk of sandstone beneath a cottonwood tree.

"I don't wanna sit."

"All right," said the girl with a shrug. "But I do."

Rebecca sat down on the rock and made herself comfortable. Joel let out a sigh of resignation and sat down beside her.

"Do you always get your way?" he asked.

"Sometimes," she replied in a teasing voice.

They sat for several moments listening to the night sounds. Each ones thoughts turned inward. Joel had rehearsed this meeting many times in his mind, but it was certainly not going as planned. For her part, Rebecca was bothered by her brother's insistence that she go away with him. For a moment she thought how nice and well-ordered her life had been before Joel had suddenly appeared on her doorstep. She wished it were still that way, a thought she instantly regretted.

"Joel..."

"Laura Jean..."

They had both spoken at once.

"I'm sorry," said Rebecca, laughing merrily. "You go first."

"No, please. It wasn't important."

Rebecca knew that wasn't true. Everything Joel could tell her would be important.

"All right," she said. "Tell me how you got away that day, and what you've been doing all this time, and how you found me."

Joel took the better part of an hour to tell his story, omitting only the part about his relationship with Isaac Delaney. Rebecca interrupted only occasionally with a question or a comment. The young man seemed almost detached as he recounted his experiences in California, Utah, and the Civil War. By the time he had finished, he was emotionally spent.

"Do you see now?" he asked in a subdued voice. "The past twelve years I have lived for only one thing...to get you away from the Mormons and then take my revenge for what they done to us."

Rebecca shook her head sadly.

"Oh, Joel. After all these years and you still hate so much."

"It was the only thing that kept me alive in Alton Prison. I've known Mormons, worked with 'em, and I've held my peace, 'cause finding you was more important. But, if I could find 'em all now," said Joel, pulling his revolver from its holster, "I'd send every last one of 'em to hell with this."

"Would you send me there too, Joel?"

Joel looked intently at his sister. He couldn't believe what he had just heard.

"What do you mean?" he said slowly.

"I'm a Mormon, Joel. Of my own free will."

A wretched, choking sound of agony escaped Joel's lips. "No! No, not you! Not my own sister!"

"It's true, Joel. I was baptized a Mormon when I was eleven."

Slowly, Joel rose to his feet, barely able to control his rage. His hand shook as he raised his revolver and pointed it at Rebecca.

"Oh, God, I can't stand it, Laura Jean. I'd sooner see you dead than be a Mormon."

There was no fear on Rebecca's face, but a look of confidence that grew out of her convictions. There was no doubt in her mind of her eternal destiny. She had no fear of someone who could only take her mortal life. Her voice was quiet, but firm, as she spoke.

"Have you looked for me all these years just to kill me?"

"No," said Joel, weakly, suddenly aware of the absurdity of his position. "I came to take you home."

"Why?"

"Because you're my sister. You're all that's left of my family."

"Did you want to kill me five minutes ago before you knew I had become a Mormon?"

"No, of course not."

"Oh, Joel, can't you see? I'm still the same person. Mormons are like anyone else. Some are good, some are bad. There are those who love and those who hate. Some are honest and others would choke on the truth. You just can't tar everyone with the same brush."

Joel was crying and he felt ashamed. The fire of revenge that had burned so brightly within him for so long had turned to ashes and was now an empty void.

"What about the massacre, Laura Jean? Good people don't do that sort of thing!"

"Sometimes good people do terrible things. You're a good man, Joel. Have you never done anything you were ashamed of?"

"I never killed anyone."

It was a lie and Joel knew it, but with a quick rationalization or two he was able to quiet the still, small voice within himself.

"Fear does crazy things to people, Joel. And they were afraid."

"Of what?" Joel demanded.

"Of us."

"Us? Farmers? Women and children?"

"Joel, before the Saints came west they were persecuted, driven from their homes, dispossessed of their lands, and the prophet and his brother murdered. They were determined that it would never happen again. Surely, you remember the threats by some members of the train to raise an army and return?"

"I remember it. And we should have done it. Well, at least I should have done it."

"The massacre was a terrible tragedy," said Rebecca. "It ruined the lives of so many good and faithful men. To this day they are filled with guilt and remorse."

Joel's mood had grown sullen.

"Good men, huh? My heart goes out to 'em," he said, sarcastically.

"Yes, good men." Rebecca had begun to cry. "I know, because I'm married to one of them?"

"You what?"

Joel could not believe what he was hearing. His anger flashed anew.

"John was there," Rebecca continued. "He was only nineteen. Did you notice the ugly scar above his right eye? He refused to take part in the killing. When he walked away he was shot...by his own father."

Rebecca wept.

Joel thought of Isaac Delaney. No wonder the man had been so bitter. In spite of his hatred, Joel felt a strange mixture of admiration and compassion for John Delaney. He returned his gun to its holster, then sat down on the rock and embraced his sister. Their lives had been destroyed that day, and at last he realized he could never go back to it. There was nothing more to say. Forgiveness would be a long time coming, if it ever did. A twelve year old hatred would not die easily.

Joel lifted Rebecca to her feet and kissed her on the forehead.

"Gotta go, Sis," he whispered.

"I know," she managed to say in spite of the sobs that were racking her body.

They started walking back the short distance to the house. Rebecca felt she would be unable to stand without Joel to support her.

"Will you come back some day?" She asked.

"Can't really say," said Joel. "Gotta make a life for myself somewhere, somehow."

"You can stay here...with us."

Joel shook his head slowly.

"No. I gotta make it on my own or not at all."

John Delaney was waiting on the porch. Joel wondered how long he had been there. At their approach, Delaney stepped from the porch and put his left arm around Rebecca's shoulders.

"I'll be going now," said Joel. "You take good care of her. She's the only family I've got."

Delaney extended his right hand.

"Good luck," he said.

Joel looked at the proffered handshake, then at his sister. Then he looked squarely at Delaney. Even in the moonlight he could see the scar on his brother-in-law's brow. There was a somber look on Delaney's face. Joel grasped the man's hand firmly.

"Thanks," he said.

The expression on Delaney's face changed slightly, almost, but not quite a smile.

"The Lord be with you, Brother," he said.

Joel nodded, then turned and mounted his horse. Rebecca came forward and, reaching up, placed her hand on his.

"Stay," she said.

"Can't do it, Sis," he said, choking on the words. "Gotta go."

"Stay."

"Oh, Laura Jean...please don't."

Now the tears were flowing freely and Joel was ashamed, but at the same time he felt proud of his sister and joy for her happiness. He tugged on the reins and his horse backed up a couple of steps. Joel turned the animal's head and urged it to a slow gallop. In a few minutes he crested the ridge a couple hundred yards north of the Delaney house, stopped and looked back. In the darkness he could not make them out, but he knew they were still there. His quest was over, but in a sense it had only just begun.

Joel had been to many places in his travels: California, Utah, Tennessee. He had worked for the Pony Express, built the transcontinental railroad, and fought in the great Civil War. Though his body had been elsewhere, his heart and mind, yes, even his very soul had never left Mountain Meadows. The Union army had held him prisoner twice, at Camp Morton and Alton Prison, but from the day of the massacre his spirit had been held captive by the ghosts of Mountain Meadows. Perhaps now, like his sister Laura Jean, he could turn from death to life, from sorrow to joy, find peace and contentment, and at last come all the way...Home from the Meadows.

www.ingramcontent.com/pod-product-compliance
Lightning Source LLC
Chambersburg PA
CBHW071156020726
47502CB00002B/429